For my brothers: Chris, Tim and Brady
With love

Alison Case received her BA from Oberlin College and her PhD in English Literature from Cornell University. A professor of English at Williams College in Williamstown, Massachusetts, she has published two books and many articles on nineteenth-century British fiction and poetry. This is her first novel.

Nelly Dean

Alison Case

b

THE BOROUGH PRESS

The Borough Press
An imprint of HarperCollins*Publishers*
1 London Bridge Street
London SE1 9GF

www.harpercollins.co.uk

Published by The Borough Press 2015
1

A catalogue record for this book
is available from the British Library

ISBN: 978 0 00 812339 0

This novel is entirely a work of fiction.
Except in the case of historical fact, any resemblance to
actual persons, living or dead, events or localities is
entirely coincidental.

Set in Minion by Palimpsest Book Production Limited,
Falkirk, Stirlingshire

Printed and bound in Great Britain by
Clays Ltd, St Ives plc

MIX
Paper from
responsible sources
FSC™ C007454

FSC™ is a non-profit international organisation established to promote
the responsible management of the world's forests. Products carrying the
FSC label are independently certified to assure consumers that they come
from forests that are managed to meet the social, economic and
ecological needs of present and future generations,
and other controlled sources.

Find out more about HarperCollins and the environment at
www.harpercollins.co.uk/green

ONE

Dear Mr Lockwood,

I don't suppose you'll be expecting to hear from me, not since I sent you the few bits of things you left behind on your last visit – you'll remember, the handkerchiefs and your carved walking stick that turned up after you left. I'm not writing about anything like that now – I am sorry to say that we never did find your other pair of spectacles. I think they must have fallen from your overcoat pocket when you were floundering in the snow that night, and got trodden into the mud after it thawed in spring. I turned the house here inside out last month, when we were getting ready for the wedding: every drawer and cupboard emptied, and the carpets and cushions and bedding all taken out to be aired and beaten. I'm sure we would have found them then if they were to be found. And that covers everything that you wrote to me was missing.

There, I said I wasn't writing about your things, and I have gone and done it anyway. It's an old habit with me, to get the chores finished off before settling down to a bit of time for myself, and those spectacles of yours have been weighing on my mind like a half-sewn shirt or a half-swept floor. Or a half-told tale.

1

It's that I'm writing to you about, Mr Lockwood: the story I told you over those long, dark nights. And about the story I didn't tell. Don't mistake me, please, I told you no lies, or not what you would call lies. Or at least — well, we'll come to that. But there were things I didn't say, things I couldn't say, then, and perhaps shouldn't now. But they've weighed on me since, and my mind has kept returning to you listening, and me talking, and I've imagined myself again and again telling you all those other things, and you taking an interest in them, as a story, you know, as you did that other tale I told. I half fancied that you might pass this way again, to pay a visit and see for yourself how Hareton and Cathy were coming on, and perhaps you might sit with me by the fire in the sitting room, and I would tell you another story altogether, a homespun grey yarn woven in among the bright-dyed and glossy dark threads of the Earnshaws and Lintons.

So when your letter came about the things you missed, and you wrote that you were to be settling in Italy for your health, I saw that that would never be. And to be honest, even if you had, I could never have told you such a story to your face. But it pleased me to think of it, and as I've said, it bothered me a bit, some of the things left out of that other story, till it came to where I sat myself down and started to write. So here I am.

It was a strange thing, telling you that story, hour after hour, pulling myself back into all those times, and sorting and choosing among my memories what to tell and what not. You asked me to tell you everything, to leave out nothing, but of course no one can do that, tell all they've seen and heard and felt, and all they've known and thought, wondered, and suspected too. And I was so afraid of wearying you! You thought it was a simple thing: you asked for Heathcliff's story, and I knew it and told it to you, same as I might have told you any current story about the doings of a neighbour here, or one of the tales of folk from the other world that we tell on dark nights. And if somewhere in the middle you'd grown weary and wanted to hear no more of it, why that would be that. Yet the story would be there with me, just the same, though untold. But the story wasn't there until I told it to you. It wasn't a story to tell, just a jumble of memories, like pictures in my mind: young Heathcliff tossing his dirty mane from his eyes like a wild moor pony; the two of them standing side by side, sullen and defiant, under one of Joseph's lectures; or later, Catherine glittering and primping in her new finery; or Heathcliff with that set, frozen look he'd get under one of Hindley's savage beatings, so that I didn't know which was the more awful: the baffled rage in Hindley's red face, that all his wild flailing with strap or stick could wring no cry nor plea from the boy, or the still hatred in Heathcliff's white one, that promised I didn't know what – all that came after, it seems to me now.

See, that's how it is when you tell a story. You can't help changing things, seeing the future lying curled in the past like a half-grown chick in an egg. But it's not so. Putting myself back there, looking at him then, Heathcliff's face promised nothing, foreboded nothing, and I felt only sickness and horror looking on it, loving them both, in my own way, as I did, and powerless to stop them. In the midst of scenes like that, Mr Lockwood – and may God grant that you never learn the truth of this yourself – there are no stories, because there is no past and no future, only now. And afterwards, it seemed best to forget them, if I could. Until you asked about the folks at Wuthering Heights, and then I thought, 'Maybe this is where you come in, Nelly Dean, after all.'

It seemed so strange that all that remained of the family I grew up with at the Heights, and my own two beloved bairns as well, should be shut up together just a short way down the road – each, as it seemed, set only on making misery for the others – and I, the one person on earth that loved them all, barred from giving any help at all. And then you arrived, a handsome gentleman of independent means, 'taking solitude as a cure' – though for what ailment you wouldn't say. But it was soon plain enough you were hungry for excitement, and could no more bear being alone than the tabby cat here, that turns up her nose and stalks away from my offered caresses, but then comes and jumps in my lap the moment I'm settled by the fire to sew. So off you went to the Heights the first fine day, and came back singed and smarting from your reception, but interested too, and curious. And you'd seen my little Cathy, as lovely and loving a girl as any man could wish, to my mind, locked up there like a princess in a tower, and only needing to be rescued.

A good servant ought to keep her mouth shut about her employers' doings, or tell only what is already generally known in the neighbourhood. But as you must have guessed by now, I am a good deal less, and more, than a good servant. When I told you that story, I wanted it to do what stories in books had so often done to me – caught me up in them until they seemed more real than the everyday world around me, and made me long to walk in them as my own sober self, to warn fools against foolishness and enlighten the deceived, to talk sense to the wicked and comfort the afflicted. To forestall disaster. To make peace. There have been times I could have flung a book against the wall, in sheer frustration that it could make me care so and yet leave me helpless to act. I thought if I could only tell the story like that, to make you feel that way, why for you there would be no barrier, nothing more than a stroll down the lane between you and the chance to make happiness out of the living tragedy. Well, it wasn't to be, though whether the fault was in the teller or the hearer – or the tale itself, for it was a strange one – is not for me to say. And it all worked out for the best.

I was always a great one for reading. I well remember when I first saw the library at Thrushcross Grange; I'd never seen so many books in one room before, or a whole room given over just to books. Mr Linton was kind enough to let me borrow books from it as often as I wished – he was glad to see a servant wishing to improve her mind, he said. At the Heights, I had to steal the books and the time to read them both, once I began work in earnest – until then I had my lessons with Cathy and Hindley. But I was as clever as any of them – I get that from my mother. Cleverer than many, between ourselves, especially the wives. Not Cathy, she didn't lack for brains, any more than for spirit, I'll give her that. But Mrs Earnshaw was a sad, silly thing, who'd made a right mess of the housekeeping at Wuthering Heights before she had my mother in to help her, and as for Frances, that Mr Hindley brought home for a wife, as far as I could tell she could scarcely read or write. I never saw her pick up a book without putting it down a minute afterwards, declaring it 'tiresome'. It was no better with ciphering: she knew that as mistress she ought to keep the household accounts, and so once a month or so she would get out the account book and all the bills and receipts, and make a great show and bustle of laying them out on the table. Then she would sit down with a pen and stare at them in a state of puzzlement, before handing them over to me with the excuse that she had a 'headache'.

They all thought he was lost in love for her – I know I told you so, Mr Lockwood, and anyone here would have told you the same. Indeed you would have thought the same yourself, had you seen them, with all the fuss and show he put on about her. And I'll not say he didn't love her. But sometimes, if I was by, and her back to me, in the midst of his fussing he would send me a long, keen look, as if all this show was for my benefit, and then he would find something to complain of, to mark the difference between us: 'Nelly, fetch more cushions for this sofa,' or 'Nelly, this tea's like dirty dishwater! My wife is used to better things. Make up a fresh pot, and don't stint the tea this time. You can drink this stuff yourself, if you like it so.' Now the mistress, she would protest this at first. She was a friendly enough little thing, really, and wanted to be loved by all, so it was always 'don't take the trouble' or 'I like it just as it is, thank you' in her mouth. It was thanks to that we didn't have to fit up a lady's sitting room for her at the start, as Hindley wished us to do.

But she soon saw where the wind lay: Hindley would frown and look dark at any friendly words from her to me, but he petted and kissed her for complaining of me and ordering me about. And to tell the truth, I did little to encourage her friendliness myself. She would have liked to make a confidante of me, I could see, and small wonder: she had no one else to talk to, poor child, with Cathy wild and scornful, and no visiting in the neighbourhood. But I was having none of it. I gave her no more than 'yes, ma'am' and 'no, ma'am' and 'if you please, ma'am', though I could see it hurt her to be put off so. You see, Mr Lockwood, when Hindley brought her back, and flaunted her in front of me as his fine lady bride, I vowed to myself that from then on I'd work for my wages, and no more. 'Never again,' I said to them all in my head, 'will I split myself in two for you, to be kin one day, and slave the next, as you see need.' And as far as she went, I kept my word, and I was well pleased with myself for keeping it. Now, though, looking back, I think how lonely she must have been, for I think, silly as she was, she saw through all Hindley's petting and praise, that his heart was elsewhere, though she little guessed who had had the keeping of it.

Yes, Mr Lockwood, if you'd come to Wuthering Heights then, you'd have seen Hindley a doting husband, and me, a bustling and solicitous servant, and Frances, fluttering and laughing as if all the world loved her. And you'd have thought the only thing amiss in the family was a brooding, dark-faced boy and a wild mischievous girl, and their endless skirmishing with Hindley and Joseph. But all the time, Hindley was using her to strike at me, and I was using her to strike at him, and she, poor thing, was battered between us, and died of it. Of all the ghosts at Wuthering Heights, hers is the one I fear, for I wronged her, and God knows she meant me no harm.

TWO

But this will not do: I am meandering about like a puppy on the moors, following after one scent and then another in every direction at once. I must make a proper start, and tell you my story in a more collected fashion.

Heathcliff's arrival was the end of my childhood.

I had lived at the Heights as long as I could remember. My mother had been nurse to Hindley when we were both babes-in-arms, so we had been nearly always together. After we were weaned, my mother returned home to the cottage she shared with my father, coming to the Heights only one or two days a week to help with the churning and other tasks too heavy for the mistress and too skilled to be left to maids. But she chose, for reasons of her own, that I should stay on with the Earnshaws, to live in the nursery and, in time, have lessons with Hindley and Cathy.

I knew that I was not really one of the family. I knew that my own parents were poor, and that when I grew older I should have to work for my bread, as they did. I knew that I was only permitted to live and be educated at the Heights because of Mrs Earnshaw's old friendship with my mother, and her gratitude for my mother's services to the family, and that it was expected of me that I would be a pleasing companion to the children and a help to Mrs Earnshaw – and to my mother too, when she came over. I knew all this, I say, because I had been told it, but it was not a truth I had before me in my day-to-day life. Mrs Earnshaw was an indulgent mistress – if anything, kinder to me than to her own children, though perhaps that was only because I tried her patience less. Mr Earnshaw was a good deal sterner than his wife, but again, not more so to me than to his own, and with him too, I felt myself to be something of a favourite. It is true that I was often called from my lessons to do chores in the kitchen, but Hindley was almost equally called upon out-of-doors, his father thinking it best to give him an early introduction to the labours required by the estate he was to inherit. For the rest, I ate, slept, studied and played with Hindley and Cathy, shared in their treats and their punishments, and participated as an equal in their games. I knew, if I thought about it, that my future prospects were widely different from theirs, but what child can think about that, when the sun is shining and the bees are humming over the blooming heather, and she and her nursery-mates have just been granted an unexpected holiday from lessons in honour of the first sunny day in a week? And looking back on it now, my childhood seems composed only of such holidays. But all that changed when Heathcliff came.

We were little prepared for such a change that evening. We had all been eagerly anticipating the master's return from his trip to Liverpool, and our minds were dwelling much on the good things that were to arrive with him. You must not think, though, that we were greedy children, always looking after gifts and treats, or that we were much attached to toys and other possessions. This was an exceptional occasion, for the master had never been gone so far or so long from the house before.

In those days, Gimmerton was the outermost limit of our known world, and Liverpool seemed scarcely less distant and magical than Paris or Constantinople. Then, too, the gifts Mr Earnshaw had engaged to bring back for us held a significance far beyond their price. For Hindley, who had asked for a fiddle, his father's cheerful promise to bring him one had come like a peace offering, for he endured much criticism for preferring all forms of play and merrymaking – which his father termed indolence – to schoolwork or farm business. Cathy, too, had been often scolded for being too wild and too much out-of-doors, when she ought to be sitting in the house with her sampler, or helping her mother. Emboldened by Hindley's success, she had asked for a whip – and took her father's smiling acquiescence in the request as tacit permission for many a future gallop across the moors on her little pony. I myself, when asked, had not ventured to request anything more extravagant than 'an apple', whereupon he called me a good girl and promised me a whole pocketful.

As the hour of his expected return approached, our excitement reached a pitch that made any pretence of rational employment impossible. Hindley, in anticipation of his fiddle, was holding an invisible one stiffly to his shoulder with his head bent sideways, and sawing the air over it with the grimmest possible expression on his face, while his feet danced merrily under him as if disconnected from the top, in perfect imitation of our best local fiddler – a performance that had even the mistress in fits of laughter. Cathy, not to be outdone, was cantering around the outside of the room as if she were pony and rider both, and, by judicious application of her imaginary whip (signalled by shouting '*Thwack!*' as she moved her arm), leaping every obstacle in her path with ease. I, with nothing more exciting to expect than apples, was trying to prove my superior virtue by sitting quietly with some plain sewing, but Hindley's glee was infectious, and I soon jumped up to improvise a dance to his imaginary tune – earning me a gallant bow from the pretending fiddler – while Mrs Earnshaw clapped the time, and Cathy galloped about to the same rhythm.

In all the riot we half forgot the object of our anticipation, so that the master's weary 'Halloo' from outside, announcing his arrival at the gate, came like a magical signal ending the revels all in a flash, as we scurried to our seats, still flushed and laughing, to compose ourselves for a more seemly welcome. In addition to the promised gifts, we had formed hopes of getting some marvellous sweets, for Mr Earnshaw never went to town without bringing us back a few small indulgences of that kind, and, with childish logic, we thought that this much longer trip, to a much larger town, would yield treats proportionately more magnificent.

But even our more reasonable expectations were disappointed, when the master appeared with nothing more to offer than that queer, filthy little child who would be named Heathcliff. Hindley could not forbear weeping when his father drew forth the shards of the broken kit, and Cathy wailed outright when her father's assiduous searching and patting of pockets yielded only the news that her whip was lost.

All this was but a poor recommendation of young Heathcliff to our affections, as you may imagine, and it was not helped by the master's too-evident disgust that his children should weigh the loss of mere 'trifling toys', as he put it, above the salvation of a human being. But the mistress's dismay at the new arrival was hardly less than their own, and as might have been expected, they all fed off each other's: the children taking umbrage on their mother's behalf, and the mistress on the children's – and all of them directing their anger first and

11

foremost at the child, as being a safer object for it than their lord and master.

As for me, of course I never tasted my apples – yet I was thrust out of the garden all the same. I have told you how I left the child out on the landing, that night, after being told to put him to bed, and how, upon the master discovering it, I was sent away in disgrace. I made light of it to you, but to my childish mind at the time it really seemed hardly less of a catastrophe than the expulsion of our first parents – and no less permanent. He had thundered at me in the manner of an Old Testament prophet, concluding with the terrible words, 'Leave this house, Ellen Dean, and never return.'

Well, I stumbled out of there, I don't know how, and set out towards home. For the first half-mile I could scarcely walk for grief, so finally I set myself down in a small hollow and gave over entirely to sobbing. I had rarely seen Mr Earnshaw so angry, and never so with me, and it seemed a terrible thing to have lost his good opinion, as I thought, for ever. But when I had exhausted the first burst of grief, the chill wind sent me on my way again. Then walking warmed and woke me, and my mind began to dwell more on what lay before me than on what was behind.

My reflections were not comfortable ones. I knew that it was at my mother's wish that I remained at the Heights, and I couldn't think that she would be pleased to see me cast out of there by my own fault. As for my father, on the rare occasions that I saw him he could scarcely look at me without raising his hand to strike me. Terrified of him as I was, I didn't like to think of what he might do if he thought I'd given him good cause for displeasure. However, the more I dawdled on the way, the less chance I had of making it home before he returned from work, and I preferred to encounter my mother's anger alone first, reasoning that it would be the less dangerous of the two, and further, that once she had got over the worst of it herself she would be likelier to take my part in defence against my father, should that prove necessary.

So I mended my pace, and began thinking how I might present myself in the best light to my mother. 'After all,' I said to myself, 'what have I done but what the whole family (the master excepted) wished me to do? Am I not bound to do as I'm bid by them, and did not Hindley and Cathy refuse to have the child in the nursery with them? The master, weary from his journey, was in bed already, and the mistress was going on at a great pace herself about how she "couldn't think what Mr Earnshaw thought he was about, bringing such a creature into the family, when who knows what nasty habits the child will have picked up in the street – most likely he'd steal all the valuables in the house, or maybe murder us all in our beds!" ("I'll murder him first!" was Hindley's reply) – so what was I to do?'

With such reflections, I had worked myself, by the time I came within sight of my parents' cottage, into feeling rather aggrieved at my expulsion than otherwise, and I almost looked forward to telling my wrongs to my mother – until the sight of her in the flesh, standing in the doorway and looking more worried than pleased to see me, drove all my fine words from my head.

'Nelly! Whatever brings you here at this time? Has something happened at the Heights? Are they all well?'

I managed to stumble out a reassurance on this point, before sobs overtook me. 'I have been sent away,' I wailed, 'never to return, because I did wrong by the orphan boy, and would have brought God's curse down on the house by turning him from the door.'

My reception was not at all what I expected. Instead of being angry at me, or sympathizing with my sorrow, she began cross-questioning me about matters that had little to do with what was uppermost in my mind, which was the fault I'd committed and the punishment I was to bear for it.

'What orphan boy was this?'

'The one the master brought home from Liverpool yesterday.'

'Liverpool! When did he go there? I saw him in church only last Sunday.'

'Aye, he left just after dinner Sunday.'

'Travelling of a Sunday! That's unlike him. And he must have half-killed his horse, to go there and back in this time. Or did he take the coach from Gimmerton?'

'Neither one. He walked all the way, and it's his feet that were half killed, as I saw myself when I brought him a basin and towel to wash them. All swollen they were, and rubbed raw and bleeding in many places. It is not wrong to walk on a Sunday, is it?' I added, a bit concerned about this point. 'How could it be, when we all walk to church and back?'

'To be sure not – though if he'd waited until Monday he could still have got there quicker by coach. Very strange that he should walk all that way. And why should he go at all?'

'He said he had business there.'

'What business could he possibly have in Liverpool?'

'Probably something about the wool, I should think.'

'No, he deals with a wool stapler in Gimmerton, and any business he had further afield than that would be handled by his solicitor.'

'Well I'm sure I don't know,' I said, beginning, perversely enough, to feel rather slighted by her focus on Mr Earnshaw's doings. 'He doesn't tell me his business. But I don't know why he'd make such a journey if he didn't need to.'

'No . . . And you say he picked up the child there? How did he come by it?'

'He said he found it in the street, half-starved, and no one to take charge of it.'

'And so he brought it all that way home? And on foot too? Strange.'

'Well, he couldn't leave him there to die, could he?' I said, now feeling rather defensive on Mr Earnshaw's part. 'Are we not bid to care for orphans and widows?'

'We are. But we needn't walk sixty miles to Liverpool to find them, when there's misery enough within a day's walk to keep the charity of ten Earnshaws occupied.'

'But he was there anyway, on business,' I reminded her, 'and he found the child there, and no one would own it, and he couldn't leave it to starve, and so . . .'

'Aye. So you said. What does the child look like?'

'Dark all over. Partly from dirt, I guess – I don't think he had ever been bathed before. But his skin was dark even after bathing.'

'How old?'

'Two or three years by size, but he seems older by his manner.'

'Can he not speak for himself?'

'Only some queer gibberish. Nothing we can understand.'

'Stranger and stranger! How does he act towards Mr Earnshaw? Does he seem to know him?'

'He looks to him all the time, and seems less frightened of him than of the rest of us,' I said – choosing not to mention that this was no doubt because Hindley and Cathy pinched him whenever they could, and I made faces at him, while even Mrs Earnshaw made no secret of her dislike. 'But he doesn't seem to understand him any better than the rest of us.'

'Hmm.' She sank into a chair, looking puzzled.

Like most children, I was accustomed to take what my elders told me as simple truth, never thinking to question it except insofar as it directly concerned myself. Little as I liked the strange new creature, and sorry as I was for the trouble he had brought on my head, it had never occurred to me that there was anything unaccountable in Mr Earnshaw's having brought him home. That he was a good, wise, and just man I firmly believed. If he thought it his duty to claim a stray child in a far-off city as his responsibility, no doubt it was so. But this did not appear to be my mother's view of the case.

'How does he act towards the child? Is he very fond of it?'

'He seems so. He fires up if anyone seems to be slighting him in any way. He was very angry when he found I'd—' I stopped, unable to speak further.

'What did you do, Nelly?'

'Nothing!' I cried, all my sense of grievance returning. 'Hindley and Cathy wouldn't have him in the nursery, and Mrs Earnshaw was in hysterics that he was in the house at all, and it was left to me to find him a place to sleep, so where was I to put him? What else was I to do? Take him into my own bed? I just left him on the landing, and hoped he'd be gone by morning.'

'Hush, Nelly. Calm yourself and stop shouting. Did you tell Mr Earnshaw this?'

'No. I don't like to carry tales, and—'

'And what?'

'I didn't want Hindley to be beaten, as I knew he would be.'

'Is Hindley beaten often?'

'I don't know. Not so very often. It's just that—'

'What?'

'Just . . . I don't like to see it. Mr Earnshaw is so angry when he does it. His face gets purple. And Hindley, he . . . I . . .' I took a deep breath, and looked at the ground. 'I feel as if it's happening to me.'

'Does Mr Earnshaw ever beat you?'

'No. If Hindley and I get into mischief, it is always Hindley who gets the blame – he takes the blame. And I never do wrong on my own. At least not until now. So how could I bring him into it?'

'What did Mr Earnshaw do when he found out what you'd done with the child?'

'He was so angry it frightened me. He said . . . he said I must leave and never come again. But I would rather he had beaten me, if only I could stay. What will Hindley do without me? He'll have no friend at all. And what will become of me?'

You may think it strange, Mr Lockwood, that a child of fourteen could ask such a question of her mother, and under her father's roof. But I was mortally afraid of my father, and my mother's care in keeping me from the sight of him, by making him unfamiliar to me, only increased my terror. No doubt it was wrong of me, but I verily believed he might kill me if he had to see me every day.

My mother sat me down in the kitchen, and shortly produced a mug of tea and some bread and butter. All the while, she was speaking to me in her gentlest tones.

'Hindley is a difficult lad,' she said, 'and has been so from a babe. Mr Earnshaw doesn't wish to spare the rod and spoil him, and doubtless he is right in that, although . . . well, it may be difficult for you to see it. Mr Earnshaw may be a hard man, Nelly, but he is a just man. If his anger has not fallen on you before today, it is because he has cause to believe Hindley is at the root of any mischief you two get into together. And that is so, is it not? Did you not say you never do wrong except with him – until now, anyway?'

I nodded silently, looking steadily into my mug of tea.

'It is generous in Hindley to take all the blame to himself,' she went on. 'It shows a good heart. But it means you have all the more duty to head him away from wrongdoing when you are with him, Nelly. That is the best way to shield him from punishment.'

'But how am I to do that if I am never to return?' I wailed.

'Leave that to me,' she said, and began removing her apron and wrapping her shawl, preparatory to going out. I rose and was beginning to do the same, but she stopped me.

'You stay here, Nelly. I am going to the Heights, and I will see what I can do to allow you to return there, but I must go alone.' I glanced towards the door, not liking to say what was in my mind.

'In all likelihood I will be back before your father returns. But if I'm not—' She began looking about the cottage – perhaps for a likely hiding place, I thought, though the rooms were too small and sparsely furnished to afford one. At last, with an air of decision, she reached down the crock of sugar, and, feeling her way to the bottom of it, pulled out a small purse, from which she drew two shillings, and put them on the table.

'Tell him you've brought him your wages,' she said. My eyes widened at this. The teaching at Wuthering Heights was strong on the Commandments, and lying to my father, I thought, would be breaking two at one blow. She must have guessed my thought, for she flushed and added, 'You needn't say an untruth – indeed I wouldn't wish you to. Leave the coins on the table, and only say "I'm getting wages now" – that should be true enough by the time you've said it, if my errand goes well.' She thought a bit more, then added, 'If he asks if that's all your wages, just say "I've given you all I got" – that's true too. The money will soften your welcome, and with any luck he'll go off with it to town straight away, and won't return until you're abed – but most likely I'll be back before he comes in anyway, as I said.'

No doubt this was a good plan, and 'with luck' might have worked well enough, but I had no intention of staying to find that out. As soon as my mother was out of sight behind a rise I got up myself and followed her, keeping well back and behind such cover as I could find. When we got nearer the Heights, this was easy enough, for Hindley and I had learned every dip and hollow all around, and prided ourselves on being able to disappear from view at a moment's notice – particularly when chores or lessons were in the offing.

I had expected that my mother would go straight to Mrs Earnshaw, her old friend and staunchest ally in the household, so I was surprised to see her seek out the master instead, and in a manner that told me she had no wish to be spotted by the mistress first. This puzzled me, until I reflected that her wish to get home before my father's return meant she must dispatch her business quickly, and that it was the master, after all, who had banned me from the house, and must be won over to agree to my return.

Mr Earnshaw had carved out an office for himself from the corner of the nearer barn – little more than a closet, really, but lit with a small window, and furnished with a desk, a couple of chairs, and a brazier for hot coals in winter. Here he kept his account books, and met with his tenants and any others with whom he had business that he did not wish to intrude on the house, where the mistress held sway.

I was not near enough to hear what was said when my mother found Mr Earnshaw in another barn examining a lame horse, but the consequence of it was that they both went into the 'office' and closed the door.

19

Under the office window was a large and fiercely prickly gooseberry bush, placed there, no doubt, so as to discourage eavesdroppers. But years before, Hindley and I had amused ourselves one lazy afternoon by constructing a 'secret passageway', low to the ground between the bush and the wall. We had carefully lined it with willow twigs and grasses, to allow us to squeeze through without being snagged on the prickles, into a space carved out of the centre of the bush, scarcely large enough for the two of us to huddle in together, but perfectly situated to render audible anything that was said in the office. We never overheard anything of real interest to us there, but, by christening our little hideaway 'the robbers' cave', and performing the like transformation on whatever we heard there – as, turning shillings into pounds, and pounds into bags of gold, or taking 'milk' as code for brandy, 'sultanas' for pearls and rubies, and 'a ewe lamb' for an Arabian mare of priceless bloodlines, we contrived to imagine ourselves as a pair of hardened bandits with prices on our heads, ruthlessly planning the violent diversion of all this precious cargo.

It had been a few years since Hindley and I had last pushed our way under the gooseberry bush together, having outgrown its accommodation for the two of us, but the passage was still there, only a little dilapidated with time, and when I had squeezed myself along it into the old cave, I found it cramped but adequate for myself alone. I carefully settled down to listen.

'So you have thrown Nelly out of the house,' began my mother, with a directness that rather startled me.

'By her own fault,' he responded quickly, and told again what she had already had from me, much dwelling on the bad heart shown in my cruelty to an unfriended orphan, so that I was like to begin sobbing all over again, but that my fear of discovery was more powerful than my grief.

'She did wrong there, to be sure. But she had seen the child bring sorrow and strife into the house – the mistress distraught and angry, and her nursery-mates dismayed, and it was that more than cruelty that made her act as she did. Whatever possessed you to bring the child home in the first place?'

'I found him starving in the street in Liverpool, and no one to claim him or care for him.'

'Aye, and could have found two or three more on every corner there, if what I hear is true. Not to mention the poor of our own parish, whom it would better become you to aid than a stranger from far away – particularly as some of them are your own tenants.'

'It is not for you to dictate to me how or to whom I extend charity, Mrs Dean. That is between me and my conscience.'

'Very well then. What was the business that brought you to Liverpool?'

'That too is between me and my conscience.'

'Ah. It's as I thought then – the "business" and the boy are one and the same.'

'I don't know quite what you mean to imply. I can assure you that the boy was unknown to me before I went, nor do I know any more of his parentage or circumstances than I have told already.' There was a short pause. 'But I will not deny to you that I had some such purpose in making this journey. And I trust that knowing this will make plainer to you the importance of treating this poor child with consideration.'

'I would more willingly grant that if you had not made him the occasion for thrusting my own child from your hearth.'

'Your child has a home, to which it is perhaps time she returned. She should come under her own father's discipline.'

'Her father's discipline was like to have killed her! For pity's sake, Mr Earnshaw, do you not remember the condition she was in when I brought her here? Her arm broken, her eye blacked, and all over bruises? If he could treat her so as a child of four, what will he do now?'

'Nelly is old enough now to avoid giving offence.'

'Do you think he will wait for her to give offence? Her very existence gives offence to him! I have seen him with her, sir, as you have not. She has but to walk into the room for him to be lit up with rage. He will take offence at the way she stands, or walks, or sits in a chair. I had hoped it would be better when our son was born, but though he doted on the lad, it did little to soften him towards Nell. And since he died,' she paused to regain her voice, 'it is as if all his grief were changed into anger at her. You would have thought she had had a hand in his death, to hear him. And this, even though I had made sure she was away from home during the whole of the poor child's illness – though it was a bitter sorrow to her that she was unable to say farewell.'

'You ought not to complain of your husband to me,' said the master, but his voice had softened.

'I don't wish to. I have made my bed, and I will lie in it. But you must forgive a mother's concern for the welfare of her child. Mr Earnshaw, please think of what this means for her. Do you think I am happy to have her so far from me, or to let her believe, as I know she does, that I bear her too little love to care much for her company? Do you think I like to see her loving your wife with the love she might have given me? For pity's sake, sir, give her back the refuge here that you promised me for her ten years ago in this very room. Far be it from me to hinder your fulfilment of any vow you may have made with regard to this strange child, but bethink you, sir: can an act of penance be acceptable to the Lord if its burden falls heavier on others than on the penitent? That were like offering as sacrifice a ram taken from another man's flock.'

A long silence followed this speech. When the master finally spoke, it was in a voice so low I could scarcely follow it.

'There is something in what you say, Mrs Dean. I have perhaps been overly hasty in sending your daughter away. But neither can I simply remit her punishment. It must be clear, not only to her but to the whole household, that this child must be treated with all the consideration due to my own son.'

'And is my—' but whatever my mother had been about to say, she thought better of it. I heard her draw a deep breath, such as I had sometimes seen her do to calm herself when angry, and when she spoke her voice was steady. 'Banish her for a day or two if you must,' she said. 'I can keep her so long at least without too much difficulty. And when she returns, let her return on the footing of a servant – the change will seem to her and your children to mark your displeasure clearly enough. And I do think it best, with this new child in the house, for her to understand her own place more clearly. She has been playmate to your children and a sharer in their lessons longer already than a girl of her . . . her birth and prospects can expect. In addition,' she added more hesitantly, 'her father expects her to be earning, but I don't want her going into the mills: that work is bad for girls – both for their bodily health and their character.'

Mr Earnshaw concurred.

'I have heard that Martha Pickerell will be leaving you soon to be married. Nell can take her place. You need pay her no more than is customary for girls her age who are new to service – a shilling a week to start with, which is a good deal less than Martha earns now – and she's a quick-witted lass and a hard worker' – I was pleased to hear a grunt of assent here from

23

the master – 'so you will not lose anything by it. I have been teaching her the dairying on my days here already, and I've no doubt that in time she will be able to manage that too, and more than repay you for all your kindness to her.'

To my astonishment, the master let out a grim chuckle. 'If she takes after you at all, Mary, I've no doubt she will manage us all quite nicely.'

'Oh yes, I have managed very well for myself, have I not?' my mother replied bitterly. This produced another awkward silence.

'Very well then,' he said at last, 'Nelly shall come back with us, say after church on Sunday, and on the terms you suggest.' Relief flooded me (making its exit in a gush of silent tears), not only that I might come back, but that, as it seemed, Mr Earnshaw's goodwill and good humour were restored – for much as I longed to return to the Heights, I had rather dreaded living henceforth under his displeasure.

I would have expected that my mother, having gained her point, would head homeward forthwith, so I was surprised to hear her broaching a new subject: 'And this new child, what place will he have?'

'I shall raise him as one of my own.'

'Do you think that is wise? Will you be giving him a son's portion? What will that mean for Hindley?'

'If Hindley cannot welcome the lad as a brother, so much the worse for him. He must do as he is bid while I am still master in this house.'

'He is your son.'

'Aye, and his mother's.'

'From whom he gets a loving heart and a merry spirit, if they be not trampled down by harsh treatment.'

'Mrs Dean, I have listened to you on the subject of your

24

daughter, and I have responded not ungenerously, I think, to your plea on her behalf. But I will not be dictated to by you about the way I raise my own children. I trust that is understood?'

'Forgive me, sir. I still have something of a mother's feeling for my old nursling, and I couldn't wish to see him slighted for a child who has no prior claims on your heart. But I had no wish to give offence. You must do as you think best, of course. And I thank you heartily for what you have done for Nell.' With this I heard sounds suggestive of my mother wrapping her shawl again in preparation for leaving.

'Will you not stop in to visit with my wife? She would be grieved to hear that you'd come and gone without seeing her.'

'Perhaps it would be best not to mention it, then.'

'Not possible, I'm afraid – the children will have brought her word already. Do go in and see her – and while you are there you can tell her of my decision about Nell. She will be glad of it – I know she has been sorely grieved by all this.' The master spoke with some embarrassment here. I guessed – what I later learned was true – that he had had hard words from the mistress over the new child and my expulsion, and he did not feel it would be conducive to his dignity or authority as master of the house to confess directly to suspending my punishment so soon. 'You are also best able to explain to her about Nelly's new duties,' he added, 'which of course it will be her task to oversee.'

'Very well then, I will just stop in briefly to speak to her.'

'While you are there, please tell her that I will be up in the high pasture this afternoon, so she should not expect me to dinner.'

With that they went their separate ways, my mother heading into the house, and the master taking off with his brisk, long

strides towards the heights behind the house – which, fortunately, lay in another direction than my own way. No sooner
had they disappeared from view than I began extracting myself
from my hiding place. This proved awkward, for my entrance
had dislodged much of the wickerwork lining the passageway,
and I was hard-pressed to make progress while detaching the
snagged prickles that threatened to tear my clothes. My dress
made it out unscathed, but my arms and face were not so lucky
– a fact that I realized would require some explanation when
I saw my mother again, as I was supposed to have been sitting
quietly at home all the while. No sooner did I emerge than
Hindley pounced on me with a shout.

'Nell, I'm so glad you're back. It would be too much to have
that filthy little horror foisted upon us and lose you too all at
one blow. But what in Heaven have you been doing? You look
like the cat's been at you.'

'Hush, Hindley – keep your voice low and come around the
corner behind this wall – I'm not supposed to be here now. I
had to scurry roundabout to get here without Mother spotting
me, and I took a tumble into some brambles on the way.' I
didn't think it wise to mention my eavesdropping, as Hindley
would insist on hearing everything that had been said, and I
knew from long experience that his discretion was not to be
relied on.

'Is your mother here now?'

'She's stepped in to see the mistress, I believe to see about
my coming back.'

'Well, let's hear them, then. Come over here beneath the
window, and I'll lift you up.'

'Better I should lift you – you're smaller than I am.'

'Nonsense! I'm older, and anyway you're only a girl.' In fact,
I was the elder, though only by a few months, but from the

time he could talk Hindley had always insisted it was he, and if anyone asked his age would always proudly claim his full years while subtracting one from mine, as in 'I am *four*, and Nelly is *three*.' At the time, this had been terribly galling to my childish dignity, but my mother would not let me contradict him. As she said, it only made folk think me forward for my age, which was no harm to me. By this time, I had grown so used to Hindley's claim to be my elder that I all but forgot that it wasn't so. So I let him grasp me about the knees and heave me up, but he staggered about so that I begged him to put me down.

'Hindley, please let's switch places,' I said. 'If your face is spotted at the window you'll get only a scolding from your mother, but I shall be in a peck of trouble with my mother and the master both if I'm caught. And anyway,' I added cannily, 'you are better at gripping the sill than I am, which takes off a good deal of the weight.' So Hindley allowed me to lift him up, and overheard just enough to announce to me with great importance the news I had already gleaned from my nest in the gooseberry bush.

'You're to come back after church next Sunday,' he said, 'but you're to be a servant now, Nell, and you'll get a shilling a week! I wish I was a servant – no lessons to do, and more pocket money than I shall ever see. But you'll share with me, won't you, Nell?'

'All my wages will go to my father,' I said, 'and if I get no lessons, there'll be no play either: I shall have to work all day, so you needn't be jealous. But hush now – I want to hear what else is said.' I lowered him to the ground, for in truth the conversation was perfectly audible from there, and easier to follow without Hindley relaying his own versions from above.

'I am so glad we are to have Nelly back with us, Mary,' the mistress was saying. 'I was sorely grieved that she should be sent away on so slight a fault. But I do verily think my husband has gone mad! How could he bring this creature here all the way from Liverpool, and then turn on our own children so? And it's worse than that – he's named the child Heathcliff, after our firstborn! It is cruel of him, don't you think? Positively cruel to bring that name before me every day!' She began sobbing bitterly. Hindley's eyes filled with tears too.

'The little beast!' he hissed. 'I shall make him pay for this – just watch me.' Poor Hindley never could bear to see his mother cry (though it was a common enough occurrence), and generally contrived to get angry at someone else, to cover his own grief for her. In this case, I saw that the new child would bear the brunt of the anger Hindley dared not show towards his father. To be honest, I was not inclined to take the new child's part either, for I still felt aggrieved myself that he had pushed me, as I saw it, from my place with the children at the Heights.

From the window came the familiar sounds of my mother soothing and cheering her old friend, as the mistress's sobs gradually subsided into sighs. 'You mustn't take it so, Helen,' my mother was saying. 'It was a good deed, surely, to rescue the poor child from starvation or worse on the streets, and now that he is here it will be your duty to bring him up to be a credit to the family. Probably Mr Earnshaw thought that giving the boy the name of your firstborn would help you to feel a mother's affection for him. I am sure he meant you no harm by it. You know you have been sad not to be able to have more children about you, and now here is another little one come to you as if by magic, like the return of your lost child. And that Nelly is coming back as a servant need not grieve you

28

either – it only means she'll be spending her days helping you instead of scampering over the moors with Hindley. Really, she'll be more like a daughter to you than ever. And I shall have to come over here more often myself, at first, to help her learn her new duties.'

'I wish you could be here always, Mary,' said the mistress with a sigh. 'Those were the happiest years, when you were here, and I have never managed so well since you left. Why did you have to get married and go away?'

'It was you who married first, Helen, long before me,' said my mother gently. 'And if I had not married and had Nell, what would have become of Hindley? He would have died like all the rest, would he not? Those times seem happy to you now because you remember what you had then and have not now, but you forget that you didn't have your bairns then, and thought you never would, and that grieved you sorely. We never get all we want in this world. We must bear the trials God sends to us, and do our duty with a cheerful heart.' Then, with special firmness, she added, 'And your duty now is to this child, to *Heathcliff.*'

'Heathcliff,' the mistress sighed. 'I suppose I must accustom myself to using it.'

'It won't take long – you'll see,' my mother replied, 'but I cannot stay longer, Helen. I've left Nelly at home by herself, waiting to hear what is to become of her, and I should prefer to be back before Tom gets home, too.'

'Send Nelly my love, then, and tell her how glad I shall be to have her back again, and she must not mind too much about the work, for I will be an easy mistress to her.'

'I'll send your love to be sure,' said my mother, 'but as to her work, I'll tell her nothing of the sort, and really, Helen, you will do her no favours by encouraging idleness, unless you have a fortune hidden somewhere you are planning to endow her with. Nelly will always have to earn her bread, like the rest of us, and the sooner she resigns herself to that, the happier she will be.'

I did not stay to hear more, for now I had to contrive to get home before my mother, and make it look as if I'd never left. 'Hindley,' I said, 'do you think you can manage to delay my mother a few minutes, so I can get well away before she sets out?'

'Leave it to me,' he said with a grin, delighted as always to have a hand in mischief of any kind. 'You know your mother can never resist an appeal from her old nursling.' He took off for the door, while I took one of our more circuitous and well-hidden routes back towards my parents' cottage.

I soon saw that it would be hard to keep out of sight and ahead of my mother all the way (though stout, she was a brisk walker), and still arrive in time to compose myself and my story for her arrival, but I thought of something that would save me a good portion of my trip, and serve as excuse for my injuries as well. I brought myself around nigh and to one side of her, climbed up on a hummock, and waved, calling 'Mother, Mother!' from a direction that was neither before nor behind her path.

'Nelly! What brings you here? I told you to stay at home. And what in Heaven have you done to yourself?' she added, noticing the scratches on my arms and face.

'I'm very sorry, Mother, but I just couldn't stay. I was . . . I had . . .' There was no need to pretend my embarrassment. 'I didn't know what I should say if Father came in, and I grew anxious, so I ran out onto the moors and came to meet you, and then there were brambles in my way, and I got tangled in them.' This was all true enough as far as it went, but I then bethought me that I ought to show some suspense about the result of her errand, and begged her to tell me if I would be permitted to return.

'Yes, Nelly, you are to go home with them after church on Sunday. But you shall be earning wages now, and must not go running off to the moors with the other children.'

'And what am I to do until then? Will I stay here with you and Father?'

'You will, for tonight anyway – but don't fear, Nell, all will be well with him, you'll see. Come with me now, and I'll tell you all about it.' She told me, of course, a good deal less than all I had heard for myself, but I listened with as much interest as if it were all new to me. The events of that day had set me thinking about a number of things I had not given much thought to until then, and had made my mother an object of interest and curiosity to me in a way she had never been before.

Dusk was approaching by the time we reached the cottage, but my father was not yet home. My mother hurried to build up the fire and set supper in motion. She was just looking at my scratches, and putting salve on the deeper ones, when we heard my father's footsteps outside. She waved me into an inconspicuous corner, where I cowered, trying to quell my fear and be ready to compose my face into a smile when he should spot me. He came in without looking around, and sat down heavily in his chair by the fire. My mother quickly brought him a mug of tea and a large slice of bread and butter. He took these in either hand and leaned back with a sigh.

'How did the job go on?' she asked solicitously. 'Did you finish it today?'

'Noo, I did not. It's bigger nor I thought – half the wall 'ill have to come down a' the north side, and be done all anew.

31

I'd told the fellow at the start he munna think it war only a hole to be filled in, if the wall round it weren't fit, and so it weren't. But he took it with an ill grace, all the same. I asked for payment today, and he were right shy of givin' it. Said as how he'd pay when the job were done, but I were having none of that. "I've earned me wages," I said to him. "Ye needn't fear that I won't finish the job – I've never left one unfinished yet, and I'm not starting now. But I've got t' buy me bread and pay me rent same as the next man, and I don't see why I should be stinted because another man's wall is in worse shape than he thought."

'"Nought a penny till the job is done," says ee. "I know your ways, and if I pay you now, you'll be drunk tomorrow, and my cows 'ill 've the cold wind on their backs another day." Can you believe that? I'd aff a mind to swing my fist at him.

'"And what are we to do without my wages tomorrow? Are we to have porridge for our Sunday dinner for the sake of your cows?" I asked.'

'Fie, Tom,' my mother interjected, her voice drifting into broader Yorkshire than she ever employed at the Heights, 'when have I ever given you porridge for Sunday dinner? There'll be roast fowl and ale, and apple pasty, same as ever, whether you get your wages tomorrow or Saturday, or not till Monday. And there's money in the house now too – look, Nelly's come home, and she's earning wages now. Here's two shillings for you, and she's to have one every week.'

I took this as my cue to emerge from the corner, and I did my best to look cheerful and glad to see him.

'Hello, Father,' I said, with a bit of a curtsey.

'Hoo, "Father" is it? Well, aren't we the fine lady,' he said, but he was hampered by the tea and bread in either hand from offering worse hostilities than this.

'Whisht, husband,' my mother chided, 'is that any way to greet your daughter who's just brought you her first wages, like a good girl?'

'What wages? I 'aven't seen any yet.'

'She's afraid to come near ye, most likely. If you can't be friendly the first time you've seen her in six months, I'll just tell her to bring her wages elsewhere.'

'Aw right then,' he said, and, balancing his slice atop his mug, he extended a large, calloused hand to me in a reasonable imitation of friendship. I came forward, at my mother's encouraging nod, and put my small hand in his great one for a brief shake, before proffering the shillings. 'Eh, you're a good enough lass,' he said, pulling me a foot or two closer and tousling my hair, at which I needed every ounce of self-control I had not to flinch. Then my mother motioned me to a stool at the other side of the fire, and handed me a mug and slice of my own before settling into the other chair herself. I had little appetite, but I was grateful for anything that would save me looking at or talking to my father, and so took to eating and drinking with a great show of earnestness, and we all sat munching in silence for some time.

His supper finished, my father rose and headed for the door.

'I'll just step out to the Ox and Plough to meet a man about a job of work,' he said.

'Aye, go then,' said my mother, with as much good humour as if she believed him. When he was gone, she put an arm around me and heaved a sigh.

'Well done, Nelly, you're a good lass. He'll drink that off at the inn, and before he's back we'll have you tucked snug into bed up the ladder in the loft, where he never goes. And anyway, he's not one of those men who become more violent with drink – quite the contrary, thank Heaven.'

It was a better end than I could have imagined to a day begun so badly, but for all that I could not help collapsing into her arms and sobbing as if my heart were broken. 'Why does he hate me so?' I wailed – rather to my own surprise, I must confess, since normally I did not think myself much concerned about what he thought of me, only provided I were out of reach of his fists. But, of all that had distressed me that day, this was the safest to express to my mother, and the likeliest to earn her sympathy, so perhaps that had something to do with it.

My mother never had much patience for tears, but on this occasion she did no more than tighten her arms and ease me down beside her by the fire, rocking gently, until my sobs began to subside.

'He doesn't hate you, Nelly,' she said at last. 'How could he? He doesn't know you at all.'

'But he acts as if he does.'

'He was . . . not kind to you when you were just a little thing, and that sits heavy on his conscience now. He's not a bad man, Nelly. I can't excuse how he has treated you, but I want you to know that in the main he is not a bad man. He has never laid a finger on me, nor done me any more wrong than to drink wages he ought to save. And then perhaps I've taken too much care to keep you clear of him, so that he feels awkward with you, and acts rough to cover it. But you got off to a good start with him today, and perhaps these few days at home will prove a blessing in disguise, and make you better friends in future.'

I could see that she was convincing herself as she spoke, but I remembered too vividly her urgency in pleading with Mr Earnshaw for my return to the Heights to feel the same confidence in her assurances. Nor had she really answered my question.

'But why me?' I persisted. 'He liked little Tommy well enough. Is it only because I'm a girl? Or is it because I was – because I'm the eldest?'

She sighed heavily, and let silence gather for a time. When she finally spoke, it was with some reluctance: 'When a man marries beneath himself, Nell – and let this be a lesson to you – he raises his wife to his level. His friends and relations may wish he had looked higher, but that just puts the more responsibility on his wife to ensure that he never regrets his choice. But when a woman marries down, she brings shame on herself and no credit to her husband. She is thought less of for it, and he partakes in some measure of her shame. I did your father no service by marrying him.'

That my mother had married 'beneath her' was not news to me – it being a rather frequent subject of querulous commentary by Mrs Earnshaw – but I was surprised to hear her own it so frankly, and it emboldened me to ask what I had never dared to ask before: 'Why did you marry him then?'

My mother flushed at this, and I could have pinched myself. I knew very well why they had married – as did anyone else who had ever looked in the parish record to compare the date of their marriage with that of my birth.

'I mean,' I stumbled, 'why him?'

'I was over forty years old, Nelly, and I had never been a beauty, even in my youth. I had no fortune aside from some little savings out of my wages, nor any prospects of any, and no family remaining who could be of material assistance to a husband of mine. It is true that I had better birth and education than many in my situation, and some claim to family connection with the Earnshaws, but that would not be enough to tempt a man of any stature unless it were backed by more tangible attractions of person or property. Thomas Dean earned day wages by the work of his hands, and possessed but little book learning, true, but his skill was much in demand and well paid, and his character was generally respected. It was said, too, that he had been a most devoted son to his mother, who was but lately dead, and perhaps it was that made him look so kindly on a plain woman eight years his elder. At any rate, he smiled whenever he saw me, and made all manner of excuses to come by the Heights to visit, and in time . . . well, I thought I could not do better, and might do a great deal worse.'

'But why should you have wished to do anything – I mean, to change your situation at all?' I persisted. I had crossed into forbidden territory already, I felt, and thought I might as well be hung for a sheep as a lamb, and ask all my questions at once. 'That is what Mrs Earnshaw cannot understand. She says you were already mistress of Wuthering Heights in all but name, because she was so often ill, and even that you had the best of it, for you got more in wages than she ever did in pin money.'

'She ought not to say such things,' my mother snapped, looking nettled. 'She forgets that I earned the household more than my wages and her pin money combined, selling the surplus butter and eggs that came out of my own good management of the dairy and poultry. Had I been mistress indeed that money would have been mine by right.'

'Please don't be angry at her,' I cried, stricken with guilt for having provoked her to lash out at the mistress, whom I loved dearly. 'Mrs Earnshaw never meant it seriously, I'm sure – it was only for a joke, and because she wishes you were still there, you know.'

'Don't fret about it, Nelly,' she said, softening. 'I am not really angry at her – I know she meant no harm. She only means that I did the work of a mistress, and held some of a mistress's authority over the servants. And she was always sorry that she could not do those things herself, as she thought she ought to, so she envied me that. But she doesn't understand, because she hasn't felt it, how it is to have the work and cares and responsibilities of a mistress without' – she paused to find the right words – 'without a mistress's honours, or privileges. I wanted a home of my own, even if it were a humble one, and children too, if that were still possible. I thought that I could give your father a better home than a woman of his own class could, and that would make up for . . . any disparities in what we brought to our marriage. And so I have done, so far as material things go. When I saw that he was prone to drinking, I made sure that I could put food on the table and clothes on our backs and make up the rent on this cottage, by my own efforts, and I have managed it in such a way that there is scarcely ever money about that he could demand of me for his own uses. But his pride has suffered from it, I think. If he knew that his own comfort and mine depended on what he brought home, if he had to face an empty belly or the threat of eviction, perhaps he would not be so ready to drink all he earns, and the need of drink would not have grown on him as much as it has. And that is why I say that I did him no favour in marrying him.'

I had never before heard my mother speak so frankly about my father or her marriage. I was much struck by the regret in her voice, and I found myself thinking more kindly of my father than I had ever done before. In that state I was bundled off to bed in the loft, and it was not until I was almost asleep that I realized that she had never answered my first question.

37

THREE

I awoke the next morning in considerable confusion, partly from the unfamiliar setting, though I soon recollected where I was, but more so because the morning was far advanced, and I was accustomed to being woken at dawn. I made haste down the ladder, expecting a scolding for my laziness, but my mother seemed cheerful enough.

'Good morning, little sleepyhead,' she said with a smile. 'Your father is off to work long since, but I thought after all the excitement of yesterday it would be as well to let you sleep in for once – we'll have you back in harness soon enough.' Whereupon she placed before me a mug of tea and a freshly baked oatcake spread liberally with butter and jam – a rare treat. And so it went on all day. My mother seemed inclined, most unusually, to be indulgent, and even make a fuss of me. She asked but little of me in the way of chores, so I found it easy to do more than she asked, and felt for the first time with her how pleasant it is to do labour that is offered in kindness and accepted with gratitude, instead of being demanded as a right.

My father did get at least some of his wages that day – or so we presumed, at any rate, from his not appearing at home until long after supper, and showing every sign that a good portion of his pay had been put to its usual use. I was already up in the loft again by the time he came in, but I was wide awake and peering over the edge of the ladder hole to watch him, counting on the darkness to hide me.

'Where's Nelly?' he asked, good-humouredly enough, and on being told that I was abed, bellowed, 'Nelly! wake up and come down from there, lass, and see what I've brought ye.'

Seeing my mother nod encouragement, I obeyed, whereupon he pulled out from under his jacket a large and somewhat sodden parcel wrapped in paper. 'Look here,' he said, placing it on the table and unwrapping it to show a sizeable joint of fresh pork, 'Braithwaite had just killed a pig, and he gev it me along wi' half of my wages, an' said he were sorry for what he said yesterday, and he hoped my Sunday dinner would be fine as ony man's. But I thought that as you'd be gone back to the Heights before then, and as the wife here has already promised me roast fowl on Sunday' – here he grinned at my mother, with a flirtatious twinkle that gave me a glimpse of what she had seen in him to marry him – 'that we'd 'ave it tomorrow instead.'

I had no need to force a smile with my thanks this time, and as for my mother, she pounced on the joint with delight and began exclaiming over its size and beauty.

'Eh, leave off, woman. It's only a bit o' pork, after all. The fuss you're making, you'd think I'd brought home the Infant Jesus.' I couldn't repress a laugh at this, it was so apt a description of my mother's rapturous attentions to the pink blob still half-swaddled in paper on the table, whereupon my father gave me a broad smile and a wink. My mother affected to be nettled by his teasing, but it was clear she was pleased. In short, we formed just then, however briefly, a plausible picture of a happy little family, and, as each of us knew how unlikely that was, we felt something like awe at its appearance, almost as if (I later thought) the humble joint of pork had been the Infant Jesus indeed, sent to bring peace and goodwill to us all.

The next day was devoted to the feast. In addition to the roast, my father had the night before given my mother a handful of coins 'for any such fixin's as ye 'aven't got about the house'. So early that morning, my mother and I walked into the little market town to do our shopping. Along the way, she practically skipped with pleasure, her delight in the occasion making her seem almost girlish despite her age and heavy form.

'It's grand to see how he's taken to you at last, isn't it, Nelly? It's just as I thought – he only felt awkward because of the temper he showed you as a little child, but he's over that now and ready to be right fond of you. It's rare for him to bring home so much of his wages as he gave me last night, and I know he did that for your sake. To think you thought he hated you! I hope you don't think that now, do you?'

'No, I suppose not,' I said cautiously, 'but do you think it will last?' I was thinking of how she had told me that he couldn't hate me because he didn't know me, and reflecting that this was scarcely less true of his affection now. And I was half afraid that in her enthusiasm she would decide against sending me back to the Heights. Glad as I was for my father's newfound friendliness – and it gladdened me more than I would ever have expected it would – I had no wish to trade for it the only home I had ever known, and the companionship of the people I had learned to love as my own family.

'Well, we shall have to be careful not to try it too much, shan't we?' she answered, seeing my worries in my face. 'You'll go back to the Heights tomorrow, and from then he'll see you only on your days off once a month, when you'll be bringing him your wages for real.'

We reached town, and bought flour, sugar, raisins, and tea, and a few bottles of ale for my father. Then she made me stay looking at bonnets in a shop window while she paid a visit to a pastrycook's shop, whence she returned with a small bundle tied up in white string. The rest of the day was spent preparing such a feast as I had never seen apart from Christmas or Easter, even at the Heights. My mother was a tireless worker, but usually steady and methodical in her work. Yet today she seemed almost frantic, as if by the sheer energy of her preparations for this one meal she could shore up and make permanent the good relations that had suddenly blossomed among us. She scoured the cupboards and garden for extra delicacies, and wound up undertaking more dishes at once than her small hearth could accommodate. At length she was driven to the expedient of making up a small fire in the yard, over which she set a pot with a suet pudding to boil and a small turnspit with the roast, leaving me to attend to them both while she concentrated on more complex matters within.

My father came home earlier than usual, having finished Braithwaite's wall not long after noon, but evidently my mother had expected this, for by the time he arrived the only evidence of our labours was the rich array of dishes crowded onto the clean white cloth on the table, and her own rather flushed and worn appearance – me she had already sent to wash and change into my Sunday best. My father seemed delighted by everything, and responded to my mother's apologies for her own disarray by sweeping her into his arms for a kiss, and declaring she looked younger than the day he married her. Then, to my great astonishment, he did the same by me, then looked me up and down and declared me

41

'the prettiest girl for ten mile around' – a patent falsehood, but I blushed with pleasure all the same.

'And for that, and because you're a working lass now, and comin' on for a grown woman, I've brought ye a bit of summat,' wherewith he handed me a small package done up in blue paper. I opened it to find a pretty pink and green hair ribbon, of the sort travelling pedlars sell for a ha'penny. It was a small thing enough, but so much more than I ever expected of him that I felt my throat closing and my eyes filling with tears as I tried to thank him. It was hard for me to believe that this was the same man for whom I had felt such terror all my life, and from whom I had heard my mother beg Mr Earnshaw to protect me, only two days before.

'She's overcome, aren't you, Nelly?' my mother said hastily, apparently fearing a misinterpretation of my response. 'Such a lovely thing, isn't it?' I nodded and smiled, but was still unable to speak.

'Overworn is more likely,' said my father. 'You must have driven her hard to get all this made since this morning. She's quite the slave-driver, isn't she?' he added aside to me in a loud whisper, at which I laughed and nodded again. 'Come, let's all eat before the poor girl faints away altogether.'

And so we sat down together, to such a meal as I had never imagined eating in that house: my father jovial, and full of a gentle, teasing wit I had not known he possessed; my mother continually looking from one to the other of us, her face lit with joy; and myself, so lost in wonder at it all that I scarcely tasted the rich pork, the pudding, the apple sauce and buttered greens, or even the magical-looking little iced cakes, adorned with tiny candied flowers, that my mother produced with a flourish at the end. When we were done it was still early after-noon. My father pushed back his chair and sighed deeply with satisfaction, then looked about, as if in some puzzlement what to do next.

'Did you ever settle with that fellow about the job, the other night at the Ox and Plough?' my mother asked innocently.

'Er, not entirely,' my father replied, his face clearing, 'but he'll be there tonight, I expect. Maybe I'll just drop by and see.' And with that he was off.

As we were clearing the things from the table, my mother turned the conversation to my new role at the Heights.

'So, Nelly, now you are to be a servant in earnest. How shall you feel about that, do you think?'

'I shan't like it,' I said frankly, 'for Hindley and Cathy will get to play, the same as ever, only I won't be able to join them any more. And how will Hindley learn his lessons, if I am not there to help him? And I shan't have lessons at all, so I will not learn anything more. I will become as ignorant as Martha, who can scarcely write her own name.'

'You would have to forget a great deal of the lessons you have had already, to become as ignorant as that,' my mother replied. 'And what is to stop you pursuing your lessons on your own? The books will still be there, and you are clever enough not to need help from a teacher, are you not? Indeed, you can still help Hindley with his lessons, and, in helping him, learn them yourself.'

'But when will I be able to do that? The servants at the Heights are up before the family in the morning, and go to bed at the same time, and they work all the time in between.'

'Oh, they will not be so hard on you as all that, just at first,' said my mother. 'And as you take on more responsibilities, you will find yourself more mistress of your time than you imagine. In just a few years you can become the housekeeper there, as I was, and a housekeeper sets her own tasks, and directs the other servants at theirs. If she manages her work well, she can always make time for herself to read and study.'

My mother meant well, I'm sure, but the more she talked, the more bleak and laborious my future looked to me. Could a housekeeper make time to roll down hills and play hide-and-seek on the moors? And by the time I became one, would I even remember how to do these things? I decided to change the subject.

'The new boy, Heathcliff,' I asked her, 'is he to be a servant, too?'

My mother sighed heavily. 'I don't rightly know what they plan for him in future, but at present he is to be raised with the children, so you must think of him as one of the family, and treat him accordingly.'

This was no more than I had learned for myself already, but hearing it from her was too much for me. 'Why am I to be cast out, and he set up as my master? He is just some filthy boy off the streets, while I have been there almost from my birth, and I am Hindley's foster-sister besides, and his kin, too, on our mothers' side!'

'You don't need to tell me that, Nell,' she said. 'But I have always told you that you were not to think of yourself as one of the family, and nothing Mr Earnshaw does for this boy changes that. He has his own reasons, no doubt, that you cannot understand.'

'Well, but I wish . . .'

'Fie, Nell, do not make wishes. If you cannot pray for it or work for it, you may be sure it will do you no good to wish for it, and it may do ill. Come and sit here, and I will tell you a story about a wish, and the trouble it brought.'

And so she did, and I will tell it to you. But to do that, I must take a fresh sheet, and give it a proper title, and all.

FOUR

The Heart's Wish

'You know that there are many stories about folk who help some magical creature – say a little man caught in a tree, or a hunted beast who turns out to be a man in disguise – and are granted three wishes in return? Well, once, not long ago, and near here, there was a man, a poor farmer on bad land, who was weary of breaking his back day after day, year after year, to put food in bellies that were never more than half full. Hearing these stories, he took it into his head that he must find a fairy or a goblin, and gain from it the wishes that would lift the burden of his laborious life, and allow him to live in ease and comfort. But he was not content to wait until he should stumble over such an opportunity, nor did he wish to waste his time and anger his neighbours by saving every hunted beast that came his way, in the hopes it might prove to be magical, so instead he resolved to catch one. Well, he gathered up every story of magical folk from all the country around, and sifted and sorted them in his mind, to determine what were their habits, where they might be found, and how he might get one into his power. Accordingly, he began leaving a

45

cup of sweetened milk and a small plate of oatcakes (which he could ill spare) on the hearth at night, and in the morning he always found it gone. His wife derided him for his efforts. "What a fool you are to waste good food and drink on idle fancies, when it might have gone into our own bellies!" she said. "It is sure to be rats who have eaten the food, and now they will be all over the house, looking for more."

"'Nay, wife," he replied, "but look at how the dishes are left: the cup scoured clean and placed neatly on the plate, and both shifted to the side of the hearth, to be out of the way. We have lured a Brownie into the house, just as I hoped."

'Well, his wife demurred, but he kept on feeding the Brownie, and soon even she was convinced of its existence, by the good effects it produced. For all at once their thin and sickly cow grew fatter and began giving more and richer milk, and when the time came for her to be bred, she gave birth to twin heifers, who both throve as much as if there had only been the one. The oats that year yielded twice the normal crop on the same ground as before; the cabbages in the garden grew larger than their own heads, and the carrots so long and thick and close together they could not be pulled from the ground, but had to be dug out with a spade (yet sweet-tasting withal), and all the other vegetables throve in the like manner. For once there was more than the family could eat themselves, so the wife took butter and vegetables to market, where their beauty and sweetness brought excellent prices. With the money, she bought a piglet and a flock of chickens, to be fed up on the excess of their produce, and these throve as well as the rest.

'Soon the farmer was able to improve and enlarge his tumbled-down cottage, and his children grew fat and strong, and were enabled to better their condition by attending the school in the village. As a consequence, they gained reputations with their neighbours as excellent farmers and managers, the more so as they were placed in such an unpromising location, so that they were treated with great respect, and their opinions sought on all sorts of questions, where before they had only been pitied for the poverty of their condition.

'Now, you might think the farmer would be happy with this, but he had not forgotten his hope of gaining three wishes that would allow him to live at ease for ever after. So the farmer conceived a plan to get the resident Brownie into his power, that he might compel it to grant him wishes. When he told his wife of this, she grew angry. "How can you be such a fool!" she said. "Since the Brownie has taken up residence in our house, everything we touch has prospered. Our larder and storeroom are full; we have money for all our needs. Our neighbours think well of us, and our children are moving up in the world. If you seek to wring more from the Brownie than he has freely given us already, he may withdraw his favour from us, and cause us to lose all our prosperity. Rest content with what you have."

'"When I first set out to bring the Brownie into the house," her husband replied, "you called me a fool, too, and told me I was wasting scarce food on old tales that no sensible person believed. But you were wrong, and now we are the better for it. Now, when I seek for more you tell me again that I am a fool. Why should I listen to you?"

'"It is true that I did not wish you to waste food taken out of our own children's bellies, and for good reason. If a man with a wife and family to provide for wishes to gamble his last penny for a fortune, surely it is his wife's duty to speak against it, and it is hardly foolish in her to do so even if he prove her wrong by winning a fortune indeed, as I cannot deny that you have done. But when you lured the Brownie into our house, it was in service of what any man has a right to wish: good reward for his labour, security against hard times, and a better life for his children. But now you seek to return cruelty for kindness, and betrayal for trust, and for what? That you may sit at ease, and have all done for you without any effort at all! Since Adam, all men must eat their bread by the sweat of their brow, and why should you be exempt? Whether it were foolish or wise to put out food that might have served only to fatten mice may be proved by the result, but in this you do wrong whether you succeed or not, and no good can come of it."

'Well, the man saw that his wife would not be swayed, so he said no more of it. But neither would he give over his plan. And so, working in secret, he constructed a cage out of the roots of a graveyard yew tree and long vines of bindweed, and wove into it watercress and rosemary to restrain magic. He made a floor for it too, of the same materials, but did not fasten it to the rest. Then he waited for the new moon, for he knew the powers of such creatures wax and wane with the moon. The day before he put his plan into execution, he coaxed his wife into going to visit her relations in town for a few days, and to take their children with her, so that she might not interfere. That evening, he suspended the main part of the cage above the hearth, artfully concealing it among the hams and strings of onions that hung from the rafters. He put the floor of it under the hearthrug just under the cage, then he set out on top of it a pork pie, iced cakes, and a tankard of strong ale for the Brownie – finer victuals than he was used to receiving – and set the trap to spring when the creature should lift up the heavy tankard. This done, he concealed himself in the pantry, keeping the door slightly ajar that he might peep out and watch the success of his plan.

'As soon as the clock struck midnight, the Brownie appeared.

He was no larger than a toddling child, but wizened and dark, like meat that's been smoked over a slow fire, with wide yellow eyes like a cat's. He appeared startled at the sight of the fine victuals laid out for him, but tossed the iced cakes into his broad mouth without hesitation, and then lifted the tankard for a draught of ale. No sooner had he done so than the trap was sprung: the cage fell down with a crash around the Brownie, and before he could gather his wits to lift it up again, the man sprang out from his hiding place and, flinging himself on top of the cage, bound the floor of it to the rest with more bind-weed and cress. Then, lighting a candle from the smouldering fire, he inspected his catch.

'At first the Brownie scuttled about inside the cage, up and down and all around, testing every inch of it and chattering incomprehensibly to himself like an angry squirrel. But he found no flaw in the workmanship: the cage was tightly made, and the yew roots, which had grown from the flesh of the dead, proved too strong for the little Brownie, whose powers were bound up with living things like crops and beasts. When he discovered this, the creature hunched himself up in the far corner, hugged his bony knees to himself, and turning his cat's eyes balefully on his captor, addressed him in a high, grating voice: "Well," he said, "this is a fine return you have made me for all my help to you. What is it you want from me: are your pigs not fat enough? Is the butter that comes in great lumps from the churning not sweet enough for your taste? What have you turned your hand to since I came here that has not thriven? And all I have asked in return is a small share of it left for me by the hearth. So what would you now?"

'The farmer was somewhat abashed at this response, but he bethought him that, whatever he did now, he had surely lost the Brownie's goodwill for ever, so if he did not want to sink back into his former penury, he had better demand his wishes, and gain wealth for himself all at once. He told the Brownie that he meant him no harm, and would release him as soon as he agreed to grant him three wishes. "Ah, so that's what you are about," said the Brownie. "You are a greedy fellow indeed, if all your comfort and prosperity has bred nothing better in you than a desire for what you have not. But what makes you think I can grant you any wishes at all? I am only a Brownie. If my magical abilities extended so far as that, do you think you could catch and hold me as you have done?"

"'Do not try to fool me," replied the farmer, "I have heard enough stories of wishes granted by just such creatures as you that I have no doubt you could give me what I ask. If you refuse, I will just keep you in this cage, and make my fortune by selling you to a huckster at a fair."

"'Please, no!" the Brownie howled. "The very touch of sunlight on my skin would burn like a red-hot coal on yours. Take pity on me, sir; remember all my kindness to you, and do not condemn me to such a fate!" Whereupon the Brownie began weeping and rocking back and forth, his whole body trembling and his eyes wide with dread, but the farmer remained adamant in his demands. "Very well," said the Brownie at last, with an ill grace, "I will give you three wishes. But I tell you again: do not imagine that I am some Arabian genie who can conjure golden coaches and chests of gems from the ends of the earth. You must moderate your wishes, and not ask for more than could be found within three leagues of this place."

'Now, the farmer had hoped to wish for just such things as the Brownie mentioned, but he was well pleased to have gained his point at all, and immediately began running over the possibilities in his mind – thinking of one man's landed estate,

50

another's bustling woollen mills, and still another's thriving grocery trade, considering which would bring him the greatest wealth and eminence with the least effort. At last he made up his mind: "For my first wish—"

"'Wait," said the Brownie. "You must take time to think of what you will wish for, and I must gather my powers to grant it, for I am sure it will be no small thing. Release me now, and I promise you that when the sun goes down on the next Sabbath, I will grant you your heart's wish. The same will I do on each of the two succeeding Sabbaths. But after that, you must make the best of what you have gained, for I will be your Brownie no more."

"'How am I to be sure that you will keep your promise?" asked the farmer.

"'I have never betrayed anyone's trust in me," the little man said, with a look and tone that clearly showed he thought the same could not be said for his captor. "The same stories from which you gleaned the knowledge to lure me to your house and capture me will have taught you that our promises are sacred to us, and not a word of mine will I abate, I assure you.

"'After the sun touches the horizon, and before it sinks altogether below it, stand on the hearthstone here and speak your desire. You will not see me, but I will hear you. By sunrise the next day, your heart's wish will be granted."

'Well, the farmer was obliged to be satisfied with this. He cut the cords that tied on the floor of the cage, and pulled on the rope to raise the trap. As soon as a gap appeared, the creature scuttled out through it, and disappeared like a wisp of smoke into the crack between the hearthstone and the floor.

'The next day, so full was the farmer's mind of all the good things that were coming to him that he scarcely noticed when the dairymaid came to tell him that one of the cows had borne a dead calf, and another was showing signs of milk fever, or when a labourer came from the fields to say that a trio of wild moor ponies had jumped a stone wall and trampled a fine crop of young oats into the ground. But, as the day wore on, the evidence mounted that the Brownie had not only withdrawn his favour from the household, but called down bad luck upon them: all the poultry were found with their throats torn out by a weasel, and the pig escaped from its pen and ran squealing away over the moors as if it were being chased by a devil. The very coal in the hearth would not light properly, but only smouldered and filled the house with evil-smelling smoke. This rather shook the farmer's good spirits – he had grown so used to having everything belonging to him go as well as it possibly could do that he had come to think such success was natural to him, so it was painful to be reminded how fragile was the prosperity of his family. "But," he reflected to himself, "that only shows all the more how wise it was of me to seek for greater security. I shall wish first for a landed estate. Rich men need not fear a few strokes of bad luck – their rents come in all the same, and it is the tenants who must tighten their belts to make up the sum, as I well remember." So he went about his work in good spirits, disregarding these ominous misfortunes with a cheerfulness that astonished and impressed the servants.

'When Sunday came, the farmer was far too preoccupied with imagining his coming prosperity to go to church, or even to say prayers at home. He thought of going for a long walk, just to pass the time, for the weather looked fair and sunny, and the heather was all in bloom, but no sooner did he step outside than a powerful wind came up and drew a pall of angry-looking thunderclouds over the whole sky. When he went inside, the sky cleared as quickly as it had clouded before, so out he went again, but the same thing happened. So he resigned himself to pacing about within the house, and thinking about his coming wish. "I wonder how the Brownie will give me what I ask," he reflected. "Will it materialize all around me during the night, or will I wake the next day to find it nearby, and only waiting for me to move in and take possession?" It then occurred to him for the first time that in either case his neighbours would surely find it strange to have an entire hall appear where none had been before. "It will do me little good to be made master of a fine estate if it makes folk think I have had dealings with the Devil," he thought; "I must be careful to word my wish so as to avoid that result."

'At last the sun touched the horizon. Eagerly, the farmer stepped onto the hearthstone and said the words he had been rehearsing all day: "I wish to be master of an estate just like Morton Hall, which is to come to me without the appearance of magic." Silence greeted this statement, and then suddenly a strong gust of wind blew down the chimney, sending smoke and ash into the farmer's face, and forcing him to step back off the hearth and retreat to the far end of the house. "If you meant to prevent my claiming my wish, Brownie," he called out, "you moved too late. The wish is spoken, and now you must keep your word by granting it."

'The farmer had expected a sleepless night, but to his surprise he slept heavily and long, and did not awake until broad day. As he dressed, he looked about the room eagerly, but all seemed just as it had been the day before. The same proved true of the rest of the house. Then the farmer went out-of-doors to see if anything new might be spied, but all he saw was his wife and family at a distance in their pony and trap, returning from their visit, as planned. The farmer set out at a brisk pace to meet them, reasoning that he had best tell his wife of their great good fortune before she learned of the many small misfortunes that had fallen upon them since the Brownie had withdrawn his favour from them. But when he came near, it was his wife who rushed forward. "Such news! Such news!" she gasped. "The most shocking thing has come to pass – the whole town is talking of it – such a terrible thing!"

"'What is it?" asked the farmer, an ominous chill touching his heart.

"'Why, just think, the whole family at Morton Hall, all killed at once!"

"'Killed! All of them! How can that be?"

"'It came about last night. They all sat down to supper shortly after dark, as usual, the parents and all eight children, but no sooner did they eat it than they were all rolling about in agonies on the floor. The doctor came, but all his labours were in vain: by morning every one of them was dead! It is thought that the food must have been poisoned, and the cook has been taken up on suspicion, though why she would do such a thing I cannot think, for she has a good position, and has been with the family most of her life, and what could she gain by their deaths? The will is to be read tomorrow, as soon as the solicitor can get here from York, and it is hoped that will cast some light on the matter. But why so pale, husband, and why do you tremble? It is a dreadful thing, to be sure, that there could be so much evil in the world, and so near by us. But it is nothing to us – we are all safe and sound, thank God."

'But this was small comfort to the farmer, as he turned and walked silently homeward beside the pony and cart. Gone now was any plan of telling his wife about his success with the Brownie. For once, the farmer longed to disbelieve in his own magic.

'His wife, meanwhile, was clucking the pony forward into a trot, eager to get home and see how her flock, her dairy, and her garden had been getting on in her absence. The farmer lagged behind, preferring to let the servants be the ones to deliver the bad news, and the cries of dismay coming from the direction of the barn soon told him she was in full possession of it. Then his wife herself appeared, tears streaming down her face, for amid all the other losses was that of her favourite dairy cow, Belle, who had been with them since their poorer days, and was like one of the family, and she felt this death of a beloved beast more deeply than the deaths of all the strangers at Morton Hall. "What evil has come upon us?" she sobbed to her husband. "It seems as if all the goodness has gone from the world at once – children murdered in the bosom of their family in town, and here it seems as if all Nature is turned against us at once, my flock destroyed, and the garden trampled, and poor Belle . . ." Then, seeing her husband trembling like an aspen, she asked more pointedly, "What do you know of this?"

"'Nothing,' he stammered awkwardly. "We have had more than our share of good luck these last few years, have we not? And now we have a little taste of the bad, to balance it, but we shall weather it all right – we have food in the house, and money in the bank, and soon all will be to rights again, you will see."

"'What of the Brownie?" she asked. "I thought our good fortune was his doing?"

"'I am a little afeared," said the farmer carefully, "that the Brownie may have, eh, heard me speak of my plan to capture him, and so he has taken offence, bringing these punishments upon us. We must let him know how sorry we are, and leave out better vittles and drink than ever, and we will soon put all to rights, I am sure."

"'Perhaps so," said his wife, "but it seems hard that my own dairy and flock should be the ones to suffer, when he must know that I spoke against your plan, and I hope he will take that into account." She spoke this last rather loudly, as if hoping the Brownie might be in earshot even then. "And as for you, you should take this lesson to heart, not to be wishing for wealth and idleness when you have prosperity enough already."

"'I have indeed," said the farmer feelingly. He was already resolved that on the following Sunday he would ask the Brownie to reverse all he had done, and then forgo his last wish altogether – which, with some tempting offerings each night, might perhaps appease the Brownie, and return him to his former complaisance. True, it seemed unlikely that the creature's powers would be great enough to bring the Mortons all back to life again – if indeed he had had anything to do with their deaths – but doubtless relatives would arrive to take possession in their place. As for himself, he thought, he would work with a good heart to the end of his days, with never a complaint, if but the burden of this horror could be lifted from his conscience.

'But this was not to be. The next morning, while the family were at breakfast, a strange young man on horseback cantered up to the door, and, with pardons for interrupting the family at their meal, introduced himself as a clerk to the Morton family's solicitor, with urgent business for the man of the house. The family's eyes widened, as the farmer, with a sinking heart, rose and went outside to speak to the clerk. There he was informed that the solicitor, in going over the papers in Mr Morton's study, had discovered a will of more recent date than the one he had prepared for his client.

"'How recent?" gasped the farmer, terror gripping him.

"'Oh, some two or three years back," said the clerk, a little puzzled at this response, "but the one my master prepared is older than that, so this newer one, which was prepared by a different solicitor, is the one that will be read this afternoon. And it seems that you are named in it, no doubt for some small bequest, so I am come to bid you be present at the reading."

'The farmer went in and told this news to his wife, doing his best to act as if it were the most natural thing in the world, while straining his mind to invent a plausible explanation. "I never mentioned it to you at the time," he said, "but some years ago I pulled young Master Morton from a bog in which he was stuck fast and sinking. It was a small enough service, but the lad had been badly frightened, and assured me I had saved his life. No doubt he told his father the same, and so Mr Morton has left me a little something in gratitude. You see our luck is turning again already," he added, forcing a smile.

'"That is lucky," his wife said, "and I only hope it is a sum of money you are left and not some useless trinket like a ring or a cane, for I shall have to buy a whole new flock at the next market day, and perhaps another cow as well, and we are pinched already, with all the trouble your foolish talk has brought upon us."

'The farmer was glad enough, after that, to escape into town to hear the will. So he found himself sitting alongside a parcel of Morton relations from a nearby town, whose genuine grief at the horrific end of all their esteemed relations at once mingled with anticipation of their own likely good fortune as a result of it. But the contents of the will astonished them all. The farmer's father, it explained, had been the natural son of Mr Morton's grandfather by a serving maid, and was hence half-brother to this Mr Morton's father. This secret had been hushed up by the girl's marriage to a poor local farmer, and the bastard child himself had grown up knowing nothing of his true parentage. But, on his deathbed, the old man had

57

repented of his neglect, and charged his only grandson and heir with making some amends to the boy's descendants, should they prove worthy. With eight children of his own to provide for, and the family honour to consider, Mr Morton had not seen fit to do anything in his own lifetime, but upon enquiring after the character of his unknown uncle's only surviving son, and finding him to be prosperous and held in high respect locally despite poor beginnings, he did alter his will to provide him with a small bequest, and, in the unlikely event that none of his own numerous children survived to inherit, with the reversion of the whole estate, as being the only other living descendant of his grandfather.

'Great was the amazement that greeted this news, and even the farmer, who had dimly expected something along these lines, knew not what to make of it. After the reading, he hurried up to question the solicitor. Was the will really so old, he wanted to know, and how could they tell it was authentic?

'"The authenticity of the will cannot be in doubt," said the solicitor. "It was prepared by a different firm, but I well know the hand and seal of the late colleague who prepared it."

'"Late?"

'"He died eighteen months ago," the solicitor replied.

'"How can that be?" the farmer stammered. "How could the will have been there all those years, and no one know about it at all? And my father, all the time half-brother to Mr Morton – can all this really be true?"

'"Please sit down, sir," said the solicitor kindly. "I fear this shock has been too much for you – the more so as it comes on the heels of this strange and sinister tragedy. Here, take a glass of brandy, and try to calm yourself a little." The solicitor then turned to attend to the disappointed relations, who were as wonderstruck as the farmer, but with whom the solicitor had rather less patience as they were not likely to become his clients, and bustled them out of the room.

'Thereupon he addressed himself respectfully to the farmer. "Good sir," he said, "it speaks well of your heart that you show such distress at news that most men would find cause for rejoicing, and that you are so solicitous to assure yourself of the justice of your claim to good fortune. Of course, none of us can know the truth about private events that took place before we were born, and the participants in which are all now deceased. But I have looked into the household and parish records, and they do corroborate what the will says – your grandmother was indeed employed at Morton Hall until just before her marriage, and your father's birth took place only six months after it. Did you know anything about this?

'"Nothing," said the farmer, beginning to recover his wits a little. "I knew that my grandmother had been in service before her marriage, but not where – she never spoke of it. And I am sure my father never had any cause to doubt he was his father's son."

'"Well, I don't doubt you," the solicitor replied, "and you may rest assured that no suspicion will attach to you in these strange deaths, for I can attest that nothing could be more genuine than the shock and distress you displayed when the will was read. I watched you closely, given the suspicious circumstances of the family's deaths, and saw that your face went suddenly ashen, and you began shaking like a leaf, when the revelation of your heritage was made. Expressions and manner may be feigned, as any lawyer knows, but the most thoroughgoing scoundrel could not counterfeit such a response. How and why the family came to be murdered, or whether it was only some horrible mishap, we have yet to learn, but you are innocent of any hand in it – I would stake

59

my life that you knew nothing of that will or its contents before it was read."

"'I thank you, sir," said the farmer. The horror that had struck him when he first heard his wife's news was now beginning to abate, as it dawned on him that he might actually take possession of Morton Hall without losing the good opinion of his neighbours, or exciting any suspicions in the town, since even his own dismay at the news was taken as evidence of his innocence and good character. "Furthermore," he thought to himself, "it appears that I am in truth the near relation of the late Mr Morton – for these are matters of record from many years ago, and surely no Brownie's magic could extend to altering the past." So the farmer reasoned, and if he could but have felt assured that his wish had played no part in the deaths of all the family, he would have been happy to believe that the inheritance was no more than was due to his parentage and proven merit, but about that his heart misgave him a little. "Even so, though," he thought, "surely I myself am innocent of these deaths, for I would never have framed my wish in such terms if I had known what would be the result. The evil in this is the Brownie's, not mine. But I have learned my lesson. I will rest content with what I have, and ask no more of the Brownie than I have already got." Gone now, however, was his plan of asking the Brownie to revoke the wish he had already made – it would be better, he decided, to leave further wishing alone altogether, for however cautiously he framed his wish, might not the cunning Brownie find a way to turn it to evil? And it would certainly be pleasant to be master of Morton Hall.

'The solicitor wished him to remain at Morton Hall and send for his family to tell them the news – offering to send his clerk again to carry the message – but the farmer thought it best to inform his wife in greater privacy. But he did have one of Mr Morton's saddle horses readied, that he might ride home in comfort and style. As he walked the fine beast down the main street of the town he saw fingers pointing and heard on all sides the wondering murmurs in which the news of his inheritance spread. No one turned aside from him or cast looks of suspicion, and if there were a few of the better-born folk who showed a hint of scorn at his sudden elevation, there were many more who smiled, and bowed or curtseyed, already seeking favour with the new master at Morton Hall. All this lifted the farmer's heart considerably. But it still remained to inform his wife of their change in fortunes.

'When he came within sight of the cottage, it was his wife this time who hurried down the road to greet him. "So he has left you a horse!" she exclaimed. "Well, it looks like a very fine one. But we will have to sell it of course. These fancy saddle horses take a good deal of care and rich feeding, and we certainly could never hitch him to the plough. Still, it is a start on better times for us, I suppose – and the more cheering that it results from your own good deed to that poor lad."

'"The horse is the least of it, wife," the farmer replied, choosing to ignore her last remark. "You cannot imagine what good fortune has befallen us. I am to inherit all of Morton Hall!" And he went on to explain about the revelations in the will, hoping that news of their elevation to prosperity and position would do away all his wife's anger and grief.

'But his wife's suspicions were roused. She had had a day to discover the full scope of the Brownie's revenge, and now she remembered too how strangely the farmer had first taken the news of the Mortons' deaths. "There is something you are not telling me," she said sharply, "what is it?" The farmer stammered out a denial, but his red face and frightened manner betrayed him. "Do not attempt to hide anything from me," she added sternly, "you know I always see through your disguises."

'The farmer saw then that nothing less than the truth would satisfy his wife, and so, with downcast face and heavy heart, he confessed to her all that he had done. But he stressed also the date of the will and the evidence of the long-ago parish records. "It has all come about very strangely," he said, "but it seems that I am indeed kin to the Mortons, and rightfully heir to their estate. As for their deaths, I wished no ill on them, nor did them any. If the Brownie has done this evil – which may not even be so – the sin is surely on his head, not mine. And I will make no more wishes, I am resolved."

'"What sort of man are you?" cried his wife. "How can you doubt that their deaths are your doing, whether you meant it or not? How did you think you could get possession of an estate of the size of Morton Hall in this neighbourhood without any appearance of magic, unless you were to get Morton Hall itself? And how might that come about, but by disposing of the current inhabitants? Their deaths are on your head, and if we take this ill-gotten inheritance, they will be on mine too! Think of it – first you betray that good little Brownie, who was the author of all our prosperity, and now ten people have died in agony, the youngest but five years old, to satisfy your greed and indolence – oh, it is horrible, horrible!" and his wife threw herself on the ground, sobbing in her grief and dismay.

'The farmer endeavoured to reason away her distress, but in vain. Her mind was clearer and her heart truer than the selfish farmer's, and she continued to reproach him with the evil he had brought upon them all.

'"No," she said, "I will tell you what we must do. We must tell the whole tale to the vicar in the village, and take his advice on the matter." This suggestion filled the farmer with alarm. Convincing as he believed his own excuses to be, he had no wish to try their force on an educated clergyman. Who knew what conclusions he might come to? It was not so many years back that there had been trials for witchcraft in the area, tales of which still lingered in those hills, and for all he knew he might still be liable for prosecution. These points he urged on his wife, and, when he saw her resolve weaken a little, followed up with the plan he had formed earlier.

'"Two wishes yet remain of those the Brownie promised me," he said. "This Sunday evening I will ask him to undo all he can of my previous wish, and return us to our former condition, and I will forgo the last wish altogether. Then, when we have made what amends we can, we will try to go on as if none of this had happened at all."

'At first his wife would not hear of it. "Look how much evil came of your first wish," she said. "How can you know the second will not bring worse?"

'"We will guard against it in the wording of the wish," the farmer assured her, "by telling him that no harm is to come to anyone in the fulfilment of it, just as I told him before that there was to be no appearance of magic." Reluctantly his wife agreed to this, only stipulating that she should determine precisely what he was to say, and that she might still go to the vicar if the results failed to satisfy her conscience. The farmer then sent word to Morton Hall that his family would take some time to settle their affairs locally before taking possession of the estate. That Saturday, the children were sent to relations in town, and the servants dismissed, that there might be no mishap or interruption when they called upon the Brownie the following evening.

'Now, when the farmer had suggested that they ask the

63

Brownie to return them to their former condition, he had meant, of course, the condition of prosperity that the Brownie had first brought about on their poor farm. So he was dismayed to discover that his wife, in the sternness of her conscience, had resolved that they must renounce even that, and return to all the poverty of their early years. But he was desperate to silence his wife's bitter reproaches (which she still made continually), and above all, to prevent her from going to the vicar, and so he agreed to whatever she suggested. His wife was anxious that there should be no mistake in the wording of the wish, so she had the farmer repeat it to her again and again, to be certain he had got it correctly, and she resolved to be present at the crucial moment, to prompt or correct him should it be needed.

'When the sun began to sink towards the horizon on the appointed day, she stationed herself in the doorway to watch for the precise moment when it touched the earth, while the farmer paced in front of the hearth, muttering bitterly under his breath against his wife's stubbornness, which would reduce them all to the direst poverty. But when she signalled that the moment had come, he stepped forward onto the hearth, heart pounding, and repeated the form of words his wife had taught him, asking the Brownie to reverse all the magic he had ever done for them that could be reversed without causing harm to anyone. No sooner had he done so than he heard a loud shriek from his wife, and she fell to the ground. He ran to her, and found she was dead!'

'But how can that be?' I interrupted in some annoyance. 'The wish said clearly that no one was to be hurt!' I disliked fairy stories with morals to them, and this one was shaping up to be of that objectionable variety.

'If you will but let me finish the story, Nell, you will find out. Now hush.

'When the farmer found his wife was dead, he cried out at once and reproached the Brownie for breaking his word – see, Nell? – To his surprise, the Brownie himself appeared on the hearth. "I have kept my promise," he said.

'"But I said that no one was to be harmed, and here is my own wife, dead!"

'"I told you to speak a wish, but I did not promise to grant the wish you spoke," the Brownie replied with a cruel smile. "You spoke the wish of your mouth, but I gave you the wish of your heart."

'Then the farmer saw that he had been tricked, and that all the while he spoke the words his wife had taught him, he had longed in his heart for everything that she would deny him while she lived. "Is my heart so evil then, that I could wish her death?" he cried.

'"Can you deny it?" the Brownie replied.

'Then the farmer fell to his knees, sobbing. "Alas, I see that it is so. But I will repent me now of my greed and my anger. I beg your pardon, Brownie, for my poor treatment of you. I will ask no more wishes from you, but will use all my remaining years to make amends for my sins, and pray to God to take away my heart of stone, and give me a heart of flesh."

'"Pray all you please," the Brownie replied, "but I told you once that I would abate no word of my promise, and so I will not. When the sun goes down on the next Sabbath, whether you are dumb or whether you speak, whether you stand on the hearth or a thousand miles away, you will be granted the inmost wish of your heart." And with that he disappeared. The farmer called and called for him to return, and pleaded with the empty air to be freed from this final wish, which he now regarded with terror, but to no avail.

'Then the farmer, seeing that the Brownie would not help him, set about to examine his heart, and bring it into a better frame, that his heart's wish would not bring such horrors upon him as it had done hitherto. But, like many another man who has left repentance to the last, he found that the time was too short; through unchecked selfishness and greed, the evil of his heart had grown too great to be uprooted in the few days remaining before the wish was granted. As the sun began to sink on the Sabbath, he could not take his mind from the shame and degradation he would face if the neighbours discovered his secret, and he grew terrified, in his guilt and despair, that in some unsearched corner of his heart he might be wishing the annihilation of the whole neighbourhood around, as he had that of his wife. So he snatched up a knife from the table and, before the sun touched the horizon, plunged it into his heart. He was found thus the next morning, and pinned to his breast was a note in a queer, crabbed hand that read, "He got his heart's wish."'

'But how could the Brownie know the wish of his inmost heart, even a thousand miles off?' I interrupted again. 'I thought only God could know that. And the Brownie said before that he could not fetch things by magic more than three leagues distant!'

'Well, you are a sharp cross-questioner, Nelly,' said my mother. 'There is no fooling you. I suppose the Brownie was not being strictly truthful there. No doubt he had heard the farmer's mutterings against his wife, and made out the wish of his heart from that, and as for the rest, he counted on the farmer's fear and dismay to cloud his thinking. A man haunted by a guilty conscience thinks everyone can see into his heart. But the tale is true enough, for all that, as is pretty widely known about here. The man was buried as a suicide, in an unmarked grave at a crossroads just the other side of Gimmerton. I have seen the place myself. When I was still a girl, there was a man going around the fairs who showed what he said was the bloodstained knife and the note, at a penny a look, and I begged my mother to let me see them, but she said he could have written the note and stained the dagger himself, and no one would be the wiser, and she would not waste so much as a farthing on such trumpery shows. But the tale itself she always averred to be quite true, to her own knowledge, and she never lied. Take it to heart, Nell, and do not get in the habit of imagining yourself entitled to more than you have earned by your own labours. Leave off making idle wishes.'

Wise advice, no doubt, to anyone who could follow it. As for me, she might as well have told me to leave off breathing. But the story has haunted me since, and in my darkest times I have wondered, was there something I did in my youth, some unfledged sparrow I returned to its nest, or a moth I freed from a spider's web, that made me the recipient, all unwitting, of some such sinister boon? How many things that my wayward heart has wished for have come true, yet in a manner crueller than their denial could ever be? That very night, I wished fervently that my father might be to me henceforth as he had been these last few days. And so he was, in the sense that I never saw him otherwise, for before I saw again, he was dead.

FIVE

Now, why did I write that? I am sure I thought nothing of the kind at the time. Indeed that friendly visit had been a great relief to my conscience, in freeing me of many a guilty unbidden daydream in which my father's death figured prominently. And though it might certainly be said that I wished for his love, it was a wish I both prayed for and intended to work for – resolving to show him in future such a mixture of dutiful respect and easy affection as would assure him I had forgiven and forgotten the wrongs of the past. How could such a wish be wrong? It is true that my mother's story came in time to haunt me, but that was years later, after other, darker events, and less innocent wishes. And I am getting ahead of myself again.

I had expected that I would see my father on my next month's day off, but in the meantime, he was called away for a large job at some distance from our home. An old friend of his boyhood – a lad as poor as himself, but with a genius for all things mechanical – had risen in the world, and was now the owner of some prosperous mills outside Brassing, about thirty miles away from us. He had bought a good-sized piece of land, and was having built for himself a large manor house, and he took it into his head that none other than his old friend should oversee all the stonework, and at pay several times what my father could earn locally. My father wished to move there outright with my mother – there would be work for at least a year or two just on the house, and he counted on getting more through the connection after. But my mother flatly refused to leave the neighbourhood so soon, not wishing to be gone so far from me while I was new to my duties, or to give up the small farm into which she had poured so much work over the years, without more certain prospects elsewhere. There were hard words between them about this, as I gathered from my mother's hints, but the result was that my father left alone, with the understanding that my mother would join him in a year or two if the situation proved as good as he thought. And so he passed from my life again, though on better terms than before, certainly. I wrote to him now and again, printing in large letters so that he could read them easily, and saying as little about the Earnshaws as possible, on my mother's instructions.

When I returned to Wuthering Heights to take up my position as a maidservant, I found my new duties easier in some respects, and harder in others, than I had anticipated. Mrs Earnshaw kept to the intention she expressed to my mother, and was an easy, indulgent mistress. Had her commands been all I had to consider, I would have seen little difference in the tenor of my life at the Heights. She had no wish to banish me from the lessons she superintended with Hindley and Cathy, for in truth they were both more refractory pupils in my absence. Hindley could not keep his mind to a schoolroom task for five minutes together, and his mother quickly lost patience with him without me there to devise games or rhymes or riddles to keep him to his task, and make him learn his lessons in spite of himself. Cathy was much better, but she was motivated primarily by a desire to outshine Hindley, and when that became easier, her own progress slowed accordingly. So when it was time for lessons, Mrs Earnshaw would generally call me to suspend whatever I was doing and join them. And then, having included me in the labours of the schoolroom, she was too kind to deny me its holidays, too, so when Cathy and Hindley were released outside to run off the ill effects of two or three hours of sedentary application, I would be told to join them.

But my mother put a stop to this arrangement, when she came to hear of it, and there were words between her and the mistress about it, too. These I did not manage to overhear, but I saw the signs of them clearly enough, in my mother's set face and the mistress's quiet tears after they had been shut up together. After that my mother made time to walk over to the Heights nearly every morning, to instruct me in household duties and set my tasks for the day. These tasks, she made clear to me, were to be performed faithfully, whatever the mistress might say to the contrary – so that, in performing my new duties, I had to fight not only my own inclinations, but those of all around me. I did not take well to the change – I could not see why, if Mrs Earnshaw thought it worth my wages to have my assistance in the schoolroom, I should be denied the benefit of being there, and by my own mother, too. After a week of the new arrangement, I finally made bold to put this to her.

'You are paid wages as a servant, Nelly, and have a duty to do the service you are paid for, even if Mrs Earnshaw is too kind to ask it of you.'

'But you don't know what it is like for her, teaching Hindley and Cathy without me there,' I protested. 'She can keep no

70

order at all, and Hindley learns nothing without me there to help him. She said herself that it is little help to her to have me shelling peas in the kitchen while she is driven to distraction by the two of them – she would rather shell them herself later, and have my assistance where it is most needed. And I want to keep learning.'

'Yes, she told me that, too.' She sighed and motioned me to sit down. 'This is hard for you, Nelly, I know. But there is not only Mrs Earnshaw to consider. The master permitted you to return on the footing of a servant, and it is he that pays your wages. He has been much occupied this week with moving the sheep to fresh pastures, but when that is done he will be looking into the household again, and there will be anger for all of us, the mistress not excluded, if he has reason to feel that we have connived in circumventing his commands. And he would have reason to feel that. You do see that Nell, do you not?'

I said nothing, but looked downward and felt my face flush. I knew she was right, but it was a bitter draught to swallow, for all that, and I should have preferred to put it off as long as I could. But that was never my mother's way: she preferred to face unpleasant duties 'head on', as she said. It was the hardest of all the lessons she taught me, but it was a good one, and has stood me in better stead than all the rest combined. So I bid farewell to the schoolroom, and took some comfort in the general grumbling at this change, without adding much to it myself.

There was actually much to learn in my new sphere: I had to know all about the proper management of a dairy, from scouring and scalding the milk pans, to skimming and churning the cream, making up the butter, and straining curds to make cheese. I had to learn how to keep the fire in the kitchen hot enough for our daily needs without making it so hot that it burned the oatcakes and wasted the coal, and how to make the smooth, thick oat porridge we ate daily, without creating lumps from too much haste in adding the oats, or burning the bottom through too little stirring – and a great many other things which it would bore you to hear, no doubt. In time, as my mother predicted, I came to take almost the same pride in my quickness and efficiency at these duties that I had in my book learning before, and I had the added comfort of knowing that these skills would allow me to earn a living anywhere – which could not be said of my command of the principal rivers of Asia, or my familiarity with the longest words in Johnson's *Dictionary*.

There were other changes in the schoolroom at this time besides that of my absence. Heathcliff too had been excluded from it at first, on the grounds that he was too young and could not speak our language – but it was really because no one in the house wanted him there – and so he fell to my charge. I soon found, though, that it was only that his accent was so queer we could not make out what he was saying, nor he us. He must have been a bright lad at base, because within a few weeks that had changed, and he and I could make shift to understand each other well enough. By that time the master was back, and he made it known that Heathcliff was to have his lessons with the other children. And so he was settled on a footstool in the far corner, and given Cathy's old hornbook to begin learning his letters. At first, both Cathy and Hindley made faces at him and jeered at his ignorance, every chance they got. But Heathcliff took no notice of it, except to turn his back to them and hunch more tightly over his hornbook, and Cathy soon tired of this sport and began to take an interest in the lad's progress. Her first kind words to him brought forth a grateful devotion: he began following her about like a puppy, and taking her commands with such joyful alacrity that it is no wonder she was soon won over to loving him.

We have a saying that 'a four-wheeled cart is steady, and a two-wheeled cart is quick, but a three-wheeled cart is good for naught but landing in a ditch'. Before Heathcliff came, Hindley and I were the two-wheeled cart, and Cathy was often left behind on our excursions, or excluded from our sports, on the grounds that she was too little to participate. Now, with Heathcliff arrived and me gone from the schoolroom, Cathy saw that the tables could be turned, and Hindley would be the third wheel. And so it fell out.

The effect of all this on Hindley's behaviour was not good. He became, as I said, more refractory in the schoolroom, and often uncontrollable out if it, except by his father, who enforced obedience with fear rather than love. Even the mistress, who had always loved Hindley best despite all his waywardness – or perhaps for it – lost all patience with him, and took to reporting his more egregious misdeeds directly to the master, something she had never used to do before, as it invariably earned the boy a beating. Hindley had always been a difficult, wilful child, but he began now to exhibit signs of real maliciousness and ill temper. And his favourite object for these was the new boy in the household. Heathcliff learned early not to carry tales to the master or mistress, except in extreme cases. Not that they were not ready enough to credit his tale and punish Hindley accordingly, but the master's bitterness too often spilled over – most unreasonably – onto Cathy as well, which Heathcliff could not bear to see. Also, every flogging Hindley received on Heathcliff's behalf only lengthened the score of the former's vengeance, and heightened his violence when the next opportunity presented itself. Cathy, for her part, would fight like a wild cat to defend her favourite, or if that failed, scurry off with him to nurse his wounds with kisses and plot some petty revenge. I would remonstrate with Hindley, and if possible interfere between them, if only for Hindley's sake, but we would neither of us carry tales, partly from the old loyalty of the schoolroom, and more because we could see that it did more harm than good. Even old Joseph, though normally he liked nothing better than to get any of us into trouble with the master, disliked Heathcliff too much to take up his defence. And so it became a more or less constant game of cat-and-mouse between Heathcliff and Hindley. Hindley knew that, if he could catch Heathcliff out of sight and hearing of either of his parents – and what was more difficult, away from Cathy as well – he could do pretty near whatever he liked to the boy with impunity, only provided he restrained himself from producing conspicuous injuries.

I saw it all with a heavy heart. Towards me, and me alone, had Hindley retained any of his old warmth and boyish sense of fun, and I felt I had still some good influence over him, but we had little time together any more.

One day, about a month after Heathcliff's arrival, we contrived to go off for a whole day together. It was the first of my monthly holidays, but my father being away, and my mother still a regular visitor at the Heights, I was not expected at home. Hindley had just succeeded (with much secret assistance from me of an evening) in keeping the whole of some hundred lines of Shakespeare in his mind at once, in honour of which achievement he had been granted a day's freedom from lessons. The day being sunny, we had resolved to go to Pennistone Crag for a picnic. Mrs Earnshaw made up a packet of oatcakes and cheese for us to take along, which Hindley put in an old sack and slung over his shoulder, and off we went. But the day was unseasonably hot, so we chose to stop instead at another favourite place about midway there, a little hollow graced by a burbling stream and a small waterfall that stayed always cool and refreshing even when the rest of the world was baking.

It was a beautiful little grotto, naturally walled with stone, where the water ran in over flat slabs of bedrock and then dropped in little waterfalls through multiple pools of varying shapes and levels. The water was coloured orange by the iron-rich soil, which also drifted to the bottom and made the pools red. There was one in particular in which a narrow fall dropped straight into still water, causing it to roil up in red bubbles. We had always called this 'the pool of blood', and avoided touching its contents with as much superstitious horror as if it had been blood indeed. At another place, the sunlight somehow came through the water from the back, though there was only stone behind it, so that the little waterfall, no more than a hand's-breadth across, danced with an orange glow like flames. We called it the 'the waternixie's bonfire', and liked to imagine tiny fairy-like creatures dancing behind it. Once, Hindley put out his hand and caught up the water's flow, so we could see behind it and 'catch them at it' as he said, but there was nothing but bare stone behind. 'Too quick for us,' I said.

We took off our shoes and sat on a rock to dangle our feet in the stream. Then Hindley scooped up some water in his hand to cool his face and neck, and I did the same. By chance, a bit of it splashed onto Hindley, and he responded by flinging some on me. Then I returned fire, and soon we were in full battle, chasing each other about, splashing and laughing until we both collapsed, sopping wet and exhausted, on the bank. In that state, we found the shaded hollow a little too cool, so we went back up into the sunlight, where we rolled about on the dry heather, and lay in the hot sun to dry our clothes. After a time, Hindley declared us 'toasted to perfection' – neither too hot, nor too cold – and said it was time to eat, so we made our way back to where we had left our provisions.

'This is a bit like old times, is it not, Nelly?' he said, as we sat ourselves on a patch of soft moss beside the stream.

'Better,' I said, 'because these days are rarer for us now, and more precious accordingly.' I was fond of wise sayings, then.

'No, not better, because even now I can't forget what I have to go home to,' he replied bitterly. Then he burst out, 'What am I to do, Nelly? Everybody hates me now, except you.'

Well I had a dozen answers on the tip of my tongue, beginning with 'Leave Heathcliff alone'. But for once I knew better than to offer them. I made no answer but to lean against him, and he was silent too, for so long that I peeked over to see if he had fallen asleep. But his eyes were open, and I saw a steady trickle of tears making a path down the side of his face. When he saw me looking at him, he made a savage grunt and turned away, ashamed to have been caught weeping. But by then I'd caught the infection, and I was soon sobbing away myself, huddling myself against his back for comfort. And then he turned round, and we held each other until the worst of it passed. There was no need to speak. We both knew what we had lost. After a while I began to busy myself with our provisions: I spread my kerchief on the ground and started to empty the sack and arrange our meal on it. When that was done, we both ate, still silent, but not so grieved as we had been.

'When I am grown up and Wuthering Heights is mine,' Hindley said at last, 'I shall marry you, Nelly. I shall send Heathcliff packing, and Joseph too, and then we will be happy all day long.'

I made no reply to his announcement, but blushed, and no doubt looked as awkward as I felt. When we were small children,

Hindley and I had often talked of marrying when we grew up, as if it were a matter of course. We had even gone a whole fortnight, once, pretending that we were secretly married already, with a 'cottage' marked out with a square of stones in a little hollow nearby. But, as we got older, we had become shy of such talk, so that there had been no mention of marriage between us for some years. I had retained some secret hopes on that score, though, and often wondered if he did the same – especially after I had transformed from play-mate to maidservant.

Hindley looked a little dismayed at my reaction.

'You will marry me, won't you, Nell?' he asked anxiously. I hastened to assure him that I loved him as dearly as ever, all my shyness dissolving in the face of his obvious distress. And then I had a marvellous thought.

'Hindley,' I said excitedly, 'I tell you what we must do. We must not grieve for the past, but think to the future, and prepare ourselves to be a good master and mistress of Wuthering Heights, as we will be some day. I am learning a great deal about that already, and you must learn too. You must ask your father if you can help him more in managing the estate, and ask him a great many questions about everything.' Hindley caught my enthusiasm, so much so that he proposed we should return home straight away to put this plan into action. And so we packed up our things and headed back to Wuthering Heights, both of us more cheerful than we had been in a month. I was particularly delighted with my own cleverness in finding a way to turn Hindley into a path more likely to win him his father's approbation, and more conducive to general peace in the household. When we were nearly home, with but one little hillock hiding us from view of the house, Hindley stopped and quickly kissed me on the lips. It was but a child's kiss, after all, but it seemed momentous to us, and we walked the rest of the way holding hands and feeling rather solemn.

Well, turning a person out of his wonted path is not like turning a sheep, to be accomplished with a single wave of a stick or a nip at the heels. It is more like trying to shift a stream out of its bed: it looks easy enough at the start, as the water will go wherever you send it, but your dam of pebbles and mud will only hold so long as you are there to tend it, and left alone the water soon finds its way into its old path again. So it was with Hindley. To be fair, it was not all his fault. He began with great enthusiasm, hovering about his father, offering his help, and asking all manner of questions. But the change was so sudden that his father was more puzzled than pleased, and suspected some hidden motive, the more so as he could not help but observe that the lad did not attend particularly well to his answers. I assured Hindley at every opportunity that the master would come round in time if he would but persevere, but in the end the father's suspicions lasted longer than the son's resolve. Not only did the waters return to their own path, but the release of dammed-up force only dug the channel deeper: to the master, Hindley's short-lived reformation seemed to confirm that the boy would never come to anything, while Hindley took his father's refusal to credit his good intentions as proof that any further effort to please his father would be fruitless. And I, who had been so pleased with my own hand in bringing this about, felt sick at heart, and feared I had done more harm than good.

Despite this, however, Hindley and I still spoke privately of our marriage as a settled thing, and I continued in my own resolve to learn as much as I could of household management, against the day that I would be mistress there, and to steer Hindley into good behaviour whenever I could, and comfort him when I couldn't.

As the weeks passed, my mother's visits to the Heights became more infrequent, and my own responsibilities increased. I was still but a girl, of course, and not likely to be placed in command of servants older and longer-serving than myself, but I soon saw that it would not be long before I attained that eminence. At that time there were two maidservants employed at the Heights besides myself: one assigned to the dairy, and the other to the kitchen and household. They were both good, obedient, hard-working girls, like most rural folk, but rather slow of mind. They grew anxious when left to direct even their own work for very long, let alone anyone else's, and, when faced with an unexpected obstacle, would come to a puzzled halt, like a sheep encountering a wall, until it was removed. Furthermore, neither of them expected to spend more than a few years at the Heights before leaving for homes of their own. When they did so, I foresaw, their replacements would naturally look to me for instructions when the mistress was not available, which was more often than not, and I would be housekeeper in effect, if not in name.

During this period, I received my first and, did I but know it, only letter from my father, all but the signature written not in his own painstaking, coarse print but in a flowing script that told me he had pressed someone into service as a scribe. I have it still. It reads:

Dear Nelly,

I hope this finds you well. I am well myself. I have five men working under me. They are all good men now but one was a lazy sot so I had to let him go and find another to fill his place. You would like to see the house I am building. It is very grand. It will have two floors above the ground plus the attics. The stones for the ground floor are very large and we

must use a tackle to move them, but they are all dressed
stone and easy enough to work with once they are in place.
They have a better sort of mortar here too, smooth as butter.
I am boarding at a house in town. It is a clean place and
the landlady is very kind but not so good a cook as your
mother. I hope your mother will come here soon. This house
will need many servants when it is done and I am sure they
would take you on if I said the word. Also you would get
better wages I guess than you do now. Meantime, work hard
and be a good girl. Be sure to save your wages and take
them to your mother.
    Your loving father,
    THOMAS DEAN

Letters were scarce in those days, so this one would have
been a prize whatever its contents, but 'Your loving father'
moved me to tears, and remained precious to me for years,
even after I realized that it was but a conventional closure,
probably suggested by the scribe. The thought that my mother
might leave soon, though, and worse, that my father might
move me to a position in his employer's household, filled me
with alarm, which I conveyed to my mother on her next visit.

'The house will be at least another year a-building, Nell,'
she assured me, 'and probably more. And by the time it's built,
God willing, your father may be prosperous enough that he
won't wish you in service at all, and certainly not in his own
neighbourhood.'

'Will you be going there yourself soon?'

'Not right away. I should like to see you better settled in
your duties, and know that Mrs Earnshaw can rely on your
abilities, before I leave you all.'

'What about the cows?' I asked. My mother had but four

cows at present, but her dairy was her greatest pride and pleasure. Though generally unsentimental, she loved her 'ladies', as she called her cows, and continued the practice, begun in her girlhood by Mrs Earnshaw, of naming them all after Shakespeare's heroines. So it was that I was plain Ellen, but her barn was populated with, at present, Rosalind, Ophelia, Viola, and Marina.

'Only Reenie and Rosie will need milking over the winter,' she told me, 'Feelie and Vi are drying off now – they're due to calve in March. I shall take Reenie with me – your father has his eye on a little house in the town with one stall that will do for a cow, and she'll bear the journey easily enough. The other three shall come here – I've spoken to Mr Earnshaw about it already. In return for feeding them through the winter, he's to have Rosie's milk and his pick of Feelie's and Vi's calves come spring. They won't overload the dairy either, for you're getting low on milkers just now. And I know I can count on you to make sure my ladies get good care.'

Accordingly, one bleak afternoon in late November she appeared at the Heights, driving three weary-looking cows before her, and looking thoroughly exhausted herself.

'Nelly,' she called out, 'come out here, my dear, and take these three into the barn. My, that was weary work! I thought to have been here hours ago, but these ladies won't be hurried – balky as mules, they were.' Despite her weariness, she was shaking her head and laughing as she spoke. Meanwhile Mrs Earnshaw had hurried out, wrapping a shawl around her as she came, and keeping up a steady stream of excited talk.

'Mary, there you are at last! And your ladies, too – is this Rosalind? Ah, you didn't think I'd recognize her, did you? But I remember her clear as yesterday – the prettiest heifer in all the barn she was, with those long legs and that little star on

81

her forehead, when I picked her out to be your wedding present. And my, what a beauty she has grown into. You say she's your best milker still, after all these years? You see I haven't lost my eye for a good cow, at any rate.'

'No you certainly haven't, and not a day passes that I don't thank you for her: Rosie's been a rare treasure to me in the dairy. And so good-natured! She's still as an owl for the milking, and an angel for temperament always: I don't think she's ever kicked in her whole life. These two here are her daughters, Vi and Feely – Viola and Ophelia, that is – you see I've kept up our old practice. Reenie – that's Marina – is back at home. She's Rosie's granddaughter, and bids fair to be her equal, but she'll go with me to Brassing.'

'Oh Mary, must you really go? Brassing is so far away, and I can't bear to think of you being gone so long.' The mistress was pulling my mother towards the house as she spoke.

'Come now, Helen, you wouldn't have me neglect my duty to Tom, would you? The poor fellow is living in paid lodgings, and eating Heaven-knows-what: tallow in the butter, chalk in the milk, and the last time the landlady served goose, it tasted so foul, he thought it must be a vulture! He was half minded to demand to see the feet, he said. And I'll only be gone until spring – I'll be back before you've noticed I'm gone.' With suchlike jollyings and reassurances, my mother led the mistress back to the house, while I turned away to attend to the cows, awkwardly shooing them towards the barn. I actually had little to do with managing livestock at the Heights – the produce of the dairy was more my department than its four-footed inhabitants – so I was in some difficulties, until Joseph spied me and came running over.

'What are ye up to, ye daft hinny? That's no way to move cattle – ye'll only get them into a fright, and have them trampling all the beds.' He snatched the stick from my hands and, with a

82

sequence of light taps, accompanied by deep cooing noises, soon had the cows moving into the barn.

'Do you know where they're to go?' I asked, trying to sound as if I knew myself.

'A-course I do – wasn't it left to me to ready the stalls for them? An' it'll be left to me to find fodder for them too, I suppose. Feeding three for the milk of one – that's a bad bargain the maister's made – but he always did make bad bargains wi' womanites, and yon canny witch is the warst on 'em.'

I had turned away before Joseph shot this parting bolt, but I turned to call back at him: 'It's nothing to the bad bargain you'd be to any "womanite" foolish enough to look twice at a sour-tempered, monkey-faced dwarf like you!' I regretted it the moment I'd said it, of course. Not for its unkindness, which was well deserved, but because Joseph was forever trying to provoke me to lash out at him, so that he could denounce me to the master for ill temper and insubordination, and I had been trying to school myself to ignore him, or at least respond with no more than dignified silence and scornful looks. Now he had just what he wanted, and was gleefully working himself up into a hopping rage before running to report to the master: 'Hoo, listen to the little hussy – she's as bad as her mother – nay worse, for talking evil to her elders and betters. The maister shall hear of this – he'll turn you out, this time, he will, for sure. It's too long he's put up with your insolence and bad ways, but now he'll see, now he'll see what she's really made of, witch bastard that she is.'

I was almost at the house by now, using up all my little stock of self-control not to reply, or give any sign that his words affected me. 'Witch bastard' was one of his favourite epithets for me, combining as it did aspersions on my character, my mother's, and the circumstances of my birth, and it usually got a response from me when nothing else could, but today I did no more than slam the kitchen door behind me and commence chopping onions with a fury, both to vent my anger, and to provide some cover for the tears that were sure to follow.

Hearing the slam and subsequent racket, my mother came into the kitchen.

'Have you got the cows settled in, Nelly?' she asked, but then seeing my face, 'Whatever is the matter, Nell? You're red as beef – and here, if you don't slow down with that knife you'll lose a finger for sure. Put it down, now. Good heavens, child, you've chopped enough onions to stew a whole ox! What brought this on?'

I did not trust myself yet for a full reply, and said only 'Joseph'. But that was a full enough explanation for anyone who knew the household as well as my mother did.

'I might have known,' she said – and then, seeing me about to elaborate, 'No, don't tell me what he said. I'm sure it was not worth hearing, let alone repeating. And I suppose you replied in kind?' I nodded, shamefaced. 'Well, he'll carry that to the master, for sure. How many times have I told you to leave him be? Just because someone pours gunpowder in your ear, there's no need for you to set a spark to it. And the worst punishment you can give that old fool is to ignore him when he starts ranting at you.'

'He called me "witch bastard",' I burst out in spite of myself. Her face went still.

'Did he now?' she said quietly, and then looked at me for a bit in silence. Then she gave herself a little shake, and said, 'Don't you think any more about it, Nell. You're not a bastard, and as for "witch", Joseph thinks all women are witches – except perhaps his sister, who's as dried up and miserable as he is himself. So pay no mind to what he says, and he'll soon tire of provoking you. Now, then, what about my cattle?'

'Joseph put them away – he knew where they were to go. Do you think he'll mistreat them?'

'If they were only my cows, I have no doubt he would drive them into the nearest bog – but I've been careful to arrange things so that it's in the master's interest for them to be well looked after, and Joseph knows it. Oh, he'll grumble about them, and at them too, most like, but he'll do all he can to be sure that Rosie gives good milk all winter and Feelie and Vi both bear healthy calves.'

'He said it was a bad bargain the master made,' I couldn't resist adding.

'And would have said the same if I were paying their weight in gold,' my mother replied. 'Now I'm serious, Nell, pay no mind to what Joseph says. And you are not to carry me any more tales about him. Do you understand?'

I nodded, and the subject was dropped. But I have reason to believe she spoke to the master on the subject, for, though Joseph continued to mutter that I was a witch, he never again called me a bastard, nor did he ever refer to my mother by any worse name than 'Mrs Dean' or 'your mother' – though he contrived to throw into the latter enough scorn that you would have thought there was no worse title to be had.

My mother would have liked to return home that evening, not wanting to leave even Reenie's milking to the neighbour's boy she had left in charge, but night was falling by the time all was settled at the Heights, and the night being moonless and cloudy to boot, it was of that inky blackness wherein you cannot see your own feet, let alone the path ahead. So she was persuaded to spend the night with us. The mistress was all for making up the guest bed for her, but my mother would not hear of it, and insisted on sharing my little bed instead. So I was very warm that night, sleeping in her arms for the first time since I was a little child. In the morning she kissed me goodbye, and promised to write to me and the mistress both, and the mistress cried heartily, and I cried a little, too, as we watched her disappear over the nearest rise.

A few weeks later, I had my first letter from her.

My dearest Nell,

You will be glad to know that I arrived safely in Brassing, and am now settled with your father in a cottage on the edge of the town. I was glad not to be in the centre, for the stench there is dreadful to someone accustomed to the clean air of the moors. I think my cowshed at home is sweeter to the nose. But I am getting used to it now. The cottage your father found was smaller than we have at home, and not over-clean, but I have got it done up now and it will do.

Reenie made the trip like a born traveller; she was only leaner and a bit footsore by the time she got here. She too has smaller and poorer lodgings than she did at home, but when I have got your father to plug some holes in the wall, and found some better straw for the floor, she will be quite cosy. It is warmer here, with all these houses to stop the wind, and everyone burning coal as well. We share a wall with a family of wool-combers, and they keep their stove red-hot all day long – they have to, you know, or the grease in the wool goes hard, and it can't be combed out.

If you ever feel sorry that you were born poor, Nelly, think on these poor wool-combers' children, who from early childhood work all day long in a hot, airless room, doing hard and monotonous labour, and live on bad bread (the bread here is shocking) and worse tea. There are six of them altogether, all sleeping on one filthy pallet, like a heap of puppies. I am doing what I can for them, at any rate. At every morning and evening's milking, they line up, from youngest to oldest, and drink each in turn a mugful of Reenie's good fresh milk. I told their father it was in payment for his stove half heating our cottage for us.

I had planned to sell the rest of the milk in the marketplace – what we don't use ourselves, that is – but I am not to have that trouble, it seems. Word is out in the neighbourhood that we have a cow, and folk just show up at the door with their pitchers and cans and their coins, and they all say they have never tasted such milk in all their lives, which I can well believe. So I am quite a feature in the neighbourhood now, and have many acquaintances already.

Your father is earning very good wages, and drinks but little of them, so there is a good deal of money in the house. But living in the town is more expensive than I ever imagined, as we must buy everything we need, even to the greens we eat – and it's no easy matter finding good ones, I can tell you. I go to the market at dawn, even before the milking, to get the freshest stuff, and pay extra for it, too. But what I meant to say is that we have enough money, so you can save your wages, and perhaps get yourself a new winter dress, as you have nearly outgrown the old one. Don't go spending your money on trifles, though, Nelly.

Take good care of yourself in this weather. Always wrap up about the neck before you go outside, and drink something hot when you come in. And never, never go about with your feet wet. And work hard, and do your duty. Send my love to the family, and to my ladies too. Your father sends his love.

Your loving mother,
Mary Dean

*   *   *

The next few months passed quietly enough. My mother kept up a regular correspondence with the mistress, so she and I exchanged shorter letters enclosed in those to save on postage, but there was little enough to tell, particularly as I did not care to comment on Hindley, who was going from bad to worse, despite all my best efforts to restrain him.

It was early March, and the snows were just starting to recede from the roads, when Cathy came running into the kitchen to announce that she had spied a pony carriage coming our way, and who could it be? We all hurried out to look, but could make out no more than that it was a woman driving, and not like anyone we knew. The mistress sent us back in again with orders to put the kettle on for tea and see to it that the house was presentable, while she ran upstairs to freshen her toilette for a visitor. When the cart pulled up, we saw that it was driven by a handsome, fresh-faced woman, perhaps thirty years of age. Her gown and pelisse were of good materials, and well made, in a simple, sober style, her only mark of fashion being a jaunty bonnet from which sprang a beautiful dark-dyed ostrich feather.

She jumped lightly down from the carriage and handed the reins to one of the lads hovering around. Cathy and I had been instructed to make ourselves scarce, so we were crouched at the top of the stairs, trying to be within sight and sound of the visitor without being seen or heard ourselves. But the lady spoke in a low, soft voice to the mistress, and we could not make out any of it. We were not left in suspense for long, though, for as soon as they had consulted, the mistress called out to me.

'Nelly, come down here and meet Mrs Thorne. She has a message for you from your mother.' I came down and curtseyed as the mistress introduced me. Then she took both my hands in hers, and I looked up and saw tears in her eyes. My heart dropped. I opened my mouth to speak, but could get nothing out.

'So you are little Ellen,' she said kindly. 'I am so sorry we should meet under these circumstances, dear child, but I have sad news to bring you. Your father has had an accident at work. A stone they were moving slipped and fell on top of him. He is badly injured, and it is not known whether he can recover. Your mother is with him now, and dare not leave his side, so I said that I would come to fetch you. I know this is very sudden, but do you think you can gather some things together and be ready to go with me, in perhaps half an hour? I should like to get back as soon as we can.'

I felt as if I had been struck with a stone myself, but I nodded mutely and turned to go upstairs. But the mistress took one look at my white face and folded me in her arms instead, and instructed the other maidservant to fetch tea for all three of us.

'There will be time enough to get ready when you have both sat down and refreshed yourselves,' she said. I sat down. I could not cry, but could not seem to do anything else either. Finally the tea arrived, which at least gave me something to do with my hands and mouth. Meanwhile, Mrs Thorne and the mistress kept up a low, soothing patter of small talk. Mrs Thorne, it appeared, was the young wife of my father's friend – I had recognized the name when she came in. She owned quite frankly that she was 'new to being a fine lady', having begun life as a factory girl, and met her future husband at the works before his career was well begun.

'It was a great relief to me to meet Mrs Dean,' she said. 'I do have a difficult time talking to the well-bred ladies I am supposed to visit all day. They talk of nothing but scandal, their children, and the iniquities of servants, whereas Mrs Dean is full of good, practical advice on everything from the planting of a kitchen garden to the best books to read, and she never tries to make me feel ignorant or crude.'

This set the mistress off on one of her favourite themes: the good sense, omni-competence, and general all-around excellence of my mother, though she carefully refrained, in this case, from interleaving her talk with the usual regrets and complaints that she no longer lived at Wuthering Heights. It was as soothing a cover as they could have hit upon under which I could recover my wits a little, and in a few minutes I had gathered enough of them to look about me a bit, and begin to stir myself to get ready. At this point, Cathy, who had been hovering in a corner, jumped up.

'Shall I pack your things for you, Nelly?' she asked, evidently eager to be of help. I was about to decline, but, before I could speak, the mistress accepted on my behalf, and Cathy raced upstairs to begin. I wanted to go up with her, not quite trusting her judgement, but the mistress kept me next to her on the sofa, saying I must rest for the journey to come. Cathy, meanwhile, came to the head of the stairs every few minutes to consult.

'You will want your new brown dress, won't you, Nelly?' was her first query, and then 'Mama, may Nelly borrow your old valise?' and next, 'What is she to do for gloves, Mama? Yours would be too small for her,' and 'Will she need a clean apron?' By the time all these questions and more had been settled, and Cathy had dragged the packed valise to the top of the stairs for Hindley to carry down, I had to acknowledge she had done a better job than I could have in my present addled state. Nor were we much behind the half-hour Mrs Thorne had allotted to us to get ready. Mrs Earnshaw hugged and kissed and cried over me, assuring me all the while that I would be back soon enough, and my mother with me. Then she dug a crown out of her purse to bestow on me, and I shook hands with all the children and the master too (he had come in in the meantime), and the master told me to be a good girl, and we climbed into the carriage, and were off.

At Gimmerton we exchanged the pony and carriage for a post-chaise, and drove on to Brassing at the fastest pace the post-boy could be coaxed to permit, stopping only to change horses again. All this was very new to me, and would have been a wondering pleasure, but in me both thought and feeling seemed stuck in one round. I didn't know which I feared more: that my father would die before I arrived, or that he would be alive, and not pleased to see me. Mrs Thorne seemed to understand something of what I was feeling, for she talked but little herself, and asked almost nothing of me.

Brassing, when we finally drew nigh, looked to be a much larger town than Gimmerton, but it had little else to recommend it that I could see. The houses were of grey stone, and crowded together all higgledy-piggledy, and the air was thick with an acrid miasma composed of coal smoke mingled with the smell of open privies. The post-boy let us down at the top of a narrow lane, next to a small public house. Mrs Thorne said we would stop in there to get ready. Inside, she carried out a whispered consultation with the landlady, who then produced a pair of pattens for each of us. Mrs Thorne pulled a packet of pins from her bag, and said we must pin up our skirts, and strap on the pattens, before venturing into the lane, for it was ankle-deep, or worse, in dirt. I was in a trembling hurry to be on our way, but she assured me, on the landlady's information, that there was no immediate cause for haste. Once equipped, we set off down the lane. Mrs Thorne kept a tight grip on my arm, which was just as well, as I was unaccustomed both to pattens and to cobblestones, and until I found my feet, each step threatened to pitch me head-foremost into the muck. From halfway down that lane, we turned into another still narrower, and at the end of it I saw my mother standing in a doorway. Mrs Thorne restrained me from rushing forward, but quickened her pace, and in another minute I was in my mother's arms. Mrs Thorne stayed only to receive my mother's thanks for fetching me, and then went on her way back up the lane.

'How is Father?' I asked, as soon as I caught my breath.

'He's resting,' she said, and then set me on a stool in the entryway and began removing the pattens and taking the pins from my skirt. That done, she declared me fit to step indoors. The cottage had two small rooms, but the door to the bedroom was shut. My mother sat me down by the small fire, and fetched me tea and some sweet biscuits. For some time, she would not let me speak, only directing me to eat and drink instead. I would have thought that I had no appetite at all, but the tea awakened it, and between it, the biscuits, and some bread and cheese that followed, I found the haze lifting that I had been in since Mrs Thorne's first news.

'Do you think Father will wake soon?' I asked at last. 'When will I be able to see him?' My mother knelt beside me and put her arms around me. Her eyes were filled with tears.

'Oh Nelly, he will never wake more in this world,' she said. 'He went to his final rest some three hours since. He asked for you near the end, though, to say farewell, and to beg your forgiveness for his early cruelty to you.' This opened the flood-gates at last. I sobbed myself into exhaustion on her shoulder, and she sobbed as well. Then a woman opened the door to the bedroom to say that all was ready – she had been engaged to wash his body and lay it out. So we went in, both of us, and I saw my father. The stone had struck his chest, so his face was his own, only paler and thinner than I remembered. I bent down and kissed his cold cheek – the first kiss I ever bestowed on him, that I remember, and the last.

My father lay in state for two days, so that his friends and neighbours could come to pay their respects. Mr and Mrs Thorne were among the first, and they spoke simply and frankly of their respect for my father, and their regret that they should have been in some manner the cause of his death, and Mr Thorne shed real tears for his boyhood friend. They also left with us a hamper of food, containing a ham, a large Dundee cake, a block of good Cheddar cheese, and a packet of fine tea, to feed ourselves and to offer to the other mourners as they came. There were a good many of them, for all my father's residence in the town had been so short – all the men who had worked with him or under him on the house, and all those whose acquaintance he had made in the pub. My mother's milk customers came too, and the wool-comber next door with his children. Their grief was very real, though I think it was less for my father himself than for the imminent departure of my mother and her cow.

My mother did not wish my father to be buried in Brassing, where the churchyards were all crowded and airless. The weather being cool, she resolved to transport him back home, to be buried in the churchyard at Gimmerton. The Thornes very kindly arranged all this, so we had only to pack up the household's few things to put in a hired wagon (not the one the coffin was in, to my relief) and tie Reenie to the back of it, before setting off home. Our progress going back was considerably slower than mine had been on the way, but another day brought us within sight of my parents' cottage. Reenie grew excited then, and threatened to overset the wagon, so my mother untied her, whereupon she tossed her head and took off at a slow, lumbering gallop towards the barn.

'Well, she is not sorry to shake the dust of Brassing from her feet, at any rate,' said my mother.

And so we settled back into our old places – I at the Heights, and my mother at the cottage, which she had resolved to keep. I used most of my small stock of savings to buy myself a full suit of mourning, and made much of my grief for my father. Had I known what was coming, I would have saved my tears.

SIX

I did not dare to speak to you of her death – the mistress's, that is – how it tore us all apart, and left wounds that never did heal. Yet if I didn't mention it to you, you might have asked about it at any time, and caught me unawares, and that would be worse. So I gabbled over it as fast as I could, and in the wrong place, too, so that I had to go back and tell things that came before it, as if they were after. But this is cool paper, that soaks up all I tell it without remark, and I am not so grieved now as I was then, either, by all that happened in those days.

It began with the measles. It was midsummer. My mother, I forgot to mention, had left her little cottage. It proved lonelier than she had expected, she said, without my father. And then Mrs Thorne, who had been much impressed with my mother's good sense and practical energy, wrote to ask if she would come back to Brassing to manage the dairy Mrs Thorne had been persuaded by her to establish. She offered generous terms, including the purchase of all my mother's cows, and my mother thought it best to accept. But her cows were not all as fresh-footed as young Reenie, and so my mother, as she put it, 'turned drover for a time', driving the cows before her at an easy pace, taking frequent rests, and boarding at farmhouses along the way.

It was only a day or two after she had left that Hindley first took sick with the measles, and Cathy caught them soon after, and it fell on me to nurse them, for I had been through the measles already, as a baby. It was no easy task: Cathy and Hindley complained vociferously of their many discomforts, and called on me peremptorily for help as if every cup of water or basin to be emptied and cleaned were the only thing standing between them and a speedy exit from this life. Heathcliff I tried to protect from infection by keeping him away from Cathy, for his own sake, and because I could not imagine how I was to manage without him to fetch things up and down the stairs and keep the coal-bin loaded, the fire burning, and the kettle full. It wasn't easy to keep them apart, but I told him that the excitement of seeing him would make Cathy's fever worse, and I took to locking the door of the children's sickroom whenever I was not there to guard it. But then Cathy's fever reached a crisis, and she began crying out at one moment that she was afraid to die, and at the next that she could not bear to live another minute. After that, nothing in Heaven or earth, I believe, could have kept him from her. I woke from an exhausted nap to find my pocket picked and the key gone, and found them both in her bed, clasped in each other's arms while Heathcliff sobbed and Cathy alternately burned and shivered. After that, Heathcliff took the infection, of course, though he hid it as long as he could, and took to his bed only when the telltale spots confessed his secret for him.

Then the mistress took the infection as well, which was odd, for she said she had had the measles in her youth. As a patient, she was gentle and undemanding, but she fretted continually, dividing her time between dreading the loss of her children and fearing that she would leave them motherless. Hers looked to be a mild case, to judge from the spots, but Mr Earnshaw was concerned about her, and called in Dr Kenneth.

He came later that day, looking harried and exhausted. The weather had turned remarkably hot – even the nights brought no relief – and this, he told us, had set off a rash of putrid fevers all over the neighbourhood, which had him running off his feet from morning to night.

This was not the Dr Robert Kenneth who attended you, Mr Lockwood, but his father, Dr Richard Kenneth. The former was a lad only a couple of years older than Hindley and me, and he had often been a playmate of ours when we were quite small, and the doctor was a frequent visitor to the mistress. At fourteen – that would be a year or two before Heathcliff came – he had been formally prenticed to his father, and after that we saw him less. His father called him Robin, and Hindley and I, through some childish corruption of that with his last name, and because he used to be so slight he could sit between the two of us on one stout pony, had come to call him Bodkin, and Bodkin he still was to us, whenever we did see him.

So Dr Kenneth came to see us, as I said. About the mistress he looked grave.

'The whole system must be weak,' he said, 'to take ill of this after having it in her youth.' He prescribed bed rest, beef jellies, and port wine, fortified with a brown mixture he left with us.

Heathcliff was only just coming out in the spots when the doctor came, while Cathy and Hindley were in full bloom. The latter were noisy and demanding patients, as I said before, but Heathcliff was quiet as a lamb, and so I had assumed his was the milder case. But Dr Kenneth clucked and sighed as he examined him.

97

'He's not of English stock, I think,' he said. 'God only knows where his parents were from. These foreign-bred folk can take our common illnesses quite hard. I would advise you to watch him closely. And don't set too much store by what he says, Nelly – I'm thinking he's one of those that suffer in silence. Judge by his spots, his fever, and his appetite.'

Dr Kenneth went into the next room, then, to talk to the master privately, and Bodkin motioned me over.

'Father claims that whenever he hears a patient moaning and complaining a great deal, he has good hopes of their recovery. He says that crying out is almost as good as bloodletting for releasing poisons from the body. I thought at first that he only said that to cheer nurses with tiresome patients on their hands, but now that I have been observing cases with him, I think there is a grain of truth in it. Look to young Heathcliff, Nelly, and don't let the other two wear you down.' I assured him that I would.

Seeing my hands full with the children, the master said he would take over the nursing of his wife himself, which he did, I must say, with great gentleness and thoughtful consideration. But everything else in the house fell onto my shoulders. Joseph, who had never had the measles and was mortally afraid of contracting them, made up a pallet for himself in the barn, and took charge of all matters in the dairy and out-of-doors, never setting foot in the house. There was no time to make cheese or churn butter, and it was too hot for milk to keep, so I made up the pots of porridge for myself and my patients with fresh milk instead of water; we set the two calves to nurse for themselves on our gentlest cow, and sent the remainder of the milk home with the dairymaid, who lived hard by with her parents and a pack of hungry brothers and sisters.

The days that followed recur to my memory now like time spent in another world. I seemed to be continually running or rushing about, except when I composed myself to attend to one of my patients, or collapsed into a few hours' exhausted sleep before waking in terror that someone had died.

Cathy and Hindley took so much of my time and attention that I all but ignored Heathcliff for a while. I was just settling them for sleep one night, when I heard a low moan from his bed, and turned to look after him. He lay on his back, still as death, and spoke not a word, but only panted faintly, his eyes wide with terror as they followed my motions, like a wounded fox that sees the dogs approach, and hopes for no mercy but a speedy end. I poured him a cup of water, and held up his head for him to drink it, and he drank greedily at first, his eyes fixed on me all the time, but swallowing seemed to pain him, and after a few gulps he leaned his head back and closed his eyes, and I laid him back down. I was speaking soothingly to him all the while – softly, so as not to wake Cathy or Hindley, but he said nothing, and gave no sign of recognition. When I felt his forehead his skin burned to my touch – Cathy and Hindley had been feverish too, but nothing like this.

My heart smote me then, that I had not attended better to Bodkin's advice. I thought, if I could not bring down his fever, he might die, and his death would be on my hands, for had I not neglected him, while attending to the others? I stripped the bedclothes off him, and his nightshirt as well. Then I wetted a cloth with water from the pitcher and washed him all over, in an effort to cool his burning skin.

I have said it was hot, but there was at this time such a heat spell as I have never known before or since. Day and night, the air was still and sweltering; there was no coolness to be found anywhere in the house, even in the stillroom. Even the water in the pitcher was lukewarm, and it only sat on the poor boy's skin like sweat, instead of drying off to cool him. I ran downstairs to fetch fresher – and, I hoped, cooler – water from the large jar in the kitchen, but it was little better. In my desperation, at length I bethought me of the well. Normally we drew our water from a shallow well in the courtyard, but the heat had caused the water in it to go foul, so we had resorted to an older well nearby, customarily used for watering the stock. It was a deep one, and water fresh-drawn from it had always the coolness of deep earth, whatever the weather. But the well was a good distance from the house, and the night black as pitch, with no moon, and stars obscured by the low haze of moisture in the air. I hastily prepared a lantern, though, and made my way as best I could to the well to draw a fresh bucketful. It was as cool as I hoped, so I filled my pitcher afresh and hurried back to the house to try its effect on my patient.

His skin was still so hot to the touch, I half-fancied I could hear it sizzle when I applied the cloths, like water on a hot skillet. But the cool cloths did seem to give him some ease. His breathing slowed and became deeper, and his eyes looked less fearful. I lifted him again for another cool drink of water, and when he was done, his lips moved to thank me, though no sound came from them, and tears welled in his eyes. I kept up bathing him with water from the pitcher, but it was not long before it grew warm again and lost its power to cool him. Then I rushed out again to fill it from the well, and began all over again.

Thus began the longest and strangest night of my life. I rushed back and forth from the well to Heathcliff's sickbed, bathing his burning skin continually except when I ran out to replenish the water in the pitcher. I stopped only to drink water myself at the well, for the rushing in and out of doors and up and down the stairs kept the sweat pouring off me in rivulets, though I had stripped myself to my shift because of the heat. By the time I saw the first glow of grey dawn in the east, my arms and legs were quivering with exhaustion, and my breath came in sobs at each new exertion. Yet I dreaded the coming of day, for fear the sun would add to the heat, and make my struggle against Heathcliff's fever yet harder.

I had just drawn up the bucket from the well when I heard the steady clump of horses' feet approaching. It was Dr Kenneth, and Bodkin behind him on a pony. I began waving my arms and shouting to them at the top of my voice, terrified that they would pass by without stopping (and that will tell you something of my state of mind, for there was no earthly reason for anyone to be on that road, unless it were to visit us). They clucked up their horses and hastened over to me, and it wasn't until they were a dozen yards away that I recollected I had only my shift on! I quickly grabbed the bucket to my chest for cover, but it was full of water, of course, which duly sloshed all down my front. This, you may be sure, improved neither my appearance nor my composure. But good Dr Kenneth's face expressed nothing but its habitual kind concern.

'Good heavens, Nelly, poor child, whatever is the matter?'

'Oh, Dr Kenneth, I didn't listen to you, and now Heathcliff has the fever terribly bad, and nothing I can do will bring it down, and I'm afraid he will die,' I sobbed out, and then commenced to babble incoherently about my long night, and my desperate efforts to cool the feverish child. Before I finished, Dr Kenneth turned his horse and hurried off to the house, pausing only to say a few words to his son in a voice too low for me to hear. His departure, and the relief that Heathcliff was now in better hands than mine, seemed to drain from me the last ounce of my desperate energy, and I crumpled to the ground and wrapped my arms around my knees, crying uncontrollably and shivering in my wet shift as if I had a chill wind on me instead of the same still heat as before. Bodkin slipped off his pony and came over to wrap his jacket around me, turning his head away as I hastily buttoned it down the front. Then he helped me up from the ground and half led, half carried me into the kitchen. There he blew up the fire, made tea, and put a mug of it before me with some oatcakes and a bit of jam he found in the storeroom. I shook my head – I could not imagine finding the strength to eat or drink.

'None of that, Nelly. This is doctor's orders. Food and something hot to drink, he said, and I'm not to leave you until you've swallowed some of each.' I did manage to take some, then, which revived me enough to remind me how hungry I was, and I set to with some eagerness.

'And now, Nelly, tell me where I may find a nightdress for you.'

'They're upstairs, in the cupboard in my room – that's the second on the right,' I said, and then added, in some confusion, 'but I can't put on nightclothes now – it's already morning.'

But Bodkin was already heading up the stairs.

'Morning for those who have been sleeping all night, perhaps,' he said, 'but bedtime for you. Again, these are my father's orders.' And then he was off, to return a minute later with one of my nightdresses. 'Here you are, milady,' he said, 'and here is your dressing room' (opening the storeroom door with a flourish). That coaxed a laugh from me.

'I can change more easily in my own room.'

'Very likely, but you have not had near enough breakfast yet, and I can't have you spilling jam on my best summer jacket.'

'Is this your best?' I asked doubtfully (it was a remarkably threadbare garment).

'My best, my worst, and my middling all, for it's my only one. Now go and change.' I thought it best to obey, and indeed it felt good to get out of the wet shift and into something clean and dry. I felt shy of coming out of the storeroom in only my nightdress though, and poked my head through the door to say so.

'You forget I am in training to be a doctor, Nell,' he said. 'Seeing folks in their nightclothes is a hazard of my chosen profession, just as getting run through with a sword is for a cavalry officer.'

'Well, call up all your professional courage, then, for here I come.'

Bodkin put some bread and cheese in front of me, and refreshed my mug of tea.

'You would be astonished at what we've seen in this heat, Nelly,' he went on. 'Some of it makes your wet shift look like a noble sacrifice to the cause of modesty.' I laughed and shook my head. 'No, truly,' he said, laughing himself, 'do you know Old Elspeth?'

'I know of her,' I said.

'Well, Father and I called by her cottage yesterday afternoon.'

'Was she ill?' I interrupted. 'It doesn't speak well of her art, that she couldn't cure herself, but had to call in a doctor to help.'

'Nothing of the sort; she's as hale as ever – it was we who needed her.'

'Really! And I thought doctors and herbwomen were at daggers drawn.'

'Not in this case. Father respects her. She serves more of the poor than he could get to if there were three of him, he says, and serves them well. And she makes a salve for the rheumatics that is better than anything. Gentlefolk won't touch it if they know it comes from her, so Father buys it from her and dispenses it as his own concoction, and thus keeps everybody happy. But to get back to my story: we rode up to her cottage and knocked at the door, but there was no answer, and then we heard her in the garden behind the cottage, so we went round there. You know she is rather deaf, so I suppose she didn't hear us coming. When we came upon her, she stood up from behind a bush, and can you guess what she was wearing, Nell?' I shook my head. 'A broad-brimmed straw hat!' he announced, making his eyes wide with feigned shock.

'Well, what is so surprising about that?' I asked, a little puzzled. 'I wear one myself, when I am working outside on a sunny day.' Bodkin gazed at me expectantly, his eyes twinkling.

'I am telling you, she was wearing . . . a broad-brimmed straw hat.' It hit me then.

'And nothing else?' I gasped.

'Not a stitch. The hat was the sum total of her costume. A woman over eighty! I tell you, I needed every ounce of my professional courage not to turn tail and flee.' I collapsed into helpless laughter, and he with me, and we both sat there giggling like a pair of naughty children.

'I would love to have seen her face when she saw you there,' I said at last.

'You would have seen little to amuse you, actually, for her face showed no awkward consciousness at all. I tell you, a savage chief from the Americas could not have borne his nakedness with more dignity than that old woman. She simply turned and strode into the cottage, then emerged later, clothed, and with the pot of salve for my father, and we all exchanged the usual pleasantries as if nothing had happened. As we were leaving, Father turned to me and asked, "So, Robin, what do you make of that?" "Well, Father," I replied, "I know that older ladies often cling to the fashions of their youth, but I had not realized that Elspeth was old enough to take hers from

Mother Eve." That made him laugh, and then we said not another word about it.'

'You are a funny fellow, Bodkin.'

'Well, laughter is the only medication I am at present qualified to dispense – that and tea,' he added, 'and the occasional article of dry clothing. And I see that those have had their usual miraculous restorative effect, so let us get you off to bed.' But, before we could head up the stairs, we met the master and Dr Kenneth coming down.

'What, not abed yet, Nelly?' the doctor said. 'Off with you, then, post haste.'

'Please, sir,' I asked, my old anxiety suddenly returning, 'how is Heathcliff?'

'His fever has broken, thanks to you,' he said, 'and he is resting peacefully. He should make a full recovery, as will Cathy and Hindley. This young woman, sir,' he said, turning to the master, 'has done heroic service for yon poor lad – all night long she ran back and forth to the old well, and up and down these stairs, to ease his fever with cooling baths – it was her own thought, and I could not have had a better one myself – and she wore herself near to collapse doing it. You have her to thank that he will pull through.'

The master looked haggard and worn himself, from worry and sleepless nights nursing his wife, but at this he turned to me, and I saw tears in his eyes.

'Come here, child,' he said hoarsely. When I came up to him, he gestured me to kneel in front of him, and put both hands on my head. 'God bless you, Ellen Dean,' he said in a choked voice, 'I think you were born to be the salvation of this house, and I swear that while I live you will always have a home here.' His hands rested on my head, and we both remained there in silence, he standing, I kneeling and looking at the floor, for what seemed a long time, and then he said again, 'God bless you,' and released me. I was weeping by then, and could scarcely rise, but Bodkin helped me up, and led me up the stairs. At the top I saw Hindley, out of bed and poking his head out of his door. He flashed on me a look of such anger and pain that I realized he must have heard every word below.

'How could you?' he hissed at me as I passed, but I was too exhausted to face him just then, so I turned away without answering, and let Bodkin lead me to my room and put me into my bed, where I fell instantly into a deep sleep that lasted the whole of that day and the following night.

*

I awoke at dawn, as usual, but with a vague sense that everything was changed, as if a whole new world had taken shape around me while I slept, so that I was startled to see the same old familiar surroundings. As I dressed, memories came back to account for this feeling: my efforts for Heathcliff, and their success, and the praise I had received for them, but most of all, Mr Earnshaw's heartfelt blessing, and his promise that I should always have a home at Wuthering Heights. I had thought that I had long since put away the bitter memory of my earlier expulsion, but somewhere in the back of my mind it must have still rankled. Now that pain was gone, as if the pressure of the master's hands on my head had been a baptism that washed away all my old sins, and made me a new person – one who belonged at Wuthering Heights, and had claims there.

About Heathcliff, too, I had new and warmer feelings. I had employed all my wits and all my strength to save his life, and I had saved it. So the doctor told me, so I believed myself, and so, I was sure, Heathcliff knew too. How could I not now value more greatly the life I had saved? And Heathcliff's need had touched me. As I had nursed him through that horrible night, I had kept up a steady gentle patter of reassurance and affection, such as a mother uses to her child. The words came naturally to my lips, and I believe I would have said the like for anyone I nursed so, but once spoken, they seemed to bring their own truth with them, and Heathcliff became no longer the troublesome brat I had always thought him, but my poor bairn, my good little laddie, my darling boy. And I saw, too, their effect on him: through the night, each time I returned to his bedside, his eyes would seek out mine and his lips move to say my name, and I saw in his face what I had never seen there for me before: trust, and gratitude, and love.

Hindley I tried not to think about, only telling myself that he could not really wish me to have let Heathcliff die, and that he would come round in time.

By the time I had thus taken stock of my mental world, I was washed and dressed. The terrible heat, I noticed, had broken at last, and all nature seemed to be celebrating it. At any rate, it was a beautiful day, of that crystalline sunny clearness we see so rarely here, that makes the very lungs leap to take in the fresh air, carries the sounds of birds for miles around, and gives the edges of objects the sharpness of a knife-blade. I went downstairs. Joseph was back in his old place – Dr Kenneth must have declared the house free of infection – but no one else was up yet. His was not the face I would have chosen to see first that morning, but my mood was too buoyant to let him affect it.

'Good morning, Joseph. I hope you slept well?' I asked cheerfully.

'Not as well as you did, spending the whole of yesterday lazing in your bed, from what I hear.'

'Doctor's orders. Same as kept you from having to lift a finger in here while I was run off my feet the whole of last week. Not that I'm complaining,' I added brightly, 'for I managed very well on my own. Dr Kenneth said I saved Heathcliff's life, and the master gave me his blessing, and told me I was born to be the salvation of the family.' This had the desired effect – Joseph scowled and turned away, but could not think of a word to say in response that would not appear to disparage these two authorities.

'Now that you're here,' I went on, 'can you tell me what happened yesterday while I was asleep? Is the mistress up from her bed yet? Or any of the children? And what of the master? He looked worn to a ravelling when last I saw him.'

'Hindley and Cathy are out of their beds, but they're to keep themselves quiet and not goo out a'doors, and t' doctor says Heathcliff's past the wust of it, but he still needs a few days rest a-bed. T' mistress is still ill, and t' master still gies all his time to nursing her. If ye want to make yeself useful, ye'll bring up a tray for both on them – thin milk porridge for t' mistress an' summat more hearty for t' master.'

'I know what they need,' I said, 'haven't I been bringing trays for them all week?' I hastened to put together the tray, adding a pot of tea and a small pitcher of milk before carrying it upstairs. Outside their room, I knocked softly at the door, as I had been instructed to do. The master opened the door, but, instead of taking the tray inside, he stepped out with me into the hall.

'She's sleeping now,' he whispered. 'Let's not disturb her. I'll eat downstairs.'

'Please, sir,' I ventured, as we went down the hall together, 'how is Mrs Earnshaw now? What did the doctor say?'

'Never mind what the doctor said. Mrs Earnshaw is still weak, but mending. Her measles are clearing up – it just took a little longer with her than with the children because she is older. She needs time to rest, and no disturbances. Trouble between the children especially frets her, and that will slow her recovery. I have arranged with the curate to take over their lessons, but apart from that I am counting on you to keep the peace, Nelly, for they are all fond of you. Do you think you can do that?'

'I – I will try, sir,' I stammered. I was flattered that he should speak to me of 'the children' as if I were not one of them, and it did not occur to me, then, that he was asking of me something I had not the authority to accomplish.

Since the master was heading downstairs for his breakfast, I decided to take the tray in to Hindley instead. True, Heathcliff was the only one of the children not yet strong enough to come downstairs for his meals, but I thought the indulgence of breakfast in his room might serve as a peace offering from me to Hindley, and allow us to make up in privacy. I knocked gently at his door.

'Who's there?'

'It's I, Nelly, with your breakfast on a tray. Are you decent?'

'I suppose so.' I opened the door and slipped in.

'Why are you bringing me a tray?' he asked sullenly, 'Dr Kenneth said I was well enough to be up.'

'I brought it up for your parents, but your mother is sleeping, and your father preferred to eat downstairs, so I thought I would bring it to you instead.'

'You should have brought it to Heathcliff. He is your favourite now.'

'He is nothing of the kind. I was responsible for his care, so of course I did all I could for him. But I will always love you best, Hindley. You know that.'

'I don't know that at all! It's all very well to say you were only doing your duty, Nelly, but I heard what Dr Kenneth said

– you half killed yourself to save him. If you had been content to do no more than your duty, that brat would be dead now, and think how much better all our lives would be.'

'I would not be better off, with his death on my conscience.'

'My conscience would not be so queasy. If I'd been awake, I could have smothered him with a pillow, while you were off fetching more water, and no one would have been the wiser – even you. But you never think of such things.'

'And neither should you! For mercy's sake, Hindley, think of your eternal soul, and banish such thoughts from your head!'

'I'd be content to go to Hell, if I could only be sure of sending him there before me.'

'And then you'd get to spend eternity with the person you hate most on earth – some triumph that would be! Can't you see that the best way to get Heathcliff out of your life is to banish him from your consciousness? Ignore him, and he and Cathy will stay out of your way, you may be sure. And we will all be the happier for it, especially your mother. This conflict is a strain on her, the master told me, and will hinder her recovery.'

'How can you accuse me of making her ill! I love her better than any of you! Father foisted this child upon her, when her hands were already full with the rest of us, and now she frets that she cannot love him, and that he makes Cathy so wild she will never learn to be a lady, and even you, you take your orders from everybody but her.'

I flushed, and spoke before I had the sense to think of my words: 'I haven't seen you making any effort to obey her – didn't she tell you day after day to just do your lessons and leave Heathcliff alone? But you never would, for all you say you love her best. You dare to be angry at me for not letting Heathcliff die. You don't know what it's like to have the

110

responsibility for all of you on my shoulders. You think only about yourself. You are selfish, selfish, selfish!' I stormed out of the room, only remembering in the nick of time not to slam the door.

I was so angry that I dared not stop in the kitchen for breakfast, but continued straight past and out of the door, only composing myself enough to look as if I were merely in a hurry. Once outside, I turned my steps towards the emptiest segment of the moors, and walked. For the first half-mile or so I was fuelled entirely by outrage at Hindley, as a steam engine is by coal, and whenever my legs began to slow I would stoke the fire by remembering his wish to smother poor Heathcliff with a pillow. But the day was fine and sunny, as I said before, and the air on the moors was breezy, and lightly scented with blooming flowers, and these things soon began to have their usual effect. With each lungful I drew in, I seemed to take in some of the freshness of the day, while each out-breath exhaled with it some of the strain and worry of the household I left behind. With greater distance – in mind as well as body – I began to see that a good deal of my anger ought rightfully to be directed at myself. Why had I allowed myself to be provoked by Hindley so easily, when I knew he was still peevish with illness, and agitated by worry for his mother? And more deeply, how remiss must I have been in indulging Hindley's disparagement of Heathcliff, that he could even think of murdering the lad outright, and imagine me a likely partner in the enterprise?

You might not think it, Mr Lockwood, but this taking of blame onto myself was actually a comfort to me, for if my troubles had been of my own making, then might it not be in my own power to fix them? I was about three miles from Wuthering Heights by the time I reached this point in my reflections, and I had slowed to an amble and begun to look about me a bit more. At length I spied a copious stand of beautiful blackberries, fat and ripe, which I decided would make a good excuse for my expedition. So I took my large kerchief from my neck and tied it into a sort of basket, which in short order I filled with the ripe fruit. I filled my mouth, too, while I was at it, for I had had no breakfast. Then I headed back to Wuthering Heights, with my mind already busy with plans. It was perhaps just as well, I reflected, that I had expressed myself so strongly to Hindley about his violent wishes towards Heathcliff – it would not do for him to continue to think me an ally in such things. But I might still make him a heartfelt apology for my vehemence, and for appearing to disparage his love for his mother, which I knew to be most devoted. And for the rest, my future conduct towards him, I vowed to myself, should be affectionate and encouraging of any good impulses, and calmly repressive of the bad.

And that, Mr Lockwood, is a fair sample of many such walks that I took, before and since, that began in anger or grief, and ended in plans for the benevolent improvement of all about me, myself included. They were not bad plans, in themselves. Their main flaw was that they required the cooperation of others in the carrying-out.

SEVEN

I was going to write how we all fared during that time: how I contrived and pleaded and stormed to try to keep Heathcliff and Cathy in good behaviour, and to appease and restrain Hindley, and how little effect it all had. But I find I have not the heart for it, after all. At the time, it seemed so important to me that I keep my promise to the master, and aid Mrs Earnshaw in her recovery, but now I see that it would have made little difference, either way. Death had marked her with his finger, and nothing we did or refrained from doing could erase that mark. We did not see it, though, but remained hopeful, clinging to each small and temporary upturn in her condition, as a sure sign of returning health.

It was Bodkin who opened my eyes to the true state of affairs. Dr Kenneth had again become a regular visitor at our house, coming every week or two to look in on the mistress and make adjustments in her treatment. He rarely brought Bodkin, though, as he said there was little new for him to learn from the case. So when, some three months after the measles, I saw them both arrive together, I was pleased, and hastened to make a pot of tea and butter some oatcakes, anticipating a comfortable chat in the kitchen with my old friend. He entered smiling, and took my hands in his.

'Nelly, my girl, you are looking very hale and rosy, as usual. We needn't worry about your health, anyway.'

'Oh, I am always well. And so are you, from the looks of you.'

'Yes, it took some time, but I am well toughened now, against rough weather and fevers both.'

'Safe from all the hazards of your profession, then?'

'Well, not all. The other day I was bitten by a child of three, as I tried to stitch a cut in his hand. See here?' He pulled up his left sleeve to reveal a nasty-looking wound. 'Father says I will bear the scar to my grave.'

'Don't you wish now you'd been a cavalry officer, after all?'

'Well, I begin to suspect they have the more comfortable life, having only the cannons and swords of battle to fear, instead of sharp-toothed brats, who may turn up anywhere.'

'Ah, but they measure their success by the number they kill, whereas you will measure yours by the number you save.'

'We'd do better by the former reckoning. If doctors were accorded respect for the number of their patients who died instead of for those who lived, we would all be national heroes – for, to be sure, our patients all die in the end.'

I laughed. 'Well, but in what other profession can you get folk to pay you so handsomely and gratefully merely for delaying the inevitable?'

'Not so handsomely, nor so gratefully as you might think.'

'Well, I don't know what we are paying you, but we are certainly grateful here, for all you are doing to help the mistress recover.' The laughter died from his face.

'Recover? Nelly, in all seriousness, you can't think that is likely, can you?'

'But why not? Today she sat up to take tea and toast, and stayed up to write some letters, for the first time in a week. Surely that means she's getting stronger?'

'Yet a month ago, she was sitting up every day,' he said gently, 'and a month before that, she would now and then come downstairs for an hour or two. She may have better days and worse days, Nelly, but on the whole she has been declining steadily, and nothing you or my father can do is like to change that.'

'Who are you to be the judge of that?' I asked angrily. 'I thought you weren't supposed to give out your father's medical opinions behind his back! Have you received your qualification since I last saw you, and set up practice on your own?'

'This is no professional opinion, Nelly, neither my own nor my father's, but simply common sense. You are all too close to Mrs Earnshaw, and love her too dearly, to see what is clear to a more distanced eye. I am not saying it is impossible for her to get better: I have seen cases no more hopeful than hers that ended in nearly a full recovery. There are miracles – God's and Nature's – and we can always hope for one here. But the more likely event is that she will continue to weaken. Her hold on life is loosening – can you not see that? She is preparing to bid it farewell. And you must prepare too.'

'Wise advice!' I said sarcastically. 'I suppose you think I should be stitching her shroud while I sit with her of an evening – and maybe we should have the carpenter in to start building her coffin in the house – or better yet, in her room! That will save us the trouble of carrying it up the stairs when it's finished, and if the sawing and hammering disturb her rest, what matter? The sooner she goes, the sooner we'll be free of the trouble of nursing her! Is that what you think? A fine doctor you'll be, with the same recommendation in every case: "Pray for a miracle, and set to work on the coffin!"'

I was breathless with outrage, and just sharpening my wits for a deeper thrust, when he put his hands on my shoulders and gave a little squeeze.

'Nelly,' he said calmly, 'I am very sorry if I spoke too strongly, and too soon. I meant to help, but I see I have done more harm than good, and that is the worst thing a doctor – or a doctor manqué, as I confess I am – can do. Will you forgive me?'

I wriggled out of his grasp and turned aside so I wouldn't have to look at him.

'Go away,' I said brusquely, then grabbed some onions and a knife, and commenced peeling. 'I have work to do.'

'We are still friends?'

'Oh, of course we are,' I said quickly. 'Just go away, please.' I feared I would begin sobbing if he stayed, and that was too humiliating. But Bodkin came round in front of me and pushed up his right sleeve to the shoulder.

'Would you care to take a bite?' he asked.

'What?'

'Take a bite out of my arm. My other patients find it relieves their feelings. And I should rather like to have matching scars.'

'Oh, *damn* you!' I said. I could not help laughing, and of course that released the tears as well, and between that and the onions I soon had my handkerchief soaked. Bodkin said nothing more, just sat down opposite me again, poured a fresh mug of tea, and pushed it over to me as soon as I looked up.

'Laughter and tea, again?' I asked.

'Laughter and tea, and' – he reached over and extracted my sodden handkerchief from my hand, replacing it with a clean one from his own pocket – 'dry linen. My tried and true treatment for Miss Ellen Dean of Wuthering Heights – cures all her ailments at once.'

'I wish it could.'

'What do you mean?'

'Oh, just that things will be difficult here if . . . if what you say is true. I don't know how Hindley will . . . he and the master are . . . well, they just don't get on well.'

'Well, but Hindley is not *your* ailment, is he?'

'No, I suppose not, but trouble is trouble, all the same. And the master relies on me to keep peace in the household.'

'He asks a good deal too much of you, then.'

'Oh no! I am happy to do my best for them all. I just worry sometimes that it is beyond my power.'

Bodkin looked thoughtful. 'You know, Nelly, you are not obliged to keep working here.'

'But Wuthering Heights has been my home for as long as I can remember. I love them bet— like my own family. I could never leave them while they need me. And where else would I go, anyway?'

'As long as you are content here, of course there is no reason to leave. But if that should change, Nelly, please don't imagine that you are obliged to sacrifice your happiness for theirs. You may be sure they would none of them do the same for you.'

'Well, thank you for that kind thought Bodkin! As I struggle through the hardship that awaits us all, and grieve for their loss as well as my own, it will be a great comfort to reflect that none of them gives a fig for my feelings.'

'I didn't mean that, Nelly, just that—'

'Please, Bodkin,' I interrupted, 'don't you think I've had enough hard truths for one day? I love the Earnshaws, and have good reason to believe they are fond of me as well. I will not leave them just when trouble comes upon them, because

I might be more comfortable elsewhere.' I forced a smile. 'If you tell me any more, I really will have to bite you.'

Bodkin shifted the talk to local gossip, then, and made his farewells as soon as his father came downstairs. But the conversation stayed with me, like a lump of cold porridge caught midway between my throat and my stomach.

During these months, we carried on a sort of triangular correspondence with my mother. She wrote to the mistress about once a week – long, chatty letters full of the pleasures and challenges of her new position – with greetings to me enclosed, and the expectation that the whole letter would be passed on to me afterwards. In fact I had them as soon as they came, for the mistress had me read them aloud to her – reading made her head ache, she said. For the same reason, it was left to me to write back to my mother and give the news of the family. This I did faithfully, as regards the frequency, but not so faithfully in the contents, for I omitted at least as much as I told.

I did not tell, for example, of the mistress's increasingly peevish remarks on my mother's oft-expressed enthusiasm for Mrs Thorne. The latter had not only entered with interest into my mother's plans for the dairy, but expanded them with benevolent schemes of her own, such as providing a cup of fresh milk each morning to the children who filed into her husband's mill to work, and another as they left in the evening – with great effects as to their health and spirits, she said. In addition, Mrs Thorne had embarked with my mother on a course of evening reading, meant to repair the deficiencies in her education, beginning with the plays of Shakespeare, of course, so as to find names for all the new cows. All this and more my mother told at length, delighted to have found a companion who shared her energy as well as her interests. But her enthusiasm grated visibly on the mistress, who felt slighted by my mother's interest in her new friend.

'She has forgotten,' she would grumble, 'how we used to look after the dairy together ourselves, and read Shakespeare of an evening, and vow that we would never be separated.'

'Of course not,' I would assure her, 'it is her memory of those happy times that gives her such joy now in reliving them, and she shares them with you for that reason.'

'No, she has replaced me entirely with this Mrs Thorne,' she replied. 'I don't think she misses me at all any more, as I do her.'

Well, I would soothe and reassure her as best I could, but I took to editing my mother's letters as I read, leaving out her praise of Mrs Thorne whenever I could, and laying stress on any little difficulties or disappointments in her new life of which she made mention, and of course on all her expressions of affection and concern for Mrs Earnshaw.

As I say, I made no mention of this in my letters to my mother. I also said next to nothing of the mistress's condition, only that she was still 'a little weak' from her illness, but mending. At first this was no more than what we all endeavoured to believe ourselves, the mistress included, but even after Bodkin had, as it were, opened my eyes to the true state of affairs, I continued to hide it from my mother. I told myself that there was no need to disturb her happiness in her new position, and that there would be time enough to send for her, if the mistress's condition should worsen further. But then, having hidden her true state for so long, it became difficult to see how I might reverse my news, and tell of her steady decline, without making clear how much I had been prevaricating already.

I don't know how long this might have gone on if it were left only to me, but one day in February, when I had just brought the mistress a cup of warm tea, she startled me by taking both my hands in hers, and looking solemnly into my eyes.

'It is time to send for your mother, Nelly,' she said. 'She must have her chance to say farewell.'

I opened my mouth to protest, but a slight pressure of her hands, and the sight of her gaunt, pale face, and the sunken eyes fixed so calmly on mine, stopped me, so I did no more than whisper, 'Yes, ma'am,' and slip away. With that compulsion fresh upon me, I sat down and wrote quickly to my mother that the mistress was 'sinking' and, we feared, past recovery, and that she wished my mother to come to her as soon as was practicable.

As expected, the letter brought my mother to us within a few days, arriving in the same pony carriage that had carried Mrs Thorne, a year before. She wasted little time on greetings, only stopping to give a brief curtsey towards the master and confirm that Mrs Earnshaw was awake, before sweeping up the stairs to her room. I had just come from there, brought out by the hubbub of my mother's arrival, so I could whisper to her on her way in that she was expected. She went in and closed the door. I hovered nearby, hoping to catch some sense of what passed, but heard only a low, soothing murmur from my mother – the mistress's voice was too soft to be heard at all. A rustling sound gave me warning that she was leaving, and I hurried to leave my post, and make it appear that I was just walking past as my mother came out. My mother was smiling and composed in taking leave of the mistress, but as soon as the door was shut she whipped round and grabbed me hard by the shoulders.

120

'Why didn't you tell me?' she hissed, pulling us both from the door at the same time. I opened my mouth to speak, but could get no words out, so overwhelmed was I by what seemed to me in that moment the enormity of my crime against her.

'I didn't know,' I burst out at last, and then collapsed into sobs.

Her face melted then, to my immense relief, and she wrapped me in her arms.

'No, of course,' she sighed, 'how could you?'

I ought to have confessed to her then, just how much I had known, and when, and how much of selfishness and heedlessness there had been in my silence. She would have forgiven me, I am sure, and we would have been closer, and had more genuine comfort from each other, in what we both knew was coming. And in what came afterwards – well, many things might have been different. But I lacked the courage.

By tacit consent, my mother took over the nursing of Mrs Earnshaw entirely. She had a little bed made up for herself on the floor – the master had moved out some weeks earlier to the spare bedroom, so as not to disturb her light sleep with his snores. I, who had prided myself on my skill in preparing nourishing foods that would tempt the mistress's increasingly delicate appetite, found my experience swept aside in the kitchen, so my mother could prepare forgotten delicacies from their youth, and honey-sweetened tisanes made up of odd-smelling herbs she went to Old Elspeth to purchase. I felt a little put out by this at first, but I soon had to concede that my mother knew what she was about, for the mistress visibly brightened and improved under her care. That, of course, only stung my conscience the more: if I had only sent for my mother sooner, might she have cured the mistress altogether? One quiet evening as we both sat by the fire in the kitchen, I ventured to put this to her.

'I wish—' I began, meaning to say that I wished we had brought her sooner, but she interrupted me.

'Whisht, Nelly, what have I said to you about wishing?'

'Very well then, I wonder, if you had come sooner, might you have made the mistress well?' I held my breath after, for this was the closest I had come to confessing that I ought to have sent for her before I did. My mother was silent for a long time, and I saw tears gathering in her eyes.

'I think not,' she said at last. 'Mrs Earnshaw has been weakening for a long time – much longer than this one illness. What you are seeing now is only a little burst of energy because she is glad to have me here again, and glad to know that I will be with her until—' She stopped, unable to continue. 'If I had come sooner, that too would have faded in time.'

I was fighting back tears myself, but if I had any inclination to throw myself into my mother's arms again to sob, she was not encouraging.

'Come now,' she said briskly, 'there will be enough weeping when the time comes – until then we should keep our hands busy and our minds on happier things.'

I picked up some sewing, and she took up a piece of knitting she had brought with her, and we both worked in silence for a little while. I cast my mind about for something to discuss, and at last hit upon something I had been wanting to ask her for a long time.

'Why do you never speak of your younger days with Mrs Earnshaw, when you were both girls together? She speaks of it all the time.'

'I don't like to talk of it,' she said shortly. 'Those days are passed and gone.'

'But you like to tell stories,' I persisted, 'and those are of days passed and gone, too. And weren't those happy times, for both of you?'

'They were,' she said, and I saw her eyes look off into the air, while her lips pressed together, and the needles stopped in their restless motion. Then she seemed to reach some decision, and the needles began moving again. She began speaking, but without looking at me.

'Mrs Earnshaw, Helen Thwaite before she married – you are called Ellen after her – was my close friend and companion in girlhood. We grew up on adjacent farms not far from here: the Thwaites' was freehold, and my father held his from Mr Linton. Our mothers were relations by marriage, and had always kept up a regular visiting between them, sharing receipts for jam and cakes, and trading gifts of butter and eggs, cheeses and chicks, back and forth, as farmers' wives do, to tide each other over, say a fox had got in among the poultry, or the cows fallen sick in the dairy.

'So we girls were often together, and called each other cousin, and as we grew older and were expected to take our share of the work at home, we took to working together at each other's houses, turn and turn about. Our mothers were happy to see it, they said, for it made our work an extension of our play, and instilled early those habits of cheerful industry that are the best dowry of a farmer's daughter. In my case, it was all the dowry I was likely to have, for my father was over-free with his money, and though my mother was a thrifty and sensible manager enough, it needed all her skill and contrivance to see to it that the rent was made up each quarter day, and my three younger brothers kept in boots and schoolbooks, without putting any aside for my establishment.

'We doted on each other, with a great deal of kissing and laughter, in the way that girls will before their attention is

123

turned to the lads. But for all we were so much together, we were not much alike, in looks, or manner, or talents. Helen was a light-hearted wisp of a girl, with sparkling brown eyes, hair that fell in bright chestnut curls down her back, and a complexion any lady might envy. Even now in her middle age and after many sufferings of mind and body both, you can still see in her face the pretty lass she had been, and how easily she won the love of all who knew her.'

I nodded – indeed, it had sometimes troubled my conscience that my heart was drawn to her more, so I thought, than to my own mother – and motioned her to continue.

'I was more solidly made than my cousin, even as a young girl, and had that sort of brown complexion and plain broad country face that is made pretty only by youth, health, and good cheer, and soon marred by the loss of any of them – much the same face you see in your own glass, Nelly. But what I lacked in beauty, I made up in quickness of mind and good practical sense, and steady health and spirits.

'I have said we shared our work, but from the start I took the lead in practical matters. Helen was clever with her hands, especially in small things, and had an excellent taste. I have yet by me a needle case she made once from scraps of ribbon and satin anyone else would have thought too small to save, all joined together with fancywork and a few stray buttons and beads into as lovely a thing as you could hope to see. But with ordinary chores it was another matter; she was inclined to be flighty, and disliked much of the daily work a farmer's daughter must turn her hand to: sweeping and scouring, straining the milk, churning and making up the butter, baking and the like, for such work, it seemed to her, was no sooner done than undone: the food eaten, the milk drunk, the pots dirtied again, and all to be done over the next day or week. With me at her side she could get through her tasks with credit enough, for we could chatter over the dough-tub and the milk pans, and if I did more than my strict share of the labour, why, Helen provided most of the entertainment. And as Helen felt in her heart no great pride in such work, she was content, too, to be assigned menial tasks and be ordered about by me as a sort of assistant, which fell in well with my love of order. So, despite our differences, or because of them, we pleased each other and our parents too, and had between us as happy and carefree a girlhood as any farmers' daughters could hope for.

'But when we came to young womanhood, our situations altered. Helen at eighteen caught the eye of the young master of Wuthering Heights, as likely a catch as the neighbourhood could boast at that time, the Earnshaws being an ancient family and the estate sizeable, though not rich. Mr Earnshaw was conscious of a gentleman's claim to a genteel wife, and he had a young man's eye for a comely face and manner. But he had also had the management of his estate long enough to know that the mistress of Wuthering Heights needs to be more than an adornment to the household. As you must have seen by now, Nelly, the farms that make up the estate are generally poor ones that owe but little rent and are often in arrears on that, and the family can only be kept up in respectable comfort by turning their own hands to the work of farming their best lands.

'In Helen Thwaite, Mr Earnshaw had reason to think he had found all he sought. He had tasted the cheese and bread made by her own hand, and seen the scoured cleanliness and order of the dairy that he had been told was her special care. He had admired the samplers and coverlets worked by her, and still more the pretty modesty with which she acknowledged that they were done from her own designs. He had heard her mother, with studied casualness, make reference to the substantial portion set aside for her from the butter-and-egg money, and the prize cow that was "Helen's own special pet" and must of course go with her "whenever she comes to marry". And if these substantial virtues were not enough (and for what young man of spirit would they be?) he saw them combined with a cheerful disposition, manners that would grace a gentleman's table, and a face and figure to gladden any man's heart.

'Helen was delighted with the handsome young man, whose habitually serious face lit with a smile whenever he spoke to her, and who treated her with a reverential dignity so different from the heavy familiarity of the sons of local farmers. But I watched and listened with a heavy heart. I was not jealous of Helen's good fortune, I don't think: I had always loved my cousin better than myself, always gladly given her the best of anything I had – and at any rate, I had long known that Helen would almost certainly marry better than I could myself – if indeed I married at all. But I saw, as neither of them did, that the courting couple had each very different visions of what their marriage would bring. He, in choosing as a wife the daughter of a farmer, believed he was gaining a mistress who would take on as a matter of course the direct management of the household, the dairy and poultry yard, and the kitchen garden: assisted by servants, to be sure, to a greater extent than in the home of her birth, but still not above getting her hands dirty, and working side by side with the help as needed. But I knew, better even than Helen herself, that Helen did not quite possess the skills she appeared to, and that she looked forward to the marriage as lifting her out of the sphere of such duties. I dropped such hints as I could to her, but Helen couldn't or wouldn't see any difficulties ahead, and finally accused me of speaking out of jealousy. So I held my tongue, and when, in

126

due time, Mr Earnshaw's proposal was made and accepted, I endeavoured to share in my cousin's joy, and hoped all would work out for the best.'

'And did it?' I asked.

'Better than I feared, and worse than she hoped, I suppose. He loved her deeply – as he still does – and if he felt any disappointment in her practical skills, he was too much the gentleman to reproach her outright. But it added, I think, a deeper shade of sternness to his character, which she felt keenly, being such a light-hearted soul herself. And then the children began coming, and that made things much more difficult.'

'But that was not for a long time, surely? You were both near forty, when Hindley and I were born, were you not?'

'Yes indeed, but Hindley was not her first, not by a long way.'

'There was the boy Heathcliff was called after, who died young, is that right?'

'Heathcliff was the first, but there were many others after who were miscarried, or stillborn, or died before they could be christened. Poor Helen! In those years it seemed she was nearly always with child, or grieving the loss of another one.'

'And where were you?'

'After my father died, about two years after Helen married, we had to leave the farm. Mother wished to keep it, with my help, until my brothers should be old enough to take it over, and really it would have been little more than we had been doing already, but Mr Linton did not believe in letting widows hold farms – he said it never turned out well, and nothing we could say would dissuade him. Mother had a brother in America who was settled on a large farm in New York. He offered to take the boys, as he had no sons of his own, and even sent the passage-money for them, and it was too good a chance for them to miss, there being little opportunity for them in England. But Mother was too old to uproot herself, she said, and my uncle had no use for girls, so she and I took lodgings in Gimmerton. She set up a little dame school there, and for a time I helped her with that, but we could not make enough to support ourselves, and so I went into service.'

'At Wuthering Heights?'

'Goodness, no. That would have been too much for my pride, then, and Mother needed me nearer by. I found a place with a wine merchant's family in Gimmerton, and soon became housekeeper there.'

'Did you see Mrs Earnshaw often?'

'Whenever she came to town, which was often at first, but as the years went by her duties and her health made it harder for her to come. I spent most of my days off looking after my mother, but every now and then I would make time to walk out to the Heights and look in on her.'

'So how did you come to work here?'

'That was a little while after Mother died, which would be, what, seven years after we came to Gimmerton.' Her face grew still. 'That was hard for me. Only eight years before we had been a family of six, and happy on the whole, though we had our troubles, and now I was all alone. But those years had taken their toll on Mrs Earnshaw as well. She had never been able to manage the housekeeping at the Heights as well as she was expected to, and that made her anxious and fretful. And then all the miscarriages and stillbirths, coming one after another, were a strain on mind and body both, and at last she fell really ill. Then Mr Earnshaw saw she must have help, and who better than myself to give it?'

'And your pride?'

'Long gone. At any rate, I was coming in as a housekeeper,

which is not quite the same as a servant. And by then I was just glad to go where I was loved and needed. But oh, the mess the housekeeping was in when I got here!' My mother laughed and shook her head. 'It took me three months to get everything running in proper order, and as it was I had to replace half the servants, who had got too set in their slovenly ways to change. Mr Earnshaw a little grudged my wages, at first, but he soon saw that I more than earned my pay through good management, and he had the comfort, too, of seeing his wife return to something of her old health and spirits under my care, and so I became a fixture here – until I left to be married, anyway.'

'But you came back to nurse Hindley.'

'Yes, I did. But no more talk tonight, Nelly. We must both be up early tomorrow. Let me light you a candle, and you can be off to bed.'

EIGHT

The good effect of my mother's nursing did not pass off, exactly: the mistress remained calmer, and happier, and brighter, somehow, than she had been before. Yet over the next few weeks her strength continued to ebb, like water dribbling from a cracked pot. We all knew she was dying – even the children had been told by then what was coming, though Hindley refused to acknowledge it at first, and railed against the rest of us, his mother included, for 'giving way' too readily. He had the decency to keep it out of her hearing, though, and in a week even he stopped fighting the truth. It was an oddly peaceful time for all of us: we no longer feared for her health, and by tacit consent we pushed aside any fears for what would follow on her death. I have often seen it since – at the death watch of a loved one, if nowhere else, we can live only for today, and accept that 'sufficient unto the day is the evil thereof'.

One scene only stands out to my memory from those weeks. Hindley and I happened both to be in the mistress's room at once, to visit with her, as we liked to do when she was awake. The wind was 'wuthering' with great force outside, and rain beat against the window, but there was a good fire in the grate for the mistress's sake, and candles lit against the gloom, though it was yet day, and the room seemed a haven of warmth and light against the storm outside, or the chillier gloom downstairs. Mrs Earnshaw was awake, and propped up by pillows, my mother by the bed as she nearly always was, when the mistress's face suddenly brightened with an idea, and she held out her hands to the two of us.

'Hindley, Nelly, both of you, come here.' We came and each took one of her hands, grasping each other's at the same time, so that we formed a small circle.

'Did I ever tell you both, how Nelly saved Hindley's life, when you were both tiny babes?'

'Helen, no,' my mother interjected, with a forcefulness that startled me.

'Whisht, Mary, why shouldn't I tell them? It's a pretty story.' My mother opened her mouth to reply, but evidently thought better of it, and turned away to busy herself at a table nearby, her face flushed and her lips tight. The mistress turned to look at her when she got no response, but seeing only her broad back, chose to take silence as consent.

'Well, Nelly, you know that when you were born, your mother was not at Wuthering Heights any more, but living with your father in their cottage. And so busy she was with you and her new household there, that I scarcely ever saw her' – a snort from my mother, whose back was still turned to us, indicated some dissent from this remark – 'and so we had to hire another woman to help me, for I was less than two months from my own confinement, and Dr Kenneth had ordered me to bed. When Hindley came, he was as likely a child as I had ever borne – ah, you were such a beauty, Hindley, big and strong, red as a beet, and kicking like a mule.' She smiled fondly at the memory, but Hindley blushed and looked down, perhaps finding this description less than flattering.

131

'I was sure that this time, at last, I had a child who would live. For the first week or so you did well enough, squalling, nursing, and sleeping by turns, like any newborn babe, but then you began to change. You were hungry all the time, cried even at the breast, and seemed never satisfied. I thought perhaps my milk was not enough for you, so we got out the bottle and teat we used for the orphan lambs, and tried giving you extra milk from that. When you spat that up, we tried sheep's milk, and then arrowroot, and sago, and some other concoctions suggested by Dr Kenneth, but none of it would you keep down. Then I said we must get you a wet nurse, and Dr Kenneth agreed, but your fath—' Here she was interrupted by the clatter and crash of a dropped saucer, over where my mother was.

'Dear me,' my mother said hurriedly, 'that's broken into bits, and past mending. I'm so sorry, Helen.'

'Never mind, Mary, it's only a saucer, after all,' said Mrs Earnshaw, but she paused in her story, and looked concerned. Perhaps she was recollecting why she had never told us this story before. But we were still there, hands clasped as before, and looking expectantly for her to continue, so she hurried on.

'Your father, for very good reasons, was unwilling to bring a wet nurse into the house, for they are often dirty, and not of good character, and some people say they do more harm than good. He was sure my milk would come in stronger in time, and he thought that the best food for you. Dr Kenneth did not wholly agree, but he was not strongly against it, and we decided to go on a few more days at least, to see if matters improved. Well, the next day who should come to visit but your mother, Nelly, with you in her arms, and oh, you were so fat and pink and lively, and you smiled, and crowed, and grasped at my finger so tightly, it was a wonder to see. But Hindley looked so pale and weak and little in comparison, it frightened me more than ever, and I cried and told your mother I was afraid we would lose you like all the rest. You were crying too, Hindley; not the lusty yells of a healthy hungry infant, but a sad, hopeless whimper you would keep up for hours. Your mother, Nelly, she handed you to me, and took up Hindley and put him to her breast. He fussed at first, but then fell to nursing in earnest, for a long time, until finally he dropped off satisfied, and fell into a deep peaceful sleep. I knew, then, that that was what Hindley needed to get well, and I begged your mother to come back to stay with us, and you with her, Nelly, of course, so that she might nurse both children together. Your mother said she must talk it over with Tom, your father, and that I must ask Mr Earnshaw's leave, too. She was going to return home, but I begged her to stay that evening at least, that Hindley might nurse again when he woke up, and at last she agreed. We sent a lad with a note and some money for Tom, to tell him she would not be back, and to get his dinner at the inn. Then I slept as I had not slept in days, knowing my babe was safe at last.'

'And that is how it all came about,' said my mother briskly. 'I moved back to the Heights until Hindley was old enough to be weaned, and poor Tom moved back into lodgings in the village, except when he came to take dinner with us here.'

'No, but Mary, you are leaving out the best part!'

'If you will but think, Helen, you will recall that there is nothing more worth telling.' But now Hindley's curiosity was roused (as was mine, but I knew better than to cross my mother) and he insisted on knowing the rest.

Mrs Earnshaw looked helplessly from one to the other of them, as if to say, 'How am I to satisfy you both?' At last my mother shook her head and turned away again, so Mrs Earnshaw continued.

133

'When Tom got the note, he did not go to the inn, but came straight here, to see his wife home through the gloaming, he said. By then Mr Earnshaw was home as well, so we had to spring our plan upon them both together. Tom looked to the master to speak first, as was right, but as soon as Mr Earnshaw said he was against it, Tom said he wouldn't have it either. Well, we tried to argue, but the two of them, united in their refusal as they were, were like a wall of stone. I don't know what I might have done; I felt so frantic I thought I must scream, or faint, but then your mother, Nelly, she got up and walked slowly across the room and put you down in the cradle next to Hindley – you were both sleeping soundly – then she came back and took me by the hand, and led me to stand with her in front of our husbands. Then she knelt on the ground before Tom. I knelt too, when I saw what she was doing, but it was your mother who did all the talking, Nell, and oh, if you could have heard her! It was like something from a play.

'She spoke to Tom first, and told him how she and I had grown up together, and that I was more than a sister to her, and all the family she had left in the world before she married him. She said that she would obey him as her husband, but that he must know that if he made her deny me this, it would tear her heart in two, and she would never rest easy after. Then, without waiting for his answer, she turned to your father, Hindley. She reminded him how many times I had been with child, and had nothing to show for my pains but another tiny corpse. She said – I will never forget her words – "To a father, his child is not real until it squalls and squirms in his arms, but to a mother, it is real the moment she feels it quicken in her womb. She clothes it and feeds it in her own flesh and blood, before she ever sees its face, and if she must bury it at last, it is not as a lost hope merely, as it is to you, but as a piece of her own being. It may be that your son would thrive without my aid, sir, but he has not been thriving, and your wife and I have seen my nursing change that. If you deny her this, and if the babe dies after – even if this be not the cause – how will she ever find it in her heart to forgive you?"

'I had my head down, sobbing, as she spoke, but when she finished I looked up into their faces, our two stern husbands, and saw them both wet with tears. What could they do then, but lift us up, and embrace us, and tell us all should be as we wished?' The mistress dabbed at her eyes, which were brimming with tears, and Hindley professed to sneeze, so as to wipe his own. Then the mistress gave our hands another squeeze. 'And that, my dears, is how Nelly came to save Hindley's life.'

It would have been fairer to say that it was my mother who saved him, I thought, but I was moved by the story. It seemed to give a deeper meaning to the master's words, that I was born to be the salvation of the family.

The whole time the mistress was speaking, my mother had never turned round, and as soon as the story finished she hurried out of the room. Mrs Earnshaw looked worn out by her efforts, and said she wished to sleep, so Hindley and I left too. I found my mother in the kitchen starting supper for the family. That was my task, normally, so I offered to take it over.

'No Nelly, I would rather be busy just now, if you don't mind, and not in Mrs Earnshaw's room.' Her eyes were dry, but a little reddened, and her voice was thick, but she seemed more angry than sad.

'Why did you not wish the mistress to tell that story?' I asked. She turned round to face me.

'Please, Nelly, you are not such a fool as that,' she snapped. 'What good will it do Hindley, now that he is about to lose one parent, to believe that the other would have been content

135

to sign his death warrant before he was a month old? A pretty story indeed! It doesn't seem pretty to him, you may be sure. But there was no stopping her once she got underway, the poor fool.'

'Is that really true, about the master?'

'Oh, Heaven knows what he was thinking. He was mad for a son, that much is sure, and very pleased to get one at last. No, of course he didn't wish Hindley to die. He had scruples, about wet-nursing, and other things. He often did have strange scruples, that he didn't always care to explain. That's how he is – we saw that with his taking in Heathcliff. But Hindley won't see it that way. You go on and find him, Nelly, and see what you can do. I'll make supper for you.'

I did not think Hindley would go outside in this weather – only Heathcliff and Cathy were wild enough for that – and sure enough, I found him in his room, hunched into a ball on his bed, with his arms wrapped around his knees, and his hands balled into white-knuckled fists. His face was buried behind his knees, and his breath came in hard snorts that rocked his whole body back and forth on the bed. I slipped in and shut the door. Hindley did not look up, but the rocking stopped.

'Mother says your father was mad for a son, and pleased as anything to get you. It was only that he had some queer scruples about wet-nursing, and, truly, he didn't believe you were in any danger.'

'Do you think I give a damn what my father thought of me when I was a squalling brat?' said Hindley angrily, uncurling himself a little. 'But that he could make my mother kneel to him, when she is ten times better than he is – it makes my blood boil!'

'He didn't make her kneel,' I objected, 'that was my mother's

136

idea. Probably she knew he couldn't bear to see it, any more than you could.'

'No,' said Hindley, '*he* made her beg, by denying her what she needed for her peace of mind. And for that I will *never* forgive him.'

I sighed, feeling baulked. 'We all of us do wrong sometimes, Hindley,' I said at last, 'and must forgive each other, as we hope to be forgiven ourselves. Isn't that what we pray, every night?'

'If Mother dies, I will never pray again,' said Hindley. Then, curling himself up, he told me in no uncertain terms to go away and stop bothering him. I obeyed, not knowing what else to do, but reported the conversation to my mother, and asked her advice.

'Poor Nell,' she said. 'Talking sense to Hindley right now feels like spitting into the wind, I'm sure. But you did right to try, and who knows? It may do some good, in time. As for his threats, don't take them too much to heart. I suspect he is only trying to shock you, and perhaps himself too.'

During that time, I often thought about what the mistress's last words to us might be. In my imagination, I put many touching sentiments into her mouth, viz, that as we all loved her, so should we love each other after she was gone, or she would not rest easy in her grave. What effect these words or others like them might have had, I do not know, for they were never spoken. About a week later, I was awoken from a light sleep by the sound of a door creaking and footsteps further down the hall. I sat up, straining my ears to listen. There was a light knocking at a door (not my own), and then my mother spoke in a low voice.

'Henry, come now. It is time.'

I waited until the further sounds of footsteps and door hinges were gone, then crept out into the passageway and down towards the mistress's room. The door was slightly ajar, and showed me the mistress asleep on her back, mouth open to aid in the breaths that came with increasing difficulty. Mr Earnshaw knelt by one side of the bed, her hand clasped in both of his, and his face buried in the bedclothes. My mother was seated on the other side, holding the mistress's other hand, but not too absorbed to spot me at the door. She made no motion to bar me, so I crept further in.

'Nelly, go and wake the children,' she said in a low whisper.

'No,' said the master, his voice choked.

'It's best for them to be here, Henry,' she said gently. 'How would you feel if I had waited until morning and then told you she was gone?' He made no answer, only moaned faintly, and she nodded to me to go ahead.

I woke the children as quietly as I could, telling them only that they were wanted in the mistress's room – I think they had little doubt what for, though. We all came in and ranged ourselves around the bottom of the bed. Hindley and Cathy clasped hands. I took Hindley's other hand, and Heathcliff Cathy's, and we all stood there, wide-eyed and silent, listening to the breaths that came each more laboured than the last. At last came an intake of breath that seemed to stop halfway, and then a little sigh, and then silence. We all stopped breathing with her, I think, so still was the room for a few seconds after. Then the master let out a harsh sob, and that opened the gates. Hindley dropped my hand, flung himself on the bed and wailed; Cathy and Heathcliff clutched each other and began crying also. My mother buried her face in her hands, and rocked back and forth in silent grief. My own eyes were streaming too, of course, but I felt strangely abandoned, and out of place. I tried to put an arm around Hindley where he lay, but he shrugged me off. I put a hand on my mother's shoulder, but she would not look up. The master was so racked with choking sobs I dared not approach, and Cathy and Heathcliff were totally absorbed in comforting each other. At last I crept out and back to my room, to cry in my bed, as much from loneliness as grief, and in that state I drifted off to sleep.

NINE

That scene was a fair presage of what followed. The master, my mother, and Hindley each withdrew into their grief alone, seeming to resent each other's competing claims to sorrow, and each of them shunning my comfort, as one with less cause to grieve than they had themselves. Hindley's grief, in particular, was all but ungovernable, and he persisted in blaming everybody, but especially his father, for adding to the strain and worry that had worn down the mistress at last. I still thought of myself as having some good influence over him, but for several weeks after the mistress's death he would scarcely meet my eyes, or reply to me with more than the minimum necessary 'aye' or 'nay'.

My mother's better intentions had resurfaced in a few days, and she made some effort then to comfort me and include me in her grief, but we were awkward together. Each of us, I think, had loved Mrs Earnshaw better than we loved each other, and were ashamed to feel so, and that made us uncomfortable together. So I was more relieved than otherwise when, a week after the funeral, she announced that it was high time she returned to her duties at Brassing.

Heathcliff was the only one of us not much stricken by the

mistress's death – after her initial revulsion towards him, she had done her best to be kind, but she had never really warmed to him, nor he to her. But Heathcliff took on any grief of Cathy's as if it were his own, and so she alone of us had real sympathy and comfort in her sorrow.

With the mistress buried and my mother gone, the household settled into new patterns. Cathy claimed the title of mistress, and I did not dispute it with her, but I paid no attention to her commands unless they coincided with what needed doing anyway, and made sure the other servants did likewise. But Cathy was content with the title, without the substance of command, and so I was housekeeper in all but name. Mr Earnshaw, for his part, seemed to avoid the house altogether. When, not long after this, one of his smaller farms fell vacant, he decided to take the farming of it into his own hands rather than find a new tenant, and that, on top of his regular duties, gave him cause to be away from home most days until nightfall, and often after. The curate, a Mr Jones by name, continued to attend Cathy and Heathcliff for lessons, but now taught Hindley at a different time, and in his own study in his lodgings at Gimmerton, as he said he needed to have his books to hand. Hindley was also given certain chores to perform outside, under Joseph's supervision, but beyond that and his studies, his time was his own.

In his general avoidance of me, Hindley had ceased to come to me for help with his lessons of an evening. This worried me at first, but as the weeks went by and no bad reports were forthcoming from the curate, I took comfort, and told myself that sorrow had tamed Hindley at last, and made him able to settle to his lessons. At least, that was what I thought until, some weeks later, I needed to go into Gimmerton to make some purchases for the household. I had timed my trip so that the completion of my errands would coincide with the end of Hindley's lesson, hoping to have his company on the walk home, and recover some of our lost intimacy. So I was startled, on passing the inn on my way to the shops, to see Hindley saunter a little unsteadily out of the door. Seeing me, he came to a dead halt.

'Hindley, what are you doing there? I thought you were supposed to be studying with Mr Jones?'

'That is exactly where I am *supposed* to be,' he replied with a rather blurry dignity, pulling me at the same time into a quieter alleyway, 'but as long as my father continues to *suppose* me to be there, I prefer to be somewhere else.'

'But what about Mr Jones? Does he know of this?'

'Mr Jones and I have reached an agreement. The effort of pounding Latin and Greek into my head, we found, was irksome to him and painful to me, and had little effect otherwise, so we left off.'

'But your father pays him to teach you!'

'No, my father pays him to *appear* to teach me. But that is only to appease his sense of duty as my father. He has never taken the trouble to enquire as to the results, which were bad enough anyway, for you know nothing stays in my head. If Mr Jones can achieve the same results – which is to say, no results at all – by leaving me alone, why shouldn't he receive the same pay? A little less, actually,' he added, 'for he gives me some of it, and that is what pays for my, ah, refreshment.'

I was struck dumb. Hindley's deceit – not to mention his drunkenness – was shocking enough, but that Mr Jones should connive in it – and he a man of the cloth! – I knew not where to begin. Hindley laughed and put an arm around me, giving me an affectionate squeeze.

142

'Look at you,' he said, 'gaping like a fish, and white as the belly of one! You are such a good and proper girl, Nelly, and I love you for it, really I do. But you needn't be so shocked. This arrangement keeps everyone happy, Father included, so what harm is there in it?'

'But the lies, Hindley!'

'What lies? I tell Father I am going straight to Mr Jones's, which I do, and coming straight home from there, which I do also, as his lodgings are on the way – convenient, that, don't you think? When Father asks Mr Jones, in a general way, about my progress, he says that I am getting on "as well as can be expected", and that contents him.'

'But if he should find out?'

'How should he find out? He buries himself so in his work on the farm, he scarcely ever comes to Gimmerton any more, and when he does he never sets foot in the inn. He has no companions to pass on the chat of the town over a glass of wine; he talks to nobody but his servants and his tenants, and they are too much in awe of him to pass on idle talk. So unless *you* tell' – here he gave me a squeeze, and a flash of his old conspiratorial grin, to assure me he was joking – 'I have nothing to fear. Now, Nelly, would you like to come in, and I'll treat you to a little glass of sherry?'

'No indeed,' I said hurriedly, 'I have shopping to do, and though I'll hold my tongue, I won't partake of your ill-gotten gains. But I'll walk home with you after, if you'll wait here – or better yet,' I added, guessing how he would spend the interim, 'come with me – you can help me carry the parcels.'

'I'll do that with pleasure.'

And so I did my little round of errands, with Hindley by my side all the way. He chatted and joked like his old, sunny self, relieved, I think, that I was in on his secret at last, and he need not hold himself aloof any more. For my part, I said little, for my thoughts and feelings were both in turmoil. I had felt so alone since the mistress died, that this return of friendliness from Hindley was like a warm fire to a frozen traveller, and drew me close to him in spite of myself. But I could not share his sanguine view of the situation; how could such a secret be kept? And when it did come out, what a storm would break over all of our heads!

You will probably think, Mr Lockwood, that I did wrong to agree to keep Hindley's secret, and ought to have gone directly to my employer with the information. And you are very likely right. But to this day, I cannot make myself feel the wrongness of it. I had great respect for the master in most things, but I had seen too often and felt too keenly his injustice to Hindley, particularly since Heathcliff had come and usurped the place in his heart that ought by rights to have belonged to his firstborn – to take the father's side against the son. Since Mrs Earnshaw's death, the master had withdrawn further from all of us, but more so from Hindley, and without the mistress's restraining presence, he was often downright cruel to him, addressing him habitually as 'oaf' or 'dunce', making sarcastic remarks on his appearance and conversation, and seizing with apparent relish on any excuse to give him a beating. My mother had spoken truly of Hindley when she said that he had 'a loving heart and a merry spirit, if they be not trampled down by harsh treatment'. I was watching the trampling daily, and with his mother dead and mine out of reach, Hindley had no one to love and comfort him under it but me. I felt I was the guardian of his better self, the more so as I believed I would be his wife in time. That duty, I told myself, must take precedence over any obligation to carry tales to his father.

Well, the secret kept longer than most secrets do, but in the end it came out, and in a manner none of us expected. One Sunday in mid-summer, Mr Jones's regular parishioners came to church to find the pulpit empty and their priest vanished. Upon enquiry, it emerged that he had fled his lodgings in the dead of night, taking all his belongings with him, and leaving behind only a few unpaid bills. We were all in a wonder as to why, for the debts amounted to little enough, but the busybodies of Gimmerton soon ferreted out the reason. What Mr Jones was failing to teach Hindley, it appears, was nothing to what he was attempting to teach some of the other local lads in his care. Their fathers, having learned of this, were just debating whether to have him arrested, or resort to more direct punishment, when Jones got wind of the discovery, and wisely took flight at the earliest opportunity.

This scandal was great enough to reach even the master's ears. Hindley's name was not mentioned in it, but Mr Earnshaw was naturally concerned, and questioned him closely about his own lessons. Hindley's answers being awkward and evasive, the master was driven at length to ask him directly if he had 'been led into abominations by that man', and Hindley was so outraged at the suggestion that he found himself confessing to one sin to avoid the imputation of a greater.

Well, that caused a storm, of course, but not so great a one as I had feared, after all. Mr Earnshaw was so relieved that there was nothing worse to tell, and Mr Jones's name was so blackened already as a corrupter of youth, that Hindley was spared much of the blame he might have had, the more so as he had confessed of his own accord. Still, his punishment was bad enough.

'Since you won't take the trouble to be educated as a gentleman's son,' his father said, 'we will stop treating you as one, and give you a trial of the alternative. For two months you will wear the clothes and perform the work of an ordinary farm labourer. You will take your meals with the workmen, and you will sleep above the stable. At the end of that time, you can decide whether it is worth your effort to learn to behave like an Earnshaw.'

'Yes, sir,' said Hindley, with his head down, in a passable effort at contrition.

'Do you have any questions?'

Hindley looked up. 'Will I get a labourer's wages?' he asked hesitantly.

'Your wages will go to repay the money I paid Mr Jones for your lessons.'

'Yes, sir.'

Hindley moved out of his room and into the stable that evening. The next day, he wore his oldest clothes to begin his labours, while the master sent me into Gimmerton to buy some more suitable to his new condition. I was not to buy new, he told me, and he budgeted my funds accordingly, so I made my way to a little basement shop I knew of that dealt in second-hand clothes of a poorer sort. I had never been in there before, and a very melancholy task it was to sort through the piles of coarse, worn garments in search of some that might do for Hindley. I was careful with my funds, though, and had enough left to add to the pile a gay red neckerchief, scarcely faded, that I hoped would add a note of good cheer to the whole. The old woman who ran the shop took my coins, rolled up my purchases, and tied them into a bundle with string.

'No paper?' I asked.

'Whatever for, missy? To protect them from dirt?' She laughed loudly at her own joke, and I grabbed my bundle and fled.

Coming out of the shop, I met Bodkin in the street. He cast a puzzled eye at my purchases.

'Buying wedding clothes, I see,' he said. 'Who's the lucky fellow?'

'Go on with you,' I said, not at all amused. 'If you must know, they're for Hindley.'

'Hindley! I smell a story. Are you in a hurry?'

I shook my head.

'Well, why don't you come by the surgery? You can tell me the whole story, and I'll pay you back one of those many cups of tea I owe you.'

'You've drunk no tea at my expense,' I said, but I smiled and fell in beside him.

'And you won't drink any at mine, either, but I don't think Father will mind. He likes you – says you're "a sensible girl", and that's rare praise, coming from him.'

'"A sensible girl"! Have a care, Bodkin. With flattery like that, I shall grow vain for sure.'

'You couldn't. You're far too sensible.'

We turned off the wide, dusty main street onto the shadier side street that held the Kenneths' pretty, modest-sized brick house, with the surgery on the side. I had been in the front waiting room several times, picking up medicine for the mistress, but now Bodkin invited me into a little back room, furnished with a small table and two chairs, and lined with shelves full of bottles, boxes, and jars. He left me seated there, then came back a few minutes later bearing a tray with tea and biscuits. He poured us each a cup, and waited until I had taken a sip or two, before leaning forward expectantly.

'Now, tell me *everything*.'

'Only if you can promise to keep it entirely to yourself, Bodkin. These are family matters and ought not to be shared.'

147

'Have no fear. Keeping confidences is one of a doctor's most sacred duties, as my father has often impressed upon me, and I consider you a patient.'

'I'm your patient, am I? I didn't even know I was ill.'

'Well then, I must be doing an excellent job.'

'Of what, exactly?'

'A complex regimen of strengthening, stimulants, and bleeding. I strengthen you with tea and biscuits, stimulate you with laughter, and then bleed off Earnshaw family confidences that might otherwise fester and make you ill. So please, let the bleeding commence. Or shall I get the leeches?'

I laughed, 'You *are* the leech, Bodkin.' But I told him the whole story anyway, and it is certainly true that I felt better for doing so. When I had finished, Bodkin shook his head and let out a low whistle.

'Well, Hindley is a bolder man than I, to pull off such a trick against his own father. It's hardly surprising that Mr Earnshaw should wish to come down hard upon him. But a common labourer for two months – and with the harvest coming too! That's hard work even for them that are used to it – and they at least have the higher harvest wages to look forward to.'

'The harvest – my God, I hadn't thought of that! How will he ever get through it?'

'Well, perhaps Mr Earnshaw will take pity on him and give him shorter days, if Hindley works with a good heart until then.'

'He won't,' I said shortly.

'You think not? I don't know him well, but Father says he has a fount of kindness hidden behind that stern exterior.'

'For his wife, yes, and for Heathcliff. And for others, some-times, perhaps. Not for Hindley, though. Not ever.'

Bodkin looked thoughtful. 'It's hard for me to imagine,' he said slowly, 'but we do see it sometimes – a parent just taking against a child like that.'

'I know,' I said feelingly.

Bodkin blushed. 'That's right. I'd forgotten you had your own experience with that. I'm sorry, Nelly, I didn't mean to bring up painful subjects.'

'Oh, that's all past and done. We parted friends, in the end. He asked my forgiveness before he died.' I forced a smile, but had to busy myself over the teacups for a few moments to recover myself. 'And how did you know about that anyway?' I asked at last. 'What happened to the sacredness of patient confidences?'

'Oh, that was common knowledge. After your mother brought you in here to have your arm set, apparently, she marched straight to the inn, where your father was drinking, and held you up, cast, bandages, bruises, and all, right in front of all his friends, and announced, "Nelly is going to live at Wuthering Heights, and if you dare to go near her there, they will set the dogs on you." Then she marched out.'

My mouth was hanging open when he finished. He leaned across the table and gently closed it. 'Did you really never hear that before?'

'Who would tell me?'

'Ah yes, I forget you live out in the unmapped wilderness, beyond the reach of the civilizing influence of gossip. Here in town, not only can nobody remain ignorant of whatever is known to the discredit of their parents and grandparents, they are never allowed to forget it. But if that was to your father's discredit,' he added apologetically, 'it was certainly not to your mother's, and she has been held in high respect here, ever since.'

149

Bodkin meant well, but I didn't want to talk about my mother. 'What about you?' I asked. 'Did you never experience anything of that sort?'

'Oh, there has only ever been Father and me,' he said, 'and we get on quite well, usually. My mother died giving birth to me – you must have known that.'

'It must have been hard, though, growing up without a mother.'

'Well, I had Tabby, of course. She was nursemaid to my father before me, so took me on as a matter of course. She was like a mother to me. But she hasn't a stern bone in her body – Father used to joke that she thought "spare the rod and spoil the child" was a commandment. She's too old now to do much of anything except sit by the fire, pour tea, and remind us both to wrap up warmly before we go out. But she does that admirably, to this day. As for Father, he started taking me about with him to cases – all but the dangerous ones – as soon as I was old enough to sit on a pony. He always wanted me to follow him into medicine, and I never wanted anything but to be as much like him as possible, so we have generally got along pretty well.'

'Except when Hindley and I dragged you into mischief.'

'Well, yes – though I would have said that it was Hindley and I who dragged you.'

'Or Hindley dragged us both. Oh, Bodkin, what am I to do about him?'

'Well, I don't see that there's much you can do. It's Hindley's crime, and he must bear his punishment like a man. I'm sure he understands that. You can smuggle him a few small comforts now and then, and condole with him on his sore muscles, but that's about all.'

The reference to sore muscles gave me an idea. 'Say, Bodkin, that salve that Old Elspeth sells you, do you think it would help Hindley with the soreness?'

'Very likely.'

'Could you get me some?'

Bodkin frowned. 'That would be very difficult.'

My face fell. 'Why?'

'Well, I should have to get up from this chair, like this, walk two steps across the room, like this, reach halfway up the wall and take down this *very* heavy little pot' – he pretended to be pulled to the ground by it – 'and carry it all the way back to put in front of you, like this.' He heaved the little pot onto the table in front of me and then collapsed into his chair, gasping with mock exhaustion. 'But for Hindley's sake, I'll do it.'

'Oh, stop it, Bodkin, you really had me worried! How much does it cost?' I had none of the master's money left, but I had brought some of my own.

'For you, *gratis*.'

'No, really, I can't be taking your father's stock like that.'

'I'll pay him for it, and you can tell Hindley it's from me. Come, it's only a shilling, and it would please me to be able to offer Hindley some comfort, too. Anyway, as I've been meaning to tell you, I must say farewell for a while, so should like to leave you something to remember me by – and what better memento than a pot of smelly ointment made by an old woman?'

'Farewell? Where are you going?'

'To Edinburgh, to complete the formal portion of my medical education. For three years I shall be watching dissections, listening to lectures, poring over medical books, and tramping the wards of a great city hospital, and if I do it all well enough, when you see me next, you may call me Dr Bodkin.'

I laughed. 'We will call you Dr Kenneth then, of course. Or to be precise, Young Dr Kenneth, so we can distinguish you from your father. But can the neighbourhood really support two doctors, or will you have to move elsewhere?'

'There will not be two Dr Kenneths in practice for long. My father is eager to pass the practice on to me. For the last thirty years he has been woken at all hours of the night, and travelled in all kinds of weather, to attend to the sick and injured for some ten miles around. He would like to retire while he still has health left to enjoy his ease, or at least limit his efforts to those well enough to haul themselves to the surgery to see him.'

'Leaving the burden of midnight rousings and hailstorm house calls to you?'

'Well, it is no more than what I have always expected. Father has certainly earned a rest, and I consider myself lucky to have a practice ready-made to step into as soon as I am qualified.'

'You are lucky in more than that, Bodkin,' I sighed.

'What do you mean?'

'Why, that what your parent would have you do, what you would do yourself, and what you *can* do, are all the same thing.'

Bodkin looked concerned. 'Do you feel that's not true for you?'

'Oh, not me. I am thinking of poor Hindley.'

'Poor Hindley! Really Nell. I am sorry that his father is not kind to him, and I condole with him sincerely on the aches and pains he is about to suffer. But taken as a whole, is there any young man on the face of the earth with fairer prospects, and who need do less to attain them, than the eldest son of an English gentleman? Enough Latin to drop the occasional phrase in polite conversation, enough arithmetic to add up the sum of his rent-roll, and enough patience to wait for his inheritance to fall in his lap – beyond that, what is really expected of him?'

'A good deal more than that,' I replied, nettled. 'What you

152

say may be true for many, but Wuthering Heights is not a rich estate. Does Mr Earnshaw look to you like a man who lives at his ease?'

'No, he looks like a man under great strain, I'll grant you that. But he seems more haunted than overworked. Does he really demand so much of Hindley? More, say, than you and I perform daily without complaint?'

This was a home question. 'When you put it that way, perhaps not,' I said carefully, 'but things that you or I can do if we try, and do well, Hindley cannot. Remember, I have been at lessons with him since we both began them, and I have seen what a struggle they have always been to him. He is not stupid – you have seen yourself what he could do with a borrowed fiddle, on which he never had a lesson in his life, and how he could learn a dance by watching it only once – and there are other things in which he is clever, too.' Bodkin nodded. 'But Mr Earnshaw never cared about those things. He only saw what Hindley could not do, and always made it clear what a poor opinion he had of him. How would you get on, if your father made no secret that he thought you a dunce, and was forever predicting that you would never come to anything? And then Heathcliff came, and Hindley was pushed entirely aside in his favour. It is not right! Is it any wonder, then, that Hindley is bitter and discouraged, and looks on his father as his enemy?' I felt myself growing more and more vehement as I spoke, as if it were the master himself, and not poor well-meaning Bodkin, I was arguing against.

'Pax!' cried Bodkin, putting up his hands, 'I'm sorry I spoke slightingly of Hindley – I had no idea I would unleash such a storm! Hindley always seemed to me a boisterous and fun-loving fellow, and I often envied him what seemed his freedom from compunction. But perhaps that was mostly bravado. And

I know he was a great favourite of his mother's, so that loss must have hit him hard.'

'It did,' I said shortly. I was fighting off the tears that threatened to follow in the wake of my anger. Bodkin must have noticed, for he excused himself from the room for a few minutes, so that I could compose myself. When he came back, I began gathering my things to leave. 'So will I really not see you for three whole years?' I asked.

'Oh, I will be home now and then, for holidays and suchlike. But not as often as I might like. It is expensive enough to pay for the lectures and my lodgings, without paying coach fare back and forth several times a year.'

'Couldn't you just ride your little pony back and forth?' I asked with a smile.

'To tell you the truth,' he laughed, 'I am hoping to leave Potsie behind for good. I have so far outgrown her, that if I don't keep my legs bent double while I'm riding her, I find myself standing on the ground, while she trots off without me!'

'What will become of her, then?'

'Oh, she's too old now to be sold on as a saddle pony, and Father doesn't like giving horses to the knacker man, so probably she'll be put out to pasture.'

'Perhaps you can bring her in the house to sit by the fire, and she and Tabby can keep each other company.'

Bodkin laughed. 'They would be well suited,' he said. 'She'd pour tea for Tabby, and Tabby would dish up hot mash for her, and the two of them would shake their heads together over the foolish men going out in all weathers, when any sensible creature would stay warm and dry at home.'

On that note we said our farewells, and I headed home with my purchases.

* * *

154

I found Hindley in the stable after supper, in a better mood than I expected. In response to my anxious queries about his first day, he assured me that it had gone well.

'I'm working with three other lads – Cal, Burt, and Jim, they are called – and today we were cutting hay. It is hard work, but I got the hang of it quickly enough, and though I couldn't keep pace with them, I worked faster than they thought I would. When we stopped for lunch they amused themselves by laughing at my "gentleman's hands" and my fine clothes, but I gave it right back to them. "Give me time," I said, "and I'll grow hooves as hard as yours. And then when I've got myself a suit of grey homespun, if I can just grow a nose as long as Burt's, and ears as big as Jim's, and bray at a jest like Cal, why, I shall be as good a donkey as any of you." How they roared! Then they asked me what wages I was getting, and when I told them none at all, they said that was a shame, and that come Saturday evening, when they are paid theirs, they would all stand me a round at the Ploughshare.'

'Well, I am glad you're getting on well,' I said cautiously, 'but have a care that you don't become too familiar with the lads, else you'll have a hard time getting their respect, when you do become their master.'

'I don't see that at all,' said Hindley. 'If Father chooses to keep me in such company as theirs, who am I to hold myself aloof? And why should I lose their respect by working as hard as they do, and showing I will take no nonsense from them, without giving back as good as I get?'

'But to let them treat you?'

'What, am I to have all of their labour, and none of their comforts? And for the matter of that,' he added jocularly, 'who are you to lecture me on the company I keep? Where would you be, if I limited myself to consorting with gentlefolk?'

155

'That's different,' I said hastily. 'I am as well brought up as you, and as well educated, for a girl, and we are kin too, on our mothers' sides. And anyway, a man raises his wife to his level – everyone knows that.'

'So he does,' said Hindley, seizing my hand and pulling me close, 'and when I have raised you up to be mistress of Wuthering Heights, you may lecture me all you please on the comportment appropriate to my station. But until then, not a word, please.' With that he kissed me, and it was no child's kiss this time. I was willing enough to be kissed, at first. But then Hindley's hands began to rove too freely, and I struggled to extricate myself.

'Please, no, Hindley,' I gasped, wriggling out of his arms at last. I felt, I know not what, angry, confused, and near to tears, all at once. 'If you – I can't—' I stumbled, my usual fluency gone. I sat down on a crate, buried my face in my hands, and burst into tears.

Hindley was instantly contrite, pouring out a stream of soft-voiced apologies and cautiously patting my back, as if afraid he might offend again. I thought this a good sign, and so I made no effort to compose myself, but let my sobs run their course. By the time I looked up, Hindley was kneeling in front of me, looking stricken and miserable, with a few tears making their way down his face.

'Please, Nelly, I am so sorry. Really I am. I don't know what came over me. Say you will forgive me, please. No one loves me but you, and I cannot bear to lose you too.'

I could not resist this, but thought I ought to show some sternness first. 'I am shocked, Hindley, that you should think you could treat me so. I may not be a lady by birth, but I am not some slattern bred in a barnyard, either, and as you hope to make me your lady in time, you ought to treat me with

156

more respect. As for you: you may be obliged to dress and work as a labourer, but you need not act like one too! Remember Ferdinand, from *The Tempest*? He was made by Prospero to haul logs, which was labour far beneath his station, but he remained a duke's son in his heart and in his manners. Prospero did that to test his character and his love for Miranda, and when Ferdinand behaved as a 'patient log-man' and passed that test, Prospero loved him as a son. You ought to take him as your model.'

'Well, I rather think my father ought to love me as a son already – seeing as I am his son.'

'Perhaps he ought. But you did do wrong, about the lessons, you know. If you show a goodwill to this work, he is bound to respect you more. And I will love you all the better for it.' With that I gave him a brief hug, and a little kiss on the cheek, just to show I had forgiven him. 'And now I must get back to my work. Oh, but I almost forgot! I brought you something from Bodkin. He is going to Edinburgh for his medical training, and he gave me this for you. You must rub it in of an evening, anywhere your muscles are sore, and it will ease them.'

'I suppose he knows all about my punishment. It must be all over the town by now.'

'Actually, I told him myself,' I said awkwardly. 'He saw me with the clothes and asked what they were for. I didn't think you would mind, as he is such an old friend of ours.'

'What do I care? Everyone will know soon enough. Bodkin must have had quite a laugh at my expense.'

'Of course not, he was concerned for you – else why would he have sent you the salve? Anyway, he wishes you all the best, and is very sorry he can't say farewell in person.'

'Well, I am sorry for it too. But I am not too sorry he is going away, for he is entirely too fond of you.'

'Me! Don't be ridiculous, Hindley. First of all, he is well known to be courting Miss Smythe, the apothecary's daughter, and second, he must know that I could never love anyone but you. He and I are only friends, who enjoy making each other laugh.'

'Miss Smythe, is it? She's a pretty little thing, to be sure, and her father's heir. It would be a handy thing for a doctor, to be heir to an apothecary shop! Still and all, I will be glad to have your laughter-making all to myself for a while. I have more need of laughs than Bodkin does, just at present.'

'Well, it takes two to jest. Don't you be spending all your merriment with your new work-fellows. Save some for me, and I will come out here of an evening to laugh over the day with you, as we used to do in the nursery long ago.'

Hindley smiled, then, with something like his old warmth. 'I will, Nelly, and I will be a "patient log-man" too, for your sake.' We shook hands to take leave, and I hurried back to the house to close up for the night, feeling more cheerful than I had in many weeks.

Hindley kept his word, and went at his new work with a better spirit than any of us expected. He had good success, too: the cleverness he lacked in schoolroom lessons he had in full when it came to learning bodily motions. Then, too, he had matured into a powerfully built lad, who took pleasure in physical exertion, so although the long hours of unremitting labour were difficult at first, he adjusted quickly, and Old Elspeth's salve fell into disuse before it was halfway expended. He continued to earn the respect of the overseer and his fellows by hard work and a ready wit. In deference to me, he declined to let them treat him; instead I gave him money each week from my own wages so that he could share a drink or two with his workmates.

Neither of us was entirely happy with this arrangement: Hindley thought it unmanly to 'take money from a girl', and I did not like to encourage his growing fondness for drink, but it seemed preferable to allowing him to become beholden to his future inferiors, or trying to ban him from pleasure altogether. Thus the two months passed peacefully enough.

The end of Hindley's punishment coincided with the finish of the harvest. Mr Earnshaw was not one for revelry in general, but he always gave a harvest dinner for his tenants and labourers not long after Michaelmas, at which the ale flowed, if not freely (for Joseph manned the tap), at least in moderate quantity. It had been an excellent harvest. The tenants had all paid their rents without difficulty, and even wiped out any little arrears, which put both them and the master in good humour. The labourers had all had plenty of work at good wages, and their wives and daughters rich gleaning in the fields after them, and their prosperity showed itself in an array of new boots, breeches, and frocks on the little lads and lasses who came with them. Hindley sat up with the family again, and looked well pleased to be there. I was too busy overseeing the food, and the crowd of women who were helping me serve it, to sit down, but I paused to listen when the master stood up to speak.

'Let me first give thanks where thanks are most due: to God Almighty who has given us this bountiful harvest, that may we use it in humbleness and gratitude towards His service,' he said, to bowed heads and respectful silence. And then, in a lighter tone, he gave thanks to all who had ploughed and planted, reaped and gathered and threshed, not forgetting those who had fed and clothed them for the work, and even those little ones whose childish prattle had 'made bright their father's eyes, and strengthened his arm to provide for them', so that there were smiles everywhere when he had finished.

After that, it was customary for the tenants each to stand to say a few words. When they were finished, the overseer of the harvest labourers stood up and raised his glass also. 'Eed joost layk to say,' he said, 'that this year we 'ad help better'n we thought on, from yoong Master Hindley, there, as is a roight foin lad, an' oon as yo should be prood on, Mr Earnshaw, eff yo don't mine me sayin' soo, an' 'ere's a toost to Master Hindley.' With that the labourers all cheered and raised their mugs. Hindley nodded his thanks back at them, and looked towards his father.

Mr Earnshaw stood up. 'Well, Hindley,' he boomed, with a broad smile, and I saw Hindley grin happily in expectation of his well-deserved praise, 'it seems you have finally found your level.'

Silence fell over the whole gathering. Even the children sensed something wrong, stopping their chatter, and looking wide-eyed towards their parents for explanation. Men and women shook their heads and looked embarrassed. The labourers all got up. Bowing and pulling their forelocks politely to the master, but with grim expressions, they left their table and departed together.

Hindley looked as if he'd been struck. His face went pale, then flushed. He pushed himself away from the table, stood up, and walked away with the awkward self-consciousness of one who knows a hundred eyes are on him. I did not wait to see what the master would do, but hastily set down the platter I was carrying and, pausing only to ask one of the farmers' wives to take charge of the kitchen in my absence, followed after Hindley.

TEN

How thick the pile of paper grows! As I turn each freshly written sheet onto the pile, its ink just dry, it sits lightly on top, but gently weighs on those beneath it, until near the bottom the leaves are as closely pressed as in a book. I turn the heavy stack over to see the first page. 'Dear Mr Lockwood,' it begins, in the large, thick script I used then, which now shocks me with its boldness, for it is only since I've been writing this that I have finally got the knack of shaving my point fine enough to write a small, close hand that conserves paper and ink both.

Why do I write this to you? You were a stranger who listened, and for no other reason than that you liked my telling, and that was new to me, I suppose. So when I imagined a listener for my own story, he had your face. But now, as I feel the weight of these pages in my hand, I try to imagine myself tying them up in whitey-brown paper and string, like a butcher's parcel, and shipping the whole package off to your address in Italy. Would you read it through? And if you did, would you share it with your friends and acquaintances? Or would you read the first few pages, grow weary, and slip the rest into the fire? And which of those fates would be worst, after all? No, I will never send it to you. I address you as 'Mr Lockwood', because I must address myself to somebody, but it could as sensibly be Mr Knockwood – for I do feel sometimes, as I think on the trials and sorrows of the past, and how fortunate I am to be done with them, that I should knock on wood – or better, Mr Lockheart – for truly, these things might be better kept locked in my heart.

If I am to stop, it should be now, before I re-enter those years of shame and anger and grief beyond all bearing – though bear it I did. But then what would be the use of this pile of pages before me? I am like a man who sets out on a difficult journey, then grows weary and decides the destination is not worth the effort, only to find that he has passed the halfway mark, and home is even further off than his goal. So what is there to do but go on, and take comfort in the feeling that step follows step, mile follows mile, and objects that loom dark and ominous on the horizon turn commonplace as we pass them by? I will go on: I have avoided this bitter ground too long.

I found Hindley in the stable, hastily stuffing his working clothes into a sack. He barely glanced round when I came in, and then went back to his work, avoiding my eye.

'Nelly,' he said hurriedly, 'could you go to my old room and fetch my grandfather Thwaite's gold watch, that Mother gave me? Also my silver penknife, and the blue silk necktie and' – here he choked a little – 'anything else you can see that didn't come from my father? And do it quickly – I want to be off before anyone comes looking for me.'

'Where are you going?'

He turned and looked at me then. His face was dirty and streaked with tears. 'Please, Nelly, just go. I can't – I can't set foot in that house. But I must have something to live on until I can get work.' His voice was desperate.

162

'I won't be long,' I said, deciding that there would be time enough for discussion when I had done what he asked. I hurried through the house, ignoring the concerned looks of the women in the kitchen, and leaped up the stairs to Hindley's room. I hastily went through his things and piled upon the bed such small things of value as I remembered had come from his mother or mine. Then I dashed to my room to grab my heaviest shawl, a few other small valuables, and the little purse of my own savings, which I tucked into my bodice. Back in Hindley's room, I piled everything else into the shawl and rolled it up. I was going to creep down the front stairs and out through the front door to avoid the curious eyes in the kitchen, but then I decided that bringing provisions was the more urgent need. So I took a deep breath and walked down the back stairs as calmly as I was able, tucking the bundle on the far side of the back door. In response to the anxious enquiries of the women, I forced a smile and made cheerful replies, then began matter-of-factly wrapping up leftover bread and meat in paper, and placing them in a basket, exactly as I would if I were taking them to a sick neighbour. 'There now,' I said when I was done, giving the basket a satisfied pat, 'that will do them nicely.' Then I picked up the basket and headed out of the door, grabbing my bundle on the way. Whether anyone was fooled by this little bit of play-acting, I will never know, but certainly it eased my pride, and signalled as clearly as I knew how that questions were unwelcome.

Hindley was where I had left him, but the energy that his anger had given him was gone now. He sat on the straw pallet that had served him as a bed, his head in his hands, his fingers clutched tightly in his hair. He barely glanced up as I came in.

'Did you bring the things I asked for?' he asked dully.

163

'Yes, and a good deal else,' I said briskly. 'Come and see.' I unrolled the shawl and began laying out my findings. Hindley shifted over to look, nodding in acknowledgement at each item, but without animation. He objected to the few little valuables of my own I had included, though (my purse I did not mention), and waved away the basket of food.

'I don't want your things, Nelly – I have taken too much from you already. And as for the food, I couldn't keep down what I've eaten anyway.' The bucket beside him had already told me that much. 'It's just as well. I shall leave here as empty as I feel.'

'Fine words, Hindley, but a man must eat, and tomorrow is Sunday. Where are you to get food, or the money to pay for it?'

'I don't care. I'll fast if I have to.'

'And sleep rough, too? In this season, and on an empty stomach?'

'Well, what would you have me do?' he said angrily. 'Do you think I can stay here, after what he did to me?'

I was mute, but I felt my lip quiver and my eyes fill with tears. I fought against them, thinking that I ought to remain calm and practical for Hindley's sake, but in truth I think my tears did him more good than any advice I might have offered. He folded me in his arms, and began talking soothingly.

'Don't fret, Nelly, please. I must leave – that much is clear now, and perhaps it will be for the best, all round.'

'But how will you live?'

'I'll find work. The harvest is still underway, to the north of here. A man can make good wages for nearly a month yet, tramping north to follow it. If there is one thing I have learned in the last two months, it is that I can work as hard as any man, and earn my bread doing it, whatever my father may think.'

I was silent. I did not share Hindley's confidence – it was one thing to work among men who knew him for their employer's heir, but quite another to seek work from strangers, and live among rough men who had neither home nor master, and were answerable to no one for their treatment of him. But to say that to him now seemed unbearably cruel. However, I formed a resolution of my own, and began to prepare accordingly.

'What are you doing?' he asked.

'Getting ready to go with you,' I replied.

'You can't come with me, Nelly. This is no work for a woman, and you have a valued place here, even if I do not.'

'I'm not running away with you, Hindley, but I can walk with you to Penniton today, anyway.'

'But how will you get home?'

'I'll walk home tomorrow: tonight I can stay with Mrs White, my mother's old teacher there – I have been meaning to visit her for some months now, and I know she will be glad to see me.'

'I would rather go alone.'

'And I would rather go with you.'

'I am telling you to stay,' said Hindley stubbornly.

'And I am telling you that I will go,' I said, as stubbornly as he. 'Come, Hindley, you are not my master yet. I have as good a right to walk to Penniton as you do, and if I choose to do it at the same time and by the same path as you, who are you to say me nay?'

'Suit yourself then,' said Hindley irritably, and, turning his back to me, stumped out of the stable. I grabbed the basket and followed.

The afternoon was still fine, though it was cooling fast, and a few dark clouds were showing on the horizon. Hindley walked quickly, hoping to leave me behind, I suppose, but I was as brisk a walker as he, and kept a few paces behind him. For the first two miles he ignored me, looking straight ahead and saying not a word, but I suppose he walked off the worst of his anger that way, for then he slowed a little and let me catch up with him. After that I ventured now and then to point out little sights as we passed – a stoat crossing our path, a kestrel overhead, a late-blooming wild rose – things of the sort we had always noted to each other before when we were on the moors together. At first he only grunted or nodded acknowledgement, but soon he began noticing things himself, and we walked along together in reasonably good fellowship.

After a while of this, I asked if we might stop and rest, and he agreed. I sat down, unwrapped the bread and meat from my basket and laid it out temptingly on its wrappings. I then picked up a piece of bread myself and began to eat. Hindley looked at the food, wavered, and then sat down by me and began eating himself. I was careful to say nothing, and avoided meeting his eye, not liking to call attention to his abandonment of principle, so we ate in silence for some time. At last Hindley, having finished a large portion, rolled up the wrappings and tucked it back in my basket with an air of finality. Then he turned his eyes on me, and I saw something like his old grin.

'When we are married, Nelly,' he said, 'will you let me win an argument now and again, if only for the novelty of it?'

'When we are married,' I said, 'I will have sworn before God to obey you.'

Hindley snorted. 'So has every other wife, I suppose, but I've never seen that they argue any less with their husbands because of it.'

'Quite the contrary,' I said. 'They argue all the more for it.

166

If wives were permitted to follow their own judgement now and again, instead of always doing as they were bid, they would have less need to convince their husbands.' I was rather surprised to hear myself say this, as I had never thought much about it before. But I was remembering Mrs Earnshaw's story, of how she and my mother had had to kneel before their husbands to beg for Hindley's life, when they knew better than anyone what the poor babe needed.

'I set great store by your judgement, Nelly,' Hindley said softly, 'and I always will. I know you are cleverer than I am.'

I looked at him, startled by the seriousness in his voice. The afternoon light had deepened the shadows on his face, setting off the darkness of his eyes and brow, and I noticed the stubble on his chin and cheeks. He was not a boy any more. I think I had always thought of marriage to Hindley as an extension of our childhood together, or in terms of our prospective occupation of the coveted places of master and mistress of Wuthering Heights. Now, for the first time, I thought, 'This man will be my husband,' and the thought was strangely stirring. I blushed and looked down, and then busied myself wrapping up the uneaten food and replacing it in the basket.

'We'd best get moving,' I said. 'It's still a good four miles to Penniton, at least.'

We set off again, walking side by side as before. The path to Penniton lay over empty moorland, dipping down into a ravine and across a stream before climbing up to Pennistone Crag, then following the ridge from there until it crossed another beck at its head. We walked briskly because of the chill, and had made excellent time as we reached the Crag. Hindley stopped to catch his breath there, where the huge outcropping made a seat, and I sat beside him, enjoying the broad view over the moors from the airy perch.

'Nelly,' said Hindley, 'what say we clamber down to the Stonegate?

The Stonegate, as it was known, was a formation just below the Crag, where a chance arrangement of boulders made a natural arch one could pass through from one side of the rock to the other. Getting there required a short scramble down part of the steep slope, but, as the same route had been taken by generations of local visitors, the path was clear and safe enough. But I was hesitant.

'We should save our energy for our walk,' I said. 'I should like to get to Penniton as early as we can.'

'There are a couple of hours of daylight left yet,' said Hindley, gesturing towards the sun.

'True enough,' I replied, 'but only if it stays clear. I don't like those clouds.'

'Oh, they are a long way off, and have scarcely moved all afternoon.'

I hesitated. Local superstition said that couples who passed through the Stonegate together would be wed within the year, so among the local folk, taking someone through it was considered as all but a formal betrothal. I was worried about the time, and the weather, but I worried more about turning Hindley loose the next day to tramp on the roads, with nothing to pull him back but the unpleasant prospect of trying to make peace with his father.

'Very well,' I said, 'but we mustn't linger.'

So we scrambled down the short, steep path, laughing as we slipped and slid on the way. Neither Hindley nor I had visited the Stonegate in many years, and we found it rather smaller than we remembered.

'It will be a tight squeeze,' said Hindley. 'I'd best take off my coat.' He did so, and I stripped off my shawl as well. Even

168

so, we could not go through side by side, but held hands and kept close together as we crawled through at an angle. Hindley was just coming through the other side when I heard a metallic clatter down the rock.

'What was that?'

'I don't know,' said Hindley, 'something fell out of my pocket, I think.'

'What was in there?' Hindley felt in his pockets.

'My silver penknife. Damn, I can't afford to lose that now.'

'It can't have fallen far. We'll find it,' I said, and we both began looking around.

Well, it was true that it couldn't have fallen far, but nonetheless, we could not find it. When our first hasty search yielded nothing, we retrieved the coat and shawl from the other side of the gate (it was getting chillier) and settled in to searching more systematically, dividing the ground into segments and poking sticks into every crack and cranny. While we were thus crouched over, I was startled to find the light fading fast. I looked up at the sky and saw that the distant clouds had made their move at last, and were on the way to blotting out the sun altogether.

'Hindley, look at the sky – we'd better make a run for it!' A distant flash of lightning and a crack of thunder answered me.

'Too dangerous now,' said Hindley. 'Out in the open, we'd be struck by lightning for sure.'

'But the Crag draws lightning even surer than we will. What are we to do?' I felt a rising sense of panic.

'What about the fairy cave?' said Hindley. 'It's a safe distance from the Crag, and will at least keep us dry.' The fairy cave, as it was known, was little more than a hollow of bare earth underneath a sheltering slab of rock. It required all the help

169

of local superstition and childish imagination to live up to the romance of its name.

'Will we even fit in it?' The cave had seemed quite large to us when we were children, but then, so had the Stonegate.

'We'll have to. Unless you can think of something better.' I couldn't, and so we made our way onto the little path that led further down and along the ravine to the cave. It was small, but there looked to be enough space for us both to lie in it, anyway. We pulled up some heather and ling to make a bed, driven to haste by the first leading drops of the coming storm. Then we wriggled into the space, drawing our feet up into the shelter just before the heavens opened.

Our nest was cramped, and though it was dry at present, we could only hope it would remain so in the downpour that now commenced. The wind howled, and the rain pounded outside, raising a strong smell of damp earth to remind us how fortunate we were not to be out in it. Lightning flashed too, giving us quick glimpses of each other's pale faces, wide-eyed and streaked with dirt. One mighty crack of lightning hit so close by that the very rock we sheltered under shook with it. We held each other tightly, and I must confess that I cried a little, from fright and cold and worry and weariness. But our refuge kept dry, and crammed in as we were, it soon warmed up as well. In a little while the worst of the storm had passed, leaving behind only a heavy, steady rain, and then we were able to feel about a little to find the outer limits of our effective shelter, and rearrange ourselves a little more comfortably within them. It was only then that I began to relax, and feel that we were safe for the night, at least.

Do I really need to tell you what happened next? Remember that my heart was sore for Hindley's humiliation by his father, and that I was his only comfort. Remember that we had crawled through the Stonegate together, and thought ourselves as good as betrothed. Remember that we were frightened and cold and far from home. And I loved him. Yes, there on our heathery bed in that little earthen chamber, roofed with stone and curtained by falling rain, I loved him with all my heart.

ELEVEN

We parted early the next morning. Walking into Penniton with Hindley now would only lead to gossip, so I thought it best to strike out over the moors in another direction. I could then return to Wuthering Heights from one Dagley's farm, where I could claim to have been visiting, as Mrs Dagley was ill, and to have taken shelter overnight from the storm. Before we parted, though, I convinced Hindley to take my little purse of savings, as a loan against the gold watch, which he gave into my keeping. I would have given him the money for nothing, of course, but he would not accept it, and this arrangement had the added benefit of ensuring that the watch would not be lost or stolen.

I tried also to encourage Hindley to return home as soon as possible, not discounting his understandable breach with his father, but stressing anew his responsibilities to me. He nodded solemnly at this, but told me that, for the sake of his pride and honour, he must have a chance to stand on his own two legs and look about him a little, by living on his own earnings for a time, before he set foot again under his father's roof. With this I was obliged to content myself. Then he untied the red neckerchief from around his own neck, and tied it around mine.

'Wear this for me,' he said, 'and think of me whenever you see it.'

'I will be thinking of you always anyway,' I said, and with that we kissed and parted.

I arrived at the Heights while the family were out at church. One of the maids was about, though, and told me that, as I had expected, the master had been told I was bringing food to a sick family, and had been caught there by the storm. There was little work to be done, for we were to sup off the leftovers of the feast. I made myself a cup of tea and settled by the fire with some knitting to occupy my hands while my mind raced over recent events, as I tried to compose myself for the family's return. By the time they came in, I had succeeded to the degree that I could rise calmly and greet them, making vague reference to the storm and the Dagleys, and reporting at the same time on Mrs Dagley's health. I had planned also to make some surprised remark at Hindley's absence, to cover my knowledge of his flight, but when the time came, I found my courage failed me. The master didn't seem to notice – he merely grunted at my remarks, and disappeared upstairs until supper.

After supper, though, he came and found me in the kitchen, where he sat down at the table and motioned me to join him, sending the other maid away at the same time with a wave of his hand. I sat down with my heart thumping in my chest like an off-kilter mill wheel. He looked me steadily in the eyes.

'Where is Hindley?' he asked calmly.

'I – I don't know,' I stammered, truthfully enough, but inwardly I was cursing the blood I felt racing to my cheeks to betray me.

'You know something, though,' he said.

I looked down and shook my head in confusion, my face flaming. I could not speak.

173

'I am not angry with him, Nelly, nor with you either,' said the master gently.

I ventured to glance upwards at him. His face looked care-worn and sad.

'What I said was wrong and cruel. I know that. I knew it the moment I said it – I should know better than to attempt a jest. And if I didn't know it then, I have been told it since by every strong-minded matron for five miles around, and half their husbands as well.' He laughed bitterly. 'The very curate today took as his text, "the labourer is worthy of his hire", and I don't think he took his eyes off me through the whole of his sermon – and he has only been here a week.'

I could not help smiling at this, but I remained silent.

'If you don't know exactly where he is, you must know something of his plans,' the master went on. 'I know you spoke to him before he left.'

This gave me some sense of where I stood, and emboldened me to reply. I told him what Hindley had told me in the stable: that he planned to follow the harvest north, finding work and lodgings as a common labourer for as long as it lasted.

'And then?'

'I don't know,' I said honestly. 'I think – I hope – that then he will come home. That is what I encouraged him to do, when . . . when I found I could not dissuade him from leaving at all.'

The master nodded thoughtfully. I took a deep breath, and felt my heart begin to settle down.

'Did he have any money with him?'

'He was going to take some things with him to pawn tomorrow, like Mrs Earnshaw's father's gold watch, and his silver penknife. I persuaded him to leave the watch with me, and to take some money I had – as a loan,' I added hastily, and at the same time produced the watch from my pocket.

174

Mr Earnshaw took the watch and looked at it thoughtfully, turning it over and over and tracing the engraving with his finger, in a way that made me wonder if he had ever seen it before.

'How much did you give him?'

'Let me see,' I said, trying to look thoughtful. I knew to a farthing what I had given him, being habitually precise in such matters, but I was afraid of seeming mercenary, so I waited a moment before responding. 'About one pound and six shillings,' I said, omitting, for the same reason, the odd tuppence ha'penny that made up the real total.

The master nodded and reached into his pocket for the money, telling the coins out carefully on the table. I shook my head and tried to refuse, but he insisted.

'Please, Nelly, I have driven my son from my home with harsh words he did not deserve. Let me at least feel that I have some hand in feeding and sheltering him on the road.' Of course I could not refuse such a plea as that, so I took up the coins and deposited them in my own pocket. To my surprise, the master then handed the watch back to me as well. I refused to take it, and must have looked as puzzled as I felt.

'Hindley entrusted the watch to you. You hold it for him. I need no security for the money.'

'Thank you, sir,' I whispered. It was as much as I could trust myself to say. I felt my eyes filling with tears, and my lip quivering in spite of all my efforts to control it. To my great relief, Mr Earnshaw got up to leave. At the door he paused and looked back at me.

'You're a good girl, Nelly,' he said. 'You've been a good influence on Hindley, always. You are like a sister to him, I know. Thank you.'

I tried to speak, but my throat was closed. He left.

As soon as he was gone, the maid entered, obviously keen to hear the news, but I was in no state for gossip. I told her hastily that I was ill and going to bed, and she must finish up in the kitchen alone. Then I fled upstairs to my room, where I could cry in private, and try to think through the tumultuous events of the past two days.

For the first two weeks or so of Hindley's absence, Mr Earnshaw did not seem too concerned, though at family prayers he never omitted to have us all pray for his safe return. In about the third week, though, he began to fret noticeably. Particularly when foul weather kept him confined to the house, he would look out of the window often, and express a hope that Hindley was well housed, at least. He questioned me again and again about what Hindley had told me of his plans, though I could only repeat what I had said many times already. Even his refer-ences to Hindley during family prayers became warmer: he was 'my firstborn child', or 'my son and heir', or, if the weather was particularly bad, 'the poor wanderer'. You would never have guessed, to hear him then, that for some years previously he had not had a good word to say to or about him. His favouritism towards Heathcliff, too, started to abate a little, and I was beginning to think that Hindley's flight might turn out to be the wisest thing he had ever done to improve rela-tions with his father.

All this was very well, but I too was becoming increasingly anxious for Hindley's return. Not only did I share the master's fears for Hindley himself, but I had a new concern of my own: that I might be with child. The thought worried me, to be sure, but it also carried a measure of excitement, and I fluttered between the two states like a shirt on a clothesline, flapping first one way, and then the other, as the winds of my thoughts

176

blew me. If it were true, it was certain that Mr Earnshaw would be angry with both of us, and disappointed in me, which was painful to think of. But I also knew that Hindley wished to marry me, and I had no doubt but that the master would expect him to do so, if I were expecting Hindley's child. His stern rectitude would never put the family's pride above a moral duty. Also, he had vowed that I should always have a home at Wuthering Heights, and I knew he had strong views on the sacredness of vows. And had he not told me already that I was a good influence on Hindley? And that I was born to be the salvation of the family? Without a child on the way, he would never permit Hindley to marry so young, but marriage and a child, I believed, were just what Hindley needed to settle down. Thus, while the short term was frightening to think of, the long term held promise, and this I endeavoured to keep in mind.

You may think that I should have felt the shame of the situation more deeply than I did. But views on this matter were not so strict among country people in those days. Folk of the lower orders were less concerned with getting a child too soon than with not getting one at all. I have seen many a young man stand proudly at the altar by the side of a bride not four months from her confinement, who would have been ashamed to show his face in the village if a year of marriage showed him with still 'no hip to his rose'. The gentry held higher standards, of course, and I had been taught better, but still, I had also seen both the master and the mistress treat my mother with respect despite the circumstances of her marriage. On the whole, then, I was neither so fearful nor so ashamed as perhaps I should have been.

For four weeks we fretted and wondered and prayed, but before the fifth week drew to a close, Hindley returned to us.

It was on a Thursday evening, after supper. A chill rain had been falling steadily all day, and kept us all confined to the house. I was in with the family, taking advantage of the brighter candlelight there to do a difficult bit of stitching on a new pinafore for Cathy. The master was dividing his attention between the fire and the rain beating against the windows, his thoughts as clear as if he had spoken them aloud. Cathy and Heathcliff were playing quietly in the corner, except when she skipped over now and then to check on my progress and make suggestions – or orders, as she styled them.

'I should like a double row of openwork hemming on the ruffles, like Mama had on her best nightdress,' she said at one point.

'I'm sure you would,' was my only reply.

'Well, will you do it then?'

'No, I will not.'

'Why not?'

'For two reasons: first, because they take so long to do that you would have outgrown this by the time I finished them, and second, because the moment I did finish you would run outside, snag one on a bramble, and rip out half my work.'

'Well, what about a single row, then?'

'That addresses my first reason somewhat, but not my second. I'll do no openwork for you until you learn to take better care of your clothes.'

'Father, did you hear that?' she cried out. 'Nelly refuses to do as I ask!'

'What did you ask of her?' he replied, looking up.

'An openwork hem for my pinafore.'

'How can you think of such trivial things when your brother may be out alone in this terrible weather?'

'What does that have to do with my pinafore?' she replied,

but she rejoined Heathcliff in the corner without waiting for an answer. There they began a whispered conversation, the purport of which (for it was perfectly audible from where I sat) was that life had become infinitely pleasanter for both of them since Hindley had left, and it would be a fine thing if he never returned. It was not the first time they had talked of this, but never before in the master's hearing. I shushed them, and motioned towards the master, to indicate that he would be grieved to hear them, but that only caused Cathy to throw me a saucy look and raise her voice a trifle higher. I just shook my head then, and pretended not to hear them, as their talk became gradually louder and bolder. I saw where it would end, but I had done my bit to keep peace, so I left them to their fate.

Sure enough, their conversation finally caught the master's attention. As it happened, it was Heathcliff speaking at that moment, saying something about 'crows picking Hindley's bones clean on the moor'.

'What did you say?' the master roared, surging out of his chair. He did not wait for an answer, but hauled them both to their feet and boxed their ears soundly. Heathcliff's eyes widened at the pain, and no doubt surprise, too, for the master had never struck him before, and Cathy began sobbing bitterly, whereupon they were both treated to a lecture on the unnaturalness of their feelings. I longed to tell the master that their feelings were only too natural – that if he had set out to sow hatred between them and Hindley, he could hardly have hit on a better plan than he had followed, these last few years. Nonetheless, I was not sorry to see the two of them punished, and the master taking Hindley's part, for once. The lecture finished, the pair were sent off to their rooms, and the master and I were left alone.

The master had just fallen back into his customary gloom, head in hands, staring into the fire, when we heard a commotion outside. The dogs that patrolled at night were growling and barking fiercely, as they would for an intruder, but then the sound changed to joyful yelping, and we heard a familiar voice calling them each by name, and sounding as pleased with the reunion as they were. The master and I both leaped up, but he reached the door before me. He flung it open, and the light from the room revealed Hindley himself, in the middle distance, soaking wet, crouched down and still greeting the excited dogs.

'Hindley, thank God you're home,' shouted the master, and rushed out into the wet to greet him. I will not say that he 'ran, and fell on his neck, and kissed him', like the father of the original Prodigal Son, but he came as close to it as his temperament would allow, embracing him heartily, and leading him towards the house with his arm around him, all with more animation than we had seen in him for some time. I hung back a little, aware of my lesser claims in the master's eyes, but I was there when Hindley entered the house. He was plainly puzzled by the warmth of his father's greeting, which was probably the last thing he had expected, and sent me a questioning look. I could only smile and nod encouragingly, to show that all was well.

'Tea, Nelly, bring the poor lad tea,' the master said hastily, for indeed Hindley looked wet to the bone.

'I'll put the kettle on,' I said, 'but I think Master Hindley should change into dry clothes first, or all the tea in China won't warm him.'

'Yes, yes, of course – run upstairs, lad, and get out of those wet clothes straight away.'

Hindley headed up the stairs, still looking rather bemused.

I ran into the kitchen to start the kettle, then came out again and started up the stairs, telling the master I would just see if Hindley needed anything.

'Do that, Nelly,' he said. 'But tell Hindley to hurry. I want to hear about what he has been doing.'

I leaped up the stairs and knocked at Hindley's door, announcing myself at the same time.

'Just a moment,' Hindley called, and then, after some rustling, 'you may come in now.'

I entered the room. Hindley had got into dry trousers, and was just buttoning up a clean shirt. His work clothes were in a sodden pile on the floor. It was the first time in months I had seen him dressed in his own proper clothing, and it was a welcome sight. He seemed taller than I remembered, and certainly broader in the chest and arms, and his face was tanned from the months of outdoor work. He gave me a hearty hug and a kiss, and then returned to his toilette.

'What in Heaven has come over Father?' he asked, pitching his voice low. 'I never expected such a greeting as that!'

I quickly filled him in on the master's change of heart, telling him at the same time to hurry downstairs, for his father was eager to hear of his travels.

'And he is really not angry with me at all?'

'Not in the least – he is angry with himself, for hurting you so.'

'How much did you tell him?'

'Only what you told me in the stable, that you were going to follow the harvest north. And about the watch,' I added, thinking the master might mention it. 'He asked me how much I had given you, and gave me the money back. But he had me keep the watch, to return to you. It's in my room – shall I fetch it?'

'Later perhaps. I should go down now and speak with him. Will you come too?'

'I'll hover about if I can, but he may want you all to himself. You can't think how eager he is to be kind to you. Why, he even boxed Heathcliff's ears for—' I stopped suddenly, regretting my words. Why reawaken the old animosity so soon?

'For what?'

'Oh nothing, for forgetting to mention you in his prayers, or some little thing like that. It doesn't matter for what – the point is that he struck Heathcliff on your account, which he never did before. It shows he is ready to give you the precedence you deserve.'

'Well enough for now. But I will hear more of this from you later.'

'Whenever you like,' I said cheerfully, glad I would have time to arrange my words more carefully. 'Have you combed your hair? Good. You go down the front stairs now. I'll go down the back, and make the tea.'

'And something to eat, please – I've been fasting since breakfast.'

'Of course. There's mutton stew I can heat up for you.'

I went back to the kitchen to put the stew on to heat up, make tea, and butter some oatcakes for Hindley to eat in the meantime, but I left the door to the main room ajar. Through it I heard Mr Earnshaw speaking in low, earnest tones to his son. I couldn't make out the words, but I guessed that he was making his apologies, and Hindley for his part was making some awkward sounds suggestive of acceptance. When I entered with the tea and oatcakes, the two seemed to have finished with that painful subject, for both were grinning with relief, and the master was just asking Hindley to tell him all about where he had gone and what he had done.

It was a pretty sight, I must say, Mr Earnshaw leaning forward and eagerly questioning his son, and Hindley, leaning back and replying with easy confidence as he detailed his movements and work over the month of his absence.

'Did you have any difficulties with the other men?' his father asked.

'At first. The travelling labourers generally go about in bands of six or seven, who come all from the same neighbourhood, so that they can look out for each other, and a man alone is in some danger from them. After my first day of work, I saw a group of them from somewhere in the south beat one man near to death and take all his money, merely for being alone, and of a different county from them. I had good reason to fear they intended do the same by me.'

'What did you do?' asked the master with some alarm. I had stopped by the door, too rapt in listening to think of my duties.

Hindley grinned. 'Well, I managed to get to the inn before they could accost me outside, and they followed me in. There, they began jostling and shoving me from one to another of them, trying to make cause for a fight. I put them off long enough to get a sense of who else was in the room, and heard some good Yorkshire speech coming from one corner. That was all I needed. I pulled all the coins from my pockets and slapped them onto the bar – over a pound, it was, which is a large sum to these sort of men. I took care in taking out the money to pull my pockets inside out, as if by accident, so it was clear I had no more on me. "Innkeep," I said loudly, in the broadest Yorkshire I could muster. "I have some orders for you, so please attend carefully." Well, the place fell dead silent – I had everyone's ears, which was just what I wanted. I split the coins into two equal piles. "This," I said, pushing one pile towards him, "is to provide care for a poor soul outside, who was beaten

183

and robbed by a gang of thugs, six against one, which is cowards' odds." I got some black looks at this from the guilty parties, I can tell you, and my heart was in my mouth, but I went on as if I didn't see them. "So the Samaritan did for a man in the same case, in our Saviour's story," I said, "and I would follow His footsteps." Now one or two of them began to look abashed, but the rest were as hard-faced as before. "I don't know who committed this act," I went on, looking each of them in the face so they could be sure I knew them full well, "but I know it was not Yorkshiremen, for no Yorkshireman would treat a solitary traveller so." At this the men in the corner cheered and raised their glasses, and I knew I was nearly home. Then I pushed the second pile of coins towards the landlord. "And this," I said, "is to provide the like care for me, should I prove to have enemies here that I know not of. But if I haven't, and all men here are my friends, it is to provide ale for every man here alike, until it is all spent, for when a man is in funds, he ought to treat his friends, as every good Yorkshireman knows." Then everyone cheered, of course, and the Yorkshiremen cheered loudest of all, and claimed me as a member of their band henceforth. So the six who had laid plans against me thought it best to abandon them and enjoy the free ale, for they had nothing to gain by attacking me.'

'That was well done,' said the master, nodding seriously, 'it was well done to imitate our Saviour by caring for the injured traveller, and to lead the other men away from evil-doing. But to spend half your money on drink, in one night? Was that wise?' There was no criticism in his voice, though – he seemed truly curious to know what Hindley thought.

'It might seem not, sir,' said Hindley carefully, 'but I had to show the men that they had nothing to gain by robbing me, for my money was all gone already. And my generosity got me something mere money could never buy – membership of a band. I travelled and worked with them for the rest of the time, and they kept me safe, and taught me much that I could never have learned for myself. And if one of us was too ill or injured to work for a time, the others would take care of him, and share their wages with him, until he could work again.'

'Did that happen to you?'

'No, I was lucky, but it well might have.' Hindley laughed. 'When you have a large group of men swinging razor-sharp scythes in a field day after day, to the point of exhaustion and sometimes past it, it's no surprise there are accidents now and again. They think little of it. If the cut is not dangerously deep, they don't even fetch the surgeon, but get two drams of whisky, "one for the wound and one for the pain", they say, and stitch it up themselves with a needle and silk they carry with them for the purpose. The man who causes the accident, be it to himself or another man, is teased mercilessly for a few days, for not being able "to tell John Bull from John Barleycorn", and you may be sure he takes better care, after that.'

'Well, thank Heaven you are home safe again, anyway,' said the master feelingly. At this point, a loud hissing from the kitchen told me that the stew was bubbling over, and I rushed out to tend to it. I was kept occupied in the kitchen for some time, for some of the stew had burned to the bottom of the pot, and I had to transfer the remainder to a fresh pot right away, or it would all taste scorched. Then I had to clean up the stew that had boiled over onto the hearth, and set the burned pot to soak, and put a basin of the hot stew outside the door for a bit, so Hindley would not scorch his mouth on it. All the while I was cursing my own carelessness, which had kept me out of the room during a conversation that might have great bearing on my own future as well as Hindley's.

When I returned with the steaming bowl of stew for Hindley, he had apparently just asked about what had been going on in his absence, for the master was telling him that we had all prayed daily for his safe return, and then drifted into the minutiae of livestock welfare, and some repairs to the high barn. The master's determination to do better by Hindley seemed to take the form, just now, of presuming that he shared his father's deep interest in farming and stock management. Hindley, for his part, was doing his best to attend, and contribute observations from his travels on how things were done on other farms in different parts of the country. But I could see that he was having difficulty staying awake. It was only to be expected, for when a man suddenly goes from being cold, wet, hungry and fearful of his future, to being warm, dry, safe, and well fed, sleep comes as a matter of course. But the master was so eager to put his own fatherly repentance into action, he could not see how Hindley's eyelids were drooping as he spoke. I decided to intervene. I took a deep breath outside the door, and put on my best imitation of a fussy older woman before bustling in, speaking non-stop.

'Oh Master Hindley,' I said, 'you must be half killed with tiredness after all your travels, and longing to get some sleep in your own bed at last, and you too, sir, for you'll be up at dawn, I know, even if Master Hindley sleeps in, as well he might, for it will be a wonder if he doesn't catch cold, with that soaking he had . . .' and on and on in the same vein. It worked. Hindley took the chance to announce himself bound for bed, and the master followed suit.

In the days that followed, Mr Earnshaw showed himself determined to go on as he had begun: to make things right with his son, and pay off all his arrears of fatherly affection and encouragement. Hindley blossomed under his attention.

His month of self-sufficiency and travel had given him more self-confidence, with less bluster in it than he had before. He had also gained a greater interest in farming in general, and some practical experience in it that in some respects differed from his father's, so that they were able to converse on a more equal footing. In the past, Mr Earnshaw had been prone to lecture Hindley about such things as the rotation of crops or the diseases of sheep, and Hindley had treated the information much as he did book-learning, with a predetermined despair at ever being able to learn it properly. Now, though, he had come to think of farming as something he might learn by doing it, as he had fiddling or dancing, and he went at it with a better spirit.

Heathcliff and Cathy looked glum enough the next morning, upon learning of Hindley's return. But Heathcliff had been startled at the master's blow the night before, and sensed that the lay of the land had shifted, so he and Cathy made some pretence of pleasure in front of the master, whatever they said behind his back, and took care to steer clear of Hindley himself, thenceforward. So upon the whole the house was more peaceful and cheerful than it had been in many years, and I would have been perfectly happy, were it not for the secret I harboured in my belly.

During the weeks of Hindley's absence, I had thought often of his return, and of our marriage and the birth of our child as following hard upon it, but I had given little thought to what lay in between. Now Hindley was home, and experiencing for the first time what it was like to be the apple of his father's eye. How would he feel to learn we had a child coming, and that he must grieve his father, and probably lose his good opinion, by telling him of it, and that soon? My heart sank at the thought, and for the first time I sincerely hoped that I might be wrong. I knew, from overhearing the talk of women in the village, that wives often would not tell their husbands they were with child for two or three months after they knew themselves, in case it came to naught, and though I dared not wait quite that long, I resolved to hold off at least three or four weeks longer before saying anything to Hindley.

As it happens, though, I did not wait quite that long. One day in the middle of November, about two weeks after Hindley's return, he begged off accompanying his father to the high barn to look after some improvements there, having twisted his ankle painfully the day before. Two men being needed for the work at the barn, Mr Earnshaw took Joseph with him instead. That took away the sharpest of the prying eyes at home, and I looked forward to a good stretch of private time with Hindley. So I hurried Cathy and Heathcliff through their lessons, and granted them a half-holiday, knowing they would use it to disappear onto the moor together. Hindley likewise limped through his chores as quickly as he might, and we agreed to meet for an hour or two in his old loft above the stable. We embraced there and talked for a while, sharing much that we had not had privacy to tell each other since his return. I had thought that private talk was all he had in mind, but it soon became clear that he had other ideas, and expected to return to our former intimacies. I refused, and told him that I had come to regret what took place in the fairy cave. He pressed me, urging that he considered us as good as married already, and assuring me that 'the lads' had told him a way to prevent me from getting with child. At this I could not help bursting into tears and telling him it was too late for that. And so my secret was out. Hindley's face froze.

'Are you sure?'

'As sure as I can be this early.'

'You mean you might be wrong?'

'I might be, or it might come to nothing – you know, end of itself.' I was blushing, not being accustomed to talking of such subjects even with women, let alone with Hindley.

Hindley let out a deep breath. 'Well, let us hope it will.' At this I felt my eyes filling with tears.

'Is that really what you most want?' I asked quaveringly. It was a foolish question, for I knew that would be best for both of us. But I craved Hindley's assurance that a child would be welcome, nonetheless. Hindley saw what was wanted, and made some effort to reassure me, but I could see that his heart was not in it. In fact, he was having difficulty restraining his irritation. My face was in my hands, but I heard him stand up, and strike the wall with his fist.

'Damn!'

'I'm sorry!' I wailed, and gave myself over to sobbing entirely. This was not the scene I had pictured.

Hindley stomped about a little longer, cursing his luck and mine, but eventually his better nature prevailed. He sat down by me again, put his arms around me, and spoke soothingly to me for a time, until we were both calm. Then we began to consider what we should do. The longer we waited to tell the master, the more chance there was that my fears might be proved groundless, and leave us nothing to confess. Yet if they weren't, and we waited too long, there would be an appearance of deceit in our not telling him sooner, and the scandal of the child's birth not long after our marriage would be that much more evident. In the end, Hindley concurred with my own calculation, and we decided that two more weeks was the outermost limit of our secrecy, during which time Hindley would do everything within his power to build on his father's new approval

189

and affection for him. At the end of that period, Hindley would break the news to his father privately, representing himself as having just learned of it from me, and suggesting that I, in my maidenly ignorance, had only just become conscious of it myself. He would say nothing of Pennistone Crag or the fairy cave, but take the responsibility upon himself for having overcome my modesty at the height of my concern for him, in this very room, before he left Wuthering Heights. We hoped that, by thus associating our failing with the immediate aftermath of the master's cruel jest, he might come to accept our news as yet another consequence of his own deeply regretted act.

Looking back on those weeks now, it seems as though I spent the whole of them with my heart in my mouth. Both Hindley and his father were doing their best to get on and think well of each other, to be sure, but they were pushing aside a lifetime of contrary beliefs and habits to do so, and the strain was beginning to tell. I would see the master clench his fists to restrain himself, when Hindley made some offhand remark, indicative of poor attention or careless thought, or I would catch Hindley flashing comical faces at me behind his father's back, while he pretended to attend to what he was saying, and hold my breath, lest the entire edifice of mutual goodwill come crashing down at once.

It was also at about this time that the master's strength began visibly failing, and his irritability rising accordingly. Heathcliff and Cathy, too, I knew were no friends to Hindley's good standing. I kept them out of the way as much as I could, but when they were about, I could see them watching for any chance to provoke an indiscretion that might bring Hindley down in his father's eyes. Much as I feared the effects of our revelation, I came almost to look forward to it, as an end to the dreadful suspense I was in.

When the agreed-upon time came, though, Hindley began to put it off from day to day, with one excuse or another, until I thought I should go mad with the delay. I had also begun to suffer from sickness, especially in the morning, which was difficult to keep hidden, and this did nothing to improve my mood. At last I told Hindley that if he would not tell his father himself, in the next two days, I would do so myself, for I could not bear to wait longer. And then something happened, to take the matter out of my hands.

Ever since his return, Hindley had been singing the praises of a breed of sheep he had encountered on a farm in the northernmost part of Yorkshire, hardier than ours, he said, yet with longer, softer wool, and mutton of a sweetness he had never tasted. His description had made enough of an impression on his father, that, farm business being largely settled for the winter, he resolved to take Hindley on a trip to see these 'woolly paragons' for himself, and if they proved as fine as Hindley's report, to purchase a ram to bring back, for the improvement of his own flock. They were to be gone a fortnight, which would bring them back a week before Christmas. Hindley was full of excitement for the trip, delighted that his father gave so much credit to his opinion, and eager to surprise the farmer, who had last seen him as a poor travelling labourer, in his new capacity as a gentleman's son and heir. He begged me to delay our news a little longer, saying that two more weeks could make little difference.

'It is not only two weeks, Hindley, but the week you have delayed already,' I replied.

'Well, three weeks, then. Anyway it makes little odds. And with Father out of the house, who is to notice your illness, and become suspicious?'

'Yes, and who is to help me as you have done, on mornings

when I can scarcely drag myself from my bed, or comfort me, when the weight of all this secrecy becomes almost more than I can bear?'

'But both the work and the burden will be less, with him gone. You will have only the children to look after, and the other servants to mind.'

'And Joseph, don't forget, who will fancy himself in charge with the master gone. He sticks his nose into everything, and already thinks I am a whore, or a witch, or both.'

'Oh, you can manage him well enough. Just threaten to cast a spell on him.'

'You can jest, Hindley, but you must see how dreadful this is for me. You promised to talk to your father a week ago, and now you want to delay still longer?'

'But if I tell him now, we will never go on this trip, and can you not see what a good thing it is for me, and how it will strengthen his respect for me? Surely that is essential, if he is to approve our marriage in the end?'

'Well, will you promise to tell him before you both return, then?'

Hindley hesitated, but I was determined.

'Very well, then. I promise on my honour as a gentleman.'

'Promise on the Bible,' I said. 'I know too little of gentlemen's honour to trust in it.' I ran and fetched the book from the house. 'Here, put your hand on it, and promise solemnly.'

'Well, since we are to be so formal about it, what exactly would you have me promise?'

'Say that you solemnly promise, that before you both return to Wuthering Heights, you will tell your father that I am carrying our child, and that you wish to marry me.'

'Very well then.' Hindley put his hand on the book. 'I solemnly promise, as God is my witness, that before I return to Wuthering Heights I will tell my father that you are carrying our child, and that I wish to marry you, for you are a marvellous girl, and will make me an excellent wife. Will that do?'

'That will have to do,' I said, smiling in spite of myself, 'and now kiss me quickly, and be off, for I have work to do.'

The next day, Hindley and his father departed on their journey, and I settled myself for two weeks of suspense as to how the master would take our news, and what he would be like on their return. Of the main result – our marriage – I had little doubt, but how far we would be in disgrace, whether we would be sent away from the Heights, and for how long, and where, and how we would live in the meantime, were all questions that spun about in the back of my mind, through all my daily duties.

I little thought, though, when I bid Hindley farewell that morning, that I would not see him again for three long years, or that when he did return, he would bring a different wife.

TWELVE

I have some difficulty in writing the next part of my story, not only because of the bitter sorrow it was to me, but because, truth to tell, I am not entirely sure what did happen, and who, if anyone, had a hand in it. I suppose I can only tell what I experienced, and what I conjectured, and leave it to you to draw what conclusions you will.

When the fortnight planned for the master's and Hindley's journey had expired, and the day came that we might expect them back, I was so agitated I could scarcely attend to my work. I had undertaken a rather ambitious dinner for their return, hoping, I suppose, to impress the master further with my usefulness, but found it difficult to stay in the kitchen. I kept finding excuses to sit in that part of the house that had a good view of the road, or to go outside and walk a little way along it, to a rise that commanded a longer view. I looked at the clock every time I passed it, and was astonished that the hours could pass so slowly. Cathy noticed my agitation and teased me for it, saying I looked as if I expected them to bring back a bridegroom for me, instead of just one for the ewes. They both laughed heartily at the joke, little thinking how near to home it was, and I responded by swinging my broom at them until they scattered, and telling them to keep out from under my feet, or I would shut them in the attic, to be sure they did.

When I finally did spy movement on the road, though, it was not, as I expected, two men on horseback, with perhaps a sheep trotting behind them on a rope, but a woman driving the same pony carriage that had brought Mrs Thorne, years before. The figure driving was too heavyset to be Mrs Thorne, though, and a closer approach soon revealed none other than my own mother! I ran down the road to intercept her, fearing I knew not what dreadful news.

'Mother! What brings you here? Do you bring news? Is everything all right?'

'All well, my dear – don't fret,' she replied soothingly, helping me into the carriage beside her. 'There has only been a change of plans.'

'What plans?'

'Well, Mr Earnshaw and Hindley stopped in York, to pay their respects to his cousins there, and they were invited to remain there through Christmas, and decided to accept. So the master wrote to me, and I got leave from the Thornes to come here in the meantime, so your own Christmas would not be too cheerless. And I come like Father Christmas himself, for I bring presents for all of you, from myself and from the Thornes, who also send their fond regards to you.'

'When will they return, then?'

'Well, I don't rightly know. They will stay for New Year at least. And then travel will depend partly on the roads, you know. But if the snow holds off, Mr Earnshaw will probably return not long after New Year.'

I knew not what to think. Had Hindley spoken to his father, and did this change of plans have something to do with that? My heart misgave me that it did. But what was my mother's

195

part in it? I searched her face, but hers was not one that gave much away.

'It's strange for Mr Earnshaw to change his plans like that. He has never gone away so long before, and I should think he would want to be home at Christmas,' I ventured.

'Well, perhaps he thought it was time to re-establish closer ties with his relations. A man often thinks of that, as his children start to grow older.'

'Do you know if he bought the ram at the farm they were visiting?'

'What ram?'

I explained to her about the purpose of their journey. 'Would they really show up to visit relations in the city with a ram in tow? It seems unlikely.'

'Well, they could always leave it at a farm outside the city, and pick it up on their way back. But his letter said nothing about a ram.'

'Did the letter say anything about Hindley? Did he seem, I don't know, pleased with him, or otherwise?'

'Why do you ask?' asked my mother, looking at me intently. But I was prepared for this.

'Since he came back, they have got on so well. I just hope that it will continue.'

'Do you have any reason to suppose it won't?'

'Well, you know, they never did before. And if Hindley was wrong about the sheep . . . I don't know. I just worry about them, of course.'

'Hmm.' My mother said nothing more.

'But the letter . . . did it say anything?'

'It said what it needed to say. No more. The master does not share his opinions with me.' It was clear from my mother's face that further questions would be unwelcome. I fell silent, calculating in my head. Even if nothing had gone wrong, this meant another two or three weeks' delay, at the least, and probably more! By the time they came back, I would be past three months, and beginning to show. Meanwhile, my mother was looking at me carefully.

'Are you well, Nelly?' she asked. 'You look ill.'

'I'm fine,' I said hastily, colouring in spite of myself. Then I remembered that, that very morning, Cathy had caught me being sick into the bushes behind the back door, a fact she would probably convey to my mother at the first opportunity. 'I have been a little ill, just today,' I amended. 'I think I ate some meat that had gone off, yesterday.'

'How many times have I told you, you cannot be too careful with meat?' my mother said, launching into one of her favourite lectures. 'If you have any doubts, chop it up fine and feed it to the hens. It will do them no harm, and will come back to you in eggs.' I longed to defend myself, since in truth I had imbibed her lessons well, and would never have served or eaten tainted meat, but I had brought this on myself, and now I must endure her close questioning about what meat it was, and who else had eaten it, and with what effects, and what I had done with it after, and so on, to all of which I must contrive likely answers. But it kept us both occupied, and away from subjects that might have proved yet more awkward, until she drew up at the house.

Joseph came out, looking anything but pleased to see my mother instead of his master, and grew sourer still when she drew from her pocket a letter to him from Mr Earnshaw, which he had enclosed in one to her. Joseph held the paper at arm's length and eyed it dubiously, as if suspicious that it might be a forgery, or poisoned, or both.

'Come Joseph,' said my mother irritably, 'you know your employer's hand, I am sure, and you can see that the seal is intact. Mr Earnshaw thought that his instructions would reach you more quickly and surely by my hand than through the post, that is all. There is nothing very dreadful inside, I can tell you, except that you will have to bear with my company, instead of his, until after New Year. Now be a good fellow, and find a lad to carry in my luggage, and put away this pony with some oats and a good brushing, until I can return him to Gimmerton tomorrow.'

'Em ee to tak orders fra the loykes o' you?' he snarled.

'Actually, you are, as you will find when you read that letter,' said my mother briskly, whereupon she handed him the reins and swept into the house. Joseph stood dumb-founded, holding the reins in one hand, and the letter in the other, as if uncertain what to do with either. I flashed him a quick smile and a wink, for his further discomfiture, before following her in.

However, I was feeling anything but cheerful. I was already worried about how I could continue to keep my condition hidden from the family, but now I had my mother's sharper eyes and daily intimacy to contend with as well. It did occur to me that I might confide in her about everything, and take her advice. Certainly it would have been a great comfort to have someone with me who knew my secret, especially one who had some experience of my condition. But I had written to her at the time of the master's words at the harvest feast, of Hindley's departure, and later of his return, all without making any mention of my part in them, so it would be awkward to tell her now. And even though I could think of no reason why it should be so, my heart whispered that she would be no friend to my marriage to Hindley. Or so I told myself. The truth was that I had grown too used to keeping secrets from my mother to confide fully in her now, with the greatest secret of my life – even though there was good reason to believe she would soon ferret it out for herself.

My mother settled in at the Heights, and took over the housekeeping as if she had never left it off. She did not sweep me aside, though, but did her best to make me a partner in the enterprise, and commended the order and methods I had maintained – always excepting the supposed episode of the tainted meat, to which, to my great annoyance, she could not stop recurring. As regarded preparations for Christmas, though, her experience far exceeded mine, and I was reduced to a mere apprentice in the compounding of fruit cakes, mince pies, and plum puddings, most of the ingredients for which she had brought with her from Brassing.

For Cathy and Heathcliff, the absence of both the master and Hindley was cause for riotous celebration in itself. I suspended their lessons, ostensibly in honour of the holidays, but really because I knew I had no hope of making them mind, without the master's authority to back me. My mother's authority they minded not a whit, and as she would neither beat them herself nor send them to Joseph for punishment, she was obliged to overlook most of their mischief. Not that they caused a great deal of trouble, really, beyond muddying their clothes and tramping dirt into the house, or stealing a few cakes and pies, which they might have got anyway, for the asking.

Our Christmas celebration was quiet. Joseph, narrow Puritan that he was, thought Christmas a 'Romish and heathen holiday' – though how it could be both at once, I was never clear – and he appeared to think that the mere consumption of its customary delicacies would render him an apostate. So we did not have his sour visage at the table – as fine a Christmas gift to us as any, my mother pointed out. The Thornes had sent rich gifts: for Heathcliff and Cathy, two silver-mounted riding whips, identical but for the initial engraved on each. They must have had my mother's advice on this, for a more perfect gift could not be conceived. Cathy still remembered the promised whip that had been lost when her father had come back from Liverpool, though she had long since reconciled herself to receiving Heathcliff instead – and now she had both together. I received from them a pretty little silver brooch set with Derbyshire spar. My mother provided what was to me a more precious gift: a copy of *Paradise Lost*. Cathy received Isaac Watts's *Divine and Moral Songs for Children*, and Heathcliff, *Pilgrim's Progress*. Cathy was always glad to receive a book, but she seemed a little downcast at the title, until my mother assured her it was full of 'lively and interesting poems', and nothing like the dry tomes Joseph imposed on us. *Pilgrim's Progress*, she told them, was as fine an adventure story as they could hope to find, with giants and castles and thrilling escapes from terrible dangers – at which they both perked up considerably. I was almost as pleased at their gifts as at my own, for I looked forward to borrowing both. My mother had read me *Pilgrim's Progress* when I was young, but we had no copy of it in the house, and Watts's poems for children I had never encountered, though we often sang his hymns in church.

We were previously unprepared with gifts for my mother, of course, but we managed to rustle up a few nonetheless: Cathy presented her with a small sampler of her own indifferent workmanship, and Heathcliff with some pretty feathers he had collected off the moors. I gave her a length of tatted lace I had been making with baby clothes in mind. She declared herself delighted with all three: Cathy's would hang on the wall of her little sitting room at Brassing, Heathcliff's would decorate her hats, and mine would adorn a cap, she said, and all three would remind her of Wuthering Heights and those she loved, every time she looked at them. And so our Christmas was cheerful enough, despite my worries.

I continued to feel ill in the mornings, and scarcely got through one without having to make an excuse to run off and be sick, somewhere out of my mother's sight. But if she noticed anything, she didn't say so. My workload was lightened, with half the household gone and my mother pitching in, for which I was most grateful, as I was fatigued easily. I was also glad that my mother was often away from the house, paying visits to friends and acquaintances around Gimmerton. I was able to excuse myself from accompanying her by pointing out that I had to look out for the children. But in fact they needed little looking after, and I seized most of the time of her absences just to lie down and rest. Further efforts to sound out my mother on the contents of the master's letter to her had yielded no information, and her habitually brisk and matter-of-fact manner was equally unreadable. I endeavoured to believe that everything was just as it appeared – that the master and Hindley were still on good terms, that the former had merely yielded to the invitation of his relatives, and the latter, with pardonable weakness, seized the excuse to delay our awkward revelation, and that the sick feeling in the pit of my stomach, which had set in with my mother's appearance, was no more than a natural consequence of my situation. But the sick feeling remained.

It was four days after Christmas that my mother came upon me being sick into the bushes behind the near barn.

'Nelly, whatever is the matter?' she exclaimed.

'I feel a little ill,' I said, thinking fast. 'I suppose my digestion is not used to all this rich food.'

'No, no, of course not,' she said hastily, 'I should have thought of that before. Come back to the house, child, and let's see what we can do for you.' I suffered myself to be led by her back into the kitchen, where she sat me in a chair and told me to put my head between my knees, and stay there. From that position I could see nothing, of course, but I heard her bustling by the stove, and pulling something out of the drawer where she was keeping her own stores. 'I have a new herbal tea from Elspeth that is excellent for stomach troubles,' she said, 'something like the mint mixture I used to give you as a child, but much better. Let me brew you up some of it – it will do wonders for you. How are you feeling now?'

'Glad to be sitting down,' I said truthfully. It was a relief not to have to hide my illness in front of her, for once, and a comfort to have her fuss so soothingly about me. She asked no more questions, and I rested in silence, until she put down a large steaming mug in front of me. I looked up.

'Drink this up,' she said. 'It's cooled enough not to burn your mouth.' I obeyed. The tea tasted strongly of mint, with other, bitter flavours somewhat masked by the addition of honey. When I was finished, she ordered me to go to bed, which I was glad enough to do. I lay down without undressing, and dozed off. When I awoke, perhaps an hour later, my mother was there with another mugful for me to drink, which tasted bitterer than the first. When, an hour after that, she came with yet another mugful, I declined, saying that the second was still sloshing in my stomach.

'Drink it,' she said, in a tone that brooked no disagreement. I complied, or tried to, but halfway through I paused again.

'It's making me feel more ill, not less,' I complained.

'It seems so at first,' she said, 'but you must drink it all, for it to work.' I didn't want to begin a dispute that might touch on the real cause of my illness, and I thought it could do no harm, so I gulped down the last of it, shuddering a little at the taste. She told me to stay in bed, that she would take care of the household for me for today. I lay back in the bed and closed my eyes. Though I knew it was not rich food that caused my illness, I had some hope that my mother's mixture would ease my nausea, all the same, for I had always had implicit faith in her herbal mixtures.

Instead of easing, though, my discomforts increased. The nausea faded, but I broke out in a cold sweat, my stomach cramped, and my bowels loosed so that I spent almost as much time on the chamber pot as in my bed. I called out for my mother.

'What have you given me?' I asked. 'I feel worse and worse!' My mother was sympathetic, but did not seem concerned.

'It's only a purgative,' she said. 'It will clean you out, and you'll feel better for it, I promise.'

'A purgative? What do you mean? What will it purge?' I was growing fearful now. 'You did not tell me it was a purgative.'

'It will purge what ails you, Nelly. Too much rich food, you said. Why, what are you afraid of?'

I searched my mother's face, but it showed nothing but mild concern. Yet my heart misgave me. 'Leave me alone,' I groaned. My mother left, after exchanging the chamber pot for a clean one, and assuring me she would be back to check on me in another hour or so. I lay back down on the bed and closed my eyes, hoping that sleep would come, and I would wake feeling better. But there was no sleep for me. Waves of cramping pain swept my lower body, growing more intense. Then the blood came, and I realized what was happening. 'No!' I wailed, in a voice that brought my mother running. When she opened the door, though, I was already up, a pillowcase stuffed where it would stop the blood.

'What is the matter, Nelly? That was a fearsome cry!'

'Nothing,' I said, 'only a bad dream. I am going out – I feel a need for fresh air.' I could barely stand, but I was desperate to get away.

'Don't be ridiculous – you're far too ill to go out, even if the weather was good.' I followed her eyes to the window, where I saw dense fog and a slow drizzle of rain, too light to make a sound on the roof. I hesitated. 'Get back into bed, Nelly.' There was a hard edge to her voice that made my heart beat faster.

'I must go out,' I said, and darted through the door before she could think to stop me. I ran down the stairs, grabbed my heavy woollen cloak, and fled out of the door. My mother was following, and calling after me to stop, but even in my illness I was quicker than she. By the time she got to the door, I had disappeared into the fog. She came out looking for me, but I knew she could not find me. She had come to Wuthering Heights as a grown woman, a housekeeper – she knew the yards and barns and gardens, and the paths that led away in one direction or another. But I had grown up there, and played hide-and-seek and sheep-in-the-pen with Hindley and Bodkin on every inch of its environs for half a mile around. The thick fog was no hindrance to me, but she would be lost as soon as she stepped off her familiar pathways. And the fog and rain hid sounds almost as much as sights. I made my way to a little hollow Hindley and I had always favoured, moving more slowly now, both for stealth and because, with the first rush of my impulse to flight faded, the pain and sickness were returning, and making it difficult to walk. Once there, I settled myself down, arranging the cloak to shield me as much as possible from the ground and the rain. That its heather grey colour would also hide me from view was an added benefit. My mother was still searching for me and calling out for me to return. I heard her increasingly anxious voice through the fog now and then, always from a different direction, but never very close to where I was.

The impulse to flee had been too strong to resist, but now that I was secure in my damp little nest, I had leisure to think about what I had done. It made little sense, I knew. Whatever I had seen in my mother's face, she meant no harm to me personally. I was sure of that. And whether she meant harm to my unborn child, or had acted in ignorance, the result would be much the same. The shuddering waves of pain that passed over me, the blood that by now had soaked the pillowcase, made that much clear. When this ended as I knew it would, I would be safer indoors, and under her care. All I had to do was answer her calls. But I could not. Looking back now, I think it was instinct that led me, the instinct that leads any animal, wild or tame, to creep off from its fellows into some hidden nook, to bear its young, or to die.

When the babe came at last, it was no bigger than the palm of my hand, and already dead. I had to feel for it amid what came with it, but when I had it, I could not bear to look. I untied Hindley's neckerchief from my neck, and gently wrapped the babe in it, folding and rolling until I had a soft, dry little bundle, which I tucked in my bosom. Then I rolled onto my knees and felt about me for a rock to dig with. The ground was not yet frozen, but even so, it took a long time to dig a hole deep enough to be safe from dogs or foxes. The soil was hard-packed, and full of rocks, each of which had to be dug round and prised out before I could continue. Many times I sat back on my heels and sobbed, longing to give over, but I could not. While I worked, the air cooled, and the fog and rain resolved themselves into gentle flakes of snow. When the hole was as deep as my arm, I took the little bundle from my bosom, kissed it, and laid it in the bottom. I put small rocks all around it, and a larger flat one on top, to make a sort of coffin. Then I piled more rocks on top of that, before filling in the soil and packing it as hard as I could with my hands – for I could not stand to stamp my foot on it. When it was filled to a small mound, I covered that with a few larger rocks, piled into a simple cairn no higher than my calf, and then eased the heather back around the spot again. Anyone coming upon it would think they saw only a little boulder poking through the heath, but I would always be able to find the spot. When I was finished, I crawled a little distance away, wrapped the cloak tightly around me, lay down in the heather, and sobbed. Even through my pain and grief, I felt sleep hovering near. I knew I should get up and go to the house, or call out, that if I let myself fall asleep now I might not wake in this world, but I was past caring. I closed my eyes, and let sleep take me.

*

When I awoke, there were two pairs of eyes looking into mine, set in two childish faces peering under the lifted hood of my cloak.

'Nelly, is that you?' asked Heathcliff.

'Of course it's her, ninny,' said Cathy, and then raised her head to call out, 'We've found her! She's over here! Quick, Heathcliff, climb up on that hillock and wave.' He hastened to obey. The multiple shouts that followed told me that more than the children had been pressed into service to search for me. I wondered how long I had slept. It seemed to be late afternoon, though with the snow still falling it was hard to tell.

Heathcliff came back shortly, and they both began plying me with questions.

'What happened?'

206

'Why did you run away?'

'Are you ill? You look ill.'

'Did you have a fight with your mother?'

'Why are your hands so dirty?'

'Why were you asleep? Don't you know you mustn't fall asleep in the snow?'

'No questions,' I said shortly. 'Can you help me to get up?' They each took an elbow and helped me stumble to my feet. Once on them, I felt weak, but in no immediate danger of falling back down. I shook the snow off my cloak as best I could without taking it off, and then wrapped it tightly around me and cast my eyes about the site. Of the whole scene of my travails, nothing was visible but a pristine blanket of new-fallen snow, with a faint undulation where I knew the heather gave way to a small pile of stones, and a bare patch where I had just been sleeping. I turned away.

'Do you think you can walk, Nelly?' asked Cathy.

I opened my mouth intending to offer a cheerful 'Yes, of course' so I was rather startled to hear from it instead a quiet 'No'. I absorbed that information. 'Wait for them to come,' I said.

'Shall we run to fetch them quicker?' asked Cathy, clearly eager to be of more active service.

Again, I opened my mouth to tell them to go, and heard instead, 'Stay here, please.' Their eyes widened at this, but they stood to either side of me like guards at attention. We were all silent, except when one of the children hollered now and again to guide the searchers. In a few more minutes my mother arrived, one of the hired hands with her. She rushed to embrace me.

'Nelly, thank God you are found. What madness made you run off into the rain like that? And you so ill, too! Poor child, you might have died,' she said, and on and on in the same vein. She was clearly distressed, but I neither embraced her nor responded, standing still as a statue. Now that she was here, I felt as if I would never speak again. 'Come, poor girl, you're half frozen. Don't try to speak yet. Here, Burt, take her other arm and we'll walk her back between us. Children, can you fly ahead and put the kettle on the hob? And put all the bed stones into the fire to heat up too – we'll tuck her up warm with them after we've got some hot tea into her.'

'No tea,' I said.

'No tea if you don't want it, of course not,' said my mother quickly. 'Hot milk with a bit of brandy, maybe, or whatever you will. Hot water and honey, if you'll take nothing else. Just to warm you up. No tea, no tea.'

I suffered myself to be led back to the house, stripped of my damp cloak, and placed on a bench near the fire. I was given a mug of hot milk and brandy, which I tasted cautiously with the tip of my tongue before I began to drink, to be sure there was nothing else in it. After a few minutes, I could feel the warmth of the fire and the hot drink beginning to penetrate me, but I was still half-stupefied with cold. I watched dumbly, occasionally sipping from my mug, as my mother poked the stones from the fire and wrapped them in rags, then tucked them in a basket and went upstairs. When she came back down, she felt my clothes for dampness, chattering to me all the while, and, having concluded that they were not dangerously damp, told me I had best sit a while longer, and drink another mugful, if I would.

'Water,' I said.

'You'd rather have hot water, dear? That's fine. Shall I just put some honey in it, to sweeten it?'

'Just water.' My stomach was already rebelling against the milk, but I felt very thirsty. I would have preferred cold water, to be honest, but I didn't think she would give it to me. But the hot water, when she brought it, was not so hot but that I could drink it quickly. Then I gathered my strength and my courage for what seemed to me, just then, a heroic effort. I stood up. 'I am going to bed,' I said.

'Yes, of course,' said my mother. 'Let me just come with you, and help you off with your things.' She was heading towards the stairs with me as she spoke.

'No.' I had been trying for just the right tone – firm enough to discourage dispute, but not so vehement that she would think I was hysterical, but I heard an edge of desperation in the word as it came out. My mother hesitated, looking disturbed. 'Please,' I said, fighting down the sobs that were threatening to rise, 'please, Mother, I want to be alone.' It was almost a whisper by then, but it swayed her.

'I'll just see you up the stairs,' she said, and took my elbow. I was relieved to have her help there, actually, for the stairs, which normally I ran up and down twenty times a day, loomed just now as a fearful obstacle. Together we made our way up, and at my door, true to her word, she left me. Once inside, I closed the door. There was no lock, so I propped my little chair under the handle. Then I began to undress. I had lifted up my skirts as I lay down on the heather, when I knew what was coming, so my dress was unsoiled except by some mud, and my underclothes not so bad as I feared. Still, I did not feel equal to explaining them to my mother, so I folded them flat and slid them under my mattress. I would wash them later, after she was gone. I poured a little water from the pitcher into the basin, and cleaned myself as best I could, then tugged my little window sash open a crack to squeeze the sponge outside. That done, and the window closed again, I slipped into my heaviest nightgown, removed the chair from the door, drank

209

most of the remaining contents of the pitcher (for I was still thirsty), and got into bed. I had forgotten that it was full of hot stones, wrapped in rags. They had warmed it up nicely, but there were too many to sleep among, so I pushed all but the one at my feet out onto the floor, where they made a dreadful clatter.

'What was that!' called my mother in alarm, so quickly that I thought she must have been listening outside.

'Just the bed stones.'

'May I come in and get them? Else the rest of us will sleep cold tonight.'

'Later, please,' I said. It was still only twilight – it would be hours before the rest of the family went to bed. I wanted to be asleep, or at least be able to feign it, before my mother came in.

'Very well,' she said. I heard her footsteps recede.

I lay in my bed. I was dry, warm, clean, and free of pain and fear for the first time in what seemed an eternity, though it was really only half a day. I had a great deal to think about, I knew, but I could not think of any of it yet. My mind was numb, and my heart ached like a fist clenched for too long. I stared at the ceiling, wondering if sleep would ever come. And that thought is the last that I remember.

When I awoke the next morning, the first thing I saw was Dr Kenneth's face. He had my wrist in one hand, and his watch in the other, and behind him hovered my mother, looking anxious.

'Good morning, Nelly,' he said with a smile, 'how do you feel today?' I pushed myself up to a sitting position, and took stock. There was some soreness, but nothing worrisome.

'I feel well,' I said cautiously.

'No aches or pains, no unusual symptoms of any kind?'

'None.'

'Good. Mrs Dean, could you perhaps leave us for a few minutes?' My mother went out, but left the door ajar. The doctor went over and closed it firmly. When he returned, he sat down and took both my hands in his. 'How far along were you?' he asked quietly.

'What?'

'How far along was your pregnancy? Do you know?'

I blushed. 'How did you know? I didn't think it showed yet.'

'You had the look. About your face. The mask of pregnancy, they call it. I saw it when you came to town.'

'Does my mother know?' We were both whispering.

'She didn't say, and her face is harder to read than yours.'

'Will you tell her?'

'Not if you don't want me to. You should tell her yourself, though. It may feel difficult now, but you will be happier for it, in the long run. Now tell me, how far along were you?'

'Not quite three months.'

'Do you know what brought on the miscarriage?'

'My mo—' I stopped, suddenly worried. Could my mother be guilty of child murder in the eyes of the law? And if so, would Dr Kenneth's discretion extend to concealing a crime? I had no idea, and didn't want to find out. I paused, and arranged my words carefully.

'My mother had some herbs, from Elspeth. She said they were a stomachic. She brewed some for . . . for herself, one night when she felt ill, and they cured her. There was some left, and I drank it the next morning, when I was feeling ill. I thought it would help. But instead . . .'

Dr Kenneth nodded, and then questioned me closely about

what had followed, while he carried out his examination. At the end of it, he pronounced himself satisfied.

'You've come through it well,' he said. 'I see nothing to worry about. You may get up when you're ready to. And send for me again if you have any alarming symptoms. Will you promise me that?' I nodded. 'Good, now let's bring your mother back.' He opened the door, and announced to my mother that I was 'sound as a nut' and past danger.

'Thank God,' she said, 'and thank you too, Dr Kenneth, for coming so quickly. I was quite worried.'

'Well, you need have no further worries – she'll be up and about today, I should think. But can you tell me, Mrs Dean – Nelly says she drank some herbal tea, a stomachic you had from Elspeth, that you had brewed up for yourself, and she went and drank the rest of it, and it made her ill. Might I have a look at it?'

My mother shot me an unreadable look. 'Oh, there's none of that left – I brewed up the last of it yesterday, and threw the leaves on the rubbish heap.'

'Do you know what was in it?'

'Why, a good deal of mint, and some fennel, but I don't know what else. Is that what made her ill, do you think?'

'More than likely. Elspeth knows her herbs, all right, but they are not to be treated lightly. Did you follow her preparation and dosing instructions exactly?'

'Why, I . . . no, I suppose not. I thought a little more could do no harm. It is only herbs.'

'*Only herbs* can kill you, Mrs Dean, if you take the wrong ones, or too much,' said Dr Kenneth sternly. 'Or do great harm to someone else, if you leave them lying about. I would have thought you knew better than that, especially with children in the house.'

'I'm very sorry, sir,' said my mother contritely. 'I'll be more careful in future.'

Dr Kenneth pronounced himself satisfied, and took his leave. He shut the door on us as he went, leaving my mother and me to face each other. My heart was pounding. What did she know, and what would she ask?

She sat down in the chair Dr Kenneth had vacated, and took both my hands in hers. 'Nelly, dear child,' she said, 'I am so sorry that I made you ill with my foolish mixture, and frightened you too, for you must have been frightened, or delirious, to run off like that! And you frightened me too, but I suppose I deserved it, and I have learned my lesson now.' She spoke quickly, and would not meet my eye. I saw how it was: she would admit nothing, and sought no confession from me. Otherwise, would she not have commented on my lie to Dr Kenneth, and questioned me more closely about yesterday? I felt relieved, but a little disappointed too. And a deeper shade fell between my mother and me.

In the quiet days that followed, though, I found myself doubting my own conclusions. My mother seemed so calm and cheerful and loving to all of us, so absolutely normal in herself, and in her behaviour to me, that to imagine her setting out in cold blood to kill the babe in my womb, without ever saying a word to me about it, seemed too monstrous to think of. It was more comfortable to think that it had all come about unwittingly, and that it was indifference, rather than guilt, that made her pass over my lie to Dr Kenneth.

The day after New Year, my mother announced that it was time for her to return to Brassing, for her duties there had been neglected long enough, and the master was due back any day.

'The master and Hindley,' I said. 'I wonder if they will bring the ram, too?' My mother coloured and looked uncomfortable.

'Sit down, Nelly,' she said. 'I have something to tell you.' I sat. 'Hindley is not coming back,' she said quickly. 'The master has decided that he must go away to finish his studies. He is worried about his progress. That was why he went to York, to take advice from his uncle and cousins on a likely place to send him.'

I jumped up. 'What! Why? Why now? And why keep it secret? I don't understand!' I was shouting.

'Sit down again, Nelly,' said my mother firmly. 'I cannot speak to you while you are shouting and flailing about like that. The master reached this decision during his trip. He had no intention of keeping it secret – he told it to me. I thought it might grieve you, so I chose to hold off telling you until after the holidays. That is all.'

'But I thought they were getting on so well! They were before they left. What happened?' I struggled to keep a rising sense of desperation from my voice.

'Perhaps the master was less pleased than he appeared. Perhaps Hindley did something to make him change his mind. I don't know.'

'How long is he to be gone?'

'Until he finishes his education I believe. A year or two at least.'

'But why . . . why so *sneaking* about it?'

'There is no "sneaking" involved, Nelly. Mr Earnshaw is not obliged to share his plans for his family with you, any more than with the children.'

'But . . . but . . .' My mind was whirling. That my mother had hidden this news out of kindness, I might just have believed, as I had managed to believe that she killed my babe unwittingly, but the two together? And yet . . . I longed to question her more closely, but I could not see how to probe her secrets, without revealing my own. And Hindley gone, too, without a word, for years perhaps . . . between anger, grief, and suspicion, I thought I would explode. I fled to my room, shut the door, and flung myself sobbing on the bed.

I had half expected my mother to follow me, but she let me be until the storm subsided. And what a storm it was! I raged, I sobbed, I stomped around the room, pounded the bed, kicked the walls, and pulled my hair – I did everything but scream out loud, or faint. But like all storms, this one passed, and in its wake I sat quietly on my bed, numb to everything but a dull ache in my breast, that felt as if it would never leave. Not long after I reached that point, my mother opened the door, and quietly came in. I buried my face in my hands, so as not to look at her. She sat down next to me.

'Nelly,' she said gently, 'have you and Hindley become fond of each other?'

'We have always been fond of each other. Ever since we were babies together. In your care. Remember?'

'You know that's not what I mean. Have you been forming romantic ideas about him?'

I said nothing.

'How often have I told you that you are not to think your-self the equal of the Earnshaws? You are a servant, Nelly, the daughter of a servant and a half-illiterate stonemason. Hindley is a gentleman's son and heir. To pursue him—'

'I never pursued him! He pursued me!'

'Young men of Hindley's age will pursue any girl who gives them encouragement. Can you say that you did not encourage him?'

Again, I was silent.

'To encourage him, then, was an act of grossest ingratitude to the Earnshaws, who have been your benefactors from an early age.'

215

I was crying again by this time, but I managed to speak through my sobs. 'You said when a man marries down, he raises his wife to his level. And I would be a good wife to him.'

'Don't bandy words with me, Nelly,' she said angrily. 'I am telling you that you cannot marry Hindley. The master would never permit it, and neither would I. It is nothing but a childish fancy, and you must put it from your mind.'

I had no answer, only sobs. My mother took a deep breath. 'I think it is time you left Wuthering Heights.'

This was too much: the dam burst. 'Is that what you came here to do?' I accused her. 'He sent you to order me away, didn't he, so he wouldn't have to do it himself, and break his vow!' That stopped her short.

'What vow?'

'The one he made after I saved Heathcliff from the measles, when he blessed me, and said I was born to be the salvation of the family, and that while he lived I should always have a home at Wuthering Heights – *always*, he said, and he *vowed* it – and now he wishes he could take it back so he sent you instead, but I don't want to leave, this is my home, I have been here always, I don't want to go anywhere else, I don't, I don't, I don't.' I was pounding my knees with my fists as I spoke, tears streaming down my face. I had lost my baby, I had lost Hindley, and I could not bear to lose Wuthering Heights too, and the family I still loved as my own. My mother grabbed my wrists and held them, hard. That made me look at her, and I saw tears in her eyes.

'God forgive me, what have I done?' she cried, and wrapped me in her arms. But I was frozen, and would not return her embrace. At length she pushed away from me, still with her hands on my shoulders, and took a deep breath. 'I did not know about this vow,' she said. 'It explains . . . some things.

The master did not ask me to send you away. That would not be like him, to take an underhand way out of an obligation he laid on himself. It was my thought only. I did not realize how deep were your roots here. I thought you might be happier with me, at Brassing, where there are a greater variety of people about, and more opportunities for a girl like you. I still do think that, Nelly, but I will not force it on you. You must make your own choice.'

'I choose to stay here.'

'Think about it, Nelly. You need not decide now. You must think on it, when you are calmer. You would not be leaving immediately, in any case – they would need to find someone to replace you, and you would need to show them what to do; it would be a matter of weeks, at the least, if not months. So take your time, and think about it.'

I said that I would. I had a great many things to think about – why not this too? But I knew I would not change my mind. It was not just that I loved Wuthering Heights and its inhabitants, but to work under my mother, or among strangers, and as an underservant, when here I was housekeeper in all but name, and manager of my own time, held little appeal. And a part of me still hoped, whatever my mother might say, that in time I could prove myself to Mr Earnshaw as a worthy wife for Hindley.

My mother left the next day, and the master returned, alone, the day after. He was gloomier than when he had left, and more distant with all of us, but other than that he treated me no differently, and I began to think that Hindley had not spoken to him, after all. I did not trust myself to ask about why he had sent Hindley away, but Cathy and Heathcliff were not so shy. I had told them already that Hindley was being sent to school, but as soon as the master came back they began pestering him with questions. And since at that age beasts interested them more than people, they began with the ram.

'Where is the ram? Did you buy the ram?'

'I did not,' was the grim reply.

'Why not? Were the sheep as fine as Hindley said? What were they like?'

'Inferior to ours, in every way,' the master snorted. 'I don't know what that fool of a lad was thinking. "Sweetest mutton I ever tasted," he said.'

'Hard labour is a great sweetener of victuals,' I said.

'Yes, well, that certainly explains why ours never tasted so sweet to him. I suppose hard labour is a great softener of wool, too.'

I held my tongue.

'Why did you send Hindley away to school?' asked Cathy.

'Because he will never amount to anything here. The lad is useless, and will learn nothing while he has his friends and amusements at home. Perhaps a schoolmaster can do better with him. At any rate, he will be no loss here.' Cathy and Heathcliff grinned broadly, and ran off together, as cheerful as if Christmas had come again. I fled to the kitchen, and chopped onions. It was going to take some time to inure myself to hearing Hindley talked about in such terms again, without seeming to mind it. In the meantime, I chopped a great many onions.

So there you have it: the secret I have harboured all these years, with such bitterness and shame – or one of them, anyway. And now that it is told, there is nothing very remarkable about it. A maidservant got herself with child by her master's son, because she was foolish enough to believe his promise of marriage. But she had the good fortune to lose the child, before it could cost her either her position or her reputation. Who would be interested in such a story, compared to the wild, destructive passions of highborn ladies and gentlemen, and orphans of mysterious parentage? Certainly not you, Mr Lockwood, Mr Knockwood, Mr Lockheart. But I can tell you, the story was vivid enough for me, while I was living it, and the tears for my lost dream none the less bitter, for shaking the bosom of a stout, plain girl in a homespun apron and cap. And that was not the end of it, either, for this story played its part in stranger happenings that came after.

THIRTEEN

They were quiet years, those that followed. For me, they began with my slow, sad adjustment to the full scope of Hindley's banishment. For the first few months, I was in daily expectation of a letter from him. I knew he could not write to me directly, but I was sure he would find a way to get a letter to me – via one of his friends in Gimmerton, perhaps. But none came. If he wrote to his father, or the master to him, there was no sign of that either, that I could see. I would have written to him myself, if I had known where to write, but the master never so much as mentioned the name of the school, or even the part of the country it was in. When I realized that no letter would come, I still expected that Hindley would be home for the school's summer holiday, but the expected period came, with no sign of him. At this, I finally gathered my courage to ask after him.

'When will Hindley be home from school?' I asked the master one day as I served him his breakfast, striving for a casual tone.

'He will spend all his holidays with his relations,' the master said, in a tone that invited no further discussion. At this, whatever shred of hope I had remaining, that Hindley's disappearance had nothing to do with him and me, was gone. Had

I understood this at once, perhaps I would have left Wuthering Heights, as my mother wished me to. But as I said, my hopes diminished gradually, over many months, so that, by the time I was conscious that they were truly gone, I had grown used to living without them.

The gloom that had settled on the master never lifted. If anything, it seemed to deepen with each passing month, and he became ever more stern and silent. The more striking changes, to me, were the loss of his energy, and the growing power ceded to Joseph. The farm the master had taken on was let again, and more and more of the business of our own farm, which he had always seen to himself, seemed to be left to Joseph to manage. With the latter's greater responsibilities, apparently, came greater influence. Joseph not only lorded it over the rest of us, but he did not even hesitate to lecture the master on spiritual matters, and especially on the state of his soul, all of which the master bore with a meekness I could never have imagined in him before. Only the subject of Heathcliff was forbidden. Joseph hated the lad like poison, and for a time he tried to turn his master against him, but Mr Earnshaw's old spirit would flare into life again at any attempt to disparage his favourite, and Joseph soon left off the attempt.

I was concerned that Joseph would now turn his energies to disparaging me to the master, but he must have realized that I had become essential to the smooth running of the household (as indeed I had), for he confined himself to harassing me personally. I had finally learned how best to deal with this, which was by wrapping myself in a hard carapace of respectful politeness to his face, which gave him no opening for complaint, and then making horrible faces at him behind his back, to soothe my own feelings. I only did this while I thought no one was watching, of course, but on one occasion Cathy and

Heathcliff happened to be peeking through the door, unbeknownst to me, and caught me doing it. They went off into gales of laughter, and Joseph whirled round to demand the cause. I put my finger to my lips to beg their silence, which made them laugh the harder, but they kept mum, even when Joseph condemned them to listen to an entire sermon, as an antidote to their insolent levity. After that, they took up the practice themselves, casting me conspiratorial looks all the while, but they were far less careful not to be seen by him. In fact, they seemed to like nothing better than to have Joseph spot them with their faces twisted and their tongues out at him, and then run off before he could catch them. But they never said a word about my part in it, and in truth it gave all three of us a good deal of much-needed amusement, during those gloomy times.

I don't know when I first truly realized that the master was in his final illness. It is not that I didn't see the signs, or even that I didn't draw any conclusions from them. It is rather that, no sooner would the thought, 'Mr Earnshaw may be ill,' or 'Mr Earnshaw may die soon,' flicker across my mind, than a number of other thoughts would follow, willy-nilly: that if he did die, Hindley would come home; that he would become master of Wuthering Heights; that there would be nothing, then, to prevent us from marrying as soon as we liked. You might think that these would be welcome thoughts, but they were anything but that: they filled me with terror. To imagine that what I most desired would follow directly from the master's death felt too much to me like wishing for him to die, and though I was not conscious of really wishing that, the fear of it was enough to make me push away any signs or hints that might otherwise have been clear enough.

I have told you that my mother's story came to haunt me. This is where it really began. I could not stop thinking about how the farmer had wished for his wife's death in his heart without knowing that he did so, and imagining the horror he felt, when his wish was granted, and he knew that it was his own heart that had done the evil. It even crossed my mind at this time, that earlier, while Hindley and I had been debating when to tell his father our news, I had wished in my heart that I were not with child, and perhaps it was that, more than anything my mother might have done, that had led to the babe's death.

I tried to reason myself out of my superstitious fear. I reminded myself that wishes, whether good or ill, did not come true just by wishing them, that 'if wishes were horses, then poor men would ride'. I told myself that the farmer in my mother's story had earned the Brownie's ill will by abusing his generosity, something I was not aware of having done to any creature, magical or otherwise. And when that did not ease my anxiety, I tried to ensure that my heart was in good trim by acting as if it were. I flung myself with renewed vigour into fulfilling every duty, and treating the master with all the deference and consideration I could muster; I prayed for the health and pros-perity of each family member nightly; but above all, I tried to avoid thinking those thoughts I believed to have evil at their roots, however innocent their outward appearance. And so it was not until Dr Kenneth was called in, and officially pronounced his verdict, that I allowed myself to think of the master as truly ill. Dr Kenneth now became a regular visitor at our house again, though not so regular as he had been with the mistress, for the master disliked frequent medical attendance.

One bright spot during this time was the return of Bodkin. At one of Dr Kenneth's visits, he mentioned that his son was back from Edinburgh, now a doctor in his own right. I asked if we would be seeing him at the Heights any time soon.

'Ah, the days when I can bring him along on my own cases are done now,' he said with a smile. 'He must manage his own cases.'

'Will he be taking over the whole of your practice?' I asked.

'Only gradually,' he replied. 'My older patients, your master, for instance, have known me too long to accept a substitute, particularly one they are not yet accustomed to seeing in long trousers. And I myself should be sorry to bid farewell to them. For now, he is managing the surgery and going out for new cases. Then we will see how it goes. But do visit him – I know he would like to see you. And he has news to give you.'

'What news?'

'I'll leave that to him,' he said with a smile.

With that as an incentive, I seized the next opportunity of going into Gimmerton for some errands, and stopped by the surgery before heading home. There were three people waiting there already – an older gentleman, a young woman, and a boy, presumably her son, with a bandage on his leg – so I feared I would not be able to do more than greet Bodkin and be on my way. Soon the door opened, and Bodkin came in, looking taller and older, and sporting a trim little beard only slightly less red than his hair.

'Nelly!' he cried on seeing me. 'How good of you to come. If you can stand to wait a few minutes, I will be at your service.'

'You seem to have your hands full with patients,' I said doubtfully.

'Ah, that is an illusion,' he said, 'for Mr Gross is only here to pick up his medicine, which I have right here,' he flourished a blue bottle which he handed to the gentleman, who thanked him and left, 'while this exceedingly brave little man is here to

224

have some stitches removed, which will only take a minute, and his mother is here to witness his bravery, so she can brag about it to all the neighbours. Is that right, Tommy?' The little boy managed a nervous smile and a nod, and Bodkin ushered both of them into the next room, where, to judge from the wails that followed, Tommy was anything but brave. But the operation was quickly finished, and the child emerged with a peppermint stick in one hand, his mother's hand in the other, and a great eagerness to be out of the place. As soon as they were gone, Bodkin came out and put up a little pasteboard sign, saying that the surgery would reopen at four o'clock (it was just after three), and then he led me through the surgery into the sitting room of the main house, stopping a small maid along the way to ask her to bring tea and biscuits, forthwith.

'Dr Kenneth,' I said.

'Oh, please don't call me that,' he said. 'I keep looking round for my father.'

'But you'll have to get used to it,' I protested.

'Yes, I will, in time, but not from you. To you I must remain Bodkin, or how am I to remember, amidst all these new responsibilities, that I was ever young?'

I laughed, and promised that he would always be Bodkin to me. Then I asked him how he liked his new practice.

'Well enough,' he said. 'Father is staying with his older regular patients for now, so mine are mostly children and poorer folks. It makes for a good deal less bowing and scraping, which is fine with me, but I am worried I will forget everything I ever learned about gout.'

'No, I don't suppose you see much of that among the young or the poor.'

'Oh, it is so far a badge of mature wealth, these days, it is almost as good as a title. In Edinburgh men who have come into money late in life will bandage a toe and take to crutches, just to hide their upstart origins. You'd be surprised how well it answers.'

I laughed. 'You seem to have a way with the children, anyway,' I said. 'Though Tommy was not so brave after all, was he?'

'No, I'm afraid little Tommy is not at all brave,' he sighed. 'The poor child cries if a fly lands on his arm, and expects imminent death if he stubs his toe. He's a trial to his mother, I know.' He smiled. 'But I try to keep on good terms with him, anyway, for he has the makings of an excellent hypochondriac, and they are bread and butter to a country doctor.'

'Your father said you had news?'

'I do, and you can probably guess what it is,' he grinned.

'You are getting married.'

'I am indeed.'

'To Anna Smythe.'

'Damn Gimmerton's gossips – they leave me nothing to tell! It's quite true. Father said there was no reason for us to wait, with the practice well established and this house sitting nearly empty, and he is keen for us to supply him with grandchildren while he is still spry enough to chase them about.'

'Gossip says it was your fathers made the whole match, with an eye to their mutual business advantage.'

'That's nonsense. Father gave me a free and full choice – between Anna and Old Elspeth.'

I laughed. 'Well, at least with Elspeth, you would know exactly what you were getting.' Bodkin affected to shudder.

'But seriously, Nelly,' he said more soberly, 'I don't like to hear you lending an ear to such talk, let alone passing it along. Anna Smythe and I have known each other since we were children, and we have always been fond of each other. As far as Gimmerton gossip is concerned, there was never a marriage

226

made in this town that was not compounded of varying parts of greed, folly, and deceit, though none of them could point to a greedy, foolish, or deceitful thing my father has ever done before.'

'Or Mr Smythe?'

Bodkin hesitated. 'He has his flaws, certainly, but they have no bearing on this marriage, except in that they made the rest of us the more keen to get Anna out of his house. She has not had an easy time of it, at home.'

'Really? He is always so unctuous to his customers – we used to call him Mr Smooth.'

'Well, I suppose his customers get the smooth, and his daughter the rough. But if you breathe a word of that outside of this room, Nelly, I will never speak to you again. Anna has a strong sense of filial duty, and she would be deeply grieved for anyone to think she complained of him.'

'No, of course not. And if anyone tries to tell me that your marriage is founded on anything but sincere affection and mutual respect, I will fly out at them in a fury, and say that Miss Anna Smythe is a sweet, generous girl with a strong sense of duty, and Dr Robert Kenneth is a kind-hearted and highly responsible young man, and they have every prospect of being extremely happy together. How is that?'

'Very well, if you mean it.'

'I do, Bodkin, and very sincerely.' And then, all at once, I felt my lip begin to quiver, and tears welling in my eyes that were not from laughter. 'I must go,' I said quickly, turning aside and fumbling with my bag, 'I have several errands still to run.' Bodkin saw how it was, and he saw me to the door without further discussion.

I walked home wondering how much he knew, or had guessed. I thought that Dr Kenneth could be trusted with my secret, and had still no good reason to think otherwise. But I could not help noticing that in the whole of our conversation, Bodkin had not once mentioned Hindley.

At home, my duties expanded to include attending a sickroom again. At first my thoughts were as wayward as ever, but seeing the master, who had always been a pillar of strength, reduced to an invalid dependent on me for the most simple services, tugged at my heartstrings, and I was relieved to find that I longed quite sincerely for his recovery under my care. He was irritable, and snapped often, and since I was usually nearest, he snapped at me as often as not. But I did not take it to heart, for I knew then that it was only his illness. He knew it too, and in his quieter moments he would thank me for my service, and beg my pardon for the trouble he gave me, which always brought tears to my eyes. During this time, he never mentioned Hindley, nor said anything to suggest that he knew of our past together, but he always talked as if I were to be a permanent fixture as housekeeper at the Heights. He would beg me to take good care of Heathcliff, and steer him on the right path, as if it were in my hands to do so, and at times he would even talk to me about tenants and rents as if I had the management of the estate. Probably it was only because his mind was wandering, but I began to fancy that he was changing his mind about Hindley and me, and resigning himself to our marriage.

My guilty thoughts of what might follow on the master's death now began to be replaced with more gratifying daydreams: I imagined myself, through some exhausting and heroic feat of nursing, rescuing him from death and entirely restoring him to health, as I had once done for Heathcliff. Hindley, recalled from school to what he believed to be his father's deathbed, would arrive to find all danger past, and myself kneeling at his father's bedside for his blessing. His father, looking up with tears in his eyes, would tell Hindley to kneel with me, join our hands, and bless us both together, and our wedding would follow as soon as the master was recovered enough to come to church.

But Mr Earnshaw's illness was no feverish conflagration to be beaten back with frantic effort, as Heathcliff's had been. It was rather a slow sapping of the vital force, like a fruit tree that withers and sheds its leaves from no visible cause, no matter how the farmer tries to save it. My daydreams were a comfort to me, and allowed me to go about my duties in a better spirit, but they did not fool me. The master was dying, slowly but inexorably.

I did think that Hindley ought to be sent for, but knew not how to bring it about. I was shy of speaking Hindley's name to the master again, and shy too, of acknowledging to his face that I knew he was dying, but whom else was I to ask? I wrote to my mother, for the first time in many months, to tell her the master was dying, and, braver with a pen than with my voice, said that Hindley should come home, but I had small hope of her bringing that about, for many reasons. At last I thought of Joseph, whose influence with his master was now at its peak. He was at his bedside almost as often as I was, not to provide comfort or ease, it seemed, but to take them away, by whispering to him urgently about matters I could not overhear. His talk made the master groan and clutch his head in anguish, so that I wished I could banish Joseph from the sickroom altogether, except that the master would not permit it. I did not like to make an ally of Joseph, now or ever, but it struck me that he was inclined to Hindley's favour, as the son and heir to the Earnshaw family, whose dignity he claimed as his own, and now he faced the prospect of Hindley becoming his own master soon. I also had no reason to think that Joseph knew anything about my former relations with Hindley, which was an added inducement.

So, one morning, as Joseph sat over his porridge at breakfast, I sat down opposite him and composed myself to be as polite and respectful as I knew how.

'Joseph,' I said. 'There is something that has been worrying me, and I wonder if you might be able to help.'

'If it's your soul, yo've good cause to worry, and there's naught I can do for yo.'

'I don't mean that,' I said, swallowing my irritation. 'But I wonder that the master has not thought to send for Hindley. Dr Kenneth says that he has not many more weeks, and it would be right for Hindley to be home before . . . to receive his father's blessing, as his firstborn.' I hoped that the vaguely Biblical reference might impress Joseph favourably.

'Hoo's got all the blessing hoo's like to get, poor lad,' said he. 'Yon black devil's child has stolen all the rest, an' hoo's birthright too, more than likely.'

'But shouldn't Hindley be at home, then, as soon as possible?'

Joseph eyed me suspiciously. 'What's it to yo?' he snarled.

'I just thought it would be right, and the master's so . . . preoccupied, I thought it might not have crossed his mind, so perhaps you could do something about it.'

'I have me orders fro' the master, and they don't cover sendin' for Hindley on the say-so of a household wench.'

I didn't argue – I knew it would only harden Joseph's position. 'You must do as you think best, of course,' I said politely, and took my leave, hoping I had at least planted a seed in his mind. If it took root, though, I never learned. Whether it was by design or by oversight, Hindley was not sent for until it was too late.

When Mr Earnshaw finally died on that chill October evening, I wept quite bitterly and sincerely. I had not loved him as deeply as I did the mistress – he was not a man to be loved so by his dependants, stern and distant as he habitually was – but he had been the head of my little world for as long as I could remember, and more like a father to me than certainly my own father had been. But even in my sorrow, I could not quell the flicker of excitement that came too, with the thought of what would follow. And so I wept for him, and for Heathcliff, who had good reason to fear for his future, but I wept too for my lost innocence, and my corrupted heart, that would never know peace again.

FOURTEEN

Hindley was expected home the afternoon before the funeral, and as you may imagine, I was not the only one agitated about his arrival. The servants were all jumpy in expectation of their new master, dropping their work and hastening to the window at each of a dozen false reports of his arrival. Cathy and Heathcliff were rocketing around like billiard balls, running back and forth to the little hill that gave the best vantage on the road, and debating continually how best to greet Hindley on his return.

'You must greet him seriously and kindly, as befits a sister who shares his grief,' I said finally. 'There is nothing difficult about it.'

'But what about Heathcliff?' she asked. 'Should he be friendly, or only strive not to be noticed?'

'Friendliness will never come amiss,' I said, 'but there is no need for him to intrude himself. Heathcliff, you must smile and nod, but you need not say anything, and you should keep a little behind Cathy.' But of course Cathy must raise objections to anything that seemed to place Heathcliff below the family, and Heathcliff must look scornful at the idea of smiling at Hindley. I affected to be irritated at all their fussing, but really

I was glad of anything that could take my mind off my own tumultuous thoughts and feelings.

It was three years since Hindley and I had parted, in the firm belief that we would see each other in a week or two, and be wed not long after. During all that time I had heard nothing from him, or even about him. What had he been told about me? Did he know I had lost our child, or even that I was still at Wuthering Heights? Would he be surprised to see me? How would he greet me? And how would three years at school have changed him? I had plenty to keep my mind occupied and my heart beating fast, and had Cathy and Heathcliff not taken on themselves the office of lookout, I would probably have been running back and forth to the top of the hill myself.

At last I heard Cathy's shrill call from the hilltop: 'I see him!'

I ran up to join them. The horse and cart were still only a speck in the distance, so far as I could see, but Heathcliff had the eyes of a hawk. He was peering intently at the speck, shading his eyes with his hands.

'There's someone with him,' he said.

'Probably a boy, to take the cart back after,' I said.

'No,' said Heathcliff, squinting intently, 'it's a woman.'

'A woman? How odd! Perhaps it's my mother,' I said.

By now Cathy was exclaiming that she saw her too, but my poorer eyesight could still make out nothing but a vague blur.

'Whoever she is, she's not your mother,' said Heathcliff. 'Too thin.'

'It's a lady!' Cathy interjected, hopping with excitement. 'She has a huge bonnet on, with a great big feather. I can see it from here!'

'Yes,' Heathcliff added, 'and she's leaning into him and hanging on his arm. Who do you suppose it can be?'

I had often heard the expression, 'his blood ran cold', but I never knew until that moment how precise a description it was. Dread washed through my veins like an icy bath. I forced myself to speak.

'We'll find out who it is soon enough,' I said brusquely. 'Meanwhile, I have work to do.' I turned to walk away.

'Oh, but Nelly, don't you want to see who it is? Whoever could it be? Could he be married? Don't you want to know?'

'It's nothing to me,' I said dully, and continued on my way. Hindley was bringing a woman home with him. She was dressed like a lady, and behaving as though she had some claim on him. What more did I need to know? I went into the kitchen, and looked about for something to do, but I could see nothing that appealed to me, and the presence of the other servants was oppressive. I wandered into the house, sat down, and took up some sewing, but my hands seemed made of lead. After a stitch or two, I laid it down, folded my hands in my lap, and tried to think. Hindley and his wife – or soon-to-be-wife, it hardly mattered which – were plodding towards the house. They would arrive in less than an hour. What was I to do?

While I was thus reflecting, the front door banged open, and Heathcliff dashed in.

'It's true!' he cried, 'Hindley's married, really and truly! The cart was plodding along at such a slow pace, we thought it would be an hour before we knew, so Cathy ran ahead to speak to them, and then ran back to tell me – what do you think of that?' He didn't wait for an answer, but turned and ran back through the door. It was just as well, for I could not have said a word.

His news did have the effect of lifting me out of my torpor, though. Whatever I thought or felt, one thing was certain: I needed to get away from the house, and everyone in it, immediately.

234

I felt a storm rising in my breast: dark clouds sweeping across the sky, the wind rising, and hints of thunder to come. Before it struck, I needed to be far away from curious eyes; I felt almost an animal instinct to flee. I grabbed my shawl and left through the back door, mumbling something about an errand. I heard some puzzled remarks, but I ignored them.

I bent my steps in the opposite direction from the Gimmerton road, towards the emptiest part of the moors, so I soon found myself on the path that led by Pennistone Crags to Penniton, the same I had walked with Hindley, three years before. Then it had been autumn too, and the sights and sounds and smells were so much the same, and brought back that walk so vividly before me, that it might have been three weeks earlier, instead of as many years. In defiance of my spirits, the weather was fair: cool and clear, with only a light breeze at my back ruffling the heather, and a thin scattering of wispy clouds high above, like brushstrokes across the vivid blue.

At first I felt only pain, my heart twisted into a hard knot that would scarcely let me breathe. I half ran, half walked along the path. I had just enough sense to get myself out of earshot of Wuthering Heights before I broke down and howled like a beast. I did not stop walking, though, I felt such urgency to get away, but stumbled forward, clutching my head and choking out tearless sobs. These and the exertion of walking gave me some relief at last, and I began to feel a measure of calm – enough, anyway, to begin picking apart the tangle of feelings that tormented me. Grief, anger, and shame were chief among them: grief at the final, decisive loss of all my dreams of a loving future with Hindley; anger at him for marrying in such haste without even waiting to see me, at the parents who had, I was now convinced, connived to keep us apart, and at myself, for harbouring hopes in spite of all my better judgement; most of all, a deep shame that my love, which I had been so sure he shared, could be spurned so casually. How arrogant my pretensions had been, and how foolish! For what was I, after all, but a plain-faced servant girl who had presumed too much on her early friendship with the heir, and imagined as some deathless love what was really only a childish fondness?

When I had left the house, I had felt that I was leaving for good. It did not seem possible that I could ever look Hindley in the face again, let alone take up my old duties in the daily presence of him and his wife. Now I began to think through my situation more carefully. Where was I to go? If I continued on the path to Penniton, I could stay with Mrs White for a day or two, but what then? Gossips in the neighbourhood would busy themselves with my sudden disappearance just when Hindley arrived with his new bride, and my absence from my late master's funeral tomorrow would be noted as well. They would draw the obvious conclusion, and I would not have even the comfort of knowing they were wrong. I could hardly seek a position in Gimmerton with that over my head, and I could not ask Hindley for a character that would enable me to seek work further off. My only choice would be to go to my mother in Brassing, and either work under her at the Thornes', or try to use their connection to find work in the town. But would they be willing to do even so much in my favour, with such a story as I would have to confess about my departure without giving notice? And the thought of turning to my mother for help was galling, when she was herself, in my eyes, one of the chief authors of my predicament. Nor would she stint in her condemnation of my foolishness, which would be hard to bear. As I turned these thoughts over in my head, I found my steps slowing. I was never a great judge of distance – looking at an object from afar, I could not tell you, as Hindley always could, if it was two miles off, or five, or ten. But a sure instinct always told me when I had gone as far from the Heights as I could go and still return by nightfall. I was approaching that point now. It was time to choose.

Looking back, I think that by the time I reached that point, I had already made my choice: I would return to Wuthering Heights, to hold my head high, defy Hindley and my shame both, and keep my place at least long enough to look about me, and decide what to do next. But I could not acknowledge that to myself then: instead, I began searching for more acceptable reasons to do what I secretly wished to do. First I castigated myself some more for my presumptions, and solemnly sentenced myself to the mortification of taking up my humble duties under the eyes of Hindley and his wife, without a word of reproach or complaint. Then I reminded myself of my concern for the children, and especially Heathcliff, who would now be at Hindley's mercy, and told myself that my prior good influence with both man and boy made it my duty to stay, and try to bring about peace between them. Finally, I reflected that the new Mrs Earnshaw would need guidance in learning how to run the household, and there was nobody fit to offer it but me. In short, I succeeded in making my return seem to myself an act of exemplary virtue and humility, when in truth it was compounded in equal parts of self-interest and pride. I turned round.

On the walk back, I focused on calming myself sufficiently to meet Hindley without emotion, and thinking up a plausible excuse for my absence. When I reached the house it was twilight, and the cart stood empty outside the stable – the horse having clearly been put away in the stable already, and the contents carried in. I took a deep breath and entered the back door, into the kitchen.

'Where have you been?' I was greeted by the little kitchen maid. 'The new master is here with his wife, and everyone wondered where you'd gone to!'

'Oh, I had no idea they would arrive so soon!' I said, affecting disappointment. 'I had promised Mrs Dagley a paper of needles – she had broken her last one, and she wanted to repair her husband's coat before the funeral tomorrow, so I walked over to bring them to her, and then of course she must tell me all about her health, you know how she goes on, and it was all I could do to prise myself away. I'm so sorry I missed their arrival! I suppose I must go in and present myself – are they in the house now, do you know?'

'Oh yes, they're drinking tea.'

I changed my apron for a clean one, and tidied myself up. Then I paused at the door. 'What is she like?' I asked.

'Very pretty and good-natured, and he is mad in love with her, it's clear. Such a happy couple they are!'

'Well, here goes then!' I said with a determined smile, and then, heart pounding, I took a deep breath and opened the door.

Hindley and a slight-looking, pretty young woman were sitting side by side on the sofa, tea things in front of them on a small table. He looked older: he had grown a beard, and had more of the gaunt look of his father about him than he had had. They were neither of them in mourning, I noted – indeed her clothes were garishly bright, adorned with a welter of ribbons and bows, and a wide collar of coarse home-made lace. His clothes looked new, but not well made – a wedding suit, I guessed, made quickly, and on the cheap. Cathy and Heathcliff were nowhere to be seen.

'Well, if it isn't Nelly Dean,' he said when he saw me, with a booming heartiness that sounded so false to me I wondered she wasn't made suspicious by it. 'Frances, my love, here is

Nelly, whom I told you about – the housekeeper, who comes a fixture with the house. And Nelly, let me introduce you to Mrs Earnshaw.' I coloured at 'fixture', but bit my tongue and managed a small curtsey in her direction. 'We were surprised to find you gone when we arrived,' Hindley went on in the same forced tone. 'I thought perhaps you'd decided to flit altogether!' He laughed as if this were a good joke.

'Now why ever would I do that?' I said evenly. 'It would scarcely be sensible.' His discomfiture was obvious, and my own anger was making me cool by comparison.

'But you're so young!' Mrs Earnshaw burst out. She turned to Hindley. 'The way you talked of her, dear, I thought she would be forty at least, but she is scarcely older than you!'

'Mr Hindley – forgive me, Mr Earnshaw, now – has been away so long, perhaps he confused me with my mother, who was housekeeper here before me.' It was a ridiculous suggestion, of course, and Hindley had the decency to blush at it, but his wife only looked puzzled.

'It has only been three years,' she said, looking at Hindley in confusion.

'Ah well,' I said, 'girls grow up fast in service, you know.' This was no more an explanation than my last, and Frances looked so befuddled that I decided she must be simple-minded. 'And now, if you don't mind, ma'am, I should be returning to my duties in the kitchen. What time will you be wanting supper?'

'Why, I . . . I don't know. When do you usually have it?'

'We always used to eat at four o'clock,' I said. 'But it is past that now.'

'Well, what would be . . . convenient, then?' She was so unsure of herself, I saw that she had never run a household before. She was looking for help from me, but I was damned if I would provide it. My good resolutions had all flown away.

'It is your convenience that matters, not mine,' I said.

'Would . . . eight o'clock be all right?' she asked tentatively.

'Eight it is,' I said.

'We'll have no more of servants and family all eating together,' Hindley interjected. 'I don't know what my father was thinking. This is a gentleman's family. The servants should eat in the kitchen by themselves after waiting on the family at table.'

'Very well, sir,' I replied, with just the faintest emphasis on the 'sir'. I turned and swept out of the room.

I am sure it was not charity that made Hindley speak to me, and of me, so insultingly, but he could hardly have devised a better method to enable me to keep a cool head through this first awkward meeting. I felt as if I had quaffed a long, refreshing draught of pure scorn for both of them: he was a narrow-minded arrogant oaf who had thrown me over for a shallow, pretty simpleton, like a child trading dull gold for a shiny piece of polished tin. A fine pair they would make at the funeral as representatives of an ancient family: she in her loud, cheap finery, and he in his ill-made suit! All the sobriety and respect at the event would have to be provided by the servants, clearly, and I told myself that I owed it to my late master to ensure that we did.

Back in the kitchen, I set to work to have dinner ready to serve by eight, which was less than an hour away. The kitchen maid, Maggie by name, had done much of the simpler preparation already, but she was only thirteen, and still new to her position, so there was plenty left to do. Maggie worked beside me, bouncing with childish excitement to talk of the new couple.

'So what do you think of them?' she asked. 'Isn't Mrs Earnshaw lovely? And her dress, so fine, too. And he seems a handsome man, and kind.'

'She is very pretty, certainly,' I said carefully. 'But I knew Hindley Earnshaw long before he went away to school – I grew up here, you know – so I can hardly have a first impression of him now.'

'Will he be a good master, do you think? My da always said that old Mr Earnshaw was a good master, for all he complained of him come rent time.'

'I am sure he will do his best,' I said. 'But he is a young man to be taking on such large responsibilities all of a sudden, and we must not expect the wisdom of age from him, just yet.'

'And her? She is so elegant, I'm sure she must be very clever.'

'Only time will tell,' I said, and turned my back to cut her off. I left it to her to wait on them at supper, too; I had no wish to experience any more of Hindley's insulting remarks, nor his wife's ignorant cheerfulness.

Grief inclines us towards sleep, I have found, even when we feel it so keenly that we imagine we will never sleep again. But anger is another matter. It quickens the heart and mind, courses through our veins like fire, and makes us too restless to lie still. Or at least, so I have always found it. I had thought I was ready enough for sleep when that eventful day came to an end, and I closed my door and blew out my candle with a sense of relief. But there was no rest for me. My mind was spinning round with Hindley's manner and Hindley's wife. I told myself that he had no right to treat me so, and I would not bear it, and so on in the same vein, but the more I travelled over this ground, the more sleep receded from me. At last I grew weary of my own anger, so I got up and crept downstairs to relight my candle at the banked embers of the fire. I brought it back to my room, and opened my copy of *Paradise Lost*, the only book I owned.

I read over again, as I had many times before, my favourite part: the stirring tale of Satan's defiance, his rebellion against the Most High, and his establishment with his fellow rebels of the territory of Hell. I had sometimes thought before that Milton perhaps erred in making Satan such a thrilling figure, that his speeches were too powerful, too compelling, for a book written to glorify the Lord. But this time I understood at last that Milton had meant for us to be drawn to Satan, so that we might recognize in ourselves the seeds of rebellion against God, and see clearly whither they would lead us. I myself, I realized, had been all too ready to overthrow all right order, and make a Hell of the place I had thought would be my Heaven. Hindley was married, and not to me. What cause for outrage was there in that? Had he not been sent away by his father to prevent precisely that? I could not even know what his father had told him on the occasion: probably he had impressed upon him deeply that the marriage was degrading and wrong; perhaps he had even made him promise never to marry me. Could I blame Hindley for endeavouring to please his father in that, if in nothing else? And if, alone and far from home, cut off from friends and family alike, he had fallen in love with a pretty girl who was kind to him, what mystery was there in that, and what wrong?

Now my thoughts turned to our reunion, and for the first time I tried to think of it from Hindley's perspective. How awkward for him it must have been, to bring a wife home and introduce her to a servant with whom he had such a history as he had with me! Small wonder he had spoken of me as if I were a much older woman. And as for calling me a 'fixture', might that not be his way of telling me I was free to stay if I wished? Many a man in his situation would have dismissed me forthwith, and many a new mistress might do the same, on mere suspicion, but he had called me a 'fixture', as though to say, 'Nelly is here to stay; you must accustom yourself to that.'

If his manner towards me was a little rough, a little slighting, as it surely was, what was that but his awkwardness, and his uncertainty as to what he could expect from me? And what help had I given him, after all, in that difficult circumstance?

By the time I had closed *Paradise Lost*, and put it back on my little shelf, it lacked but an hour or two of dawn, and I had brought myself to what I hoped was a better frame of mind than that with which I had retired to bed. I had recovered the good intentions with which I had returned from my walk the previous day, but with more sincerity and true humility, and a firmer grasp on my duty, than I had had then. Or so I believed. The truth is that I trod this same path, or one very like it, many times over the months and years that followed.

FIFTEEN

Well, the young couple made a better showing for the funeral than I expected. The mistress had her little fit of hysterics about the preparation, as I told you before, but at the event itself they were both in mourning clothes, at least, and treating the occasion with the solemnity it required. Hindley's suit looked worn and a little tight, which puzzled me. I later learned that he had been forwarded funds, via the cousins in York, to buy a full suit of mourning, but had used them instead to buy a wedding suit, and have his old one dyed black. Her dress looked older too, and grey rather than black, though sober enough in style. I thought that perhaps she had bought it second-hand, but she told me, as we walked beside the coffin to the churchyard, that it had been bought at her mother's death, two years earlier.

'I was sorry not to be wearing it when we arrived yesterday,' she confided, 'but it is my only one, and I was so afraid it would get soiled or torn on the journey, and not be able to be made ready for the funeral today. Hindley says he does not like to see me in mourning, anyway,' she added. 'He says he does not see why I should wear black for a man I never met, and whose loss I can scarcely mourn. And I do have a horror of black, as you saw yesterday. But I told him I must wear grey

at least, so that I would not be made a byword in the neighbourhood at the start, by not showing proper respect.'

'That was very right of you,' I said, as she obviously expected.

At the service itself, Mrs Earnshaw showed so much respect
that she even contrived to weep – in sorrow, she said, that she
had never had an opportunity to meet such an estimable father.
Hindley seemed less than grief-stricken on the occasion, but
that was hardly surprising, considering how his father had
generally treated him, and I could not hold it against him. I
myself wept copiously, to the great annoyance of Joseph, who
continued to insist loudly that no grief was needed for a man
who had gone to his reward, and was now a saint in Heaven.

Both Dr Kenneths, father and son, were present at the service,
Bodkin with his new wife at his side. The elder came up to
Hindley afterwards, to offer his condolences, but Hindley
himself sought out Bodkin, clapped him on the back, and
introduced him to Mrs Earnshaw – grinning broadly the whole
time, in defiance of the sadness of the occasion. I was not near
enough to hear what was said, but I guessed by their gestures
that Bodkin was giving the news of his own marriage, and
receiving his friend's congratulations thereupon, while the two
wives made each other's acquaintance.

Afterwards, as the crowd dispersed, I remained in the churchyard, to look at Mrs Earnshaw's gravestone, to which her
husband's name and dates were soon to be added, and the sad
little row of stones that marked their dead children. Then I
wandered over to visit the far corner where my father was
buried, under a stone much larger and more ornate than his
circumstances might seem to warrant, which had been paid
for by the Thornes. Bodkin soon joined me there.

'It is a sad day for you,' he said.

'Yes,' I said, 'for all of us. But it had been coming on a long time. And Mr Earnshaw is with his wife now, whom he loved so – I suppose we ought not to grieve for that.'

'And the new master has a wife now too. That must have been a great surprise.'

I looked at him quickly, wondering if he meant anything more than usual by the remark, but his face showed nothing. 'It was unexpected, certainly,' I said carefully. 'But Mr Earnshaw can do as he likes now, I suppose, and his wife seems a good creature. He is certainly very fond of her.' Then I thought to turn the conversation. 'I did not think you owned a mourning suit,' I said. 'I hope you have not had a death in the family?'

'Oh no, it is only for funerals. It was the first thing my father gave me, when I came back ready to take up my own practice. He said he always attends his patients' funerals, unless he is called away on some emergency, and that I should do the same. "It shows that you care about them as more than a piece of medical business," he said, "and that you are confident you did your best for them."'

'That sounds very wise.'

'It is indeed, though I'm not always sure I share his confidence in my own performance. But when I don't, there is no better place than the funeral to reflect on my mistakes, and resolve to do better in future.'

'And how is marriage agreeing with you? I saw you introducing your wife to Mrs Earnshaw.'

'Oh, marriage is a highly agreeable institution, I find, particularly if one has the sense to choose a pretty and sensible girl.'

'And if one can convince the pretty and sensible girl to accept, I suppose.'

'Yes, I have been fortunate in that.'

'And how are your father and Tabby taking to the change?'

'Father is delighted. He likes Anna very well, and loves having a little more life in the house, as he says. Tabby was rather more put out than I expected, just at first, but Anna is so kind to her, and defers to her so about everything in the household that now she is as fond of her as the rest of us.'

'Well, I suppose I must take a lesson from that, not to be too put out by my new mistress,' I said. 'She seems well-intentioned enough, but I don't know that she's had much experience in running a household.'

'Very little, I would guess,' said Bodkin. 'But she cannot do better than to consult with you about it. If you like I will say something to Anna to that effect, and I am sure she will pass it on. Mrs Earnshaw seems eager to pursue the acquaintance.'

'That's very kind of you,' I said, 'but I'm sure it won't be necessary. Did you find out anything about her family, by the way? She said nothing except that she lost her mother two years ago, and we are all rather curious, the more so since Hindley kept the marriage from his father.'

'She said nothing to me, nor did Hindley – it was only a brief conversation. But I should tell you, anything I discover later will likely come under the doctor's seal, as she will be my patient.'

'What, is she with child already?' I asked – not without a certain unchristian thrill, I must confess.

'Oh no, but surely you can see it?'

'See what? She seems well enough, a little slight, but with good colour in her cheeks.'

'Ah yes, I forget not everyone sees with a doctor's eyes. Let's just say that I'm not as convinced of her good health as you are, but I hope I am wrong.'

I tried to prise more out of him, but he met me with a firm, polite resistance that I soon realized would not budge. Whatever rights to confidence our long friendship had given me, I saw, his medical principles were stronger. I was glad to see it, actually, though it disappointed me in this instance. Who knew what future confidences I might need him to keep?

At this point we spied his wife heading in our direction, and Bodkin moved off to join her.

'Come meet my wife,' he said to me.

I laughed. 'I know her already,' I said. 'You forget that for many years I was chief errand-girl to the apothecary shop.' All the same I went with him.

'Ah, you knew Miss Anna Smythe, but you have never met Mrs Robert Kenneth. She is a different personage entirely.' We had joined Mrs Kenneth by then, and Bodkin performed the introduction with the greatest formality.

'Good day, Mrs Kenneth, I am very pleased to make your acquaintance,' I said with a curtsey.

Mrs Kenneth looked puzzled. 'But we have met already, surely – aren't you Nelly Dean?' She looked at her husband. 'Is this one of your jokes? Am I to pretend that I don't know her?' She seemed very eager to please, but uncertain of what was wanted. Bodkin and I both hastened to reassure her that nothing was expected of her.

'My wife is unaccustomed to life with a comedian,' Bodkin explained. 'I am forever discomfiting her with my poor attempts at wit.'

'I am very glad that you can find so much to laugh about,' she said. 'There is so much that is serious in a doctor's work, and so many occasions for sadness' – here Bodkin gestured towards his clothes, in confirmation of her words – 'I am sure that relief is very welcome. It is only that I often have a hard time telling when you are serious, and when you are not.'

'I shall get a little flag to keep in my pocket,' Bodkin said. 'I can pull it out and wave it when I am not serious, so you will always know. Let me see, what colour shall it be? Not red certainly, that would send the wrong message, nor white either.'

'Motley, of course,' I said.

'Yes, motley! I shall keep a motley flag in my pocket – or better yet, perhaps a fool's motley cap, with bells, that I can clap on my head. How would that be, my dear?'

Mrs Kenneth smiled. 'I know you are joking now, about the cap at any rate. It would never fit in your pocket, and it would look very silly anyway, to be always taking it on and off. I wish I could have the flag – it would be a great help to me. But I ought to learn for myself, really, since it pleases you so, and I should like to do whatever pleases you.'

I saw a brief flicker of sadness in Bodkin's face. 'What would please me most would be to make you laugh yourself, without feeling it your duty to do so,' he said. 'It's a poor kind of wit that is only laughed at from a sense of duty. No, it is my job to find what will make you laugh, not yours to laugh at what doesn't amuse you.'

'Between Dr Kenneth's determination to amuse, and Mrs Kenneth's determination to be amused, I am sure you both will soon be laughing all day long,' I said. 'I shall take it upon myself to sew you a little motley flag, as a wedding present. And may you never know worse strife in marriage than the puzzle of how much to laugh, and when.' I made my goodbyes then, and set off back to Wuthering Heights. The conversation had made me a little sad, though whether it was for Bodkin or myself, I could not have told you.

The will was read the next day. After a legacy of thirty pounds to Joseph and ten to me, it left everything to Hindley, but charged him with supplying Cathy with five hundred pounds on her marriage, and with providing 'a suitable education' for

Heathcliff. My heart sank at the vague words, and Hindley snorted.

'Suitable,' he said under his breath. 'Yes, I'll suit him. He'll get a thoroughly suitable education from me.'

Cathy pouted and Heathcliff scowled, but there was no further discussion with the solicitor present. I only hoped that the responsibilities of marriage and mastership would mature and settle Hindley's character, and that his largely unencumbered inheritance would soften his resentment of Heathcliff. It didn't, as it turned out, but you knew that already.

I had my first trial of all my good resolutions, not long after the funeral. Hindley was spending a good deal of time out-of-doors, walking the land with Joseph – consulting him, he said, but I suspect it was mostly to bask in his new sense of possession. His wife moped about the house, looking bored. For a week after the funeral, she was in daily expectation of 'callers' from town, and was quite cast down when they failed to appear. Finally she made mention of it to me.

'How am I to know whom I should visit,' she asked, 'if no one comes to visit me?'

'We are too far out for casual visiting, ma'am,' I explained. 'People don't come out here, generally, unless they have some reason to.'

'But I am the new mistress of Wuthering Heights,' she said. 'I should think that would be reason enough, don't you think? They should all wish to meet me.'

'They have mostly met you at church, already,' I said. 'And if they haven't, they will have an opportunity next week, or the week after. Folk are in no hurry, here, to expand their acquaintances.'

'But what do the ladies do all day, if they do not pay calls, and receive callers in turn? What did Hindley's mother do?'

'I can't speak of the ladies in Gimmerton,' I said, 'but Mrs Earnshaw always had plenty to do, what with teaching the children, helping the poor in the neighbourhood, sewing, looking after her poultry and her garden, and so on. She would go into Gimmerton now and again, when she had errands there, and while she was there she would call on her friends, but that was not above once in a month, and less in winter.'

Mrs Earnshaw looked crestfallen. 'I can't teach the children,' she said. 'They are too big and too wild for me to manage, and anyway Hindley said that the curate has them in hand. As for the poultry: the hens seem nice enough, but the rooster tried to peck me, and the geese are so fierce, I am afraid to go near them. And I hate paddling in the dirt.'

I assured her that the rooster and the geese would be less threatening, once they knew she belonged to the household, and that there was no need for her to work in the garden, if she didn't like it.

'But what do you mean by helping the poor? We used to have beggars come to the back door, sometimes, and Mother would give them some food, if we had any to spare, but I have not seen any beggars here.'

'We don't get beggars here much, for the same reason we don't get visitors,' I said. 'We are too far from town. But we have poor folk who live here, in our own cottages – decent, hard-working people, for the most part, who yet cannot make ends meet, for one reason or another, and the mistress always did what she could for them.'

'What sort of things?'

'Well, she had a little chest of infants' clothes, that she would keep in good repair, and bring by when someone had a new baby. When they are that small, you know, they grow out of clothes faster than you can make them, and it's a great expense to keep making new. There is a christening dress in there too, quite a nice one that she worked herself. The mothers keep the chest for the first three or four months – sometimes longer, if they can – and then it comes back here to be furbished up for the next baby.'

'Where is the chest now?'

'Out with Mrs Hearne – she had her third child last month. I kept it up myself after the mistress died, as best I could. I had less time to spare, though, and I'm not so fine a needle-woman as she was. Shall I give it to you, when it comes back?'

'I suppose so,' she said doubtfully. 'What else did she do?'

'Oh the usual: bring food and medicine for the sick, give out flannel in winter where it was needed, that sort of thing. Oftentimes she would bring some small children home here for a day or two, if the mother was sick or injured and there were no older children to look after them. She liked having little children about, if they were not too noisy.'

'But how did she know what was needed?'

'From the servants, generally. Most of them don't live here, you know, but only come in by day from nearby cottages. It's really only Joseph and I that live here, for the most part.'

'So I am not to go visiting, and find out the news of the town from my equals, but instead my servants are to bring me news of their people, so that I can act as dressmaker, nurse, and nurserymaid to them? It does not seem very ladylike to me.'

I was annoyed, in spite of all my good resolutions.

'You asked me what my late mistress did, ma'am, so I told you,' I said. 'You are mistress here now, and can do as you think best. But I will say that Mrs Earnshaw was loved and admired by all who knew her, your husband included, and no one ever thought she was less than a lady because she cared for those who were worse off than she, instead of running off to town every day to gossip.'

She had the sense to look a little abashed at this, and I regretted my strong words.

'You must remember that during the time I knew her, Mrs Earnshaw had always her own children to look after,' I added more gently, 'to teach and to guide and to set a good example for, and of course they were her main concern, and took most of her time. Perhaps she had more time for visiting her friends before then – I couldn't say, for that was before my time here. When your own children come along, your duties will expand accordingly.'

'Of course they will,' she pouted. 'And in the meantime I have a duty to make acquaintance with the better class of my neighbours, I think. Hindley's mother grew up in the neighbourhood, he told me, so of course she already knew everybody, but it is different for me.'

'You are the best judge of that,' I said.

'But give me the chest when it comes back,' she added, 'and I will look it over and see what needs to be done. It will be good practice for making my own baby clothes in time. And if you hear of any beg— any poor cottagers who need something, will you tell me? Then we can consult about what to do, maybe. I shall rely on your advice a good deal, Nelly, you know. I have a feeling you and I are to be great friends, for all I am your mistress.'

I was resolved that she would be nothing of the sort, but I told her I was happy to advise her as to what was needed for the poor, though I rather suspected I would end up furnishing a good deal more than advice in that area. This proved to be the case – Mrs Earnshaw preferred to let me be the one to visit the poor in their cottages, talk with them, and deliver whatever little things would ease their difficulties. I had been doing this already, since the mistress died, so it was no addition to my duties – besides which I liked the walks, and the chance to gossip, and the gratification of being able to confer benevolence at my master's expense. And it made me popular with the tenants. Whatever I gained by it, though, she lost – at least as regarded the respect of the tenantry and the neighbourhood at large. It did not go unnoticed that she 'would not take the trouble' to attend to her charities herself, but delegated a servant to do them for her.

To fulfil her self-imposed duty of amusing herself with constant visits in town, Mrs Earnshaw convinced Hindley that she needed a pony chaise of her own, which he willingly provided. And then, when, on the return from her first foray in this vehicle, the staid little pony broke into a trot unbidden, in its eagerness to be home, she grew frightened, and decided she also needed a boy to drive for her. I made an effort to get Heathcliff to take on this duty, thinking it would please him and build goodwill between them, but she declined to be driven by him, and Heathcliff also objected, so one of the other farm lads was pressed into service instead, to his great amusement, for as he said, he had never heard of anyone needing a coachman for a pony chaise before. In this contraption, Mrs Earnshaw made it her business to go to town some three or four days a week, to shop and pay visits.

All of this cost money, of course. Mrs Earnshaw, to her credit, at least declined Hindley's proposal to redecorate the house and fit up a parlour for her, saying she liked everything just as it was. But still there was the pony and chaise, and the boy to drive it, and then she spent a great deal on millinery, and had expensive consultations with a dressmaker at regular intervals, to have made up all the finest possible gradations of her

254

mourning. Hindley in turn laid in a large stock of French wines and fine brandy, to establish 'a proper gentleman's cellar', and then had to hire a carpenter to fit up shelves to hold them, and a locksmith to fit a lock to the door, though none of us were like to steal it. Then Mrs Earnshaw evinced a dislike to porridge, and so that staple was banished to the servants' table and the nursery, while the master and mistress ate fine white bread and rolls, fetched twice a week from the bakery in Gimmerton.

The late master had been a saving man. Like all people, great and small, who derive their livelihood from the land, he well knew what a few bad harvests could do to the household finances. He also had a healthy horror of debt, having seen many times how the first easy steps in that direction could lead inexorably down to ruin. The estate yielded little to spare above household expenses, but that little went to the bank, with the aim of maintaining there a sum that could tide us over any lean years to come. The income from the estate had suffered somewhat during the master's final illness, when he could not see to things himself, but Joseph had tightened his fist on household expenditures accordingly, and we had all dined on porridge and roast onions, while the mutton went to market. As a result, there was still a good sum of money in the bank, even after the legacies had been paid. A sensible man would have left it there until he learned how to add to it, or at the very least set aside the sum that would be due to Cathy on her marriage. But Hindley had always been under such constraint, he was like a dog kept on a short chain, who suddenly finds a link give way, and takes off like a hare, determined to make up for a lifetime's captivity all at once.

I said nothing. I had concluded that both duty and interest bade me confine myself to the work I was paid to do, to give advice only if it was asked for, and not involve myself in

255

concerns that were nothing to do with me. Of course, now would have been the time to give my notice and start seeking another position, while Hindley was still feeling generous with his love and his money and his freedom. Yet I kept finding one reason after another to put it off a little further. Had you asked me then why I stayed, I would have given you one or another of these reasons, in the full conviction that they were all that motivated me, but the truth was that I did not want to leave. Not that I was happy there, particularly, nor that I could not see trouble coming – I would have had to be blind not to – but I had come to feel, deep in my heart, that my fate was bound up in that of Wuthering Heights and its family, and all my bitter experience had yet to shake that feeling.

Not long after Hindley's return, my mother came to visit us for the first time since that ill-fated Christmas, three years before. She came officially to visit Hindley and meet his new wife, but she had another purpose that became evident as soon as she had me alone.

'Leave their service, Nell,' she said.

'Why should I?' I said, my heart beating faster. 'I couldn't get so good a position elsewhere, at my age.'

'You could, in fact. There's a wool merchant's family in Brassing now, looking for a housekeeper, who'd count themselves lucky to get you, knowing me as they do. You'll get better wages and better treatment there, for they know the value of an intelligent and honest housekeeper, and being in trade themselves, they don't expect to get more than they pay for.' But when she saw me looking stubborn, she put her hands on my shoulders and spoke more seriously: 'Hindley's married, Nell. What was between you is over and done. You'll do no good to them here, nor they to you, if you stay. There's no worse sin you can do than to come between man and wife.'

'Come between them!' I cried hotly. 'What are you accusing me of? I could no more come between them than I could between a dog and his skin! Hindley hovers over her as if he was her cloak, and he scarcely speaks to me but to complain I'm not waiting on Her Ladyship fast enough.' I was fighting to keep back tears, now, but I'd rather have died than show my mother that, and to hide it I showed her so sullen and defiant a face you might have mistaken me for Cathy, or Heathcliff himself.

'Hush,' she said sharply. 'Nelly, you well know what I mean. There are things between you and Hindley that he can't share with his wife.'

'Which is true whether I'm here or not.'

'But which your being here keeps always before him.'

'If he doesn't like it, he can give me notice.'

'He won't. You know that. He could never find another housekeeper to do all that you do here, for double your wages, or treble even. I'd guess he doesn't pay you the whole of what he owes you now, does he?' I looked down and said nothing, but the colour that rose in my face gave away my answer surely enough. Recently, Hindley had given me only about a third of my wages in money, and the rest in his note of hand, and managing the household accounts as I did, I couldn't see how he was like to do better, or as well, in future.

'Do you want to become like old Joseph, hoarding up the lengthening score of your unpaid wages, and fancying yourself rich because you have what can do you no good in this world or the next?'

'So that's what he keeps in that old Bible of his!' I cried, glad enough to find something to laugh about, and change the subject. 'He won't let anyone else touch it, Mother, but snatches it away, mumbling that he's been a "servant of servants, and laid by treasure in Heaven".' I declare, he's gone mad, and thinks he'll collect his unpaid wages after death!'

'It wouldn't surprise me, though I doubt the final reckoning there will be much to his liking,' she said. 'But you're the last one ought to laugh at him, Nelly, when you're headed down the same road yourself.' Her words stung, more than I liked. The truth was that I'd treasured Hindley's note of hand more than I ever had my wages, because it held him to me, will he or nill he, and I'd imagined myself, a year or two hence, with a handful more to add to it, maybe giving me a bit more respect in the household. I didn't like to compare those thoughts to the picture of old Joseph clutching his Bible and mumbling his strange toothless mixtures of prayers and curses at us all.

So I dropped that subject, and instead began trotting out all the reasons I had been telling over to myself, for why I ought to stay. I spoke of my fears for how Heathcliff would fare under Hindley's authority, and recalled the master's request to me to look out for him, which I described as a deathbed promise from me to him; I mentioned the new mistress's ignorance of housekeeping and her reliance on my judgement, and my new role as her almoner among the poor in the neighbourhood. I represented to her more generally how careless both she and Hindley were of household expenses, and hinted at how easy it would be for a new housekeeper, with no ties of duty or affection to the family, to take advantage of their carelessness, and line her own pockets at their expense.

'In short, you have no intention of leaving, whatever I may say,' said my mother irritably.

I opened my mouth to deny this, stopped, and then shut it again. If she ordered me to leave, would I obey her? And if not, why encourage her to try? I looked steadily at my feet. 'I think it is right for me to stay,' I said softly.

My mother sighed. 'I don't think it is right at all,' she said, but there was no argument in her voice. 'I suppose I ought not to be angry that you are eager to stay where you know you are needed, and that you see a duty here. And if I thought duty was all your motive, I would be at peace with it, though I still think you could do a great deal better elsewhere. But it is not all your motive, is it?'

I continued to stare at my feet. My face was burning, and I felt tears welling in my eyes. 'It is,' I insisted. 'The rest – all that, you know – it's over now. I swear it is.' I made myself look her in the eyes. 'I have learned my lesson; I know my place now.'

'It's only your place whilst you are here, Nelly,' she said gently. 'Among manufacturing people, places are not so fixed. Why, thirty years ago I would have considered Mrs Thorne my inferior, and her husband was your father's playmate in youth, as you know. Now she is my mistress, and could easily place herself as above me, yet I count her my friend, and she treats me as an equal. You would make your own place there. And you're a comely lass yet, Nell: it wouldn't surprise me, in a few years, to see you mistress of a snug household of your own.'

'I don't want that,' I said miserably.

'You think not, now, Nelly, but give yourself time. I won't tell you to leave, but think about it. Remember that you can give your notice at any time, and come to Brassing to find a new place.'

'I will,' I promised, with as much conviction as I could muster. Then I turned back to my work, relieved to have the conversation over with.

*

Mrs Earnshaw's taste for visiting in Gimmerton abated a good deal after Cathy's five weeks' residence at Thrushcross Grange, that I told you of before, brought the family into regular communication with the Lintons. They were the first family of the neighbourhood – a good deal wealthier than the Earnshaws, though the family name was not so ancient – and Mrs Earnshaw had longed to be on visiting terms with them. But she had received no encouragement in that direction until Cathy fell into their hands and Mrs Linton decided to make a project out of 'civilizing' her. This could not be accomplished without the connivance of her female guardian, of course, and so Mrs Linton was obliged to draw Mrs Earnshaw into her circle of acquaintances.

That she did so with some reluctance I found out a few weeks after Cathy's return home. Heathcliff had just been beaten and sent off supperless to sleep in the cold stable for some fancied 'insolence of manner' towards Mrs Earnshaw. Cathy was ordered to remain in the house, but she refused to stay in the room with the master and mistress, and soon crept into the kitchen to complain to me. She got my sympathy readily enough – I felt Heathcliff's wrongs hardly less keenly than she did – but when she tried to parlay that into permission to sneak out to the stable and visit him, I had to say no.

'My instructions were very clear, miss, that I was to bid you stay with me if you would not sit with them, and that if you attempted to go out, I should bar the door, and call out to them straight away. I let you go once before, you recall, and got in a peck of trouble for it when Hindley found out. If I do it again, I might lose my place.'

'But why should he find out? I would be gone only a few minutes. He'll never notice.'

'You said that last time, too, but you were gone an hour, and we both got caught. I'm sorry, but I just can't risk it again.'

260

Cathy crossed her arms and scowled. 'I hate them both,' she announced. 'An "insolent manner" indeed! What is that? And who is she, anyway, that Heathcliff should bow and scrape to her?'

'The mistress of the house,' I said reprovingly, 'and the person most concerned with helping you grow up to be a lady, so you both owe her some deference.'

'She is no lady, really, or so the Lintons said. I overheard them talking once, when they didn't know I was near, and Mrs Linton called her "a vulgar little thing, with no family and no manners", and said she hated to encourage her, but she had no choice if she wished to help me. I've a good mind to throw that in Hindley's face, next time he goes after Heathcliff for not showing her enough respect.'

'You'll do nothing of the kind, if you have any sense at all,' I said vehemently. 'It's a cruel thing to say, and would wound her deeply. And she has been such a good friend to you too, these past few weeks – just think of that new bonnet and gloves she bought you, only last week.'

'I don't care what she buys me,' said Cathy, 'she's no friend of mine if she's not a friend to Heathcliff, too, and she isn't – she only encourages Hindley to hate him more. And he is so high and mighty now, it would do him good to be taken down a peg.'

'It would do no good at all,' I said angrily, 'and if you won't hold back for her sake, then do it for Heathcliff's. If you humiliate Hindley and make him angry on his wife's behalf, he'll only take it out on Heathcliff, as he always does, and you'll have no one but yourself to blame.' This argument seemed to strike her better than my other, and she promised to keep her information to herself. I had little hope that she would keep to her resolve, though. She was so little accustomed to controlling her impulses that this nasty bit of gossip was like a charge of gunpowder, that needed only a spark to set it off – and they flew all too frequently in our volatile household.

Sure enough, not a week had gone by before Hindley again seized some trifling excuse to punish Heathcliff, and then, when Cathy rose up to defend her favourite, declared him 'not fit to be under the same roof as ladies, even as a servant'. I saw in her face what she was about to do, and sent her a stern look and a tiny shake of my head as warning, but it was no use. The bomb was exploded, and Mrs Linton's cruel words were repeated in detail.

When she was finished, Mrs Earnshaw's eyes widened, and then she flushed deeply and looked down at her sewing. She tried to act as though she had not heard, but I could see that she was fighting off tears. Hindley stopped dead, and the colour drained from his face. Then he slowly raised his hand and slapped Cathy sharply across the cheek.

'You are a poisonous little bitch,' he said coldly, and slammed out of the house.

Cathy stood still a moment in shock – Hindley had never struck her before – and then burst into tears and ran to kneel in front of her sister-in-law, who by now was sobbing likewise.

'I didn't mean it!' she cried miserably. 'I never meant to say it, and it's not even true! Oh, I wish I could take it all back!'

'Well, you can't,' I said angrily, and I turned on my heel and left them to give each other what comfort they could.

Hindley did not return that night, but Cathy crept into the kitchen about an hour later, still red-eyed and pale, to ask for some hot milk. I complied, for I was glad to see her so contrite, but as soon as she was recovered a little, she was back to her old ways.

'I wish you had stopped me, Nelly,' she said peevishly. 'Why didn't you?'

'Stop you!' I cried. 'Good heavens, miss, have I the government of your tongue? If you can't heed your own conscience at such times, you certainly won't heed mine. Why I've a good mind to slap you myself, for even suggesting it!'

'But I can't help it!' she wailed. 'When I get angry like that, I act without thinking.'

'That is because you have no training in self-control,' I said sternly. 'If you would practise self-denial in small things, every day, you would be better able to hold yourself back, when it is a matter of consequence. That is what your mother would have taught you, were she still alive, as my mother taught me.'

'I don't want a lecture from you, Nelly.'

'Well if you won't listen to sense from me, then don't expect me to prevent you from acting foolishly, that's all I can say.'

SIXTEEN

It was not long after this that Hindley began to feel straitened as to money. I had begun keeping the household accounts, as I told you before, though they were still nominally in Mrs Earnshaw's hands, so it was easy to see that the money was flowing out at a higher rate than it ever had before, but that was only half the difficulty. Hindley appeared to think that the rents due to him from the tenants would roll in like magic whenever they were due, without any effort on his part, but of course they did nothing of the sort. I was surprised at his ignorance, for we had both heard enough from our hideaway in 'the robbers' cave' to get some idea of the effort required to get anything like the full value of the rents from the tenants. But apparently only one of us had learned from what we had heard.

The late Mr Earnshaw had taken the time to know his tenants well: their characters, the size of their families, the yields of their plantings and livestock, and all the yearly ups and downs of their prosperity. When, as often happened, one or more of his tenants came into his office to confess that they could not make up the full sum of their rent, he knew how to tailor his response to each individual circumstance. One man he might berate for improvidence, and ask him, if he had not the money for rent, why had his wife come to church last week in a new bonnet so resplendent it made Mrs Linton blush? If he had not the cash to pay his rent today, he would be told, he must send over the fat pig he had been rearing all summer, to make up the difference, and when his family sat down to their Sunday dinner of plain porridge, they could put the bonnet in the centre of the table, where the roast would have been, as a lesson to them all. But then, when the reluctantly surrendered pig had been slaughtered, the master would like as not send me over with a quarter of it to return to its original owners, to soften the bitterness of the appropriation. Another man, blessed with a large and increasing family that threatened to outgrow his ability to feed it, might be told to send a couple of his older children over to help out at the Heights, where they would get their dinner and some wages to help make up the shortfall, and might learn something of farm or household management at the same time. We usually had two or three such lads or lasses about, of varying degrees of usefulness, in light servitude for their parents' debts.

The tenants liked to grumble at the adroitness of this approach, and among themselves they called him Squire Hide-th'-ham, joking that if he walked into their cottage of a Sunday and saw a roast on the table, he would be sure to tuck it under his arm and take it away with him, in lieu of back rent. But they knew he was a just man, and always charitable to the truly unfortunate. He was conscientious, too, about encouraging improvements, and a tenant who came to him with a proposition for rebuilding a barn or shed, or adding a room to his house, could be confident of having a large portion of his expenses applied against the rent.

During Mr Earnshaw's illness, these duties had devolved

onto Joseph, who had none of his master's subtlety in judgement, let alone his charity. His uniform response to any shortfall in payment was to harangue the offending tenant as a liar and a thief, and threaten him with eviction and damnation both, those apparently being equivalent punishments in his eyes, and equally in his power to administer. And he did indeed evict two of the tenants, and would have evicted a third, a good steady man who had suffered extraordinary reverses in just one season, had I not gone behind his back to the master to appeal for clemency. But of the two cottages that were vacated, only one had been let again, and that at a reduced rent, for the evictees had spread the story of their harsh treatment throughout the neighbourhood, and frightened away potential tenants.

This then was the state of affairs when Hindley came into his estate. At first Hindley left the rent collection to Joseph, not wishing to take the trouble himself, but when this failed to yield the expected sums, he decided to look into the matter.

'I have been looking over the rent-book,' he announced one evening, as Frances and I both sat by the fire in the house – she had called me in to keep her company – I knitting a stocking, and she working on some embroidery. 'It is plain that things have been going downhill since Joseph began collecting the rents – why fully a third of the tenants are in arrears, I find, and some by almost a year! And there is one cottage that has been sitting empty for nine months now, that ought to have paid three pounds in that time!'

I explained about the evicted tenants.

'Well it is no use evicting people, if you have no one to take their place. You will never get back the rent they owe, once they are gone, and then if the place stays vacant, you are worse off than ever! I wonder Joseph didn't show more sense.'

I opened my mouth to tell him that if no one was ever to be evicted, it might be rather harder to convince the tenants that the rent must be paid, but thought better of it. Why should I defend Joseph to Hindley?

'You should talk to the tenants on rent-day yourself, dear,' said Frances. 'They all respect you so much, I am sure, much more than they do that horrible old man.'

'I believe I shall. I am master here now, and it is time I took things into my own hands. If a man cannot pay me what he owes me, let him look me in the eye and tell me so: that will put a different complexion on it, you may be sure.'

We got our first taste of the effectiveness of Hindley's methods the following rent-day. Two or three of the best tenants had always made a point of paying their rent a day early – to avoid the ruckus, they said – and Mr Earnshaw had been in the habit of rewarding them by inviting them into the house to take a cup of tea or a glass of cowslip wine with himself and the mistress. This privilege was highly valued, and such tenants often brought their wives with them to share in it. The custom had been kept up even after the mistress's death, when it fell nominally to Cathy, but really to me, to pour the refreshments and assist in entertaining the wives, and it had only fallen into abeyance when the master fell ill.

Sure enough, the day before rent-day brought one of our best farmers to the Heights in the early afternoon. His wife was with him, dressed in her Sunday finery, so evidently they were in hopes the old custom would be revived. Hindley hurried to the old office to receive him, but when they emerged a few minutes later, the man was dismissed with little more than a curt nod at him and his wife. I tried to make up for it by being as hospitable as my position allowed, which is to say that I invited them into the kitchen for a cup of tea and a slice of seed cake. They came willingly enough, but it was evident that they were rather put out.

'Ey'll tell tha soomthing, Nelly lass,' the farmer said, when they were settled with their tea, 'a mon dusn't loyke et mooch, when hoo comes early to pay hoos rent in good gold an' siller, an' not in hanks o' homespun or baskets o' eggs as soom folk mun do, an' when hoo has not shorted a farthin' of hoos rent these last five year or more, to hev the maister look back through the rent-book groombling, an' make oot the receipt at last, as though hoo were sorry not to find ony arrears to charge hoo with, an' be sent awa' loyke ony other mon, without so mooch as a handshake.'

'Not to mention which hoos wife has coom with oom to pay her respects to the new missus,' his wife interjected, 'and given up a good half-day's worth o' work to do it, an' is sent to the kitchen instead, which I mean tha no disrespect, Nelly, for tha knows I'm always happy to see tha, lass, but it isn't right, is it?'

I soothed them as best I could, reminded them that Hindley was new to his duties, and predicted that he would not be long in recognizing the value of such excellent tenants as themselves. They went away somewhat appeased, but still grumbling, and I sighed to think of how far their story would spread, before a week was out.

The next day brought the bulk of the tenants, to pay what they could, and explain what they could not. Hindley duly established himself in the office with the rent-book, and as the tenants trickled in over the course of the day he called them in, one by one. I had arranged my work to keep me in and around the dairy a good deal, so that I might overhear a little of what was being said, if not in the office itself, at least among those coming and going from it.

268

My main impression from those who came out was of a great deal of grumbling, though it generally went silent whenever I passed near enough to hear what was said. But from the scraps I could hear, I gathered that Hindley had shown himself insufficiently appreciative of those who had paid in full, while raging at those who could not. Excuses had all alike been dismissed, and suggestions of payment in kind spurned. I thought I had better do what I could to stem the tide of resentment, so I abandoned my post as eavesdropper and set myself up in the kitchen instead, providing cups of tea and a sympathetic ear to a steady stream of tenants, and where possible, making private arrangements to purchase provisions for the household.

I was in the midst of one such negotiation, when we heard Hindley in the yard, roaring with laughter, and went to the door to see what was up. Hindley had his arm around a little man, Hoggins by name, who was one of our least respectable tenants, prone to drinking his earnings and beating his wife. He had skirted eviction these many years only through the efforts of said wife, who was far better than he deserved. He was the last person I would have expected Hindley to be pleased with on rent-day.

'That is the best story I've heard in years,' Hindley was booming. 'You must tell it to my wife – it's worth a glass of brandy, that one. And never mind about the arrears. Squire Hide-th'-ham indeed! Come inside and tell my wife.' And so the grubby little down-at-heel man was ushered into the house, looking sheepish at the unexpected honour. I hastened to attend to them there.

Poor Mrs Earnshaw looked rather flustered for her part in having such a specimen foisted upon her for entertainment, but she did her best, smiling kindly and offering him tea, which

Hindley forestalled by pouring him the promised glass of brandy, as well as a generous one for himself.

'You must hear this story Hoggins tells about my father, my dear – it will make you howl, I promise you. Come, my man, tell the story to my wife.'

Both Hoggins and Mrs Earnshaw looked as if they would have preferred to dispense with this, but the former took a large swig of the brandy to fortify himself, and plunged in.

'Ee wor joost tellin' th' maister as how we used to call hoos faither Squire Hide-th'-ham, meanin' no disrespect, ma'am, but joost that hoo allus seemed to know what a mon could spare t' gie hoom, ef hoo couldn't pay hoos rent.' Hoggins finished the brandy, and Mrs Earnshaw forced herself to smile and nod.

'Oh, come now, man, that is not what you told me. Tell it all.'

Encouraged by the brandy, and seeing that Hindley would not be satisfied with less than the whole story, Hoggins carried on. 'It wur said that one day th' old maister cum to th' house of one of hoos tenants, an' hoo walked right in to where the mon and hoos wife were sitting.

'"Where's my rent?" hoo says.

'"I ha'nt got it," says the tenant.

'"Well then, I'll just tek this soocklin' pig here, for my dinner," says th' maister.

'"That's noo soocklin' pig," th' wife cries, "that's my son!"

'"Well then," says th' maister, wi'out missin' a beat, "do you joost feed hoom up another ten years or so at yur own cost, an' I'll take hoom then."'

Hindley roared again. Mrs Earnshaw forced herself to laugh, but it was so evidently false that even he noticed, and ushered Hoggins out of the house, post-haste. When he returned, he was treated to an angry lecture by his wife, the details of which

I did not hear, for I had left the room, but the words 'low' and 'disgusting' figured prominently in it. Hindley was evidently apologetic, for he replied in soothing tones.

This episode had two effects, neither of them good. One was that Hindley promised never again to bring tenants into the house to meet his wife, a ban that of course included the more respectable class of tenants by whom that privilege had always been respected. The other was that the remaining tenants concluded that the best way to 'get round' the new master was to put him in a good humour with scandalous stories and drink. A basket of eggs or a piece of salt beef was no longer acceptable as a set-off to the rent, but the gift of a bottle of spirits, they found, was always welcome, and produced reductions far beyond its cost, and since Hindley generally opened the bottle immediately to share a glass or two, the tenants got to 'give their gift, and have it too'. Squire Hide-th'-ham was no more; Hindley was Squire Bring-th'-bottle.

The results proved satisfactory to no one, however. The income from the estate continued to decline. Some of the tenants, to be sure, were too proud or too honest to resort to the accepted method for mollifying Hindley, but they were embittered by the advantage gained by those they saw as beneath them. And since Hindley was too straitened ever to agree to contribute to the cost of repairs or improvements, their houses and barns began to suffer from dilapidation. Even those who did 'bring the bottle' often had reason to be dissatisfied with the result, for however agreeable Hindley might be in his cups, he often forgot to write down the results, and then on sober review he would be outraged at the arrears, and threaten all manner of dire punishments.

For all my determination not to involve myself in such matters, I soon found myself drawn in anyway. One by one, the tenants, great and small, began contriving ways to deal with me rather than with Hindley or Joseph. It began with my purchase of kitchen provisions, as I said, but soon extended to other matters, such as the hiring of lads and lasses to help out in the household and the farm. When one of the tenants married a baker's daughter, I employed her to come one day a week and bake for us, at considerable savings over deliveries from the bakery in Gimmerton. I paid them all with chits that I signed, which I told them to present to Hindley against their rent. They all assumed I had prior approval for these arrangements, but in fact I held my breath on the first rent-day at which they were to be presented. I thought it likely that Hindley would honour them, since he had certainly had the things for which they paid, and at a saving, too, but if he didn't, I was prepared to make them good out of my own funds, for I had no wish to get anyone into trouble. The day passed without any difficulties – in fact Hindley never said a word to me about the chits, good or bad. I took the absence of objections as tacit approval of my efforts, and kept on.

Up to that point I had been careful not to handle money directly: I negotiated for goods or labour, and signed chits in return. But then, on one of my visits to Mrs Dagley, which happened to fall two days before the rent was due, her husband asked if I would convey the funds to Hindley for him. 'If tha can joost write me a receipt, as tha did for the eggs before, that's good enoow for me, and 'twill save me half a day's work, not having to bring it in myself.' I took the money and the chits for the eggs, and gave it to Hindley that afternoon, being careful to do so while his wife was present, in case there was any question later. He pocketed it immediately, and thanked me.

'You'll be wanting to enter it in the rent-book, sir, won't you?'

'Oh yes, of course,' he said, but instead of going to the office to do so, he tossed me the keys. One was to the office, and another to the great heavy safe set deep into the stone floor.

'Will you be wanting me to put the money in the safe, sir, while I am there?' I asked.

'Eh, not this time,' said Hindley. 'I have a use for this. But in future you should. And be sure to keep good records of everything you do.'

I went into the office, and opened the rent-book to make the necessary entry. It was a mess. Notes were scrawled every which way, sometimes illegibly, and sums added and subtracted with no very high degree of accuracy. I longed to sit down and put it all to rights, right then, but I had other duties to attend to. I opened the safe, too, to see what was there, and found a surprisingly small sum. I had intended to return the keys to Hindley as soon as I was finished, but the condition of the rent-book gave me a new resolve. I would keep the keys until Hindley requested them back, and see if I could take on the duties of rent-collector more directly.

I arranged with Mrs Earnshaw to borrow her pony chaise the next day – it had fallen into disuse once we began to exchange regular visits with the family at Thrushcross Grange, for they always sent their carriage for Cathy and the mistress. That day I rose well before dawn to get an early start on my household duties and set tasks for the house- and dairymaids before setting out. Then I got the rent-book from the office and began paying calls on the tenants. I went first to those that were apt to pay a day early, and those I had had dealings with for provisions. I told them that Hindley was very busy over the next day or two, and I wished to save them the trouble of coming to the Heights themselves. Most of them were glad enough to pay their rent directly to me, and see their payments

273

and credits entered conscientiously. For those who could not pay in full, I took what they could pay and then talked over with them how we were to make up the difference, and I wrote the results directly into the rent-book also, borrowing the methods I had found in the earlier entries in the book, from the days of my late master.

When I returned that afternoon, Hindley was in the house with his wife, taking tea. This was excellent news: I wanted a witness to what would follow. I was nervous – it was a bold move I had made, after all, and if Hindley wanted a reason to send me away, my taking such a liberty as this would give him a perfect one. I was counting on his old trust in my competence and honesty, and what I hoped was some dissatisfaction with his own performance as rent-collector. I took a deep breath, and entered the room with the rent-book.

'Good afternoon to you sir, and madam,' I said as respect-fully as possible. 'I'm sorry to interrupt, but some more of the tenants asked if they might pay their rents to me today, as I was calling on them – I believe they got the idea from Mr Dagley yesterday – and so I took them, and entered it all in the book. Here are the book and the money both. If you have a moment, sir, might you look them over, and see that all is in order?'

Hindley scowled, but he took the book and glanced over my entries.

'Fine,' he said. 'Go and put it back in the office, with the money.'

'If you please, sir,' I said, 'I need for you to count the money, too. I shouldn't wish it to be said later that the amounts didn't match up properly.'

Hindley grumbled, but he took the box, opened it, and counted the money. 'It's all here,' he said.

'Could you just sign in the book there, by the total, then?' I handed him a pen and ink, and he scrawled his name. 'Thank you, sir. I'm sorry for disturbing you. I'll just go and put these things in the office. Will you be wanting dinner at the usual time, ma'am?' She nodded, and I made my exit. I brought the things to the office, put the money in the safe, and left the book on the desk, open to the correct page. Then I went back to the house and gave the keys back to Hindley. He said nothing, but nodded slightly in acknowledgement. I breathed a sigh of relief – it had gone as well as possible. I had reason to believe that many of the tenants would prefer to deal with me, and that, as word spread of today's proceedings, more and more of them would contrive in future to pay me instead of Hindley. I hoped that the sight of my good results, in contrast with his own, would incline Hindley to acquiesce, as gradually more of the rent collection fell into my hands. But things moved rather faster than that.

The next morning was rent-day. I rose at dawn, as I usually did, and began preparing breakfast. The mistress nearly always slept late, but Hindley was still an early riser. When the weather allowed, he would often take a mug of tea and a slice of bread outside for an hour's walk on the moor, as a prelude to breakfast. Today was no different. By the time he returned, most of the household was up and about, and I was dishing out the porridge for breakfast. The others were out in the courtyard, performing their morning ablutions, so I chanced to be alone in the kitchen when he came in. He reached into his pocket and laid down the keys on the table in front of me. I looked at him in surprise.

'Go on,' he said in a low voice. 'You want to do it, and God knows you do it better than I can. So go on. But see them here – it is not safe for you to be on the road with that much money.'

And with that he gave me just a hint of a rueful smile, and took his plate of porridge with him into the next room.

I stood staring at the keys for some time, until the sound of the others coming through the door warned me to put them out of sight in my pocket. I am almost ashamed now, looking back, to think how much that little gesture touched me. I was like a starving man, who falls on a crust of bread as if it were a feast. I, who not long before had confidently expected to be Hindley's wife, and mistress of Wuthering Heights, was now moved to tears of joy by the honour of being permitted to perform all her functions and more, without any of the benefits.

So the tenants who filed into the office that day to pay their rent met me instead of Hindley. Most were glad of the change – even some of those who had profited by Hindley's weakness before. Farmers have so much uncertainty attendant upon the nature of their livelihood, they prefer as little of it as possible in their other dealings. It was a great strain to them to have a landlord who proved as unpredictable as next year's weather.

On the whole, I believe I performed rather well in my new role. To be sure, my age, my sex, and my status in the household were all against me when it came to exerting authority over refractory tenants. Pounding my fist on the desk and lecturing them on their shortcomings, as the late master had done, was clearly out of the question. But I found a great deal could be accomplished merely by telling them, in the mildest possible manner, that I didn't 'feel able to agree to that on my own authority, but I should have to consult with the master, to see if it were agreeable to him', but if they could just see their way clear to add thus-and-such, there would be no need for that. There were a few who rebelled, and insisted on speaking to Hindley themselves, but they found this of little service. If he was to be found at all, which was not always possible, he would be thoroughly jovial and friendly with them until they brought up the matter under dispute, whereupon his face would close down and he would wave them back to me.

I was strict in my accounting to Hindley at the end of the day. As before, I made sure that he read the entries in the rent-book, counted the money, and signed the book to indicate his acceptance of my efforts. He would have liked to skip this stage altogether, but I was adamant on this front, and on giving him back the key to the safe when I was finished with the collections for the day. I knew how quickly the cash dwindled in the safe, and how poor were Hindley's records of how he and his wife spent it, and I wanted no accusations coming my way if he found it empty sooner than he expected.

Unlike my late master, who had accepted payment in kind only as a last resort when tenants could not scrape together the rent by other means, though, I encouraged the practice whenever I could. The tenants liked it, for it saved them the time and expense of finding another market for their produce and their labour, and I liked it, for it allowed me to plan ahead to supply the needs of the household, and at a lower cost than I would otherwise pay. More importantly, it kept more of the rent money out of the hands of Hindley and his wife, for whom it was only a temptation to thoughtless extravagance, and saved me having to ask him so often for cash for necessary household expenses, which was always an awkward proceeding.

It would have been shamefully easy to line my pockets at Hindley's expense, he was so careless of money, and so inattentive to the price of goods or the quantities consumed in the household. The tenants, too, were eager to curry favour with me now, and often offered me tokens of their esteem, which were really little better than bribes. But I refused all such. I was so wary of seeming to take advantage of my situation, in fact, that I would not even deduct my wages from the money I collected, but left it to Hindley to pay me out of his own hand, even though that made payment considerably more irregular.

There was one area in which I knowingly deceived Hindley about money, however, and that was to keep Heathcliff decently clothed and shod. He was growing like a bean, and outgrowing his shoes and trousers even faster than he wore them out – and that took some doing, I can tell you. Yet Hindley would have been content to see him in rags – and this although he had put the poor lad to work to earn his keep, without paying him a penny of wages. I thought this a great wrong, both to him and to my late master, and a discredit to the family, and so I found ways to put aside money without Hindley's noticing, that I might use to buy what was needed. So when Mrs Earnshaw tired of her visits in Gimmerton, for example, and Hindley asked me to dispose of the pony chaise for whatever I could get, I was able to sell it to a milliner in town for a good price, but I told Hindley I had got less, and put the remainder aside for new winter clothes and boots for Heathcliff. I would have liked to keep this a secret from Heathcliff as well, and let him believe Hindley had at least enough concern for him to keep him decently clothed, but I needed his connivance to hide the purchases from Hindley's notice, by muddying his new things when he first put them on, so their newness would not be so obvious. And I little thought, then, that Heathcliff was storing all such wrongs up in his mind, to be paid back with interest at a future date.

If I thought that Hindley's gesture of trust, in giving me the keys, would usher in a new period of greater friendliness between us, I was mistaken. He still avoided speaking to me or looking at me as much as he could, made a great show of adoring his wife when I was about, and discouraged her from treating me in any way as an equal. But when he was obliged to consult with me, he did so respectfully, and on the whole he was not so rude as he had been at first. That, and the charm of my great responsibilities, was enough to keep me satisfied with my place on the whole.

SEVENTEEN

We were not long into that first winter when it became evident that Mrs Earnshaw was with child, and we were all told that she expected her confinement in July. I thought back to my conversation with Bodkin at the funeral, and concluded that whatever he thought he had seen then, that had concerned him, was nothing more than the earliest stage of this condition, which of course he could not have known then. Certainly she looked blooming and happy. She was not strong, and was often too weary to rise until late afternoon, but I remembered my own experience, made allowance for her greater opportunity to indulge in leisure, and concluded that this was nothing unusual.

As her pregnancy progressed, Hindley became, if possible, even more attentive and affectionate than he had been before, and more distant and dismissive towards me. It was hard to bear, at first. When I had told my mother that I had accepted Hindley's marriage and my own position in the household, I had meant it, and believed it to be true. But watching them now brought vividly back to me my own experience of that state, so very different from hers, and it was hard not to feel bitter.

One afternoon, not long after Easter, I was sweeping in the kitchen when I heard a sudden outbreak of crashing, shouting, and screaming coming from the house that made me dash in, expecting I knew not what catastrophe. When I opened the door, my first impression was that they had all suddenly gone mad: Heathcliff was leaping about on the furniture, Cathy was shouting and struggling to follow him, but was held fast by Frances, who was cowering on the sofa shrieking, and Hindley, most frightening of all, was waving a gun about, and making as if he would fire it. I soon saw the cause: a falcon had flown into the room through an open window and was flapping wildly about trying to escape. Frances was screaming to Hindley to kill it before it attacked her, Cathy was begging Heathcliff to save it at all costs, and Hindley, clearly inebriated, was getting ready to shoot, unconcerned that he was more likely to hit Heathcliff than the bird. I took it all in at a glance, and acted before I thought. I wrenched the gun out of Hindley's hands and flung it aside, then struck the bird with my broom as it swooped by, and, when it fell stunned on the floor, whipped off my apron and rolled it up inside. The whole time I was shouting at them all that they were as great a pack of fools as I had ever seen in my life, to make such a fuss and be ready to kill or be killed over a terrified creature that meant them no harm. I was in a white rage, and must have impressed them with it, for they all froze still and silent until I had the bundled-up bird in my hands. Then the spell broke.

'Give it here, Nelly,' Hindley cried, 'and I'll dash its brains out, for frightening my wife.'

'Don't let her do it, Heathcliff,' sobbed Cathy, still trying to prise herself free from Frances's terrified clutches. Heathcliff looked ready to leap on me, in obedience to Cathy's command.

'Nobody's doing anything with it,' I said. 'It's my captive and I'll dispose of it. Hindley, you had much better take care of your wife, and you too, Cathy. She's had a bad fright, thanks to you all. Heathcliff, come with me.' And with that I strode briskly out of the door. Heathcliff followed at my heels, promising Cathy that he would make sure I did the bird no further harm.

Once outside and clear of the house, I paused, and peeled back the wrapping just enough to free the creature's head so it could breathe, making sure to keep my fingers well away from the sharp beak. It was awake, but, bound tightly and unable to move, it seemed oddly calm, the deep black eye in its gold rim fixed on me unmoving. Heathcliff hovered close.

'May I touch it?' he whispered.

'Only if you want to lose a finger,' I said. 'Come, we'll go a good distance from the house and let it go.' I set off walking at a brisk pace, and Heathcliff half walked, half ran alongside, keeping close by the bird. I could have let it go nearer by, no doubt, but my blood was up and I needed the walk. I also thought it best to keep Heathcliff out of the way until things were settled down inside, lest Hindley take it into his head to relieve his own feelings on the poor lad's backside. So we walked about a mile, to the top of a little rise, and then I stopped. I took hold of the corner of the apron, planning to shake it out like a sheet and release the bird that way, but Heathcliff begged to do it, so I let him take it. Ignoring my warnings, he unwrapped the bundle slowly in his hands – to make sure, he said, that the bird was not hurt – and sure enough, as soon as the falcon was free enough to struggle, it raked his arm with its talons. But Heathcliff took no notice except to curse. He took hold of the bird with both hands, holding its wings into its body and ignoring the small wounds it continued to inflict with its beak, and launched it upwards into the sky as you would a pigeon. It exploded into flight, and he watched it steadily as it winged its way into the distance.

'He won't be back,' I said. 'But good God, Heathcliff, what were you thinking to handle him so? Look at your hands!'

He looked. Two parallel tracks were opened along one arm, from which blood dripped down to join that from several deep nips on his hand, and the other hand was also bleeding freely. Heathcliff shrugged, and we both began walking back.

'I don't mind,' he said. 'I promised Cathy that I would see to it that the falcon was unhurt, and so I did.'

'You mean you would as lief have them as not,' I snorted, 'so you can prove your bravery to her.'

'And why not?' he said. He held out his arms again, and surveyed his injuries with satisfaction. 'What do you think young Edgar Linton would do, with wounds like these?'

'Scream for the doctor, and take to his bed, most likely,' I said. 'But then, he would probably have the sense not to get them in the first place, so where does that leave you?'

'That only shows he's a coward as well as a milksop.'

'There's no cowardice in taking sensible precautions,' I replied. 'But have no fear, I won't tell Cathy how gratuitous your injuries are. You may brag of your battle scars with no interference from me.'

We walked the rest of the way in silence. When we came near the house, I told him to come into the kitchen with me, and promised I would fetch Cathy to him there. I left him sitting at the table, dabbing away the gore with a clean cloth and some warm water, while I ventured into the house to see how things were there.

Frances was still on the sofa, with Hindley kneeling beside her, stroking her hair and murmuring comforts to her. She looked pale and shaken, and whimpered now and then, but between Hindley's ministrations and a cup of hot tea, she seemed to be recovering. Cathy sat in a chair opposite, looking annoyed. She jumped up when I came in, and began pestering me with questions about what I had done with the bird. This set Frances to crying again.

'Be quiet,' I hissed to Cathy under my breath, 'can't you see you're upsetting her? Go into the kitchen – you're needed there.' She took the hint and left, and I went over to Hindley and Frances.

'Is it gone?' Frances asked.

'Far gone,' I replied. 'We took him a mile from the house, and he flew further off as fast as his wings could carry him. He's probably in Scotland by now.' I forced a laugh. 'However badly he frightened you, my lady, we frightened him much worse, I can assure you. We won't see him again.'

She managed a feeble smile.

Hindley pulled me aside, looking anxious. 'I've sent for Kenneth,' he said under his breath. 'What else should I do?'

'That's good,' I said in the same tone. 'Just keep her calm, and perhaps see if she will take a little glass of wine, to settle her nerves. Don't let her see that you're worried: that will only worry her more. When Dr Kenneth comes I'll tell him to pretend he just happened by.'

Hindley nodded, and I went back to the kitchen, where I found, as expected, that Cathy had taken over cleaning Heathcliff's wounds, and was listening with rapt attention to his description of the creature's release.

'I wish you had let me come, Nelly,' she said peevishly. 'I have never seen a falcon up close before. I should have liked to hold him.'

'Your hands would look like Heathcliff's if you had,' I said, 'and anyway, your sister-in-law had need of you, or she would not have held you so tightly. She's in a delicate condition, you know, and mustn't be upset. If you want to be a lady, as you say you do, you must learn to put others' needs before your own, sometimes.'

'I am,' she said. 'I am putting Heathcliff's needs first. If I had been there to help, I might have saved him a few of these cuts – I shouldn't mind being cut myself.'

'Well I should,' said Heathcliff. 'Your hands are so delicate, I should hate to see them marred – a few more scars on mine won't make any difference, they are so calloused already. I'm sorry you didn't get to see the falcon, though. But if you want to see one up close, I know where we could catch one – there's a nest near Pennistone Crag, remember?'

'I don't want to catch one,' pouted Cathy. 'I want them to be free. I love to watch them hover, and then drop like a stone to strike. I only wanted to be close to it, before it flew away.'

I left them to their discussion, for I had other duties to attend to. Soon I heard noises outside, suggestive of Bodkin's arrival, so I went out to waylay him and tell him how things stood. He agreed to pretend he had come by for a social visit, and promised also to stop in the kitchen afterwards, for I wanted him to take a look at Heathcliff's cuts, and see if any needed stitching. With that I retreated to the kitchen myself. Bodkin came into the back about an hour later, and was able to assure us that Mrs Earnshaw had taken no lasting harm from her fright, and that Heathcliff needed no stitches. He could not stay to talk though, he said, for his father was laid up at home with a bad cold, so he had all his patients to attend to, as well as his own.

'When he is up and about though,' he added, 'I am asking him to take over Mrs Earnshaw's case, so you will not be seeing me here any more. You'll have to come to see me in town, Nelly, if you want to gossip.'

'Why is that? I thought you had agreed that you should take all the new patients?'

'I am concerned it may be a difficult birth, Mrs Earnshaw is so slight. Father has much more experience than I do in these things; I think it's best if he attends her.'

After he left, and the children had run off, I sat down in the kitchen with a cup of tea, to catch my breath and collect my thoughts. I had scarcely thought at all while it was happening, but now, looking back, the whole scene moved me strangely. I felt again the stillness of the bound bird in my hands after its wild flailing in the house, the odd lightness of the bundle for its size, saw the fierce face with its black eye fixed on me, and most of all I remembered the explosion of flight out of Heathcliff's arms, the confident power of its wings as it found itself again in its native air.

It came to me, then, that the trapped bird was a good figure for any of the three of them: Hindley's rage, Heathcliff's desperate love, Cathy's hunger for freedom – whatever drove them, it seemed to drive them each past sense and reason, past any care for the battering they gave to themselves and to each other. And further, I thought, each of them, there in that room, had sensed that, had seen themselves in that falcon. And so Hindley had tried to destroy it, Cathy to free it, Heathcliff to make it an offering to her. I thought to myself, 'I am not like them,' and it was like a revelation to me. Oh, I had bruised my wings on those ancient beams a few times, to be sure, but I had learned my lesson from it: folded my wings and resigned myself to walking about with my two

286

sturdy legs on the ground, like a sensible hen. I did not have it in me to fly wildly at a window again, and yet again, and yet again. And no doubt that was a good thing. But for all my pride in my own good sense, I could not help being sad at the thought.

EIGHTEEN

Mrs Earnshaw's labour began in the evening. I had thought I knew what to expect, for I had been with my mother when my brother Tommy was born. But my mother was a strong, resolute woman, who had given birth before and assisted other women at theirs, and the mistress was none of those things. The moment the pains began, Dr Kenneth was sent for with great urgency, and he arrived jacketless and breathing hard, having galloped his horse all the way, thinking it an emergency. He was not pleased to find it nothing of the sort. But when he tried to leave, saying he would not be needed for many hours yet, Mrs Earnshaw grew so distressed that Hindley barred the door and forbade him to go. Dr Kenneth took it in good humour. He helped himself to a glass of Hindley's brandy, and made himself comfortable on the settle.

'It will be a long night of it for all of us, if you carry on this way at the start,' he said, 'for I might as well tell you now, it will get a good deal worse than this before it gets better.'

'All the more reason to have you close by,' said Hindley.

Kenneth shrugged, and only asked that Heathcliff be sent to town with the message that he would probably not be back until late the next day.

Kenneth was right – it was a very long night. Despite all his efforts to reassure her and explain to her what was happening, Mrs Earnshaw persisted in treating each wave of pain as a new and terrifying crisis, and Hindley took his cue from her. The doctor was a kindly man, and had developed great patience with the peevishness of suffering, but at length even his good nature was worn away, and he grew quite snappish with them both. So first we would hear her scream, and then stomping and curses from Hindley, followed by a few choice words from Dr Kenneth, then silence, and then the whole sequence would repeat itself a little while later, in a way that would have been comical if we were not all so exhausted. A few hours into this, Cathy and Heathcliff took advantage of their elders' preoccupation to sneak off to the stable, where they could sleep in peace. I would have liked to join them there, but I knew I might be called upon at any time to provide refreshments, clean linens, and so forth. I soon gave up on my efforts to snatch some sleep between the outbreaks of noise, and crept downstairs, thinking to keep Dr Kenneth company and work on some sewing. But I found Hindley there instead, he having at last been banished from the birth-room altogether. He was pacing anxiously, and drinking brandy at a rate that did not bode well, so I retreated to the kitchen with a candle. There, for the nonce, I was left alone with my thoughts. Deprived of sleep, and agitated periodically by the ruckus upstairs, I was perhaps not in the best state to reflect soberly upon my future, but reflect I did.

It had been hard to accept Hindley's marriage, but I thought I had succeeded. Now, listening to his wife's cries, I realized that the babe to come – and more to follow, no doubt – would bring a whole new set of pains for me to endure in silence. I might manage the whole estate for them, and Hindley would scarcely notice or care, so wrapped up would he be in his new family. I had been so sure that I belonged at Wuthering Heights, that I was needed – nay, loved – there, as I would be nowhere else. But now, it seemed to me, my illusions were stripped away, and I saw that I had been pouring out my heart in return for a handful of promissory notes that would never be paid. My mother had been right: I should leave Wuthering Heights – it was only a matter of hanging on until a little while after the birth, when the household would be sufficiently settled for me to give my notice.

By the time dawn came, I was ready to seize any excuse to leave the house, so when Joseph announced at breakfast that Heathcliff and Maggie would both be needed again for haying in the far field, I hastened to volunteer myself in the latter's place. Maggie was delighted at the prospect of being left in charge of the kitchen.

'You needn't fear that I'll be put out by the birthing upstairs,' she assured me. 'I've been with Ma through her last four, and I'm ever so good at helping. My ma calls me her "little midwife", and Dame Archer said I had the makings of a good one.'

'Don't go intruding yourself,' I warned her. 'Keep out of the room unless you are asked to come in. Ladies are very particular about whom they have around them at such a time. Keep the large kettle aboil, and keep hot tea and buttered oatcakes and cheese ready in the kitchen, to bring in whenever Mr Earnshaw or Dr Kenneth come downstairs – there'll be no regular meals today. Beyond that, just take your orders from Dr Kenneth, and be a good girl and keep your questions to yourself. Can you do all that?'

'Of course I can,' she said proudly. 'I just wonder that you can bear to leave at such a time.'

'I've been at my post all night, so I'll be glad of a change, and some fresh air,' I said, truthfully enough, but I was gladder still to get out of reach of those screams, and to have work to do heavy enough to drive thought from my mind.

When Maggie came running out to the field to tell me of Hareton's birth, and announced that I was to have sole care of him as his mother was not expected to live, it struck me like a blow to the chest. I stood shocked and bewildered, listening to little Maggie's rapturous description of the baby, trying to take in what I had heard.

'Did the birth go badly, then?' I asked.

'It went as well as could be expected, Dr Kenneth said, but she was too weak to start with, and the consumption's got hold of her good now,' she said, growing more composed now that her subject was a gloomier one.

'She's consumptive?'

'Why yes, I thought you knew that,' Maggie said, puzzled. 'I thought everyone knew, and we weren't to speak of it 'cause it made the master fly out so. That's what my ma said, anyway. I know the look of it, for my older sister Abby went that way, you know, she just wasted away, just like the mistress is doing, but she hadn't so much to keep her here, for her sweetheart had died the year before, and she couldn't get a position being ill like that, so she felt a burden on us. It's different for Mrs Earnshaw, with such a likely babe, and a loving husband, and being mistress of a fine house, and all that. I don't think I could bear to die, if I had all that.' Maggie chattered on, as she was wont to do, and while her endless stream of talk had often been an annoyance to me, I was grateful for it now. I listened with only half an ear, while my mind whirled, struggling to digest the momentous news. All my plans were upended in a moment, my thoughts in turmoil. And beneath it all, like the drumbeat of distant thunder, the not-to-be-thought: did I wish this?

After I had made my greetings to Hindley and Mrs Earnshaw, and paid my compliments to the infant for the latter's benefit, Dr Kenneth gestured me out into the hallway and shut the door before gently depositing the bundle in my arms.

'I told Hindley he could not do better than to give the child into your care, Nelly,' he said in a low voice. 'You know I have a high opinion of your capacity as a nurse.'

'Did he agree to it?' I asked anxiously.

'Well, he didn't much like hearing that his wife must not nurse the child herself. He's a doting fool about that poor lass, and imagines that motherhood is just the thing to restore her health, when anyone can see she's sinking fast. I'm counting on you to see to it that she spends as little time with the child as can be gently managed – it will make it easier for both of them when she goes, and that will not be long now.'

'I mean, did he agree to it being me – instead of someone else?'

'Well of course – whom else could he want? But you must not expect him to take much interest in the babe, just yet – fathers generally don't, until the child starts running about and babbling at least, and he has other things to think of.'

The whole time I was speaking with Dr Kenneth, I was looking at the little creature in my arms. We call a newborn baby 'beautiful' if he is good-sized and red, squalls loudly, and has all his fingers and toes, but most of them have little other claim to the title, as their faces are generally bruised and misshapen from the birth. It takes a few days, if not weeks, before they are at all pretty to look on. Hareton was no exception to this rule, on the whole. But his eyes were beautiful: almond-shaped, wide open and dark, and he stared out at the

world with solemn stillness, as if he were in awe at the strange-
ness of it all, like a much older child.

I would like to tell you that I was besotted with him the
moment I met those eyes, that in their steady, liquid gaze any
doubts I might have had about taking on this charge dissolved
like the morning dew. And in time that was true. But it was
not true then. I was terrified. The child seemed at the same
time so fragile and so momentous a charge, and I sensed that
accepting it would be the end of all freedom of choice, whether
to stay or to go, yet I knew not how to refuse it now. No, it
was not love that made me reach out my arms that day and
accept the burden laid in them. Mostly it was habit: the habit
of doing as I was bid, of accepting without complaint any duties
laid upon me. And there was some vanity too: at Dr Kenneth's
faith in me, at Maggie's jealousy, even at Hindley's acceptance
that I was the most fit person to have care of his son.

Later that day I undressed him for the first time, to bathe
him and change his clothes. In the creases of his neck and
limbs, the moisture of the womb still lingered. It turned the
cloth pink when I wiped it away. It gave me the strangest feeling
to find it, as it brought before me so vividly the place he had
but lately come from. For months he had lain curled under
his mother's heart. And now he would lie on mine.

Dr Kenneth left a jar of cows' teats preserved in spirits, and
a booklet for me, titled 'Raising By Hand: The Most Approved
and Hygienic Method', by a Dr Theophilus Perkins, which I
looked into as soon as I had a moment to spare. Strangely, the
bulk of it was taken up with a long diatribe against wet nurses,
supported by many grievous examples. They were in general
women of low morals, he wrote, who too often had come to
motherhood by no honest means, and were usually diseased
as a result. They were not uncommonly addicted to drink, so

that their poor charges 'might as well be sucking at a gin bottle'. A wet nurse, if she left her own infant at home to nurse a stranger for pay, must be an unnatural mother, and hence no fit guardian for an infant. But if she nursed the two infants together, she would be sure to give the lion's share of the nourishment to her own offspring, to the detriment of her paid charge. A mother who had lost her own child, however, posed an even worse threat: she might become so attached to the child that she would be unwilling to leave it when the natural term of her employment ended. Such women had been known to steal the child they nursed, and either disappear with it for ever, or, facing certain capture and prosecution, kill both themselves and the poor infant, rather than be separated from it. I read this section with great curiosity, though it was hardly relevant to the task before me, as it cast some light on what had always puzzled me in Mr Earnshaw's strong resistance, years before, to allowing a wet nurse for Hindley.

Dr Perkins was of the opinion that the fittest nourishment for most infants was to be had at their mother's breast, and that 'too often' a wet nurse was engaged from 'mere vanity of figure' on the mother's part or a 'selfish desire of convenience' on the father's. However, he allowed as how there were instances when, 'for reasons of health or through the intervention of tragedy', this nourishment was unavailable. In that case, he said, the task of hand-feeding an infant should be delegated to 'a responsible woman of cleanly habits, firmly attached to the household and the family', who could be trusted to follow religiously the procedures he outlined in the remainder of the booklet.

Now at last we came to what I needed to know, instructions for the feeding of infants from birth through their first year, with recipes for the appropriate mixture of milky, sweetened pabulum needed at each period of their growth. Throughout, Dr Perkins laid a great emphasis on the importance of 'scrupulous cleanliness', as in the scouring and scalding of all utensils and containers with every use. This was very much like what I had already learned at the dairy, where the slightest failing on that front could turn the milk so that the butter would not come, and I had long prided myself on my success in that area, so I felt confident that I could manage it. Still and all, the milk pans only required cleaning once or twice a week, while the infant would need to be fed every few hours for months yet. I was lucky, I reflected, that he had been born in early summer, as it meant that my late-night risings to creep downstairs and prepare his feedings would not be too chilly, nor very dark either, for in fact we have but little darkness at that time of year.

Mrs Earnshaw wanted to name the child Fredrick, which had been her father's name, but Hindley said that all the Earnshaw men must have names beginning with H, that it had been so for as far back as anyone could remember. So then she suggested that they call him Hareton, after the name over the door.

'Think what it would be like for him, to grow up reading his own name carved in stone above the door of his own home, and to know that the house has been destined for him, from all those years ago! Hindley, when was the last time there was a Hareton Earnshaw in the family?'

'If there has been one since the one that built this house, I haven't heard of it. We are all Henrys and Harolds and Hindleys and Harrisons, that I know of.'

'And Heathcliff,' interjected Cathy.

Hindley snorted. 'He's no Earnshaw.'

'He was named after the firstborn son, who would have been heir had he lived.'

'I wish he had lived – then maybe we wouldn't have been saddled with this one.'

'Well I wish it too – then you wouldn't be master here.' This salvo earned a raised hand from Hindley, and Cathy scuttled from the room. Then Frances began to cry, and Hindley apologized, and the result of it all was that the child was named Hareton.

I don't know how I can describe to you what that first week or two was like. He was with me both day and night, and I never had more than a couple of hours when he did not need my care, so of course I slept but little. I could not attend to many of my regular duties, and the loss of those familiar routines made my new state seem that much stranger. It seemed as if time slowed to a snail's pace, in which hours felt like days, and days like weeks. I remember on one occasion, Maggie made reference to churning the butter with me 'the day before yesterday'.

'Oh, no,' I said, 'I have not been able to do the butter since Hareton was born.'

'But that was yesterday!' she said.

I opened my mouth to correct her, but closed it again as I realized that indeed, it had been only a day since Hareton came to me. At the same time, I could not seem to remember that this period of all-consuming care would not last more than a few months, for I would catch myself fretting about how it would be to manage Hareton's midnight feedings in the depths of winter, or whether Maggie could manage the Christmas baking without my help.

The nights were particularly difficult. Any new baby requires feeding every few hours, of course, but that is not too much of a difficulty for a mother or wet nurse, who has the right food always fresh and ready to hand. I had to rise and carry the crying child downstairs, hastening to get out of range of the master's room, or he would storm out and yell at us both for disturbing his wife's sleep. Then I must boil water to clean the bottle and teat, changing him while I waited, then heat up his mixture and cool it to the right temperature, all before he could even begin to be fed. Finally, if all went well, I would creep back upstairs with him, praying that he would go to sleep quietly until the next feeding. But sometimes he would not, and then I would have to pace back and forth with him in the tiny room we shared, for going out into the hall was sure to bring Hindley down upon us. I felt almost desperate sometimes, and had to fight the urge to shake the poor babe in sheer frustration. At those times I often felt that I loved him not, that his care was too great a burden, and that when morning came, I would tell Hindley to find someone else to do it. But then the morning would come, and Maggie would arrive, eager to make me breakfast and beg the privilege of an hour's custody of Hareton. The master would come downstairs and make a few flattering remarks about how the baby was coming on, and joke about the strength of his lungs the night before – for Hindley was always at his most cheerful in the mornings – and Hareton himself would turn his wide dark eyes on me, and I would decide to manage for another day at least.

I was helped, too, by the steady stream of local matrons who soon made it their business to call on us, to pay their respects, take a look at the new baby, and of course, offer advice. The better sort came to the front of the house, and the lesser to the back, but in both cases it fell to me to entertain them, both because I had charge of the child, and because Frances generally preferred to conserve her strength to sit with Hindley in the evenings, knowing that he would be sorely grieved if she couldn't. These ladies, great and small, liked nothing better than to reminisce about their own 'firsts', and from them I learned that there was nothing very remarkable in my experience.

'Ah, the first month feels as if it lasts a year,' they liked to say, 'but after that, it all goes by in the wink of an eye.' On the subject of hand-feeding, though, they were less helpful, for their information was generally second-hand, and not encouraging. 'I never knew an infant yet to thrive on it,' one said bluntly, and then, when my face fell, added, 'though a few do muddle through, if they're strong to start with, and he looks likely enough.'

'Still and all, though, I'd take hand-raising over hiring a wet nurse,' said another. 'My brother had one in, when his poor wife died in childbed, and she spent every penny of her wages on gin, and smelt so bad, he couldn't be in the room with her without gagging.' Then would ensue a lively debate on the merits of hand-raising versus wet nurses, with a great deal of worrisome evidence brought to bear on both sides, and the dispiriting conclusion that both were bad, and that it was God's will, whether a child would live or die.

I must say that my heart warmed to Frances during those weeks. I had always thought her frailty largely imaginary, indulged or ignored by her as suited her convenience. Now that I knew how ill she really was, I was more impressed by her usual good spirits, and made allowance for her occasional peevishness. She was delighted with Hareton, and sometimes, propped up comfortably on the couch, she would hold him for as much as an hour, seeming content just to look into his face as he slept. But she never interfered with my management of him in any way, as I had very much feared she might, or evinced any jealousy when it was time for me to take him away. And if she felt any grief that her time with him was like to be short, she did not show it.

During those first weeks, Hareton was, upon the whole, what we call an easy child, which is to say that he cried mostly only when he was hungry or wet, and he slept a great deal. He seemed to take well enough to the bottles of warm, sweetened milk I prepared for him, too. His appetite was small, or so it seemed to me, but neither Dr Kenneth, who stopped in occasionally to look at him, nor anyone else, seemed much concerned about this.

When Frances died, though, Hareton gradually took a turn for the worse. Instead of thriving on the milky pap I fed him, he grew increasingly reluctant to take it, and showed signs of distress, after. I hoped this would pass soon, but instead it only grew worse. By the time a week had passed from the death, it had got to where every time I tried to feed him, he would turn his head away from the bottle and wail, and when I could coax him into taking some, he would spit up most of it, soon after.

Hindley was mad with grief and drinking heavily – he only ordered me out of his sight and hearing if I tried to talk to him about it, so at last I sent Maggie for Dr Kenneth myself.

When he arrived, it was only mid-afternoon, but Hindley was already drunk. Kenneth made the mistake of knocking at the front door. I tried to smuggle him into the back without Hindley's noticing him, thinking the master not fit for company, and I had reason to believe I'd been successful, for I had got Dr Kenneth settled at the kitchen table and just beginning to examine little Hareton, while I anxiously described his symptoms.

Then the door banged open, and Hindley charged in, red-faced and shouting.

'It's not enough that you frighten my wife into her grave with your dire predictions, but now you must go after my son, too?'

Dr Kenneth had risen and fallen back a step in the face of this assault, but his voice was steady.

'I said nothing to your wife, Hindley,' he said calmly. 'I told you what to expect, believing that, as her husband and the head of the household, you had the right to know it, and the fortitude to bear it. I am very sorry for your loss, but Mrs Earnshaw was in a consumption before you married her, and bearing a child hastened her end. Now, if you will excuse me, I will do my best to save your son from the same fate.'

'My son was fine before you started meddling with him,' Hindley roared. 'Now get out of my house before I throw you out, with a black eye to send you on your way!' He was waving a fist as earnest for his threat, so Dr Kenneth thought it best to obey, while I hastily gathered up Hareton from the table. At the door the doctor turned back to say hurriedly, 'Try a different milk.'

As soon as he was gone, Hindley turned to me.

'I ought to send you packing too,' he snarled, 'and I will the next time I catch you sneaking behind my back like that.'

But I was not so easily intimidated. 'I thought you not . . . *fit* to be disturbed,' I said pointedly. 'Hareton is not well, and frightening away the doctor won't cure him.'

'Hareton was fine before you got hold of him,' said Hindley. 'Even Dr Kenneth said he'd never seen a likelier lad.'

'He was fine until his mother died,' I replied, 'but now his food won't agree with him. We must do something – if you won't take Dr Kenneth's advice, perhaps we should employ a wet nurse.'

It was a mistake to try to reason with Hindley in this state, though. He slammed his fist on the table so hard that I jumped, and Hareton began to cry.

'I won't have it!' he said. 'Do you think I can afford to pension off every lazy slattern in the neighbourhood? If you can't take the trouble to manage him, get out of the house, and I'll give him to Maggie – she's keen enough.' With that he swept out of the room, but turned at the door to add a final threat. 'And don't you try some other sneaking thing, either. Do you think I don't notice all your tricks and connivances?' Then he slammed the door before I could get a word out in my own defence.

I sat down to soothe little Hareton, and tried to collect my thoughts. 'Try a different milk,' the doctor had said. Did he mean a different recipe for the mixture I fed him? Or the milk of a different beast altogether? I remembered reading something about this in the booklet, so I took Hareton up to my room to search it out. Sure enough, it offered up two alternative recipes for the milk mixture – one with toasted flour, and another with barley malt – which I resolved to try. At the same time, it informed me that in some cases infants could not tolerate cow's milk at all, and in these instances goat's milk might do better. We kept no goats, but it occurred to me that sheep's milk might do as well. The lambs were mostly weaned already, but there were one or two late-bearing ewes that still let their little ones suckle. Still, to obtain milk from them would be difficult without Joseph's assistance, so I resolved to try the new recipes first.

The results for both were the same: at first, Hareton took to the new mixture with a hungry eagerness that lifted my heart, but within minutes he would spit it all up, and then wail with colic for hours. So the next morning I gave Heathcliff a clean, fresh-scoured milk-pail, and promised him a penny if he could bring me half a pint or so of sheep's milk before midday, without Joseph noticing. He laughed at the challenge, promising to be

301

back with the prize in less than an hour. He was as good as his word, so I got to try its effects on my charge before the morning was far advanced, but alas, it was no better than the other. I was growing desperate now, and I worried that this constant switching of foods was only worsening Hareton's digestive difficulties. It had got to where the only thing he could keep down was boiled sugar-water, and I knew he could not hold out long on that. At last I resolved to defy Hindley, and try the effects of a wet nurse.

The difficulty was where to find one. I could not ask our own tenants to defy Hindley, and the one or two other poor cottagers that I remembered to have seen with babes at the breast appeared filthy and often visibly drunk. At length I hit upon one Mrs Dodd. She was a kind, sensible woman, whom I knew from before her marriage. She lived on a remote farm tucked up against the moors, and her husband had the reputation of a decent man. They were tenants of the Lintons, which I hoped would mean that Hindley's disapproval held no terrors for them, and their farm was not so prosperous but that a little extra money would be welcome. The greatest difficulty was that they were a brisk hour's walk away from us. To sneak Hareton over there every time he needed feeding, I would need to be carrying him to and fro almost unceasingly, day and night. Still, I thought the most urgent need was to get some food into the poor babe that he could tolerate, before his health declined further, and with that aim I bundled him up that very afternoon, tucked some of my own savings into my purse (for I dared not spend Hindley's money on this), told Maggie something about an errand at a nearby farm, and set out.

When I came within sight of the Dodds' cottage, Mrs Dodd issued from the door and began hurrying down the path towards me.

'Why if it isn't Nelly Dean,' she cried out cheerfully, as soon as I was near enough to be recognized. 'What a pleasure to have you here – and is this the little motherless Earnshaw babe? I had heard about him, poor fellow, and that you were to be his nurse.'

'Mrs Dodd,' I began, but she would not let me finish.

'Oh, call me Emma, as you always did,' she said. 'Marriage has not changed me that much, I hope!'

'Emma, then, I have something to ask of you.'

'Come inside first, and sit down for a cup of tea. You are all out of breath. There's time enough to tell me what you need, when you've had a chance to catch it. Besides, I've left my own little Jonnie in his crib asleep, so I must hurry back, before the cat settles down to sleep on his face.'

I followed her in to the little cottage, which was satisfyingly neat, and as clean as a dirt-floored cottage can ever be. Sure enough, a large tabby cat had just jumped into the cradle and set it rocking. Mrs Dodd shooed it off unceremoniously with a sharp slap on its nose, motioned me to a chair by the scrubbed deal table, moved the kettle onto the hob, and then sat down opposite me.

'Kitty is an excellent mouser,' she said, 'and I am glad enough of her company, up here by myself all day, but she cannot resist jumping into the crib with Jonnie, every chance she gets.'

'Why don't you set up a cat's cradle over the crib, to keep her off?' I asked.

'Oh I do, at night or whenever I need to leave him for any length of time, say to work in the garden. But it is too much trouble to be setting it up and taking it off again all the time, when I am right here anyway to shoo her off. You would think she would know by now that she is not allowed there, but there is no training a cat.'

'Not to stay away from a warm spot to sleep, anyway,' I agreed.

'So what brings you out here?' she asked at last. 'Not that I am not glad to see you at any time – it is lonely up here during the day, when John is off in the fields, but I am not such a fool as to imagine folk will walk all the way out here just to keep me company.'

'I would if I could,' I said truthfully, for I had always liked her. 'But as I said, I do have something to ask of you, and it concerns this same motherless babe.' I explained to her what had happened to Hareton, since his mother died, and what efforts I had made to find something he would eat, though I omitted mentioning Hindley's views on the matter. While I spoke, the kettle began to boil, and she motioned me to continue speaking while she prepared the tea. When she had sat back down again with the teapot, and poured me a cup, she loosened her top and took up Hareton, before I had even reached the question of payment.

'Well, here is your tea,' she said, 'and now it is time for this little man to have his.' She put him to the breast, and he soon settled down to nursing in earnest. His eyes were closed, and his tiny hand rested on her breast, the picture of contentment. As I watched him, I felt my eyes fill with tears. Mrs Dodd was too occupied with Hareton, at first, to notice, and I struggled to control myself before she did, but she chanced to look up just as a large drop gathered and fell down my cheek.

'Poor Nelly,' she cried, 'this must have been terribly hard for you.' It was the first gesture of real sympathy I had had, and it loosed the floodgates. I put my head down in my arms and sobbed in earnest, as I had not done since Hareton's troubles began.

'Shoosh, shoosh,' she said soothingly, patting my back with her free hand. 'All will be well now, you'll see. Just look at your

304

little one: he's eaten all he can and fallen fast asleep, peaceful as can be. I'm going to tuck him up in the cradle next to Jonnie, and then you and I can enjoy our tea in peace.' She got up to do as she said. While she was at it, I had drawn a few deep, quivering breaths to calm myself, and wiped my face with my apron.

'I don't know how to thank you enough,' I began, drawing my purse from my bodice.

'Oh, go on with you,' she said impatiently, waving it away. 'There's no need for that. My Jonnie is fat as a pig, thank the good Lord – just look at him!' she added proudly, and indeed he looked to be three times Hareton's size, and round as a barrel. 'And he's already begun taking the odd spoonful of porridge. He can well spare a bit for a hungry neighbour.'

'What's this about a hungry neighbour?' came a man's voice from the door. I looked up to see John Dodd in the doorway.

'Oh John, this is Nelly Dean,' said Emma, as we both rose.

'So it is,' he said with a friendly smile, as he offered his hand for me to shake. John Dodd was about ten years older than his wife, and I knew him mostly by reputation, as an honest, hard-working man.

'Good day, Mr Dodd,' I said politely.

'No, no, call me John. We are none of us silly enough to stand on ceremony like that. Is that a fresh pot of tea, Emma? I should be very glad of a cup, if it is.' Emma assured him that it was, and hastened to pour him a cup of his own. While she worked, she retold all I had told her about Hareton's troubles, and my errand there.

'Is Mr Earnshaw looking for a wet nurse, then? I'm afraid we can't help there – Emma has duties enough at home.'

'Not exactly,' I said carefully. 'Mr Earnshaw is still quite lost in grief . . .'

'Drowning in it, if what I hear is true,' said Dodd frankly.

'Yes, rather, and I have not wanted to disturb him with requests about the household – at least, well, he doesn't like it if I do, so I have been trying to take care of things myself. I thought if I could just see for myself whether wet-nursing was what Hareton needed, or if anything else would do, I would be better able to make what arrangements were needed.'

Dodd looked thoughtful.

'I wonder that you didn't go to Mrs Hoggins. She's a good deal nearer by, and I should think she'd be glad of some extra money.'

There was no doubt that John Dodd was a sharper questioner than his wife, and under his examination I was growing increasingly flustered. Now I flushed and stammered like any schoolboy caught in a falsehood.

'Come now, Nelly, you are not telling us everything, are you,' he said firmly, though not unkindly. 'Let's have the whole story, or we can't help you.'

I thought it best to make a clean breast of it, so I told them everything, from Dr Kenneth's expulsion to Hindley's threats against me. Emma looked horrified, and made little sympathetic noises to encourage me. Dodd merely looked grave. When I was finished, he leaned back in his chair, and let out a low whistle.

'Well, that is a fine pickle,' he said.

'I am so glad you came to us,' said Emma, reaching across to press my hand. 'I am sure we are glad to help, aren't we, John?'

'I don't see that we can help much,' he replied to her. 'You can't be going there, and for Nelly to come here every time the lad needs feeding, she'd spend the whole day running back and forth, and Mr Earnshaw'd be bound to notice that.'

'It's only for a short time,' I said hastily, 'while I search out something better to feed him with myself, or see if Mr Earnshaw can be won over to having a wet nurse come to us – perhaps Mrs Hoggins, as you said. I would only bring him by once a day, so I can be sure he's got one good meal in his belly, at any rate. And I would pay, of course,' I added, pulling out my purse again.

'Is that Earnshaw's money?'

'Oh no, it's my own savings. I may go behind his back for his son's sake, but you can't think I would spend his money on something he has forbidden.'

'I'm glad to hear it, else I couldn't take it in good conscience. Well, Emma,' he said, turning to his wife, 'what do you say? Are you willing?'

'Of course I am,' she said eagerly. 'It will be worth it, just for the pleasure of having Nelly here every day for company.'

'How much should I pay you?' I asked.

'A shilling a day,' said Dodd, at the same time as his wife said, 'Nothing at all.' They looked at each other awkwardly.

'The Lord bids us be charitable to those in need,' Emma ventured.

'Yes, but I don't think that applies to a wealthy gentleman's son,' said Dodd.

'But Nelly would be paying from her own wages!'

'I'm happy to pay,' I interposed hastily. 'I always expected to. A shilling then?'

'Sixpence,' said Emma, sending her husband a stern look. He hesitated.

'Say ninepence, then,' I said.

'Sixpence,' she said firmly, 'and not a penny more. Else I shall be so ashamed of myself the milk won't flow.' We both looked at Dodd, then, and he looked down.

'Sixpence it is, then,' he said, 'if you will have it so. It's all for you, anyway, my dear.'

'Well, that is the strangest bit of bargaining I ever did,' I said. 'I wish the tradespeople on market day bargained as you two do.' They both laughed at that, and gave each other such a warm look that it made my heart ache. I made ready to leave, then. Emma tried to coax me to stay, offering to feed Hareton again when he woke, but I thought it best to get back before my absence grew too conspicuous. Before I left, though, I asked if they knew anyone nearby who kept goats for milk.

'Smith keeps a few. You may not know him – he's another six miles further on from here. His wife's a Frenchwoman, and she makes a kind of cheese from the milk that she fancies, as it reminds her of home. I tried it once, and couldn't abide it, but there's no accounting for tastes, is there? Why do you want to know?'

'I've been told that babies who can't tolerate cow's milk may thrive on goat's. I thought if Hareton took to it, I could buy a nanny goat, and solve the problem for once and all.'

'Well, Smith would be willing enough to sell one, I think,' he replied. 'His wife was sure there would be a ready market for the cheese, since she thinks it superior to anything we have here, but most folk here like it no better than I did. So they have more than they need.'

This was hopeful, and between it and Hareton's peaceful sleep and full, round belly I felt quite cheerful on my walk home.

Almost a week went by before I could make an expedition to the Smiths', though. Maggie came down with a bad cold, and I banished her home lest she pass it to the baby in his weakened state. Without her to cover for me at the house, it was much harder to find time even to sneak off to the Dodds' every day, let alone to make the longer trip six miles beyond them. In the meantime, and with one good feeding a day to fall back on, I resolved to see whether there was any other sort of milk nearer to hand that might sit better in his stomach. Mare's milk and sow's milk were both tried, with no success. I even made an attempt to milk our mastiff bitch, who was nursing a litter of puppies, but she let me know in no uncertain terms that she was having none of it. At last Maggie was sufficiently recovered to return, and at that point I claimed a long overdue half-holiday, and made my trip. I brought the nursing bottle with me, thinking I could try Hareton on the fresh milk right there. If he liked it, I could purchase a nanny goat to bring home that very day. I planned to stop at Dodds' on the way there, to get directions for getting to Smiths', and for a light nursing, so he would not be in discomfort from his long fast. He would not be happy to be torn from the breast before he was finished, but I wanted him still hungry enough to try the new milk. If he didn't take to it, I could stop again at the Dodds' on the way back.

Emma took Hareton eagerly when we arrived, and settled in to nurse him, but she seemed anxious and unhappy.

'Is something wrong?' I asked. 'You seem distressed.'

'I am, a little,' she said reluctantly.

'If it is something you can share with me, I am happy to listen,' I said.

She paused for a moment, and then burst out, 'I'm afraid it is something I must share with you.'

'What do you mean?' My heart was pounding – I guessed something of what she would say, but dreaded to hear it.

'John says I must stop nursing Hareton. He says Mr Earnshaw becomes such a madman when he's in drink, the whole county is talking of it, and John is afraid of what he might do, if he found out we were crossing him. He says it was only ever to be for a short time, anyway. I am so sorry Nelly, I truly am.' Indeed, tears were streaming down her face as she spoke. I opened my mouth to plead with her, and then shut it again. Even if I could convince her to go against her husband's judgement, what right had I to bring strife into an otherwise happy marriage? She looked miserable enough already.

'I am sorry to hear it,' I said, fighting to keep my voice level, 'but I understand. And I thank you for all you have done already. God willing, Hareton will take to the goat's milk, and all will be settled that way. If he doesn't,' I hesitated, 'would it be all right for me to bring him by here again today, on my way home?'

'Of course it would! And for another day or two yet, until you can make other arrangements. I didn't mean to banish you instantly – that would be too cruel altogether. I only wish we could keep on, as long as you need me.'

'It's all right, Emma. John is quite right in one sense – even without Hindley's threats, we could not keep going on at this rate. A baby cannot thrive on just one good meal a day.'

It was hard to pull Hareton away from her and set off on another long walk, knowing how much rode on what we found at the end of it. So many expedients had failed me already, I was beginning to feel that failure was fated – that perhaps God, for my many sins (which I enumerated to myself as I walked), was punishing me by letting me come to love this child as my own, before taking him from me to rejoin his true mother in Heaven. I tried to feel more hopeful, remembering that it was goat's milk, after all, and not that of a mare, ewe, or sow, that was specifically recommended by Dr Perkins. Nonetheless, it was a weary walk, made no easier by Hareton's wails at being denied half his breakfast. I talked to him continually, telling him again and again that he would get the rest of it, soon enough, but of course he couldn't understand that.

At length a farm, meeting Emma's description, appeared before me. Cows dotted one pasture, and what I took to be goats, as they were taller and thinner than sheep, were scattered about another. A row of straggling grapevines, trained over a fence, claimed a south-facing patch of hillside, and I guessed that goat's cheese was not the only French comestible Mrs Smith was attempting to cultivate in Yorkshire. As I approached, a woman in ordinary clothes, but a queer-looking cap, emerged from the house and greeted me in an accent as odd as her headgear. Half a dozen children, ranging from a toddler of three or so to a young fellow who looked about Heathcliff's age, clustered around her. I introduced myself and Hareton, and explained my errand. She nodded, and turned to give rapid orders to the older boy, in a language I took to be French. 'Yes Mum,' he said, respectfully enough, but for some reason this unleashed a torrent of angry French from his mother. He mumbled something I couldn't hear, and then his mother waved him off.

'The childrens do not like to speak my tong,' she explained. 'They say the other childrens tell them they are traitors to England if they do. But if that is so, why do they teach it to the yong ladies and gentlemens? Speaking a different tong is not making one a traitor, is it?'

'I don't think so. But country children have narrow views.'

'That is so. My boy Onry' (so I understood the name) 'has gone to bring in a milker for you. We do not milk them for some hours yet, but she will have enough for your baby to try fresh. Come inside – would you like to try the shev?'

'Shev?'

'The cheese of the goat's milk. Is delicious. I will give you some in a way that you will like.' She saw me hesitating. 'Onry will be back soon, and we will get the milk for the babe then. You will please me by trying the shev?' She smiled encouragingly, and tilted her head towards the door.

'Of course,' I said. John Dodd's report had not been encouraging, but I thought for politeness I could make myself swallow a bit. Besides, I was starving – I had not eaten since an early breakfast, and had walked many miles since. Inside, Mrs Smith commenced to cut a slice from an ordinary-looking baker's loaf. This she spread with a layer of soft white cheese from a crock she reached down from a shelf. Then she took down another crock and spread a layer of what appeared to be gooseberry jam over the cheese. She cut the slice into four triangles and arranged them, points outwards, on a little flowered plate. This she set in front of me, and then sat down opposite me and gazed at me in happy expectation. 'At least she is not feeding me frogs,' I thought to myself. I picked up one of the slices and took a tentative bite from the tip. It was wonderfully good. Perhaps it was only my hunger, or my expectation of tasting something foul, but it seemed like the most exquisite food I had ever eaten.

'But this is delicious!' I exclaimed in happy surprise. Mrs Smith positively clapped with joy. I finished the slice with gusto, and willingly accepted a second, as it was clear my hostess was even more pleased to supply it than I was to get it.

'You will tell others, that is good, yes?'

'That I will, with pleasure. We are not in a populous neighbourhood, but I will certainly do my best to spread the word.'

'Thank you so much. I am very happy that you like it. And now I hear that Onry is back.'

She picked up an empty pitcher and started to go out of the door, but I stopped her.

'Could we scald it first?' I motioned to the kettle, and mimed swirling water in the pitcher.

'Wee-wee,' she said, to my great puzzlement, but she did as I asked. I had brought the bottle and calf's teat with me, wrapped in clean paper, and I took them out now. Onry was leading the nanny goat with a rope halter. She was a pretty thing, all white, with a dainty face and delicate legs. I had not thought a goat could be so pretty.

'This is Celeste,' said Onry, with no trace of his mother's accent. 'She's our best.'

Mrs Smith crouched down by the goat's side, and quickly obtained a half-pint or so of milk, which she handed up to me.

'Is enough?'

'Yes, that's plenty,' I said. I was still carrying Hareton, so we both went into the house, and I gave her the baby to hold while I poured half the contents of the pitcher into the bottle, tied on the teat with some string I had brought with me, and then took Hareton back to see what he thought of it. He grabbed the teat eagerly as ever, and this time he did not spit it out, as he had done so many times before. Instead he drank almost the whole of what was in the bottle, and then drifted off into a peaceful sleep. My heart lifted, and Mrs Smith smiled happily.

'How much to buy her?' I asked directly.

'Celeste?'

'Yes, I want to buy her, to bring home with me.'

'I cannot sell Celeste, she is . . . is special to me. Another milk goat you can buy. We have many.' But I had my heart set on Celeste. It was her milk that Hareton had taken to, and after the last few weeks' experience, I was taking no chances. Besides that, her dainty form, pure white coat, and angelic-sounding name made her seem the perfect antidote to my superstitious fears. I tried to explain some part of this to Mrs Smith, but

313

she seemed to grow confused. Eventually she called in Onry to translate for her. She chattered to him for some time in French, and then he turned to me.

'Mum would never sell Celeste,' he said bluntly. 'She is our best breeder, and improves the whole flock. And her milk is the sweetest.'

'But that is just what I'm afraid of!' I cried. 'If the others have inferior milk, the baby may not take to it so well.' Onry translated this to his mother, and she shook her head and replied.

'She is sorry, but she cannot let Celeste go. She would sell you Celeste's daughter; her milk is almost the same. And all goats' milk is healthy for babies.'

I stopped and thought for a bit. 'I only need her for a few months, until Hareton can be weaned,' I said at last. 'I could bring her back to you before she needs to be bred again. I will pay you well.' Onry explained this to his mother, and a rapid conversation ensued, after which the boy left the cottage.

'Onry has gone to bring my husband to us,' she said to me at last. 'He will talk to you, and then we will decide what is best. No?' I asked how long it would be before her husband returned.

'Not long, he is only three fields away. He will come straight away when Onry finds him.' With this I was obliged to be content. She offered me a cup of tea while we waited, so we settled indoors, with Hareton on my lap. She made a large pot, and the rest of her children clustered around to get a cup each. She spoke French to her children, and the two littlest happily babbled it back to her, but the rest followed the example of their elder brother, and answered her in good Yorkshire English. The children then clustered around me to look at the baby. They all exclaimed at how tiny he was, and how skinny, until their mother, seeing how the remarks distressed me, said something sharply in French, and they all dispersed. After that, Mrs Smith and I laboured away at discussing the weather and comparing the contents and progress of our respective vegetable gardens. I asked about the grapevines, and she informed me that, while the vines grew well enough, they bore no fruit, for the frost always killed the blossoms.

'I wonder you don't pull them out, then,' I said. 'It's a fine bit of land they are on – you could put apples or pears there.'

'Ah, I have not the heart to kill them. They remind me so of my home. If we have a mild spring sometime, perhaps they will bear. And the leaves are useful to wrap the shev.'

Soon after this, Mr Smith arrived. He was a smallish man with dark hair and eyes, who looked more quick than strong – rather like one of his goats. Evidently his son had filled him in on the purpose of my visit, for he wasted no time in coming to the subject.

'So, you have taken a liking to our Celeste, my son says, and wish to, what, lease her? For a season or two?' I nodded. 'Well, I would like to help you, but she is the queen of our little flock, you know. What security do I have that you will take good care of her, and bring her back as sound and healthy as she leaves us? To be frank, I hear things of your master that worry me.'

'Mr Earnshaw will have little to do with her,' I said hastily. 'She will be under my care – I have charge of the dairy and the household both. I will see to it that she is well fed and looked after.'

'The dairy, the household, and now an infant too? You look rather young to be carrying all that.'

'I grew up in the household – my mother was house-keeper before me. Besides,' I added, 'it is no more than your wife manages.'

'True enough,' he said. 'But I will need more than just your assurances. In addition to the price of the lease, you will need to leave us with her full value as security against her safe return.'

'How much?' He named a price that made me gasp. I had seen cows sold for less, and said so.

'Ah, but they were not Celeste, and my wife tells me you will have no other but her.'

I wavered, but in truth he was right, and it left me little room to bargain. Still, I managed to knock a third off his price, to bring it within what I had brought with me, and further gained the assistance of young Henry (as I discovered his name to be) to lead her home with me, and the right to recoup some of the lease money, as well as my security, if I brought her back early.

I was just counting out the coins from my purse, when Hareton woke up, suddenly vomited out the whole contents of his stomach, and began to scream in distress. I hastily cleaned him up and took him outside to walk up and down, with a little bouncing step that often soothed him, but it had no effect this time.

The Smiths came out to join me.

'I don't suppose you'll be wanting the nanny now,' said Mr Smith sadly.

'No,' I said, choking back tears.

Mrs Smith said something to her husband, and he took Celeste's halter and headed with her back to the fields. His wife reached out her arms and gestured for me to give her the baby. I handed him over. She took him inside and sat down with him, and then, to my great surprise, untied her tucker and gave him her breast. He was instantly calm, and commenced suckling with an earnestness that told me his efforts were not in vain. I looked around the cottage, thinking I must have missed sight of a crib somewhere, but there was none.

'How,' I began. Mrs Smith smiled.

'My little one, Marie,' she said, 'she still likes to nurse sometimes. It is not so strange, where I come from. And why not? It is pleasant to me. I am sorry the goat's milk did not agree with this one. It would be best if it had, no? But at least I can give him something, so he will not go home hungry.'

I thanked her as best I could, and bought a jug of the goat's milk anyway – it had stayed longer in his belly than anything else I had tried, so I still had some hopes for it. Mrs Smith also insisted on giving me a little packet of the goat's cheese, wrapped in vine leaves and then in paper to keep it fresh, to take away with me. But I was bitterly disappointed – and frightened, too, for I had lost my last expedient, and it was ominous to hear what was being reported of Hindley. The two worries mingled in my mind as I walked, as if Hindley's excess of intoxicating drink were somehow the cause of his son's refusal to drink milk, the one offsetting the other like some terrible devil's bargain.

Instead of going directly home, I turned aside to go through Gimmerton. Hindley might decline to call Bodkin in to see his son, I thought, but there was nothing to stop me taking the child to him. The waiting room in the surgery was nearly full, to my disappointment. I had already been gone more than half the day on my expedition, and I was not sure how much longer I could be absent without raising suspicions. Hindley was inattentive, and disinclined to interfere with my management in general, but he was not completely insensible. But Bodkin must have guessed something of my situation, for when he next poked his head in the room and saw me, he called on me immediately.

317

'Ah, Nelly, thank you so much for dropping in – it will save me a trip, as I said,' he said smoothly, making it appear that I was there at his request. 'I know you must get back to your duties, so why don't you come in now?' I hurried through the door, and Bodkin ushered me into the little room where he kept his supplies. 'Will you take some tea?' he asked, ringing a bell for the servant and then pulling out a chair for me.

'Perhaps a bit,' I said, for I was weary, 'but I don't want to keep you too long. Thank you for bringing me in that way, though – I was dreading the long wait.'

'I guessed as much. Now, what brings you here? How is the little fellow?'

I took a deep breath and began a reasonably calm disquisition on Hareton's symptoms, but in the midst of it the weight of my worries overcame me, and I began sobbing out my fears. 'Ever since his mother died, he can keep down nothing. It is as if he wants to die, and go to her. He needs a wet nurse, but Hindley will not hear me on it. He flatly refuses – he talks as if I don't want the extra work, and says if I will not take the trouble, he will give the baby to the kitchen maid instead, but though she's eager enough to help, she's a mere child and has no idea what to do. I have tried everything else, everything, but nothing works.'

Bodkin listened until I finished, nodding quietly and keeping his eyes fixed on mine, as if he sought to steady me with his look. When I finished speaking, he lifted the babe from my arms and unwrapped him to examine him, then placed him in the scale.

'He has lost weight, to be sure,' he said. 'But you say this started when Mrs Earnshaw died? He must be keeping something down, or he would be in worse shape than he is.'

'I have started walking to the Dodds' cottage, once every

318

day, and paying Emma Dodd to nurse him, and the rest of the time I give him boiled sugar-water, and he keeps a little down,' I explained. 'But her husband doesn't want her to keep it up – he is afraid of what Hindley will do, if he finds out I have been going behind his back, and it takes three hours to walk there and back – I am running out of excuses.'

'There's no one nearer who can nurse him?'

'Not in secret. They are all Hindley's tenants, and dare not go against him.'

Bodkin sat back and sighed. 'What would you have me do?' he asked.

'Can you not give him something, to make him keep the milk down better?'

'I have no such thing. I am no magician. If I were, I would make up a potion to make Hindley see sense – that would be the surest cure, I think, for a great many problems at Wuthering Heights.'

'But Hareton will die! How can you stand by and let that happen!'

Bodkin looked stricken. 'I have stood by and watched children die before this, Nelly,' he said sadly. 'I have no power to make a parent take my medical advice against their will and judgement. Nor am I so certain of my skill, that I would force it on them if I could.'

'Will you talk to Hindley, anyway?'

'I can try, but I doubt it will do any good. Hindley already blames my father for his wife's death – he seems to think that if my father had not told her she was ill, she would have borne up better, and come through it. I'd guess he won't thank me for bad news about his son's health. But I will make the attempt, and that soon. I suppose it cannot make things worse. In the meantime, keep on with the sugar-water, and try adding just a little of the goat's milk to it – say one quarter to start with. Then if that stays down, keep on with it, and then try a third the next day, and so on. We will see if we cannot coax his digestion into tolerating it.'

'Thank you,' I said, beginning to wrap up the babe and myself to leave. 'What do I owe you for the visit?'

'Nothing at all,' said Bodkin. 'I only wish I did have some medicine for the case, that I could charge you for. This is merely a friendly visit.'

'I don't like to take your time without paying you,' I said anxiously.

'And I don't like to be paid to tell people I can't help them,' he replied firmly. 'No more of that, Nelly, or I shall be angry.'

I had a sudden thought. 'Have you ever had goat's milk cheese?' I asked. 'Mrs Smith, from whom I got the goat's milk, makes it. She is French, and got the taste for it at home.'

Bodkin looked startled. 'Why, actually I have, in Edinburgh, and I liked it very much. I didn't know it was to be had in these parts.'

'Take it then,' I said, hastily extricating it from my bundle. 'She gave it to me, and I am sure no one at home will eat it.'

'I will, with pleasure,' said Bodkin.

'And if you like it, you will find her or her husband in town on market day, selling more.'

Bodkin thanked me, we shook hands, and I left.

I was sorely disappointed, but I had got some little straws of hope to cling to from the visit anyway, and I was clinging to them with all my might. Yet, I might as well tell you, before the next day was gone, both were swept away: Hindley refused to hear a word from Bodkin on the subject of his son, and Hareton spat up the goat's milk as fast as I could get it into him. And then, in my desperation, I thought of one final resource. Bodkin had told me that he had no magic potion that would change Hindley's heart or his son's digestion, and of course he did not. But there was someone else who just might.

NINETEEN

At dawn the next day, I again wrapped Hareton in my shawl, tucked the purse with my dwindling savings in my bosom, and left the house, heading for Elspeth's cottage. I had never met her in person, but I knew the cottage well, as Hindley and I had passed it often in our wanderings. Children in the neighbourhood had long liked to frighten themselves by calling her a witch and running screaming from the sight of her, and Hindley and I had been no exception. Their parents had more respect, and those of them who could not afford the more expensive treatments of Dr Kenneth or Mr Smythe relied on her for remedies she compounded from the natural apothecary she cultivated around her cottage, and gathered from the moors and woods nearby. But it was whispered that there was more to her potions than herbs, and that, if asked in the right way, she would provide cures for problems the doctor and his ilk could never touch: philtres to be sneaked into some loved one's food or drink, that could turn an unwilling heart or steady a troubled mind, and even darker remedies, whose purposes were only dimly hinted at. I had outgrown my childish fear of Elspeth, only to have it replaced by a deeper dread after the fateful dose of her art my mother had given me, and nothing less than my present state of desperation could have induced me to direct my feet to her door. But by now Hareton's tiny fingers were twined deep in my heartstrings, and for his sake I would have sought her help even if I had believed her every inch the witch our childish fancy painted her.

Such sinister imaginings seemed merely silly, though, in the face of the neat little old woman who answered my knock at her cottage door. Her face was deeply seamed with age, and weathered from a life spent out-of-doors, but the lines were kindly ones, though the eyes were sharp and penetrating.

'Nelly Dean,' she said calmly. 'Tha'll be Mary Dean's daughter.'

'Yes,' I stammered awkwardly, a little taken aback, as I had planned to begin by introducing myself.

'And this little bundle, I'm guessing, is the motherless Earnshaw bairn – am I right?'

'Yes, this is Hareton – I am his nurse.'

'So I heard, missy, so I heard. Please, coom inside and sit tha down. Wilt tha take soom tea? It's only the ordinary sort, from Hobson's shop,' she added, seeing me hesitate.

'Yes, thank you, I would,' I said, relieved. She turned and busied herself at the hearth.

'Oatcake too?' she asked, with her back still turned.

'No, thank you, just tea,' I said. I fussed over Hareton to hide my nervousness – he had been lulled to sleep by the walk, as he usually was, and I was trying to settle him comfortably in my lap without waking him.

Soon Elspeth returned to the table with the tea and poured us each a mug.

'Now, child, what is it tha wants?'

'I need something that will help the baby keep down his food,' I said. 'He keeps nothing down.'

'What art tha feeding him?'

'Cow's milk, to start with,' I said, and went on to detail all I had tried, and how little success I had had with it. In the course of it, I had to explain, too, about Hindley's intransigence on hiring a wet nurse, and my efforts to get round it.

'So tha's been going behind his back, and sneaking off to pay a nurse out of thy own pocket, just to keep the poor lad alive?'

I nodded. 'I didn't know what else to do. But it's not enough, you can see that, and now the nurse doesn't want to go on, either, and I don't know what else to try. I was hoping you had something that would help him, or maybe—'

'Maybe what?'

'Something . . . for Mr Earnshaw. I know he loves his son, or he would, but he's troubled in his mind, since his wife's death – he can't think clearly. If you had something . . .'

'Ah,' she smiled, 'a little powder, is it, that you could slip in his porridge, to give his mind the right turning?'

'Yes,' I said eagerly, 'that is just what I want!'

She shook her head. 'Poor child,' she said. 'If I had a powder that could give men sense, and make them do better by their bairns than they often do, the world would be a much better place, and I a rich woman. But I have no such magic. Not for this wee babe, either, I'm sorry to say. There are some who just won't thrive on aught but mother's milk, and it seems he is such a one.'

But I was not going to give up my last hope so easily. 'There must be something you can do,' I begged. 'There must! You must help me, or he will die – I will pay anything, do anything, please, you must!'

'Must, child?' she said sternly. 'Who art tha to tell me what I "must" do, when tha's never come to my door before today. I am sorry for thy trouble, but I owe tha nothing.'

'But you do,' I said, struck with a sudden thought, 'you do.'

'And how is that?'

I looked at her steadily, though my heart was pounding. 'You killed my baby.'

I expected her to protest, or demand an explanation, but she did neither. She held my gaze a long time, her expression unreadable. Then she nodded, ever so slightly.

'That would be about three years ago, wouldn't it?' she said. 'The herbs I gave thy mother?'

I nodded. 'A stomachic,' I said. My throat was almost closed with grief – it was all I could do to get the words out. 'A purgative. It purged . . .' I stopped, unable to say more.

'Yes,' she said softly. 'It would. How far along were you?'

'About three months.'

'And it was Hindley's child?'

I nodded. She was silent.

'So you will help me?'

'Let me think,' she said.

And think she did, staring off into the dark eaves of the cottage for so long that I feared she had gone into some kind of trance. It was Hareton's cries that brought her back, the sad little whimperings that were all he could manage these days, in his weakened state. She shook herself, and turned to me with an air of decision.

'Show me the child.'

I started to pass her the whimpering bundle, but she declined to take it, indicating that I should unwrap him myself. I did so, and, discovering his clothes to be wet, I commenced changing him into the dry clothes I had brought with me. Always when I did this, however tired or hungry or fussy Hareton might have been before, as soon as I began the operation he would become calm and still, and hold my eyes with that wide, dark stare of his, and I would be taken with him into another world, where there was only him and me, as I chattered and crooned to him an ever-lengthening string of pet-names: my bonnie nurseling, my wee little laddie, my beautiful boy, and more in that vein, ending, as I always did, with the same ones: Hareton, my little hare, my leveret, my love.

When I was finished, I glanced over to find Elspeth watching me intently.

'He is clean now – do you want to take him?' I asked.

'I can see what I need to from here,' she said.

'Will you help him?'

'I will help tha both. But it will be difficult.'

'I will pay you . . .'

'I don't mean for me. It will be difficult for tha. Tha must put thy whole heart into it, no matter what happens. And it will frighten thee.'

It was true then! Elspeth was a witch! I felt as strange then as the farmer must have, when he saw the actual Brownie before him.

'I am ready to do anything,' I said.

'Go then for now.' As she spoke, Elspeth was taking down a jar from a crowded shelf, together with a small piece of paper from a store of them weighted with a rock. She reached her hand into the jar, and put a few generous pinches of its contents onto the paper, folding it into a neat packet. I watched intently, imagining that I saw the means of Hareton's salvation before me.

'Take the babe to Emma Dodd again today,' she said.

'But I don't know if she . . .'

'She will. Bring her this,' she handed me the little packet, 'and tell her it is from me. She will know what it is, and she'll help thee a few more days, for my sake.'

'But after that?'

'Come back tonight, after dark, as soon as you can get away. Tell nobody of this. Nobody. And bring a lantern – the moon is waning, and there'll be but little light.'

I nodded solemnly, my heart pounding. 'Of course,' I thought, 'this work must be done in darkness, and in secret.'

'And what must I bring?' I asked, imagining eye of newt, the finger-bone of a suicide, or God knows what.

'Thyself, and the babe, and thy purse.'

'I can pay you now,' I said, relieved, and beginning to extract it from my bosom.

'No, bring it with thee tonight.'

So I bundled Hareton into his shawl again, bid Elspeth goodbye, and set out on my long walk to the Dodds' cottage, in the strangest jumble of triumph and self-doubt, hopefulness and dread, that I have ever experienced.

The summer evening felt endlessly long as I waited for nightfall. Hindley had already left, for what was now his routine of nightly drinking at the nearest inn, but I needed to wait for the children and then Joseph to go to bed before I dared leave the house. I only hoped my return would not coincide with Hindley's. As soon as all was quiet, I crept downstairs and prepared the lantern we used for night calvings and the like, then covered it over until I should be clear of the house, softly unlocked the door, shushed the dogs, and set out on the path that led by Elspeth's cottage. It was a familiar one, fortunately, for the moon had waned to a nail pairing and shed but little light. I met with no mishap before I was over the rise and it was safe to unswathe the lantern.

In truth, I was a good deal frightened by what I was doing. There was the fear of being found out, of course, as I imagined

327

trying to explain to Hindley why I had sneaked out of the house with his heir in the dark of the night. But I had greater fears about what lay ahead. Was Elspeth really a witch? And if she was, what forbidden arts would she use to give me what I asked for, and at what cost to me or the child? The story of the Brownie and the farmer was only one of a great many my mother had told me, the burden of which was always that all those who attempted to wield magic to their gain invariably came to a bad end. The local clergy's teachings had been simpler, but hardly more encouraging: all such arts were dismissed as 'superstition', harmful only in duping the credulous, and luring them from the surer hands of true religion and medical science. True, I had the Kenneths' warrant for Elspeth's general run of practice being competent and above chicanery, but this was clearly outside the general run, undertaken only under strong pressure and long reflection – and under cover of darkness. In short, I don't know which I dreaded more: that she could really work magic, or that she couldn't, and my errand was in vain. But I was desperate, and willing to grasp at any straw.

When I came nigh the cottage, I saw a candle glimmering through the window that told me Elspeth was awake, and waiting for me. She must have heard my footsteps, for before I could knock on the door I heard the sounds of her undoing the latch, and then the door opened. She was the same Elspeth I had met in the morning, but lit from below by the lantern, her face looked stranger, and more sinister. My heart pounded.

'I've come, as you asked,' I said, speaking softly, for Hareton was asleep.

'So tha has,' she said, as quietly as I. 'Come in and sit down.' She took the lantern from my hands as I entered, and put out the flame, so that the room was lit only by the candle on the table. 'You'll need this for the walk home,' she said.

I sat down at the table, which had a number of items ranged around the candle. I saw two small pots of the sort she put her salves in, an earthenware jug that looked to hold about a quart, a mug with some milk in it, a cloth bag, a yellow lump I took to be beeswax, and a tangle of thread that, on closer inspection, proved to be a jumble of embroidery silks in a variety of colours. It was a puzzling array, but there was nothing obviously sinister in it, at any rate. I sat down cautiously.

'What are you going to do?'

'It's mostly what tha'll do that matters. I can only give tha what tha needs, and get tha started on it.'

'On what?'

'Binding the child to tha.'

'What do you mean?'

'The mother that birthed him is dead and gone, and he pines for the milk she could ha' gi'en him. Naught else will save him. So we must make tha his mother, and he thy babe. Then the milk will come to tha, and tha canst feed him thyself. Give thy whole mind to what I'm telling thee, for it is no easy thing we are going to do.'

I nodded solemnly. Had she told me that morning that this was her plan, I would have dismissed it as an impossibility, but now, in the dark, the low timbre of her voice and the strange shadows from the candle seemed to have cast a spell already, that made anything seem possible.

'First, tha must pay me.'

'How much?'

'A gold sovereign.'

It was a large sum, by Elspeth's standards, but I was prepared for that. I pulled out my purse and dug out some coins, but the two or three sovereigns I had were not among them. I laid out four crowns instead. 'Will this do?'

'Tha has no sovereign?'

'I do, but this is the same amount,' I said, puzzled.

'Tha cannot pay for a binding with broken coins, lass. I must have only the one.' So I emptied the whole purse and pulled from the pile the brightest of my sovereigns to give to her, then returned the rest to my purse. She took it and held it close to the candle to examine it, turning it over and over before tucking it into her bosom.

'That will do,' she said, then pushed the jug towards me. 'Drink this.'

'All of it?'

'As much as tha canst. It's not full.' I picked up the jug, and found it was less than half full. I uncorked it and took a cautious sip. It was some kind of herbal tea, sweetened with honey, strange tasting but not unpleasant, with a hint of liquorice and a peppery aftertaste that felt warm in my mouth after I swallowed it. I took a deep breath. Either I must trust Elspeth, or give up on the child, that much seemed clear. I tilted up the jug and drained it.

'Good,' she said. 'Now, tha'll bring the jug home with thee empty tonight, and every morning tha'll make up a brew to fill it, with a level teacup full of what's in the bag here boiled in a quart of water for as long as tha wouldst soft-boil an egg. Be sure to mix up the herbs from the bottom of the bag through to the top before you scoop them, so none of them settle out. Then take the pot off and let it cool with the herbs in it before tha strains it into the jug. Tha may add honey or sugar or whatever tha likes for the taste, only excepting wine or liquor. Drink it throughout the day, spacing it out so that tha takes the last of it just before bedtime. Is that clear?'

I nodded and repeated the directions back to her.

'Very well. Now on to the next thing.' She removed the cover from the smaller of the two pots, and pushed it over to me. 'Work this into thy teats five times a day.' I flushed, not being accustomed to discussing that part of my anatomy, but nodded. 'Let me see thee do it,' she said. I flushed deeper.

'Do I really need to?'

'Do as I say.'

The salve appeared to be a familiar mix of butter and beeswax, infused with something aromatic. Rather hesitantly, I undid my tucker and gingerly dabbed a bit of it where she had said.

'Not like that. Work it in.'

I made a further attempt, but it did not satisfy her, for she reached over and kneaded that tender point with a roughness that made me gasp and pull back. The shock disturbed Hareton, and he woke up and began crying.

'Like that,' she said. 'Tha'll feel a stab straight to thy belly, when tha does it right. I told thee it would not be easy. Now gie the child to me, and do the other one.'

I did as she asked, shuddering against the queer pain it brought, and feeling very near to tears.

She jiggled Hareton calmly until his cries settled into a low whimper. Then she opened the other pot and passed it to me. It was a sort of golden cream colour, but a little translucent, and it wobbled like a jelly – it looked like nothing I knew, and after my recent experience I was rather dreading learning its use.

'What is it?' I asked.

'It's summat the bees make to feed their grubs. Not honey, but summat else. They make but little of it, and that not all the time. I had to open every hive I have to gather this much,

331

and tha must guard it like gold – nay, more than gold, for when it's gone, gold itself wouldn't buy thee any more. It goes on thy teats too, but tha needn't work it in – it's for the child.'

'I don't understand.'

'Come, it's clear enough. Tha must put it on thy teat, and let the child suckle it off. About a teaspoonful, a little at a time, half on each breast, every time he is hungry. It won't fill his belly, so tha must go to the sugar-water after, and still get him to Emma Dodd each day, for another three days yet. But do this first, always, and get four or five spoonfuls a day of this into him by that means. After he's suckled, work in the other salve – not before as we did today. Now, then, let me see tha do it.'

I took a fingerful of the strange mixture and smeared it onto my breast. Then Elspeth handed Hareton back to me, and I put him to my breast to suck, as I had seen many a mother do. He fastened on and sucked lustily. It hurt, especially on top of Elspeth's rough treatment, but there was something pleasant to it also, and altogether, between the drink, and the salve, and the sight of the babe with his tiny fist resting on my breast, it was the strangest thing I had ever felt. Elspeth nodded her satisfaction.

Hareton soon finished what I had put on, and then Elspeth gestured me to do the same on the other side, and so, back and forth, one more time. While I was doing that, she reached over and pulled a few hairs from the scant supply on Hareton's head, and three or four from my own head also. I watched as she twisted two separate skeins of hair, each with a mix of Hareton's and mine. These she stretched out into two parallel lines on the table. Then she picked up the bunch of silks and brought the candle close, and I saw her working it with her crabbed fingers, with surprising delicacy, to disentangle and pull from it the colours she wanted. Two strands of red, and two of white, were added one each to the skeins of hair on the table. She then got up and fetched a saucer from the cupboard, which she placed between the two piles. She handed me the cup of milk, and I took it with my free hand, the other still holding Hareton to my breast.

'Take a small sip of the milk, but dunna swallow. Only swish it around in your mouth, and then spit it out into the saucer.' I did as she said. Hareton finished, about then, and looked ready for sleep, so I began settling him more securely into my shawl. Before I was done, though, Elspeth came over with a little tin spoon and collected a bit of his spittle, which she mixed with the milk in the saucer. One at a time, she picked up each of the white threads and ran them through the mixture in the saucer to wet them. Then she wiped the saucer clean, took out a needle, and held its point in the candle flame. I eyed the red threads. It was not hard to guess what was coming.

'Gie me thy thumb,' she said. She pricked it hard, and I cried out in spite of myself. Then she squeezed several good-sized drops of blood into the saucer, where they formed a small red pool.

'You're not going to do that to the babe?' I asked anxiously.

'Not like that,' she said, wiping off the needle and holding it in the flame again. 'We'll need only a wee drop from him. He'll scarcely feel it.' She was as good as her word, and soon one bright drop of Hareton's blood joined mine on the saucer. Elspeth stirred it with the needle, and then ran each of the two red threads through it before returning them to their piles. Then, one at a time, she took up each of the two piles, made a knot at the top, and braided the red, the white, and the hair together. I was astonished at how dextrous she was – she was

333

bent double over the threads, and I could scarcely see the fingers move, yet the braided chain emerged from them with surprising speed. The whole time she worked, she was mumbling to herself, but I could not make out any of what she said. I sat spellbound. Between the tea, the salve, and Hareton's nursing, I felt the strangest tinglings and disturbances all over my body, and that, combined with the oddness of being secretly away from home at this late hour, and Elspeth's eerie form in the dim candlelight, had lulled my usual sensible scepticism to sleep, and left me firmly believing in the power of Elspeth's magic.

When she was finished, each chain was a little less than a foot in length, and fixed with a knot at either end, and an inch or two of loose thread trailing beyond that. When she was done, she handed them to me.

'What are these for?' I asked.

'One for thy wrist, and one for the babe's. His will have to go twice round. That will seal the binding.' I took one of the chains and pulled out Hareton's wrist to begin.

'Not now, child! The binding canna happen here. I haven't that sort o' power. Tha must ask the stone for that.'

'The stone?'

'Aye, what they call Pennistone Crag. I can get tha ready for it, but the stone itself must bind thee. It's always been that way.'

I must have looked as confused as I felt.

'Does tha know the stone?'

'I was there many times as a child – not so much since.' I felt my face burn as I spoke, remembering the circumstances of my most recent visit, but if Elspeth noticed, she said nothing of it.

'Then tha knows it is a powerful place.'

'I know there are some . . . beliefs around it. Like that couples who go through the gate will get married in a year. But I have good reason to believe that an empty superstition.'

Elspeth snorted. 'Marry! Is that what they told thee? Ah, that's what comes of growing up with the gentry. They never teach what anyone in a cottage could ha' told thee. Folk don't go to the stone to make marriages, lass. They go to it to make children.'

My heart seemed to stop. I went cold all over. Elspeth eyed me appraisingly.

'And I'm guessing that's how tha got the bairn tha lost. Am I right?' I nodded. 'Poor lass, tha was sorely misguided, that's sure. And tha's paid heavily for thy mistake, too. But tha must see, now, that the stone is a powerful thing.'

I took a deep breath. 'What must I do?'

'Tha must offer payment to the stone, and make thy request, then spend the night there with the babe, in the fairy cave. Tha'll have to wait three more days to go there, until the night when the new moon first shows in the sky – tha can't do this sort o' magic on a waning moon. Full would be best, and gie thee more light, too, but beggars can't be choosers: the babe canna wait so long as that, and a new moon is next best – tha'll have the whole of its waxing after, to help bring up the milk, and that's no bad thing, either.'

'How much do I pay?' I asked, pulling out my purse, and assuming that this was only a roundabout way of claiming more money for herself.

'Put thy money away, child – I'm not the stone,' she snorted, 'and it won't be money that's needed either, the stone don't want that, not from thee, anyway.'

'What does it want, then?'

'Tha must work that out for thyself. Now hold thy tongue

and listen. When I'm done tha may ask all the questions tha please.'

I nodded, and Elspeth proceeded to give me very detailed instructions for all I should do – except in the one particular of payment. There were so many details, I took out a pencil and asked for paper to make some notes, but she bid me put it away, saying I must keep it all in my head. When she was finished, she had me repeat it all back to her. I did so, while she corrected two or three little inaccuracies that had crept in.

'Now repeat it again.'

This time I got it all right.

'Now again,' she said again.

'But I thought I got it right that time.'

'That's so. And I'll have thee get it right two more times, before I let thee leave. Then on the walk home tha must repeat it to thyself seven more times. That makes ten,' she said, spreading her fingers wide, 'one for each finger of the hands, and then tha'll have it grasped tight, and it can't slip from thee.' And she clenched her fingers together and mimed pulling something to her chest. 'That's my mother's saying, and everything I learned from her I learned that way, for she could neither read nor write.'

'When I have done all that, how will I know if it has worked?'

'Tha'll know. Tha'll feel the milk in thy breast.'

'How long will it take? Will I feel it right away?'

'If tha's done everything just as I say, the milk will come with the morning sun, if not before. There will be little enough, at the start, but it will come in stronger a few days after.'

'And if it doesn't work?'

She shrugged. 'Tha asked for my help. This is what I have to give thee. If it fails, tha must look elsewhere. But I've watched

336

thee carefully: thy bond with this child is strong already. It will work.'

'What did you mean by saying I must work out for myself what I give the stone. How am I to work it out? What sort of thing is it?'

'Small enough to carry with thee, of course.'

'But what *sort* of thing? Can you not give me some idea? Should it be something of value, or food, or some sort of charm?'

She seemed mildly amused. 'Tha must work it out for thyself. If I gave thee ideas of what other folk have paid, it might gie thy mind the wrong turning. Don't think about it tonight – use thy time to repeat what I told thee, else it will get lost in thy sleep after. Starting tomorrow, just think on it until the right idea comes to thee. Tha will know when it does.'

'How will I know?'

'By the sinking of thy heart.'

She sent me off then, with good wishes for my success, and I made my way home, repeating her instructions all the way.

The three days that followed taxed my ingenuity to a considerable degree: I still needed to walk Hareton to the Dodds' cottage once a day, whilst also finding time to brew and drink the potion and put Hareton to my breast four or five times a day, all in strictest secrecy. The strange stuff Elspeth had given me to feed Hareton seemed to be good for him – at any rate, he always took it eagerly, and seemed better for it. As for me, between the tea, the salve, and Hareton's suckling, my body was in a very queer state. I was constantly aware of that part of my anatomy, and felt that things were strangely stirred up inside me.

How to absent myself with the child for a whole night was

a puzzle. Hindley would be easy to deceive, provided I did not leave before he took off for his now nightly drinking – even if he noticed my absence on his return, he probably would not remember it in the morning, or could be convinced he was mistaken. But Joseph was another matter. Here a bit of luck came my way, though: Joseph suddenly announced the following evening that he was going away for two days, to the wedding of his nephew in another town. We were all sitting at the table in the house, family and servants both, as we had gone back to doing after the mistress died – all but Hindley, who was out drinking already. We were surprised that Joseph had not mentioned this sooner, as he must have known it for some time, and said so.

'I see noo sense gi'in yo all more time to plan yor mischief fer whilst I'm gone. I know what sort o' tricks yo all get into when I'm not here to keep an eye on yo.'

'Well, if you can tell exactly what we get up to when you're away, what difference does it make whether you stay or go?' said Cathy saucily. 'It is obviously no impediment to your surveillance. Have you a magic mirror, that you can see into, to spy on us?' Her manners had not much improved since her friendship with the Lintons, but her vocabulary had.

'I need no truck wi' magic – that's the Devil's business – to guess what's done when my back's turned.'

'So you don't *know*,' said Cathy, always delighted to quibble with authorities, especially this one. 'I wonder you don't fear for your soul, Joseph, to be stretching the truth like that. Why, for all you know, you might be bearing false witness against us, and that's against a Commandment. Number nine, I believe – perhaps you should look it up in your Bible.'

Joseph slammed his fist on the table, his face purple with rage. 'I know my Commandments a good deal better than yo,' he

338

sputtered, 'and yo'd do well to study them for your own good. Especially the fifth, that tells ye not to talk back to your elders.'

'Honour thy father and mother,' said Cathy. 'What, are you my father? I wonder my mother never mentioned it.' Heathcliff laughed loudly at this, and Cathy soon joined him, as Joseph stormed out of the room in disgust.

'You ought not to provoke him like that,' I said reprovingly.

'Oh come now, Nelly, he deserves it, the old hypocrite. And you know you enjoy it too – I saw how you buried your mouth in your napkin just now, to stifle a laugh.'

'Well at least I have the sense to stifle it. There's enough strife in the household already, without you adding to it for your own amusement.'

'Joseph will be sour and mean-spirited whether I tease him or not. Why shouldn't I lighten the mood for the rest of us, when I have a chance?'

'Push him too far, and he'll decide not to go, just to spite us. Or talk Hindley into staying home to watch us.'

'And you want him gone too, do you? What, have you a sweetheart you're planning to meet that night?'

I didn't contradict her, as I didn't want her guessing anything closer to the truth, but tried to change the subject.

'Well, don't worry about us,' said Cathy laughingly. 'Heathcliff and I have been wanting to camp out up on the moor for some time, and if the weather stays this fine, we'll do it. It's the new moon night after next, so the stars will be brilliant. We'll stay up all night, and count them all, won't we, Heathcliff?'

'Every one,' he said.

This took me back a bit. True, it would get those two out of the way of noticing my absence, but it would also leave no one in the house at all when Hindley came home. What if, instead of tumbling straight into bed as he often did, he called out for company? But the alternative would be to take Cathy and Heathcliff into my confidence. I didn't doubt their good-will in any scheme to deceive Hindley, but I was far less certain of their discretion – especially Cathy's. At length I decided that the risk of Hindley noticing the house was empty was less than that of counting on Cathy to keep a secret. I planned to lock my door before I left, hoping that if he tried it, Hindley would conclude the baby and I were asleep. As his drinking had increased, Hindley had ceased to be such an early riser – I might be able to get back before he woke. But in case I didn't, I would tell Maggie to come early the next day on the grounds that I had to be off at dawn for an errand. That would have her in place to provide breakfast when Hindley awoke, and able to offer an explanation for my absence, without requiring her to lie on my behalf.

You may wonder, sir, that I was not more concerned about letting my young mistress go off for the night with Heathcliff, unchaperoned. But strong as the bond was between those two, I had not as yet detected any sign that there was more to it than the attachment of childhood playmates. And even if I had, Cathy was left to her own devices so much, and I had so much else on my hands already, that chaperoning her times with Heathcliff would not have been possible even if I had wished to do it. Indeed, their affection for each other seemed still so innocent, I thought it best not to put the subject into their heads at all.

Through all my secret plans and preparations, and all the strange stirrings in my bosom, one nagging puzzle remained. With what was I to 'pay the stone'? I knew that it had to be something small, for the 'payment' consisted of burying it nearby – about which Elspeth had given me very precise instructions. And she had told me that I would know when I thought of it, by the ominous sign of a sinking heart. My worried mind ranged over many possible objects, precious, sentimental, or grotesque, but none produced the desired effect. The day before my adventure was to begin, I had still not arrived at a conclusion, and I was just debating whether I could squeeze in a trip to Elspeth to beg for better instructions, when it suddenly came to me. And she was quite right. My heart sank, and I knew.

TWENTY

The morning of my great adventure dawned sunny and fair, with a faint breeze freshening the warm air. I was up before anyone: Hindley was snoring loudly in his room, and without Jöseph to knock on their doors and order them up, the children were still asleep also. Maggie would not come for another two hours yet. I tied Hareton into my shawl, stopped in the kitchen and the barn to collect a few things, and then made my way to a certain little hollow not far from the house, where a stone peeking out of the heather would reveal itself, on closer examination, to be the top of a small cairn.

I settled Hareton, who was sleeping soundly, into the dry heather nearby. I spread a cloth beside the cairn to kneel on, so as not to dirty my clothes, gently removed the stones, and began to dig. The first time I had dug there it had seemed a great ordeal. This time it went much more quickly: I was strong and healthy, I had a trowel to dig with, and there was nothing but soil to get through, all the rocks having been cleared out previously. In a very few minutes, the hole was nearly at the depth I remembered, and the trowel was scraping on the stone at the base of it. I stopped, suddenly overwhelmed, dropped the trowel, and sat back on my heels, feeling sick. I closed my eyes and took several deep breaths, breathing in the bitter sorrow of memory, and exhaling inarticulate prayers to the nameless being I was about to disturb. When I felt calmer, I went on. I dug around the stone, and down the outside of the little ring of stones I knew were underneath it. Then I spread a clean handkerchief atop the heather beside the hole, took another deep breath, and lifted off the top stone. I could not bear to look closely at what was underneath, and my eyes were too full of tears to see clearly anyway – a quick, vague glimpse of a dirty bundle was all I got. I took up the trowel, and scraped it along the stone at the base, to lift it, and then I gently deposited it on the handkerchief. I wrapped it up quickly and tied it with a little bit of ribbon. It formed a neat, clean little parcel, which I tucked deep into my bosom. Then I filled in the hole in the ground, and piled the cairn over it again, though it now marked only the memory of a grave.

I gathered up Hareton, and was back in time to brew the day's herbal tea and nurse him at my breast, and with the sugar-water after, before Maggie arrived. Elspeth had said I was not to go to the Dodds' today, which left my day a little more free than it had been of late. When Maggie arrived, and asked as usual if she could take Hareton for an hour or two, I readily agreed, but instead of heading out to the dairy to catch up on chores there, I told her I was taking a nap.

'Hareton kept me up all night,' I said, which was true enough, though not of the previous night in particular.

'Oh the poor bairn!' cried Maggie, giving the baby an extra bounce, as if to make up for his discomforts the night before. 'Of course, you go and catch up on your sleep a bit. I'll manage things here well enough.' I left her with strict instructions to wake me in an hour, or as soon as she heard Hindley stirring, whichever came first, and retired to my room. I had meant this only as an excuse to begin preparing the bundle I was to take with me later in the afternoon, but when I got to my room, I suddenly felt my knees weak with tiredness. The truth was that I had been driving myself with frantic energy for weeks now, with neither adequate rest at night, nor a sympathetic ear in daytime, to ease the constant strain of mind and body both. I lay down on the bed, thinking to take just a few minutes of waking rest, and fell into a deep sleep.

I woke of my own accord, and a glance at the sun streaming through the window told me that the morning was far advanced. I leaped out of bed and rushed downstairs. Maggie was shelling fresh peas in the kitchen, with Hareton sleeping soundly in his cradle next to her.

'Why didn't you wake me up?' I cried. 'There is so much to do! And where is Mr Earnshaw?'

'Don't worry,' said Maggie happily, 'I've taken care of everything, to let you sleep a bit more. The master came down not long after you'd gone to your room – I couldn't have gone to get you first, for he surprised me in the kitchen before I knew he was up – but he didn't ask after you anyway, just took a big slice of bread and butter and said he was going to the high pasture, and not to expect him back until late afternoon. Then I thought that as there was little enough to do at home with him and Joseph both gone, and Hareton was sleeping nicely for once, I would just let you sleep a bit more. You looked as if you needed it badly!'

I sat down, my heart knocking and my brain racing. 'But the dairy,' I exclaimed, 'there's still the milk to be skimmed, and the butter to be churned!'

'It's nearly all done!' said Maggie, almost bouncing with excitement. 'I skimmed the milk myself, and scoured and scalded the churn just as you taught me, and then did it all over again, just to be sure. I tried to do the churning too, but it is too heavy for me, so I had to leave that for you, but that's two or three hours' work taken care of already. Now you sit right there and I'll bring you some breakfast. You've earned a rest.'

At another time, it would have amused me to hear such maternal tones of concern coming from that childish mouth, and combining themselves with her childish glee at accomplishing grown-up tasks all by herself, but I was still flustered at her disruption of my careful planning, and it was all I could do to show any sort of appreciation for her well-intentioned efforts. But that I must do, I knew. Accordingly, I forced myself to sit still and let her bring me a mug of tea and a plate of porridge, and to express all the surprised gratitude I ought to feel for her efforts, whether I felt it or not. And in truth the rest had done me considerable good.

While I ate, Heathcliff and Cathy came into the kitchen for some food, having just returned from a long morning's ramble on the moors. Joseph's absence had freed Heathcliff temporarily from his unpaid labour, provided he kept well out of sight, for Hindley would only assign tasks for him if he was reminded of his existence by chancing to see him. Normally I would not interfere with his impromptu holiday, thinking it well earned, but today the sight of him gave me an idea for something that would both please Maggie and give me an hour's privacy to nurse Hareton again and make my preparations.

'Heathcliff,' I said, 'could you help Maggie to turn the handle on the churn today? She's done everything up to that point all by herself, and I should like to see her go through the whole process, but she's not strong enough to turn the churn alone.'

345

'You've no right to order him about,' Cathy interposed, before Heathcliff could respond.

'Nor am I,' I said carefully. 'I am asking him a favour.'

'And why should he do you a favour?'

'And why are you taking words out of his mouth?' I replied. 'Do you not think he can speak for himself? Heathcliff knows a good deal better than you do whether he owes me any kindness, don't you, Heathcliff?'

'I am willing enough,' said Heathcliff, more to Cathy than to me. 'Come, it will be fun. You can watch us, or take a turn yourself, if you like.'

'And when you're done you may all drink as much of the buttermilk as you like, before giving the rest to the calves, and there'll be some jam to have with the fresh butter, on oatcakes,' I added.

The three of them left together – young enough, all three, that they still seemed like a gaggle of children off to play. I nursed Hareton again, as soon as they were gone, drank more of the tea, and applied the salve according to the directions. Elspeth had figured her quantities carefully: I had used up the last of the herbs for the tea this morning, and both of the little pots were coming to the end of their contents. The ointment might see me through another day or two yet, but the bee jelly, as I called it to myself, would run out tonight. Whatever it was, it was good food, and Hareton had done better on it, in combination with the sugar-water and his one daily nursing with Mrs Dodd, than he was doing before. But I had no way of getting any more. If tonight failed – well, I was trying not to think of that.

Once Hareton had drifted off to sleep, I laid him in the cradle and quickly began wrapping up the food I would bring with me that night – a hunk of bread and another of cheese, and a jug of fresh water, all of which I conveyed up to my room and wrapped into my bundle. Then I slipped back downstairs. Hareton was still sleeping soundly, so I left him for a bit to check on the children in the dairy. I found them taking turns, one at a time, to turn the handle, while the other two counted the turns. Evidently they had made it into a game, to see who could turn the longest before collapsing. I stood unnoticed at the door and watched them for a bit. Heathcliff was winning, of course, but, to my surprise, Cathy was running a close second, while poor Maggie struggled to keep up. I had not stood there long before the sloshing of cream in the churn turned to a telltale thumping.

'That's it!' cried Maggie. 'That's the butter – it's come, I can hear it!'

'Thank God,' said Cathy, whose turn it chanced to be. 'I think my arms would fall off if I had to do another turn. What's my score, then?'

'Two hundred and three for you, and two hundred and thirty for Heathcliff,' said Maggie. 'I have only one hundred and seventy-eight.'

'We win then, and Maggie must pay the forfeit,' said Cathy triumphantly.

'You mean Heathcliff won,' I interposed. 'And Maggie will pay no forfeit, unless it's to try her hand at making up the butter by herself. Can you do that, Maggie?'

'I think I can – I should like to try.'

'Good girl. And when that's done, you may all come in for your treat, for I'm sure you've earned it.'

'Heathcliff and I will have ours now,' announced Cathy. 'We don't want to stay until the butter is made up. We have other plans.'

'Oh really, and what are they?'

'I told you before, we are going to sleep out on the moor tonight. We will want our supper wrapped up for us, to take out there.'

'Where are you planning to go?' I asked, struck by a sudden thought.

'Up towards Pennistone Crag,' said Heathcliff. 'The view is best there. Why do you ask?'

I had to think quickly. This could disarrange all my plans. 'Only so that if you are both eaten by the Gytrash, we'll know where to search for your bones,' I said coolly. 'You know he haunts that area of the moors particularly.'

The Gytrash, Mr Lockwood, is a storied beast of this area, a great black dog with eyes like burning coals, who haunts solitary ways, and preys on the unwary.

'I am not afraid of the Gytrash,' said Cathy, though her face belied her. 'He only attacks lone travellers, and we will be two together.'

'Perhaps he will make an exception for you. He loves the taste of children.'

'And how do you know that?'

'Nelly feeds him children,' said Heathcliff. 'She is meeting him tonight at Pennistone Crag to feed him Hareton. That is why she wants us to go elsewhere.' I flushed in spite of myself.

'I should much rather feed him you two, though,' I said, playing along. 'Then I can keep my little nurseling here to myself, and get you two out from under my feet, both at once.'

'I have my clasp-knife, and will fight him off if he comes,' said Heathcliff. Then we will bring home his skin, for a trophy. How should you like a Gytrash-skin coat, Cathy?'

'I would rather not meet him at all,' said Cathy, who was getting more anxious as the conversation progressed.

'Well, you will do as you like,' I said, 'but I would not go near Pennistone Crag on the very night of the new moon if I had any choice in the matter. It is the second most magical night of the month, you know, after the full – and much the darker of the two, besides. There is no telling what may come out to get you, if you stay near the Crag.' I was not wholly teasing here, for I was a good deal frightened myself, and so my voice carried the ring of truth.

'I hadn't thought of that,' said Cathy, turning to Heathcliff. 'Perhaps we shouldn't go there after all.'

'I am not afraid of any demons,' said Heathcliff, twisting his face into a good imitation of one. 'But if you would rather go elsewhere, there is the hill up beyond Moor End – the top of that has a good view as well, and it is the other way from Pennistone Crag.'

'And it's not so far from other houses but that we can get help if anything goes awry,' said Cathy. 'Now that I think of it, that would be the best spot.'

'I am glad of it,' I said feelingly.

'Why, Nelly, I do believe you really were frightened for us!' exclaimed Cathy.

'It's a dangerous place on a dark night, Gytrash or not, with those steep cliffs and gullies,' I said. 'I shall rest easier knowing you are on safer ground, and nearer to human habitation. Now, if you like, I'll help you put together a supper to carry with you.'

I assembled a good repast for them – a good deal better than the one I had put away for myself – and wrapped it up neatly in paper and string. Then I helped them roll it into a couple of old blankets, and stuffed the whole thing into a large basket fitted with straps to go over the shoulders. I helped Heathcliff hoist the basket onto his back, and waved them off at the door, breathing a sigh of relief as I watched them disappear over the rise.

I went into the dairy to find Maggie struggling with the butter. But when I offered to help, she begged me to let her finish on her own, and so I did, only staying a little while to watch and offer suggestions as needed, and keeping one ear cocked for Hareton in the kitchen next door. Maggie was a willing worker, eager to please and proud of her accomplishments – just such a one as I had been at her age. At length I heard Hareton waking, so I left her to her labours.

'Leave aside half a pound or so for the house before you pack it into the moulds,' I told her, 'and bring that in to me when you're done, so we can have it fresh on the oatcakes for tea.'

Then I went inside to feed Hareton, for the last time before we left. He was just finishing the bottle of sugar-water when Maggie came in with the butter. She was eager to chatter over tea, but I discouraged her – I was in no mood for talking.

'You are worried, aren't you?' she said suddenly.

'Worried, why should I be worried?'

'Well, Hareton's not taking his food properly, is he? Isn't that why you sneak off each day, to take him to a wet nurse? Why must it be a secret? Does the master mind?'

I was struck dumb for a moment, internally cursing her quickness. When I finally spoke, I did so slowly and solemnly. 'Maggie, dear child, please understand: if I do not tell you something, it is because there is good reason not to. For example, if Mr Earnshaw were to ask you something, I should not wish you to have to lie to him. And there may be other reasons also, which I cannot explain to you. You are a quick girl, and so you may have made certain guesses. But that is not the same as saying that you know those things, is it?'

'No, it is not,' said Maggie, her eyes wide.

'Then if you are asked questions, you will answer only with what you know, and not what you guess, is that right?'

She nodded solemnly.

'Good girl. You are a great help to me, Maggie, and it is comforting to know I can rely on you.'

'I'm sure I hope you always will,' said Maggie earnestly.

I smiled at her. 'Here now, let's wrap up the rest of this butter for you to take home and show your mother. She'll be right proud to hear of what you've done today.'

'But it's early yet for me to be leaving, isn't it?'

'You've worked so hard today, you deserve a bit of time off while there's still plenty of daylight to enjoy it. And also, I've a favour to ask of you: could you come extra early tomorrow morning? As soon after dawn as you can get here? I must leave before dawn for an errand of my own, so I'll need you here to make up the fire in the morning and prepare breakfast for the household. Do you think you can do that?'

'Yes, of course I can!'

'Good. And if anybody asks where I am, you'll tell them just what I told you?' She nodded. 'And one more thing,' I added. 'If I am not back by noon, you must go and tell Old Elspeth. No one else, just Elspeth. She will know what to do.' Maggie's eyes widened still further. I did not like leaving her with such a mysterious secret, which could only be a temptation to gossip or investigation, but since my conversation with Cathy and Heathcliff it had occurred to me that it was unwise of me, too, to go off to a dangerous place overnight with no one knowing where I had gone but Elspeth, who was unlikely to be consulted if I did not return.

When Maggie had left, I sat down at the kitchen table to gather my thoughts. Everyone was gone, except for Hareton and me, and soon we would be leaving too. Hindley had said he would be back for supper, but if experience was any guide, he was more likely to go straight to the inn for his night's drinking instead. Whenever he came home, be it early or late, he would find the house empty, but if it were late, and he were drunk, there was a good chance that he wouldn't notice, or if he did, would forget it by morning. That was what I counted on, though it felt strange to be hoping, for once, that tonight would not be the night he decided to mend his ways. If instead he returned early, and relatively sober, the whole scheme would blow up in my face, with Heaven knows what consequences. I felt as if I were staking Hareton's life on a roll of the dice, but I saw no good alternative. I knew not even how to pray for the success of my enterprise, for, so far as I knew, it violated the laws of both God and man.

'God save thee, little one,' I said at last, 'and protect thee from the foolishness and ill-doing of thy elders – myself included.' Then I loaded myself up as if I were a donkey, tied Hareton into a shawl in front of me, and drew another one over my head to cover my face, and set on my way to Pennistone Crag.

To one accustomed to dancing along a path with all the energy of youth and health and spirits, it was a weary walk. The weight I was carrying hunched me over for balance, and obliged me to take small steps, especially where the path went uphill, as it mostly did. Then, too, I was so draped about with bundles, I could not feel the cooling breeze, so I quickly grew overheated, and had to take frequent stops to catch my breath. It was a little as if I had suddenly been transformed into an old woman, bent and hobbling, obliged by the weakness of her frame to creep slowly where once she ran. I had allowed extra time for my journey, but now I feared it might not be enough.

Normally as I walked I would sing songs, aloud or in my

head as circumstances allowed, or let my imagination wander into self-made tales of wonder and adventure, but heat, weariness, and worry seemed to have driven that capacity from my head. I could think only about putting one foot in front of the other, and anxiously calculating my progress against the too-quick decline of the sun. Then the path levelled off for a time, and I decided I was past the place I might encounter other walkers, so I took off the shawl from my head and tied it about my waist. This allowed me to mend my pace a little, and I began to feel more hopeful. By the time I had reached the most difficult portion of the path, where it wound down into a narrow gully, over stepping stones across a rushing stream, and up the other side towards the Crag, it was clear that I would have at least a half-hour of daylight at the end of my journey – less than I had planned for, to be sure, but perhaps enough for my purposes.

By the time I got to Pennistone Crag, little Hareton was awake and crying for a meal. But Elspeth had told me on no account to feed him until certain rituals had been completed. So I made him as comfortable as I could in a little heathery dip near the cave, apologizing to him for leaving him to his cries for the time being. I spread an oilcloth on the floor of the cave, and spread the bedding out over it as best I could. Then I patted the little bundle that was still nestled in my bosom, to make sure it was secure. Elspeth had told me I must carry it around the stone three times widdershins, before burying it in the shadow cast by the sun. If you have been to the Crag, you will know that this was not as simple as it sounded, for the stone jutted out from the edge of a steep cliff, so my circuits involved much careful scrambling. Through it all, Hareton's increasingly frantic cries tore at my heart. At any other time, such cries would have made me drop whatever I was doing and rush to gather him up and soothe him, but I dared not. By the time I had finished my third circuit, my eyes were half-blinded with tears, and the sun was approaching the horizon. I positioned myself in its shadow and looked about me for a stone to dig with – Elspeth had said I must not bring a trowel, but only use what was nearby. I found a sharp-edged rock and began working frantically at the sod with it. The action brought back that earlier burial vividly, so that Hareton's cries seemed merged with my grief for that earlier child who had never drawn breath, and I wept outright.

My efforts quickly dislodged a loose piece of sod, which I set aside according to instructions. The soil underneath it was much less tightly packed than I had expected, and I soon found out why. Mine was not the first 'payment' to be buried there. I came upon several small items: a baby tooth, a paste brooch, a scattering of tiny bones that looked as if they came from a small bird, and a half-rotten leather pouch, the contents of which I did not examine. These also I set aside until my hole was ready, only stopping with each one to throw a pinch of soil over my left shoulder and mumble an apology through my tears, as Elspeth had told me to do. When my hole was deep enough to hide my little package, the sun was just touching the horizon. I put the dislodged objects at the bottom of it, and went to gather up Hareton, whose outraged cries had softened into a piteous grizzling monotony that wrenched my heart even more than before. I settled him on my lap beside the hole, and then pulled from my bosom the small parcel containing what I had unearthed that morning. Wrapped in snowy white cotton, and tied with a gaudy ribbon like a precious gift, it seemed a fit object to lie among these other mysterious items, earlier offerings in return for who knows what desperate requests. I kissed it, my eyes streaming, and laid it in the hole,

354

piling the soil over it again and replacing the piece of sod. Then I pulled from my pocket the paper containing the threads Elspeth had woven for us both. I wrapped one twice around Hareton's thin wrist and knotted it loosely. Then, working awkwardly with one hand in the fading light, I tied the other around my own wrist, touching Hareton's finger to the crossed strings before I finished the knot, as Elspeth had instructed.

By now there was only a small arc of sun above the horizon. The moment it disappeared was to be when I spoke my request. I had thought that this part would be the most awkward for me: this addressing of myself to an outcropping of stone as if it were a sentient being, and asking it 'with all my heart' to complete some mysterious 'binding' between Hareton and me. I had even prepared a stiff little form of words for this purpose, and practised saying them to myself. But now that the moment was come, my spirit was so raw from the merging of old griefs with new fears, my heart yearned so towards the tiny being crying in my lap, who needed desperately what I could not give him, that words poured out of me unbidden.

'Whoever or whatever you be,' I sobbed out, 'help me to save this child, Hareton Earnshaw, and make him in truth what he is already in my heart, mine own child. Do this for me, and I will cast out all repining for the dead child of my body that I give you here in payment, my firstborn, and devote myself henceforward to the care of this little one.'

I sat for a moment after, exhausted by emotion, feeling the stillness of dusk descend on me – even Hareton's cries were momentarily hushed. Then he began wailing louder than ever. I bound him tightly to my chest with the shawl, only making sure that he could breathe, so that he would stay in place without my hands to support him. Then, for the second time in my life, I crawled through the Stonegate. I had some difficulty getting out onto the ground after, without landing on the baby, but I managed it by rolling slightly to one side, with my arms locked stiffly around Hareton to keep him safe. In the process, my old dress tore in the back, exposing my bare skin to a patch of nettles that chanced to be there. By the time I had got us both upright, my back was burning, and the pain merged with the stinging tingle in my breasts from several days of the ointment and Hareton's nursing, and the soreness of my back and shoulders from my laden walk hither, and the sharp ache of grief that Hareton's cries caused to twist my heart and tighten my throat, and it seemed altogether more than I could bear.

'Please, please, please,' I murmured through hiccuping sobs, not even knowing whom I was addressing, or for what, as I fumbled in the dwindling light for the pot of jelly to feed Hareton. At last I was ready, and put him to suck. He fell to with the fierceness of hunger, his little fist clasping and unclasping in rhythm. It was such a relief to still his cries, it was as if he were drawing all the pain from my body. While he suckled, I prepared the bottle of sugar-water that was to fill his belly after – an awkward proceeding in the growing dark, and holding Hareton in one arm all the while. Before I had left home, I had filled a jug with sugar-water as hot as I could make it, corked it tightly, and then rolled it into the centre of the blankets, hoping it would still be warm enough by the time I needed it, for I would have no means of heating it. I was relieved to find that the jug was still hot to the touch; perhaps the liquid would even need some cooling off before I gave it to the baby. I took the bottle and teat out from the clean linen in which I had wrapped them, then poured in the liquid and tied on the teat – by far the most difficult part of the proceeding, under the circumstances. When I was done, I found the contents still a little too hot, so I commenced shaking it to cool it, stopping now and then to test the temperature again.

All this took a good deal of time and concentration, hampered as I was. So it was not until I had finished that I noticed that Hareton had remained nursing contentedly at my breast far longer than usual – long after the bit of jelly would have been gone. I froze, and all but stopped breathing, as if this thing I had hardly dared hope for were a hare, paused within arms' reach, that would start at the least sound or movement. In the still darkness I heard, faintly but unmistakably, the sound of Hareton swallowing as he sucked. At the same time, I became aware that my other breast ached with a feeling that, though new to me, told its meaning with all the simple eloquence of the senses, as surely as the pangs of hunger or cold, or a call of the bowels – the same feeling that hurried the cows home every evening, lowing anxiously to be milked. I was still taking this in, when Hareton let out a little gasp – not a cry – and let go of my breast. I shifted him over to the other side, omitting the jelly this time, and he nestled in to nurse as steadily as I had ever seen him do with Emma Dodd.

And so I got my miracle. Whether it came from God, or Nature, or a pact with the Devil himself, I could not have told you. In time that question would cause me a great deal of concern, but that night I felt none. I sat and nursed my little Hare, whom I had snatched before he could flee this earth, my falcon who had struggled so to get free, and now lay calm in my arms. I watched as the stars winked into view above, and a hairline sliver of new moon rose in the east, and I listened to the faint chirrupings and rustlings of the night. Then he dropped off, satisfied, so I wrapped a warm blanket around us both, wriggled backwards into the fairy cave with him clasped in my arms, and slept.

357

TWENTY-ONE

I awoke in the night to Hareton's cries, and an answering ache in my breasts. I put him to suck, and drifted back to semi-sleep, marvelling at the ease of it. He woke once more to nurse before dawn, and by the time he was done it was light enough to see. I crawled with him out of our earthen nest, and looked about me. The sun had not yet peeped over the horizon, but I could see that the sky was clear, and presaged a fair, warm day. I changed Hareton into clean clothes, and rolled up the soiled ones inside the oilcloth. To my eyes, he seemed healthier already. He was awake, but quiet and alert, in a way I had not seen him in weeks.

'Well, little man,' I said to him cheerfully, 'it seems I am your mama now. What do you think of that?'

'Eh!' he said, waving the arm that held the string.

'Yes, I have one too, see? Here it is. And now you must sit quiet, and look about you, while I eat some breakfast, for I forgot to eat my supper last night. And from now on, little Hare, if I don't eat, why, neither will you!' Of course, he understood nothing I said, but his eyes followed me so intently it seemed as if he did. I was ravenously hungry, and rather regretted now that I had provisioned myself in so Spartan a fashion. A little of the cold fowl and seed cake I had packed up for Cathy and Heathcliff would have been a welcome addition to the bread, cheese, and water I had brought for myself. Still, hunger is the best relish, so I ate every crumb, and then, on a whim, drank the remains of Hareton's sugar-water also. I then tidied my hair and clothes as best I could, and began packing up our things for the walk home. Once laden again, I tied Hareton into a shawl in front and draped another loosely over my head, and set off home.

The walk back to Wuthering Heights was a good deal easier than the one the night before, for the path went more down-hill than up, and the provisions were now in my belly instead of on my back, but most of all, my heart was lightened. Hareton was safe, and I had saved him. It was true what Mr Earnshaw had said, that I was born to be the salvation of the family.

Had someone I knew chanced to pass me in the first mile or so of my walk, I would have joyfully blurted out the whole story of my success, I am sure, but it did not take long before more sober reflection kicked in. How was I to explain this miracle? So far as anyone but Elspeth knew, there was only one way a young woman could qualify herself as a wet nurse, and that was by bearing a child herself. If word that I was nursing Hareton got out, all sorts of speculation would ensue. True, I had not been seen to be obviously with child, but I had thickened about the waist in recent years, and in the absence of other believable explanations, it might well be concluded that I had concealed a pregnancy and then disposed of the infant. Nothing could be proved, of course, but it would set a cloud over my head that I would be hard-pressed to dispel. Explaining what I had actually done would be little better: half would disbelieve me, and the other half condemn me for dealing in witchcraft – even Elspeth might suffer as a consequence. And

359

who could say how Hindley would respond? There was nothing for it, then: I must maintain strictest secrecy on the matter. It was a depressing conclusion – I was already weary of dealing in secrecy, lies, and half-truths for Hareton's sake, and it saddened me, too, that I would have to shut myself out from the fellowship of other mothers, who loved to share stories and advice about the nursing of children, and whose cosy confabulations I had often envied.

At the first sign of dejection, though, I began upbraiding myself: 'What a greedy heart you have, after all, Nelly,' I said to myself. 'A day ago you were prepared to give anything, do anything, if only you could find a way to save this child, and now, the minute your unlikely boon is granted, you begin repining for the next thing you have not!' This was a salutary line of reflection, and I pursued it for a mile or so, to good effect. Then Hareton began crying, and I stopped to nurse him. I needed no better reminder of how much I had to be thankful for, and for the remainder of my walk I did not dwell on the difficulties of my situation, except to consider how they were to be managed.

When I arrived home it was mid-morning, and only Maggie was about. She seemed glad to see me, and immediately offered me tea and porridge, and took Hareton from me so that I could eat and drink, all of which was very welcome.

'Is Mr Earnshaw up yet?' I asked.

'Not yet,' she said, sounding relieved. 'And neither are Cathy nor Heathcliff, strange to say.'

'Oh, they are out already,' I said. 'They left as early as I did, to be sure of being gone before the master could give them something to do.' Whether Cathy and Heathcliff would sustain this story when they returned, I had no idea, but I thought it best to preserve Cathy's dignity so far as I could.

'And how is this little one?' asked Maggie. 'Was your errand this morning something to do with him? Or is that something I ought not to ask about?'

'It was, and it is,' I said. 'But I will tell you this much: it was successful, and I will be able to feed Hareton at home here from now on, with no further difficulties.'

'Oh, I am glad of that!' exclaimed Maggie, but I could see that it was hard for her to contain her curiosity about the details.

In truth, I reflected, Maggie would be my greatest difficulty in keeping my nursing of Hareton a secret. She was much with me during the day, for most of the work she did was under my supervision, and now the very qualities that had first led me to employ her – her cleverness, curiosity, and eagerness to be of help – seemed likely to be fatal to the maintenance of my secret.

Soon we heard movement upstairs, suggestive of Hindley's rising, and Maggie hastened to make fresh tea, and prepare the bread and butter with which he usually preferred to start the day. She had just readied the tray to bring into the house, when the door to the kitchen opened and Hindley came in instead. He looked dreadful: haggard and bleary-eyed. We both froze, expecting some orders from him, but instead he collapsed into a chair and held his head in his hands.

'May I get you some tea, sir?' asked Maggie tentatively.

'Yes, tea – hot and strong,' he replied hoarsely. She hurried to obey. Hindley raised his head and looked at me, his expression unreadable.

'I had a very strange dream last night,' he said at last.

'What did you dream?'

'I dreamed that I came home late at night, and called out for someone to help me take my boots off, but no one came.

I thought you were all asleep, so I bellowed louder, to wake one of you, but still there was no answer.'

My heart was pounding. Then I saw the door from outside open a crack, and Cathy's face peek through. She caught sight of Hindley, and I shot her a warning look, so she gently closed the door again without coming in.

'I went upstairs, then,' Hindley continued, his voice still strangely expressionless and his eyes fixed on mine, 'and began throwing open doors to get someone up, but all the rooms were empty, the beds unslept-in. Except for yours, Nelly, and that was locked fast. I banged on it and called for you, but you did not answer.' I held his gaze, willing myself to look only mildly interested, but I felt the blood draining from my face. I could scarcely breathe. Maggie brought the tea then, and Hindley stopped to drink some, so I was able to take a few moments to collect myself.

'That is strange indeed,' I said carefully, inwardly praying that he really thought it only a dream.

'That's not the strangest part,' said Hindley. 'I stopped banging, and put my ear to the door, to try to hear you within, but instead I heard wailing coming from down the hall, in the direction of my own room. I walked down there slowly, for the wailing filled me with dread. In my room, there, in the bed, was—' Here Hindley stopped, and buried his head in his hands again. 'My wife,' he choked out. 'She was lying in the bed, and it was she who was wailing. "My baby," she kept crying, "where is my baby? They have taken my baby away!" I looked around, and saw the cradle in the corner of the room, with the child in it, wrapped in blankets. "He is right here!" I cried, and snatched him up and gave him to her. But when she put aside the blankets, it was not Hareton there, but a stone, wrapped up in swaddling clothes. She

362

screamed then, and I was afraid for her, for she mustn't excite herself, the doctor said so, and I held her and tried to calm her, but she screamed and screamed. God help me, I still hear her screaming.'

Hindley's hands raked and clutched at his hair, tugging it so fiercely I wondered he did not pull it out, as his breath came in ragged gasps. Maggie had stopped, looking frightened, halfway to bringing Hindley his breakfast. I was struck dumb, too, overwhelmed with the relation, until at last pity for Hindley's pain moved me to speech.

'Hareton is right here, sir,' I said soothingly. 'See? Here is your son, real and alive – he is no stone, is he?' Hindley looked up to where I had perched Hareton on the table for him to see.

'He is so small,' he said wonderingly. 'Why is he so small? He looks smaller now than the day he was born.' Hindley seemed dazed, as if he were still unsure whether he were dreaming or waking.

'No smaller, sir, only not much larger,' I said. 'He went through a bad patch with his digestion, for a couple of weeks there – that is why I called in Dr Kenneth, you remember – but he is past the worst of it now, and should be putting on weight fast enough from here on.' I had adopted a brisk, matter-of-fact tone, deciding that this was the best way to reassure Hindley, and I motioned Maggie to give him his breakfast. 'But that was certainly an odd dream, sir, and I don't wonder that it gave you a bit of a turn.'

'A bit of a turn, yes,' said Hindley, shaking his head as if to dispel the vision. 'Maggie, fetch me a dram of brandy to put in this tea. That'll clear my head.'

'I've never known brandy to clear anyone's head, sir,' I could not resist saying, 'especially not when it's begun at breakfast!'

363

'Nonsense! It's the best thing there is for driving out the cold horrors – I should know. Spirits against spirits, to keep up the spirits – that's the thing, eh, Maggie?' Poor Maggie only curtseyed and fled the room, presumably to fetch the brandy. Hindley was back to himself, apparently, or at least to the self he had been of late. I was sorry to see it, and could not resist saying so.

'It's small wonder your wife haunts you with fears for her child, when she sees how you abuse yourself with drink since she was taken from you,' I said. 'Take warning while you still can, sir, and devote yourself to building a good life for your son. That is the best way to ensure that Mrs Earnshaw's spirit will rest in peace.'

'I'll thank you to leave my wife's name out of your reproaches,' said Hindley coldly. 'It's not your dreams she's haunting, but mine.' He got up then, and turned to go into the house. He met Maggie in the doorway, holding the brandy bottle; he took it from her, and continued on his way. Not long after, we heard the front door slam.

Maggie turned back to me. 'What was I to do?' she whispered. 'If he asks me for it, I must obey, mustn't I?'

'Of course you must,' I sighed. 'You did nothing wrong, lass.'

'But that was a queer dream, wasn't it?' she went on. 'What do you make of it? Do you think that it was really his wife's ghost, who came to him?'

'And that all the rooms in the house were empty, and Hareton a stone?' I forced myself to laugh.

'Well, perhaps they were empty,' Maggie said. 'With Joseph gone, perhaps Cathy and Heathcliff had gone out – they do like to sneak off sometimes, you know, and—'

'Nonsense, child,' I said sharply. 'You forget I was home myself. Do you think I wouldn't have heard him, if he were banging on my door? It was only a bad dream, brought on by too much drink. It's a wonder he doesn't have them more often.'

'Of course,' said Maggie apologetically. Decidedly, the girl was too quick.

Cathy and Heathcliff crept down the back stairs, then, having determined that Hindley was in front. Evidently they had sneaked up to their rooms while Hindley was with us, to hide the evidence of their adventure. At any rate, Cathy, at least, was in fresh clothes, and both had washed and tidied their hair.

'I suppose you two will be wanting some breakfast,' I said, 'though you have both *slept in* so late, I should more properly call it lunch.' I glanced at Maggie as I spoke, and Cathy caught my meaning clearly enough.

'We are both positively starving,' she said. 'All that *sleeping* gives one quite an appetite, you know.'

I sighed. Cathy's arch manner was like to give them away as fast as if they spoke of their adventure outright. Asking her to keep a secret was like asking a basket to hold water.

'Maggie, would you go out and pull weeds in the north-east corner of the garden today? I passed by it as I was coming in, and the kale is quite overgrown with them.' Maggie nodded and moved towards the door. 'And don't forget the straw hat,' I added, as she headed out without it, 'the sun is shining today.'

'So now, let us tell you about our adventures,' said Cathy as soon as the door was shut.

'Let me guess,' I replied. 'The night was warm, but very dark. The Gytrash did not make an appearance. The stars were bright and extremely numerous, and you fell asleep before you could finish counting them. Is that close?'

'Close enough,' said Cathy, somewhat annoyed, 'but that is not the most interesting part. For after we fell asleep,

Heathcliff and I both had exactly the same dream, and a very queer one, too.'

'Stop right there,' I cried. 'I will hear no more dreams this morning!'

'But it was about you, and baby Hareton.'

'All the more reason not to hear it. I have just heard Mr Hindley's nightmare on the same subject, and I still have the horrors from it. It is bad luck to hear so many bad dreams in one day. It will turn the milk.'

'I didn't say it was bad, only that it was queer. And I never heard that telling dreams could turn milk – I think you made that up just now. But what was Hindley's dream, that it has frightened you so?'

'If you want to know that, ask your brother – or Maggie,' I added, fearing she might take me at my word, 'she heard it too. But don't tell her yours, for you will be sure to let slip where you had it, and she ought not to be asked to keep secrets from the master.'

'But whom am I to tell, then? It was so strange that we should both have just the same dream on the same night!'

'Not so strange, really, for you had been together all the day before, seen all the same sights, and had all the same conversations. And the memory of dreams is very pliable on waking – probably you started to tell yours, and Heathcliff caught at some little similarity with his own, and imagined the rest to be in perfect concordance. There is no surprise in that.'

'If it is all so perfectly rational and unsurprising, I don't know why you are afraid to hear it. You really are very inconsistent, Nelly. One minute you are full of superstitious fears, and the next you are the height of rational scepticism.'

'Well, we are all like that sometimes, aren't we?' I said, putting down their breakfast in front of them. 'You are not very consistent yourself, for one minute you order me about like a servant—'

'Which you are,' Cathy interjected.

'Which I am – and the next you want to confide in me as though I were your dearest friend, which I am not. Come, miss, surely it is enough that I connive in your adventures, and keep your little secrets from my master, without you making me the repository of your dreams as well.'

'Leave it be, Cathy,' said Heathcliff irritably, 'she doesn't want to hear it, and why should we share it with anybody but each other?' Cathy made a sour face, but after that they both ate in silence.

I commenced preparing a bottle of milk for Hareton – for of course I needed to keep up the appearance that I was feeding him by hand. Then Heathcliff slipped off to wash, and Cathy seized the chance to sidle up to me.

'I think that Edgar Linton is coming to visit later today,' she whispered, 'and it might be better if Heathcliff were not here. Can you think of something to get him out of the way for a couple of hours, before two o'clock today?'

'I can't promise anything, miss,' I said, shaking my head at her duplicity, 'but I'll do my best.'

'Thank you, thank you, thank you!' she said, and then gave me her prettiest smile, and a little hug.

I had an errand I had planned to do myself that day, which was to let both Elspeth and Bodkin know that all was well with Hareton. On reflection, though, I thought this task might equally well be performed by Heathcliff – and certainly I would be glad to spend a quiet day entirely at home. I washed out the jug and the two little pots Elspeth had given me, and filled the former with fresh milk, and the latter with butter, put the cork in one and the lids on the others, and tied them all up with paper. These would convey my news as clearly as if I told her of it myself. What to send Bodkin was more of a puzzle, until I remembered the motley flag. I had indeed started to sew one for him, but never finished. I found it in the bottom of my workbasket, and settled in for a quiet half-hour's sewing to complete it. Then I purloined some writing materials from Hindley's desk, and wrote in my finest hand, 'Dear Bodkin, thank you for your advice. All is well. Here is the flag I promised you. Long may it wave. Sincerely, Nelly Dean.' I folded this up with the flag inside and sealed it with a wafer, then wrote 'Dr Robert Kenneth', on the outside.

Heathcliff came in for some oatcakes and cheese when it still wanted about a quarter-hour of two o'clock. Cathy was nowhere to be seen.

'Heathcliff, I wonder if you might run a little errand for me this afternoon,' I began. 'I need you to take this bag to Elspeth, and then deliver this letter to young Dr Kenneth in Gimmerton.'

'Might as well,' said Heathcliff gloomily, his mouth full of food. 'She wants me gone. That pasty-faced little worm, Edgar Linton, is coming over.'

'Did she say that?'

'She didn't have to. I can always tell.' He slammed the table. 'What does she see in him?'

'Manners,' I said, 'and education. Both of which you might gain for yourself, if you would take the trouble.'

'Fine clothes, and a rich estate, you mean,' Heathcliff snorted, 'neither of which I am likely to gain for myself.'

'I wouldn't say that. Look at Mr Thorne, my mother's employer in Brassing. He began life with fewer advantages than you have had here.'

'And had less standing in his way than I have now, I'll wager,' said Heathcliff. 'I can't leave Cathy, yet as long as I stay, Hindley will grind me down, and Linton outshine me.'

'If you'll take my advice,' I began.

'I won't. I tried that before, and it only got me a beating. Give me the things, now, and I'll be off. I should hate to cross paths with Linton coming in.'

'Off with you then, lad, and here's a shilling for you to spend in Gimmerton.' In truth, I did feel sorry for him.

The rest of the day passed without incident. Edgar and his sister Isabella came and were received by Cathy with as much elegance and decorum as if she had not spent the previous night on the moors with her rough companion. Hindley stayed away all day. Hareton cried to be fed every two or three hours: evidently my milk was not yet plentiful enough to satisfy him for longer, or perhaps he was only making up for lost time. At any rate, I had to use all my wits to keep Maggie occupied elsewhere, every time I needed to nurse him. Joseph came home before nightfall, and the household returned to what then passed for normal. I never did find out what Cathy and Heathcliff had dreamed.

TWENTY-TWO

Two days after Joseph returned, the question of how to manage my secret in Maggie's presence was solved for me. Maggie came in that morning at her usual time, but instead of settling straight in to her duties, she stood in front of me looking at the ground, twisting her apron in her hand, and generally looking anxious and miserable.

'What is the matter, Maggie?' I asked gently.

'Please, miss, my da says I am not to work here any more after today. I am sorry about the short notice and all, and my da says I must lose some wages for it, but that's all right with him.'

'Why does he want you to leave?'

'It's the master, miss, he's got so wild. Not that I told him anything about . . . about how things are here, sometimes – I wouldn't do that, you know. But Mr Earnshaw is at the inn in the village most nights now, and the way he talks and acts there, well, word has gone round. So now my da says it's no place for a girl my age. I am so sorry, miss, for I do like helping you and all, and you have taught me so much, and I shall miss little Hareton, and I don't want to go and leave you to manage all by yourself—' Poor Maggie here dissolved into tears. I hastened to reassure her.

'It's all right, child, I understand. Of course you must do as your father says. I can manage well enough by myself here – there is not so much to do as there was when we had a mistress here, and regular meals to serve to the family.' I was a little downcast, though. Even after what I had heard from the Dodds, I had hoped Hindley was not making so much of a spectacle of himself in public as he did at home, but evidently he was.

'But you'll have no help with Hareton, especially in the mornings after you've had a bad night with him. I did ask my da if I might come here just in the mornings, but he said I must look for a regular position somewhere else.'

'Hareton is doing much better now – he won't need feeding in the night for much longer.'

'Thank you, miss,' she sniffled, 'for taking it so kindly and all. I was afraid you would be angry at me.'

'Of course not child, I am not angry at all. I will miss you, Maggie, for you've been an excellent helper, but I'm sure you will get a good position somewhere else, and use all you've learned here.' I would miss her, it was true. But I was also somewhat relieved to have the matter taken out of my hands, and in a way that would not hurt her feelings, either.

Maggie was the first to leave, but before long, as I told you before, the household was deprived of all servants but Joseph and me. No one wished to stay in a household so strange and violent as ours had become, particularly when their wages were so uncertain. I continued to manage the rents as best I could, but I was hampered in my efforts by Hindley's constant demands for money, money, money. Nothing but cash would serve him to buy drink, and as long as he had that, he cared not what the rest of us lived on! The dairy was reduced to two cows, as I could not manage more without the help of a dairy-maid. I had endeavoured to press Cathy into service in that area, on the grounds that her mother had not been above it, but she was having none of it. Isabella Linton, she said, had never touched a cow in her life, nor set foot in the dairy either, and what she would not do, Cathy would not do. And so I had to struggle on by myself.

Still, though, I had my little Hare. My milk had indeed waxed with the moon, and before a week was passed Hareton was sleeping longer at night, and spending more of his days in cheerful wakefulness between feedings. It was not long after that when he began smiling at me, and then crowing with delight at anything that caught his eye, but always looking back to me, to share his pleasure. In short, he was such a joy to me, that I would have tolerated worse than I did, for his sake.

As a young child, I had once seen, at the house of an elderly lady in town, a large glass bottle, turned sideways, in which she had laboriously planted a whole living garden in miniature – as great a wonder to me then as if a ship in a bottle had floated on a real little sea, and swarmed with tiny sailors. It was winter at the time, but though snow and wind howled out-of-doors, it was always summer in her fairy garden. Now, as I stretched myself thin to cover and protect my little bairn, I thought of myself as like the glass skin of that bottle, creating for him a whole little world of warmth and safety amid the storm all around him.

I had weighed him not long after my return from Pennistone Crag, in the hanging scale in the barn that we used for fleeces. It was not very accurate, but it would do to tell if he was gaining weight, which was of course a great concern to me. I weighed him weekly after that, and the results were encouraging. When he had gained a whole pound, I thought to myself, 'That pound came from my own body, just as the flesh he was born with came from his mother.' And when a few more had been added, I thought, 'Now one-third of him comes from me.' When at last his weight had more than doubled, I felt a secret delight in the fact, as if now my claim on him as my own child were sober fact. As I thought it, there came before my mind's eye the image of Frances in Hindley's dream, unwrapping the clothes and finding, not her baby, but a stone, and I had a flash of compunction. 'But what was I to do?' I addressed the ghost silently. 'I could not let him die, could I?'

And did I think, ever, of how Hindley had once wished to marry me, and wonder if he might yet do so? Ah, that is a difficult question to answer. I believed that I ought not to think of it. I had promised, at Pennistone Crag, that if I were granted the great boon of making Hareton my own, so that I might save him, I would never repine again for what was passed and gone. To be sure, I was uncertain to whom this promise had been made: was it to some local demon like the Gytrash or a Brownie? Was it to the King or Queen of Faerie, who were said to rule the fairy cave and its environs? Was it to the Devil himself, as Joseph would aver? Or to Nature, who Bodkin had told me does miracles of her own? Or was it, after all, to God, who hears and sees all we do, and knows the secrets of our hearts, as we say in the prayer, better than we do ourselves? Whomever was the recipient of that desperate promise, they had certainly carried out their end of the bargain, and so it was surely up to me to carry out mine. Still, it is one thing to believe that it is wrong to harbour certain wishes, and quite another to expunge them from your heart and mind. Over the years, I had grown used to living much in daydreams of what the future might hold. They filled the monotony of my daily labours, and comforted me in all my disappointments and sorrows, little and great. So how could it not cross my mind, willy-nilly, that as I was now Hareton's mother, and Hindley his father, it would be well for all of us if we married?

Still, there was little enough in Hindley's behaviour to encourage such thoughts. I had hoped, at first, that Hindley's heart would be warmed towards both of us, by seeing us so happy together, but I soon realized that the opposite was true: the sight of us together seemed to irritate him more than either of us separately, and anything that showed the child's affection for me or dependence on me enraged him. And so came the habit of tucking Hareton away out of sight when Hindley came home. Usually I could manage it so that Hareton was asleep and tucked into his crib upstairs by that time, but Hindley was unpredictable in his comings and goings, so I was not infrequently obliged to resort to hiding him in the cupboard, as I think I told you before.

Even when Hareton was not about, though, Hindley's behaviour towards me was not pleasant. For the most part he just ignored me, or gave orders as shortly as he could, but every now and then his cruel streak would surface, and he would set out to distress me.

'Look at our Nelly Dean,' he said one day, when Cathy and Heathcliff happened to be by. 'Strong as a mule, and just as good-natured, isn't she? She will make a fine catch for some hard-working man, if he's not too particular about her breeding. It's a wonder more of them don't come knocking to seek her out. Have you a sweetheart, yet, Nelly? Or shall we try to find one for you? I shall put up a notice at the inn: "Healthy girl of fine peasant stock seeks mate with similar qualifications."'

I had found in these situations that defiance answered best. 'Better a sober peasant than a drunken squire,' I replied coolly.

'I wouldn't know – I have never met a sober peasant.'

'Perhaps you are looking in the wrong place, then. They are not generally to be found in a public house.'

'But your father was, wasn't he? Why, you were practically bred in a public house.'

'All the more reason to marry outside of one.'

'Ah yes, it won't do to marry where you are bred, will it?'

'That must depend on circumstances, of course, sir.'

'Oh ho! So you have your eyes set on someone in the household! Well, pickings are slim here, to be sure. There is Joseph, of course – he is certainly sober, but a little old, and I doubt he'd have you. I have detected in him, now and again, some slight hints of an aversion to you, strange as that may seem. How about Heathcliff? He is on the young side, to be sure, but he will grow, he will grow. Or is his gypsy blood too low even for your taste?' But when he turned to where Heathcliff had been, he found that both the children had fled. 'Oh dear,' he said sarcastically, 'it appears Heathcliff is no more eager for the match than Joseph. Well, what are we to do, then?'

'I am not looking to marry at all, sir, but if I ever do, I certainly will not seek your services as a matchmaker.'

'But I know you so well!'

'Not as well as I know you. Come, sir, there is no one left here to be amused by your teasing, and I have work to do, even if you do not.' Then I turned my back on him and left to go to work in the dairy.

That was a fair sample of many such conversations, if they can even be called conversations. They all had this in common: they were intended to wound me, and they did so by harping on my 'low' birth and scant qualifications for marriage.

'There is no mystery here,' you will say. 'Hindley is making it as clear as he possibly can without saying it outright, that you are not to think of marrying him.' True. And yet, and yet . . .

375

why did he keep recurring to the subject? And why was it that, the drunker he was, the more improper his teasings became? I tell you, sir, though you will think me mad with self-regard to say it: I think he loved me yet, and that he was fighting the feeling, not only when he lashed out at me, but in all the wild dissipations into which he flung himself. He would stumble in, bleary-eyed, fouled and stinking with mud or worse, and push himself into my face with his nasty remarks and crude insinuations, and seemed as though he were saying to me, plain as words, 'There is no depth I will not sink to, no degradation of body or spirit that I will not embrace, except you. Except you.' I think that his love held him as a steel trap holds a fox, and he was gnawing at himself to get free. And he tore so deep as he did because the trap had bitten deep, so that when he finally got free he could only drag himself off, bleeding, and fall prey to the first beast that came his way. When I think back on those scenes now, Mr Lockwood, the tears spring to my eyes, though I was dry-eyed then, and to this day I do not know whether they are tears of anger, or shame, or love. For yes, I loved him still. Not with the romantic passion of a green-sick girl, nor yet with the steady joy of one who holds a confirmed mutual affection, but with the sad, anxious love a mother has for a wild and wayward child, who hurts her most when he hurts himself.

And while I am confessing to you (for I will never send this to you, Mr Lockwood, Mr Knockwood, Mr Lockheart) I will say this too: that whatever promise his father had extracted from him, or whatever solemn vow to God he made at his behest; whatever faith he was still holding towards his late wife, or however low or degrading he believed a match with me to be, he would have been in every way a better man had he denied them all, and married me. There. It is written, in black and white. Of course I wished it, however hard I tried not to.

Of course I dreamed of it, even as I tried to push the dreams from my mind. It would have been best for Hareton, best for Hindley, best even for Cathy and Heathcliff, and certainly best for me. How could I not?

Then he dropped my baby from the top of the stairs, and everything changed.

Did it really happen all in one night? That Cathy pinched me and slapped Edgar, that Hindley stuck a knife in my teeth, told me he had just drowned Bodkin in a bog, got hold of my bonny, winsome nurseling and threatened to cut his ears off, and then, dear God, *dropped him*, in front of my eyes? That Cathy sneaked in later, and confessed to me her love for Edgar, and her deeper love for Heathcliff, and poor Heathcliff heard only the former, and ran off that very night, and Cathy made herself ill with searching for him? It seems impossible that it was all compressed into one fateful evening, a few hours that changed the whole future for all of us, did we but know it. I remember it so, now, but perhaps that is only because I told it to you that way, compressing into one night what took place over many. To save time, for it was growing late, or perhaps only to stuff something, anything, into the space between Hareton's fall and what it did to me, for my heart stopped dead in that moment, and when it started up again, when Hareton landed safe in Heathcliff's arms, it beat to a new rhythm henceforward.

The image of his fall is seared into my brain, yet I know that what I see when I think of it cannot be what really happened. I see a scene with figures stiffly posed in exaggerated positions, like the illustrations to a book, or the players in a village pageant: Hindley at the top of the stairs, arms wide, hands still in position as if they held his son, staring down at the falling child with his face frozen in a look of shock and anguish that in reality he had no time to assume; Heathcliff poised beneath, face solemn, arms already cradling the space where the child would be, and between them, about midway down, Hareton, seated serenely on the empty air, with one hand raised in blessing, like the Christ child in a picture.

Afterwards, I screamed at him, as I told you – I made one final, desperate effort to reach him, but I could not. So I turned my back on him and wrapped myself over the child, weeping and rocking and crooning all the love words I had hitherto taken such care to keep from his father's ears, whispering over and over again, 'Hareton, my little hare, my leveret, my love.'

How Hindley took this demonstration I had no way of knowing, for he said nothing, and I would not so much as look round until the sound of his boots on the stairs told me he had gone up to bed.

Much later I finally mounted the stairs myself, Hareton fast asleep on my shoulder. When I reached the top, the door to the master's room opened, and Hindley stood there. If I was startled it was only for a moment, for there was nothing to fear in his face. Drained of the anger and sarcastic mirth into which it had so often been twisted, it looked, not quite like his boyhood self, but like a ghost or memory of it. He said, 'Nelly.' Just that, 'Nelly.' Said it, not pleading or demanding, but as if it were simply a fact, a truth he had finally brought himself to see.

How often had I imagined that scene, and how many responses to it had I rehearsed to myself in my mind? But whether they were angry or tearful, exuberant or calm, brief or long-drawn, my mental scenes had always ended in the same conclusion: myself, with Hareton, in Hindley's arms, his face looking down on us both, suffused with a peaceful joy in my simple presence that I had not seen there in many a long year. Yet when the moment came in sober fact, all my imaginings and rehearsals went for naught, for I spoke without thinking at all. 'Goodnight, Hindley,' I said. I heard my voice as if it were a stranger's: sad, calm, firm, kind. And that was when I knew my heart had changed. I walked past him to my room, entered it, and closed the door. Afterwards, lying in my bed in the dark, listening to the soft snufflings of Hareton's breathing next to me, the reaction came. Long into the night, tears streamed down my face, and my body shook with silent sobs. That is what I wished to forget. That is why I merged that awful night with Cathy's confession and Heathcliff's flight. As if I could have sat there in the kitchen after what had just happened, catechizing Cathy on her two loves and offering sage advice.

It was a momentous thing for me, to have the greatest dream of my life extinguished – or rather, to know that I had myself extinguished it. I thought, when I rose the next morning, that the change would have somehow suffused the whole household, as if lightning had struck the house and torn down a wall while we were sleeping. Yet everyone went on as if nothing had happened – as indeed for, most of them, it had not. Even Hindley seemed unchanged, when he finally rose from his bed. Perhaps he was a little more distant to me, but that may have been only my imagination, for he was usually so in the mornings.

No, it was Cathy's feelings that brought upheaval to all of us, as ever – not mine. It could not have been more than a day or two later, for Hindley was still fresh in my mind, when I had to listen to her saying that marriage to Heathcliff would 'degrade' her, and so she would marry Edgar instead, but keep Heathcliff by her as a hanger-on, so that he could serve her with his whole heart, and be fed in return with the scraps of her affection, as I had been by Hindley, all this time. Is it any wonder I loved her not?

I was glad that Heathcliff had left. It made the house a little less violent, though not by as much as I might have hoped. And though Cathy grew quite tyrannical, as I told you before, she was at least more predictable in her demands, as there was nothing to compete with her desire to impress and attach young Mr Linton – which, for that matter, Hindley wished also. As for Heathcliff himself, wherever he had gone, I could not imagine that his situation was worse than it had been before. I believed he was gone for good, and I thought him wise to break his tie with Cathy, and shake the dust of Wuthering Heights from his feet, to make his own way in the world.

One great sorrow during that period was the sudden debility of old Dr Kenneth. Only a few months after Cathy took sick (as she did just after Heathcliff's departure, you may recall), he had a stroke that left him unable to speak or walk. He could get about a little, pushed in a wheeled chair, and could communicate laboriously with pencil and paper, but of course he could not see patients any more, so Bodkin had to take over the practice entirely. He and his wife had a son of their own by then, a few months younger than Hareton, named Richard after his grandfather. As soon as I heard of the good doctor's trouble, I made it my business to go into Gimmerton and see how the family was doing. The surgery was open, but nobody was waiting, so Bodkin called me in straight away. Then Anna came in, and took Hareton away with her to play with Ricky, so Bodkin and I could chat at leisure.

'I am so sorry to hear about your father,' I began. 'How is he doing now?'

'He is as well as can be expected, as regards his bodily health,' said Bodkin, 'and in spirits, a good deal better than we have any right to expect. He is very determined to give us as little trouble as possible, so he has been working hard to learn to dress himself and manage the chair without help. Still, it's hard to see such an energetic and capable man as that bending all his store of energy and concentration merely to putting his arm into a shirtsleeve, or writing a note to ask someone to draw the window shade. Anna has been wonderful, though – she is always thinking up new ways to give him ease, or make it easier for him to do things for himself.'

'She has presumably given up working for her father?'

Bodkin snorted. 'Yes – I would have thought Ricky's birth would be enough to see to that, but Mr Smythe persuaded her to keep coming in, and bringing the babe with her. And would you believe it, after Father's stroke he still tried to suggest that we should hire someone to look after Father, so that Anna could keep working for him, gratis! But she refused, thank Heaven. Even she was shocked by his selfishness then, and she has spent her whole life making herself blind to it. So then what does the old monster do, but go and marry his house-keeper! And now he has her helping in the shop too – and of course needn't pay her either.'

I laughed. 'But she's not much older than us, is she? I wonder she would have him.'

'Well, she's a hard-favoured woman, with a character to match, is Zillah – I doubt she could do better. And of course he's promised to leave her everything now, as she took pains to point out to Anna at the wedding.'

'So Anna gets nothing after all? That seems most unfair.'

'Well, I don't care about it for myself – we have enough, really. But poor Anna was grieved. She worried that I had married her under false pretences about what she would bring us. I told her I had never trusted the old man's promises anyway, and that I would gladly have taken her without them. Really he has done us a favour by casting her off, for, between you and me, he robbed me shamefully on the drugs I bought from him, and was not over-scrupulous about the quality either, yet I felt I couldn't go elsewhere. Now I can get what I need whole-sale through a supplier in Brassing, and know I am getting the best quality, too. And Anna is a great help with the measuring and compounding.'

'You must both be very busy, with your father's care, and all your father's patients on your shoulders now too.'

'Busy enough, to be sure. But my father managed it all alone for many years, you know, so we cannot complain.'

'Hindley says you are too busy ever to go drinking with him any more.'

'It was a handy excuse, really. The last time I was out with him – it would have been not long before Cathy's illness, I suppose – he took umbrage at something I said, and tried to drown me in a ditch! He was too drunk to succeed, fortunately. But I came home filthy and damp, and with a good display of bruises, and Anna was so frightened, she made me promise never to go out with Hindley again. I can't say I made any resistance to her. I had only kept with him for old time's sake, and in hopes of having some good influence, but I think he really is past that now.'

'You know he came home and told us he had killed you outright? It gave me quite a turn, though I could not believe it was true, for I thought you too sensible to let him do anything really threatening.'

'So did I, to be honest, but he came a little too close for comfort, there.' He smiled ruefully. 'It seems we are both in the habit of underestimating just how badly Hindley can behave. I would ask you why you stay, but I have seen you with little Hareton, and there's really no need to ask.'

'No, I couldn't leave him. He's like my own child, and the poor thing gets no kindness from anyone else in that house.'

'Not even Cathy?'

'Oh, she's not unkind to him, really, but she takes no interest in him either. And she has grown so peremptory since her illness! She seems to think it her duty now to think of no one but herself, and expects us all to do the same.'

'She was in a very bad way there, for a time, you know. Father thought it essential that nothing should upset her, until she was fully recovered.'

'But could he really have meant that none of us must ever gainsay her again, for the rest of her natural life?'

Bodkin laughed. 'Is that how she understood it? I'm sure he didn't mean that – only that she must be kept clear of distresses for a few months – or at any rate, of distresses over and above those that could not be helped. She took Heathcliff's departure very hard, I understand.'

'To be sure, she did, though it was partly her own doing. She spoke to me of planning to marry Linton, saying Heathcliff was too low for her, when she didn't know Heathcliff could hear her. After that, what was there to keep him?'

'And you have heard nothing about him since?'

'Not a word – and we made more effort to find him than you might think we would, precisely because Cathy was so ill with worry. It's plain he has left the neighbourhood, and has no desire to be found. But to return to Cathy, may I tell her from you that her health no longer provides a warrant for her unchecked tyranny?'

Bodkin looked taken aback. 'I don't know that I can say that on my own authority, Nelly. Though I presume she will be my

383

patient now, I have not had any consultation with her since Father's stroke. If I am called in to see her, I will be able to form my own judgement on that matter, and will certainly communicate it then.'

I sighed. 'Well, let us hope she sends for you soon, then.' The surgery was beginning to fill up again at that point, so I went to join Anna and the children in the house, and to pay my respects to old Dr Kenneth. He was a sad sight, to be sure, but he managed half a smile when he saw me, and leaned forward in his chair.

'He cannot speak,' said Anna, 'but I can assure you his mind is as quick as ever.'

'I don't doubt it,' I said, nodding to Dr Kenneth and to her. The two boys had retreated to a corner, where Ricky had a few small, brightly coloured toys, which seemed to fascinate Hareton. There were still a few toys in the nursery at home that he liked to play with, but they were old and faded, and like all small children he was drawn to the bright colours. At one point Ricky snatched a toy from Hareton's hands, and the latter began to cry. Anna immediately came over and knelt by the children, taking the toy from Ricky and talking gently but firmly to him as she returned it to Hareton.

'Hareton is our *guest*,' she said, 'and we must always be kind to *guests*, and share our toys with them.'

'Atta,' said Ricky.

'Yes, Hareton is his name, and Hareton is our *guest*.'

Ricky gazed at Hareton, seemingly more interested in this strange concept of 'guest' than concerned about the toy. 'Atta gess,' he announced.

'Exactly!' said Anna delightedly, as Ricky grinned with pride. 'He's only just begun putting words together like that,' said Anna to me. 'It's quite fun to watch, isn't it?'

'Delightful,' I said, forcing a smile. 'And equally delightful to watch you teaching him the principles of hospitality at such a young age.' I was remembering the first time Hareton had put two words together. I had left him playing in the yard while I did some work in the dairy, stepping out to check on him now and again. He was engaging in one of his favourite activities: carefully arranging sticks and pebbles according to some inner logic of his own, while carrying on an incomprehensible running commentary to himself. Then suddenly he rushed into the dairy and hid in my skirts. Hindley's voice from outside, uttering a string of foul language, soon told me the reason. When we were sure he had passed, we came back out again, to find that Hindley had kicked apart Hareton's arrangement, scattering the sticks and pebbles in every direction. I looked at Hareton, expecting him to burst into wails, but he only began silently gathering up his materials again. Then he looked up at me.

'Dada naughty,' he had said, as calmly and matter-of-factly as if he had been saying that fire was hot, or water wet. It was the first time he had ever said 'dada'. ('Nana', which I had taught him to call me, was the first word he ever spoke).

We watched the two children a little longer, while Anna and I chatted lightly about what they were eating, and how quickly they outgrew their clothes. I noticed how careful she was to include her father-in-law in the conversation despite his inability to contribute to it, addressing herself as much to him as to me, so I made every effort to do the same. When I perceived that Hareton was growing tired and irritable, I bundled him up and took my leave, not wishing to test Ricky's new-forged hospitality too strenuously.

On the walk home, Hareton slept on my shoulder, and I reflected sadly on the contrast between the Kenneths' household and our own. Hareton had such a loving, generous spirit born in him, but where was he to learn hospitality, or charity?

I said almost nothing about those years to you before, Mr Lockwood, for I had been cut off from the poor child so long, and feared so for what he was becoming under Heathcliff's rough tutelage, that I could not bear to speak about it beyond what absolutely must be told. Now that that awful time is passed and gone, and I have them both under my wing again, I thought that I would be able to tell all about it. Yet I have sat here, day after day, pen poised, unable to begin. What is there to tell? Mostly the stories any doting mother will tell of her first child: that he took his first steps at thus-and-such an age, and spoke his first word at another; that he was forward at learning his numbers, but more backward at his letters, that he loved currants, but could not abide gooseberries – or the other way round. What is the use of writing all that down here? The knowledge is precious to me, but it will only sound commonplace to your ears. Cathy might like to know these things, when she can compare them to her own child's progress – but I do not write this for her.

Well, I will write what I can. Such a bonny, sweet child he was! He feared and disliked his father, as well he might, but when Hindley was not about, which was most of the time, as I managed it, his naturally loving and trusting character held sway. You have never had children, Mr Lockwood, so I can scarcely hope to make you understand what it is like to be with a child day and night, as he grows from a helpless babe-in-arms to a proper little man running about in short trousers. How he flung himself with all his spirit into his little joys and sorrows, in a way that brought back to me the intensity of my own feelings as a child, so that when I shared in the former, and comforted him in the latter, it was as if I was caring, too, for that long-lost child that I was myself. I was not merely his nurse, but also his teacher, his parent, and, when I could snatch the time from my duties, his playmate too. His favourite game with me was one we called 'sack of oats'. He would climb into a burlap sack, placed somewhere that I would be sure to see it, and lie quiet until I came upon him. Then I would pretend to be puzzled by the find.

'What is this sack of oats doing here in the path?' I would exclaim, poking at it with a finger. This would elicit a number of barely stifled giggles. 'What a strangely noisy sack of oats this is!' I would say. 'Perhaps it has mice in it! Well, I had better bring it back to the barn where it belongs.' Then I would pick up the sack and sling it over my shoulder, pretending not to notice as Hareton wriggled and shrieked with glee. 'What a *heavy* sack of oats this is!' I would say. Once in the barn, I would fling the sack down on a large pile of hay, pretending to be careless, but really making sure the child landed safely, then turn on my heel and walk away. Then, a few minutes later, the sack would reappear somewhere else, and I would begin all over again, acting more and more puzzled about how this same sack of oats kept ending up in odd places after I had taken the trouble of putting it away. 'Joseph must be very careless to leave sacks of oats lying around,' I would say, or 'I think that naughty cow has been up to her tricks again, dragging sacks of oats every which way.' At other times I would blame the dogs, the horses, or even the cat: the more unlikely the culprit, the more he laughed. Hareton would happily have played this game all day long, I think, but I rarely had time or energy for more than a round or two. When I wanted to end it, I would announce that this sack of oats was so troublesome, I was going to feed it to the horses, straight away. I would go to their manger and start to take hold of the bag as if I were going to empty it, and then Hareton would pop his head out and declare himself in triumph. 'Why if it isn't Hareton!' I would cry, as if astonished. 'And I thought all this time, you were a sack of oats!'

His faith in me was touching – he really thought me not only the kindest, but also the bravest and strongest being on earth. He loved to compare the monsters in the stories I told him, wondering, could an ogre defeat a Gytrash, or the other way round? But whichever one I said would triumph, he would add, 'But *you* could make it go away, couldn't you?'

'To be sure I could, if it were threatening you,' I would say. 'I would hit it over the head with my rolling pin, pour boiling water on it, and scold it so viciously, it would run away and never come back.' Then he would nestle safe in my arms and ask for another story, 'A *really* scary one this time.' Ah, those were happy times for us.

No, I find it racks me still, the years I did not have with him: all the missed caresses, the little triumphs unshared, the troubles uncomforted, and lessons untaught. It was his loss too, that I see yet. He is so diffident, so loving and yet so uncertain of his claim to love, it tears my heart to see it. Such needless pain we both suffered, and all for the selfish whim of a girl, and the careless cruelty of a drunken beast. It was a terrible crisis in my life, when Hareton was torn from my arms, and it brought me as near to madness as I have ever been.

TWENTY-THREE

With Heathcliff gone, it was inevitable that Cathy would marry Edgar Linton in time. The only surprise to me was that it took as long as it did: some three years passed between his proposal and the wedding. The sudden death of both of the Linton parents had been a great blow to Edgar and Isabella, and they took to mourning with great solemnity. Edgar was too young to assume management of the property himself, so an uncle was made their guardian, and even after the mourning period was over, he thought Edgar a deal too young to be marrying. He wished him to go to Oxford to complete his education, and see a bit more of the world (especially, I suspect, its female portion) before deciding to settle down, as he said, 'with the only pretty girl in the neighbourhood'. But Edgar refused to go – he owed it to his sister, he said, to remain in residence, and to himself to devote his energies to learning the management of his own estate, which would be more use to him than studying Latin and Greek. But I don't doubt that Cathy had a great deal to do with his refusal, for she told him frankly that his departure would make her ill again.

When Cathy first suggested, a couple of months before the wedding, that she would like me to come with her to Thrushcross

Grange on her marriage, I thought little of it. I had no intention of leaving Hareton, and I thought I only needed to say so, for the plan to come to naught. After all, I was not some American slave, to be passed on from one family member to another like a prized cow or a silver platter, whether I wished it or not.

Cathy tackled me first. 'I have grown so fond of you, Nelly,' she said coaxingly, 'I cannot imagine going without you. When I move to Thrushcross Grange, everyone there will be a stranger to me, and you would not want me to feel so alone, would you? Besides, with me gone and no other lady in the house, it is improper for you to be here by yourself.'

'You will hardly be alone, miss,' I said, 'with your husband and your sister-in-law for company, and you have spent so many weeks in residence there, at one time or another, I am sure even the servants are not really strangers any more. But if it is loneliness you are imagining, how do you think it would be for little Hareton, if I left, and he had only Joseph and Hindley to look to for comfort? As for propriety, miss, do you really imagine that you have been chaperoning me, all these years? It is rather the other way round, don't you think?'

But Cathy was not so easily put off. She still clung to Dr Kenneth's words, that she must not be crossed for her health's sake, and nothing Bodkin could say could be permitted to countermand his father's authority – not, certainly, when that authority was so convenient to her! She pouted and cried, and refused food for a day or two, and Edgar grew alarmed.

'I am astonished that you could wish to stay here in this degraded mad-house, when your mistress shows such a need for you as she has done,' he said to me sternly. 'You will be much better off at Thrushcross Grange: we have a large servants' hall, and everything is orderly and well managed. As for your pay, I will double whatever Hindley is paying you.'

'Thank you, sir,' I replied. 'I have no doubt that Thrushcross Grange is well managed, and am therefore the more confident that you have no real need of my services there. This household may be degraded and mad, but that is all the more reason not to leave a young child unprotected here. If I leave, you may be sure Hindley will not replace me, and what will become of little Hareton then?'

'Hindley's natural affection will lead him to do his best for the child, you may be sure.'

'Pardon me, sir, but I have seen, as you have not, how far "natural affection" goes to protect a child when his father's wrath is up. I have the scars to prove it, and if Hareton does not, it is only because I have been here to protect him. If you won't take it from me, ask Dr Kenneth how many of the children he treats for broken bones, burns, and bruises are victims of their parents' "natural affections". And while you are there, ask him whether Miss Earnshaw's health still requires that we all bow to her every whim. The answer may surprise you.'

'I am not concerned with the brutality of the lower orders.'

'I have seen things in this very house, sir . . .'

'Which you ought not to speak of, to anyone. Have you learned nothing of a servant's duties?'

'I have always done my duty here, sir, and generally a great deal more.'

I had thought Edgar Linton a sensible man – as he generally was, on any subject but his love – and so I had spoken to him frankly, thinking that persuading him would settle the matter for good. I little realized that I was only providing him with the means to destroy me. He went straight to Hindley and gave him a lecture on the proper running of a household, and the importance of nipping in the bud any tendencies towards insubordination by servants, quoting me at length to prove his points.

'I don't give a tinker's damn what you think of my household, Linton,' Hindley replied angrily, 'and I'll thank you not to meddle in it.' But the damage was done. It always galled Hindley to have his authority and competence as master questioned, and the idea that I was speaking slightingly of him behind his back worked in him like a slow poison. So the next time Cathy began wheedling her brother about bringing me to Thrushcross Grange, in my hearing, Hindley announced that I could leave for all he cared, he wanted no more women in the house, with their underhanded meddling ways.

'But who is to look after Hareton, if I go?' I asked.

'The boy has been under petticoat government for too long already: he's in danger of becoming a thoroughgoing milksop. Every time I see him he is running to hide behind your skirts. Get you gone, and Joseph and I will make a proper man of him in no time.'

'And his lessons?'

'The curate can teach him, by and by.'

'He is learning his letters now – he will forget them if the lessons are not kept up.'

'Then let him forget them. There's no need for him to be a prodigy of reading – he can learn his letters when he needs them.'

'You'll have to pay the curate for his lessons, you know.'

Hindley slammed his hand on the table. 'Then I'll pay him! With the money I'm saving by not paying you for the privilege of listening to your insolence!'

I opened my mouth to tell him he paid little enough of my wages as it was, but then shut it again, turned on my heel, and went upstairs. I had had a sudden idea. I went to my room, and dug out the little pocketbook where I kept Hindley's notes of hand. They came to well over fifty pounds. A few days later, when I found Hindley alone and still reasonably sober, I confronted him.

'If I am to leave with Cathy, you must pay me all my arrears of wages. I have over fifty pounds in your notes of hand that must be paid before I leave.'

'Nonsense, you know as well as anyone that I have no such sum about me.'

'Then perhaps you should not be so hasty in complaining of how much I cost you working here. Come, Hindley,' I said pleadingly, 'you know how little you actually pay me, and how much I do for the household for that little. You must know that your income will be lower, and your expenses greater, without me than with me. I am worth far more than I cost you. But I stay for Hareton's sake, and will stay yet if you but let me. But if I go, I must have my back wages.'

Hindley looked hesitant, and I pressed my advantage. 'Do you really want to live on Joseph's cooking?' I said with a smile. 'You and I have had enough of that for one lifetime, surely. And if you think the boy is too much with me, why that is easily remedied. He only wants a little kind attention from you, and he will be as ready to follow you and look up to you as any son can be. I know that for certain.'

Hindley scowled and waved me off, but he did not dispute what I said, and I was confident that I had swayed him. I did not hear Cathy's next conversation with Hindley on the subject, but I guessed the purport of it when, on his next visit, Edgar took me aside to remonstrate with me about using Hindley's debt to me as leverage over him.

'It is ridiculous to make this into a dispute about money, Nelly – I have already offered you much better wages than

Hindley can, and I can assure you they will be paid in full. I would never give a servant a note of hand in lieu of wages.'

'Be that as it may, sir, I don't think it right that I should be told to walk away from fifty-four pounds that is owed to me already, and I won't do it.'

'But you must know that you are not more likely to get it by staying here – the debt will only pile higher. It makes no sense at all.'

'Well, I certainly won't see it if I leave, sir. Come, you know it is not really about the money with me – I don't want to leave Hareton, and don't think it right that he should be left with no one to care for him. I have only tried to tip the balance for Mr Earnshaw by reminding him of how much I am worth to the household, and how much it will cost him if I leave. Surely I have every right to do that. The debt is real enough – you don't dispute that.'

'It is not a fit subject for dispute with you, Nelly. It only goes to show why no gentleman should get into debt to his servants. It is a violation of all right order.'

'I am sure your views on what gentlemen ought and ought not to do are very strict and correct, Mr Linton,' I said, as humbly as I could manage, 'but I do not think Mr Earnshaw always shares them.'

'That is very certain,' snapped Edgar, and with that he left me. I thought him annoyed because he had lost his point, and felt quite pleased with myself for having gained mine. I underestimated what he was prepared to undertake on Cathy's behalf.

As I told you before, Cathy was entitled by her father's will to five hundred pounds on her marriage. When he was reminded of this, Hindley announced that he couldn't possibly pay it, as he had no money on hand. This had caused quite a storm. Edgar wanted no part of a fight with Hindley, and said Cathy herself was all the treasure he needed, but Cathy grew passionate on the subject – Hindley had already deprived her of so much that was precious to her (she did not specify Heathcliff, but it was clear enough that that was her meaning), she was damned if she would give up her birthright too. She would have the law on him, she said, and bankrupt him, if need be, but the money must be paid. Edgar was far more concerned about the public scandal that would ensue than about the money, but he was always eager to please Cathy, and so he had undertaken negotiations with Hindley for him to transfer some land to Cathy's name that would return to Wuthering Heights if Cathy had no heirs. These negotiations were still underway at this time, the precise piece of land and the exact terms of its future transmission being still unsettled. I had paid little heed to the details, not thinking it a matter of much concern to me, one way or the other.

I was taken aback, then, when, two weeks later, Hindley poked his head into the kitchen and said, 'Nelly! Fetch your damn notes, and meet me in the office.' I hurried to do as he said. When I arrived, he took the handful of notes and began to leaf through them. But the effort of adding the sums in his head was evidently too much for him. He handed me a fresh sheet of paper and a pen. 'Make a schedule of these, with the dates and amounts, and add up the total,' he said.

'What is this about?'

'Just do as you're told.'

I finished the schedule, which came, as I already knew, to fifty-four pounds, six shillings. I handed it to Hindley, and he glanced at the total.

'Right,' he said. He picked up an odd piece of paper and pushed it at me. 'Here is a cheque from Edgar Linton for fifty-four pounds sterling, and here' – he dug into his pocket and pulled up a handful of coins – 'are six shillings.' He snapped them down onto the cheque, one at time, smiling nastily all the while. 'Now I'll thank you to write "paid in full" on your little schedule there, and sign your name to it. Then we can burn these notes.'

'I don't understand,' I said, my heart thumping.

'It is perfectly clear,' said Hindley. 'You are paid up, paid off, cashiered out. Take your money and go.'

'But this is Mr Linton's money.'

'Mr Linton and I have concluded our negotiations. He has taken a piece of land off my hands, and in return . . . well, he is also taking you off my hands. A bargain at both ends, come to think of it.'

I sat dumbfounded.

'Go!' he said.

'You want me to leave . . . now?' I could barely speak.

'This office, yes. The household you need not leave until Cathy does, next month. For her sake, Mr Linton is very keen to employ you at Thrushcross Grange. I suggest you take him up on the offer, though I don't much care one way or the other. But you will have no further employment here.'

I got up and stumbled out. I had been so sure of my success that the blow came as suddenly as if the subject had never come up before, and I found myself unable even to think. I went into the kitchen and began preparing myself a cup of tea, hoping that would clear my head somewhat. No sooner had I sat down with it than little Hareton popped his head in.

'Can you play with me now, Nana?' he asked. 'We have not played "sack of oats" in such a long time.'

'No, dear child,' I said, struggling to smile. 'I have work to do. And you are getting so big now, that sack of oats is too heavy for me.'

'Maybe the sack of oats could stand up and jump into your arms. That would be easier.'

'What a strange sack of oats that would be! But I really cannot play just now.'

'Are you sad, Nana?' he asked, coming and clambering into my lap. 'You look sad.'

'A little, child, but I will be better soon.'

'Did Dada make you sad?'

'Let us not talk about sadness. Go and fetch your hornbook, and you can work on your letters while I start dinner.'

'May I do that later? I want to go outside and play.' I had scarcely noticed the weather when I went to the office. I looked outside now. The sun was shining and the air was balmy. What did it matter if Hareton did his lessons now or later, or indeed never?

'Go on,' I said, 'but don't go further than you can hear me.'

I went about my work like an automaton. I still could not quite believe what I had heard, but the truth of it was beginning to sink in. Cathy had outflanked me. Between Edgar's wealth and eagerness to please his love, and Hindley's pride and greed for cash, I was trapped. All my cleverness, and more, all my years of loving sacrifice and all my real usefulness to the household, were powerless against those weapons. What was I to do?

I will tell you what I did: over the next few days, I appealed to each of the three of them alone. I went down on my knees, I sobbed and begged, with all the hysterical desperation of a mother pleading for the life of her child, for I really believed his life was at stake. I will not write of those scenes: each was different, but they all ended the same way. Then Hareton learned what was coming – I hid it from him as long as I could, for pity's sake, but his father and aunt had no such compunction

397

– and he soon added his wails and pleas to mine. Nothing availed – in truth, it seemed that the more desperately we both begged, the more convinced the three of them became, each in their own way, that it was right for us to part. Cathy, under the Lintons' tuition, had learned to think of both children and servants as beings not entitled to their own judgement, but fit only to follow the guidance of their elders and betters – and her guidance was of course based on what she wanted herself. That she was little more than a child herself apparently did not cross her mind. So then I swallowed my pain and my anger, told them I would come to Thrushcross Grange, and tried to look and act resigned to my fate, while inwardly I paced the walls of my enclosure like the Brownie in his cage, testing for any weakness by means of which I might make my escape.

I thought of stealing away with Hareton, and hiding us both in some faraway town. I had cashed the cheque and added the resulting banknotes and sovereigns to my own modest hoard. Together they came to over seventy pounds. Surely that was enough to begin a new life somewhere? I could take a small house and let lodgings, or hire out as a dairywoman – I was young and clever and strong, and I felt confident that I could support us both by my efforts. But further reflection showed me the dangers of this proceeding: I would be a hunted woman, obliged to conceal my name and my origins, and requiring poor Hareton to do the same. Even if we escaped for a time, would we not live in terror of discovery? Then, too, while I might manage to put food in our mouths and a roof over our heads, I could not make up to Hareton for the loss of his birthright, or give him an education fitting his station. Did I have the right to condemn him to a life in the lower orders, when he was born to be a gentleman and a squire?

If I could have known for certain that Hareton would die if

left with his father – which I certainly feared, and not without reason, as you know – all these risks and disadvantages would have been worth braving, for his sake. Yet I knew not how to weigh the one set of risks against the other. Hareton was not a helpless baby any more, and though he still feared his father, he had gained some skill in avoiding the dangers he posed. I, on the other hand, had never been a fugitive, and knew not how far the tentacles of the law might extend themselves to find me, or how long and resolutely Hindley would keep up a search. And if we were discovered, I would hang for sure, and Hareton be carried back in grief and ignominy, in a worse condition than ever. I kept thinking of the stories in Dr Perkins's pamphlet, of wet nurses who had been mad enough to steal away their charges, and had come to a miserable end, often taking the babes with them into death. Now I understood too well what had driven them to such desperate acts. But did I really wish to share their fate, and be reduced to a mere cautionary example in his next edition? Reluctantly, and with great misgivings, I let go of this plan.

At last another thought crossed my mind, which ultimately decided me: was it not possible that Hindley would tire of the trouble and expense of keeping a young child? And if he did, what was more likely than that he would send Hareton to live at Thrushcross Grange? Edgar would be eager to have his nephew raised under his more civilized care, I did not doubt, and Cathy was unlikely to object either, for she was fond enough of Hareton, provided that he did not inconvenience her. In that case, if I were there already, what a joyous reunion Hareton and I would have, and how much better off would we both be henceforward, than we ever were at Wuthering Heights! Deep in my heart, I think I knew that this dream was but a will-o'-the-wisp that would lead me astray, but I was desperate for some sliver of hope to guide my judgement. That it also guided me to the path that was easiest for me to take, because the one most in keeping with my long habit of obedience, only strengthened it the more.

TWENTY-FOUR

Hope is but a thin broth to live on, when there is nothing of substance to add to it, and so I found it, over those last remaining weeks before the wedding. Poor Hareton was tormented by fears that, alas, I thought all too reasonable, though to comfort him I tried to make light of them. So it was that our last few weeks together were spent under the shadow of that looming sorrow. I tried to offset it with every indulgence and pleasure I could manage. I neglected my household duties shamefully, hoping to give Hindley a taste of what life would be like without me, and instead spent my days playing 'sack of oats' with Hareton, or going on long rambling picnics with him over the moors. I could lift his spirits this way, for he was young enough still to live mostly in the present moment, unweighed by thoughts of past or future except when something occurred to remind him of it. But for me each peal of glee at our game, or excited wonder at the discovery of a bird's nest or a butterfly, was like a knife in my chest, and it was all I could do to keep a smile on my face, and tears from my eyes.

And then there were the dreams, nightmares that tortured me so that I dreaded going to sleep. In all of them, Hareton was again a babe-in-arms, dependent on me for everything, and in each I would be ordered to relinquish him in some terrifying circumstance. In one, I might be directed to lay him down in a pit where prowled a slavering lion. I would be given the order casually, in passing, as if someone had asked me to fetch him a cup of tea or a clean towel. It would be Cathy or Hindley who gave the order, but there were whole crowds of people who milled about indifferently in the scene. I would remonstrate, pointing out the danger to the child, but as soon as my desperation showed through, their faces would close and they would turn away. And so I would struggle to speak calmly, reasonably and respectfully, carefully framing my commonplace reflections on the natures of lions and the vulnerabilities of babies, and drawing logical inferences therefrom, while tentatively pointing out that there was no good reason to leave the baby in such a place. But not only would Hindley and Cathy be unconvinced, but all the people around would give looks of distaste and disapproval, as if my efforts were not only wrong, but incomprehensible. That was the real horror – not only that I must deliver the child to this beast, but that nobody but me saw any danger at all, but thought this command the most ordinary and sensible thing in the world, so that I felt that either I must be mad, or the whole world was. Then Hindley would point sternly to the place where the child must be laid, and the lion would growl and snatch, and I would clutch the babe and look desperately around for a way to flee, but the wall of people would close around me, and I would cry out – and wake. In another, I might be directed to put the baby into a basket shaped like a cockleshell, and launch it into a raging sea, where it was plain it would be overset by the first wave that came against it. Again I would plead and reason, and again the uncomprehending crowd would frown on me with disapproval. There were many more dreams in the same vein:

my sleeping imagination was horribly fertile in the invention of dangers for the child to be consigned to against my will, and always they ended the same way: with the indifferent crowd closing in on me to compel me to the act, whereupon I would cry out, and wake myself up.

When we wake from a nightmare, there is a moment or two when the heart still pounds and the terror still holds us in its grip. Then gradually the real world reasserts itself, and we experience the sweet relief of knowing that the nightmare was *but* a nightmare, that its horrors cannot touch our waking life. But for me, that moment of relief would be quickly followed by the returning knowledge that my waking reality was but another version of my nightmare, so that I knew not which was worse: the shadowy horrors that came to me in my sleep, or the solid, daytime horror I woke to.

You must understand, Mr Lockwood: they put him in my arms still wet from the womb. I would have sold my soul to keep breath in his body. Indeed, there were times when I thought I had done so, in sober truth. How could I bear to leave him?

Contrary to custom, the wedding breakfast was held at Thrushcross Grange, it being more convenient to the church, and better suited to supply the elegance deemed fitting to the event. Both Hareton and I were expected to attend, but Hareton understood all too well what the event portended, and howled so at the prospect of seeing it that I was able to beg off for both of us, and spend our last morning together quietly at home. The wagon was to come for Cathy's things at two o'clock, and I, and the trunk that contained all my worldly possessions, were to go with it.

Our parting was not a pretty one. Hareton clung to me and

wailed that he would not let me go, so that Joseph had to come and prise him from me, then hold him while he struggled, screamed, and tried to bite him. I could not manage the cheerful smile I hoped to wear for his sake, but promised Hareton through my tears that I would visit him soon and often. Then Joseph carried Hareton inside, still struggling, and I climbed up onto the seat next to the wagon driver and slumped down with my shawl over my face, sick with misery and unable even to sob, let alone speak or move. The wagon moved slowly off. After a time, the driver spoke.

'We're out o' sight o' the house now, if ye'd like to put yer head up,' he said kindly. 'The fresh air might do ye some good.' I lifted up my head, but then felt so sick that I asked him to stop the wagon. My throat was so tight I could scarcely speak above a whisper, so I had to ask twice before he understood what I wanted. He stopped the wagon and hopped off to help me out of it. I climbed down and whispered my thanks, then knelt in the grass beside the road and vomited up all the contents of my stomach, choking and sobbing all the while. The driver knelt beside me and rested his hand gently on my back. He said nothing until I sat back on my heels, quivering and gasping for air, but apparently finished. Then he dug out a small flask from somewhere in his clothes, removed the cork, and offered it to me.

'Take a mouthful of that and swish it around to wash out yer mouth,' he said. I obeyed. The contents were some sort of strong spirits – I could not tell what – that burned my mouth and tongue, but they took away the taste of the vomit, anyway. I tried to hand the flask back, but he waved it away.

'Take a swallow or two first,' he said. 'It'll settle your nerves a bit.' Again I obeyed, though the strong liquor made me cough, and brought tears to my eyes. The driver took a swallow himself, then recorked the flask and tucked it back into his clothes.

'I can see you're a kind-hearted lass,' he said, 'so I know you'll not mention that to Mr Linton. He wouldn't approve.' I nodded, and then let him help me to my feet, and back into the wagon.

'Keep your head up now, miss,' he said, when we were underway again, 'and breathe deep. That's the best way to keep off the sickness.' Then, when we had gone on a little further in silence, he spoke again. 'That were Mr Earnshaw's child, that's Mrs Linton's nephew, is that right?' I nodded. 'What's his name?'

'Hareton.'

'How old?'

'Almost five.' I kept my answers short, hardly trusting my voice.

'And you've had the rearing of him, since he were born, is that what I heard?'

'Yes.'

'Eh, that's hard,' he said, shaking his head. 'But he's a likely lad enough, anyone can see that – a lively little monkey, and he knows what he wants, don't he?' I nodded again. 'He'll do all right, miss, you'll see,' he said consolingly. 'He's a little man in his own eyes, you may be sure, for all he still seems a babe to you. He'll find his feet well enough.' I said nothing, but only let the tears stream down my face unchecked. The driver lapsed back into silence, then, and so we continued for some time. But I was grateful to him, for he was the first person I had spoken to who had seemed to understand something of my pain and my fears, and tried to ease them.

When we were within half a mile of Thrushcross Grange, he pulled out a small earthenware jug from under the seat, and handed it to me.

'This here's just water,' he said. 'If you've got a clean pocket handkerchief, you'll want to use some to clean up your face a bit, for what with the dust and the tears I think it's not the face you want to show your new master and mistress.' I did as he said, and then dabbed my eyes with the cool cloth to take away some of the redness. 'Now show me a smile,' he said, smiling himself, and I managed a ghost of one. 'Ah, you're a brave lass,' he said. 'You'll do well enough here. Mr Linton is a bit of a cold fish, between you and me, but he's a good master and a fair one, and there's many a lass hereabouts would be overjoyed to get the place you're stepping into. You don't feel it yet, and I don't blame you for that. But you will, I promise you.' I nodded, not feeling equal to speaking.

'Now I've the advantage of you, for I know you're Nelly Dean, but you don't know me. My name's Thomas Overton – call me Tom – and I'm a groom here.'

'Thomas was my father's name,' I ventured.

'Well, ain't that a coincidence, for I've a daughter named Nelly, too, though she's a deal younger than you,' he said. 'My wife Bessie and I live hard by the stable, and we've two other little ones beside our Nell. If you ever find yourself in need of a cup of tea and a shoulder to cry on, look us up.'

'Thank you, Tom, you've been very kind.'

A manservant came and took up the trunk, telling me to follow him. We came to the back door, and the housekeeper, Mrs Phillips, was there to greet me. She introduced herself to me and suggested that we take a cup of tea in her sitting room, so we repaired to there. She struck me as a woman of middling sort, in every way: neither short nor tall, thin nor stout, kind nor hard, and of middle age, though more elderly than not. I found out later that she was nearly sixty, and had been a servant at Thrushcross Grange for forty-five years, and housekeeper for thirty.

'You are younger than I expected,' she began. 'How long have you been working for the Earnshaws?'

'All my life,' I told her. 'I grew up in the house, and have been in service since I was fourteen – that is eleven years now.'

'You don't look much like a lady's maid, I must say,' she said bluntly. 'How long have you been one?'

'I haven't, really,' I said. 'I helped Cathy to dress, but most of my work was elsewhere, in the kitchen, and the dairy, and in managing the household generally.' I did not trust myself to mention Hareton yet.

'So you were housekeeper there?'

'In practice, if not in title.'

'And how many servants were there in the establishment?'

I explained how the household had declined after the mistress's death, until it was composed of only Joseph and me.

'Dear me! From housekeeper to maid-of-all-work – I wonder you put up with it! Why didn't you leave as well?'

'I was – I am – very attached to the family. I grew up there, as I said. Mr Earnshaw was my foster-brother. And there was – a child.' The last word came out in a whisper. Mrs Phillips appeared to take no notice – perhaps she already knew that this was like to be a sore subject for me. Instead, she proceeded to interrogate me minutely on my skills: could I wash and dress hair, mend lace, sponge silks and furbish up drooping bonnets? I answered as best I could, but in truth my skills in this area were not far advanced.

'Well, you're a strange choice for a lady's maid – that's all I can say. But you are Mrs Linton's choice, so we must make do. We must get Wilson – she's Miss Linton's maid – to teach you what you need to know.'

'Please, ma'am,' I said, 'must I be Mrs Linton's maid? I could do more good, I think, in the kitchen or the dairy. Perhaps one of the housemaids would like the place instead?'

'It's not my decision, nor yours either. Mrs Linton asked to bring you here as her maid, and she is mistress now. Besides, with the wages I've been told we must pay you, I could not put you in any other place in the household without causing resentment among the others. Thirty pounds a year for a kitchen maid! Why, the cook herself makes barely more than that. However, when your mistress doesn't need you, we will ask you to turn a hand to other work in the household. I suppose you'll be more useful than most ladies' maids at that.' I thanked her.

'You will need to dress more smartly,' Mrs Phillips went on. 'Do you have any better clothes than you are wearing?'

'These are my work clothes,' I said. 'I have a Sunday dress too, in black silk.'

'You must wear your Sunday dress for now, then, to wait on your mistress. When you are finished dressing her in the morning, and finished tidying her dressing room and making any necessary repairs to her clothes, you will change into a housemaid's uniform to help out downstairs, then back to your good dress for your evening service to your mistress. You had best set to work on a new Sunday dress for yourself – something a little brighter and smarter in style, though not so bright or smart that it looks as if you wish to ape your mistress – a blue or green stripe, with a plain collar, would do nicely. The uniform we will find for you.' Mrs Phillips continued on in this vein for a time, explaining the order of the household, the times of rising and going to bed, meals, and so forth. I tried to listen, but I was still dazed and shaken from my parting with Hareton. Now that I was

408

not expected to form coherent answers to questions, I found it increasingly difficult to attend, or to hold back the rising tide of sorrow that threatened to engulf me. At last she came to the subject of holidays and half-holidays, and my attention was roused again.

'On Thursdays you may take the time between finishing the morning dressing and beginning the evening undressing for yourself. On the first Thursday of every month you may take the whole day, and Wilson will do for Mrs Linton. The second Tuesday of every month is Wilson's day, so you must do for Miss Linton then.'

'So this Thursday will be my first half-holiday?' Today was Saturday.

'Well, we'd be in our rights to wait until you'd worked at least a week, but if you work hard until then I will let you take it.' Five days until I could see Hareton again! It seemed an eternity, but it gave me something to aim for, at any rate. Mrs Phillips then led me up to the attic to show me my room – a tiny one, but as the mistress's own maid I was to have it to myself. The trunk was already in it, and Mrs Phillips left me there to unpack it and change into better clothes, after which I was to report to my mistress. As soon as the door was shut, I sat down on the bed and cried heartily, but I was not accustomed to indulging my feelings, so I soon roused myself to put away my things and complete my simple toilette. Thus began my work at Thrushcross Grange.

On Monday morning, I was helping Cathy to get dressed for a morning ride, when she discovered that she had left her whip at Wuthering Heights.

'I am sure there are spares in the stable,' I said, 'or Miss Isabella would let you borrow hers – she rarely rides.'

'But I am used to that one,' Cathy pouted. 'It's the one the Thornes gave me, that matches Heathcliff's, and it always reminds me of him. I will ride with no other. I will have to send a boy to fetch it – I am sure it was left in the stable, on the nail where it is usually hung.' I was struck with a sudden idea.

'Send me instead, miss,' I said eagerly. 'The whip may not be where you think, and I know my way about the place, so I will be better able to work out where to find it than a stranger would be.'

Cathy looked uncomfortable. 'That won't do,' she said.

'Why not? I promise I'll be as quick as any lad.'

Cathy took a deep breath, and then spoke quickly. 'You are not to go back to Wuthering Heights. Edgar and Hindley think it best for Hareton not to see you.'

I felt the blood draining from my face. 'For how long?'

'For good – you must not go back ever.' The words were like a blow. I gasped and swayed on my feet. Then my mind failed, my head swam, and I fainted dead away.

TWENTY-FIVE

When I came to, I was lying on my little bed in the attic, and Bodkin was holding my hand.

'How are you feeling?' he asked gently. With returning consciousness came the memory of what had caused my collapse.

'They say I am not to see Hareton ever again,' I said dully.

'Is that why you fainted?'

'I suppose so.'

'Do you feel able to get up now?'

I took stock of myself. I felt drained of any power to move. What parts of me were not racked with pain felt merely dead. 'No,' I said simply.

Bodkin felt my forehead. 'There is some fever,' he said. 'Do you mind if I examine you?'

'Leave me alone,' I said. I turned my back to him and faced the wall.

And now I must tell you something that may shock you: I had never weaned Hareton. Oh, he ate regular food with the rest of us – there was nothing wrong with him in that regard. But he still nursed in secret. There are children – little Cathy would prove such a one – who wean themselves not long after they start taking solid food: the wide world is so full of interesting

411

objects, and their new diet so wholesome and pleasant, that they will no longer take the trouble of suckling. Others are pushed off the breast by a younger brother or sister, or else the mother refuses it because nursing interferes with her work – or if nothing else, because other mothers tell her that is what she ought to do. But none of these things had occurred with Hareton. Nursing was a sure comfort to him, in that house of terrors, and it would quiet him when nothing else would. It was precious to me, too, and perhaps he sensed that: he was a loving, thoughtful child, even then.

When I had learned I must go, I knew that I ought to wean him off gradually before I left – for my sake more than his – but I could not bear to deny him anything – and perhaps I wanted the pain of my overfull breasts, to counteract the deeper pain within. I did bind a cloth tightly around my bosom, as I had overheard women advise for cases where nursing must be left off suddenly, and in the privacy of my room – when I could get there, which was not often – I would press out what I could, to relieve the pressure, but even so, it was not long after my arrival at Thrushcross Grange that they grew painful, and began to trouble me. I could no longer press anything out – evidently they were blocked, as I had sometimes seen happen with cows' teats, so that the milk built up and festered within. If they could not be unblocked, I knew, milk fever was likely to follow – had probably followed already, if what Bodkin said was true. But I was not going to confide in him – my nursing of Hareton was a secret so deeply kept that I could not imagine sharing it, nor could I explain how it had come about without other confessions still more disturbing. And so I turned away.

'Nelly, please,' said Bodkin gently. 'I cannot help you unless I examine you.'

'You cannot help me anyway,' I said. 'I am never to see my baby again. I promised him I would visit him. I said goodbye to him, and I thought I would see him again in a few days, and now – he will think I have abandoned him. He has no comforts, no safety, even. He could die out there, and I would not know!' Sobs overtook me.

'Dear God in Heaven,' I heard him say under his breath. 'That was cruel,' he said to me softly, 'and I am very sorry for it. But you are ill, Nelly, and I must examine you, or you may get worse.'

'I don't care. I cannot live this way. I want to die.'

'Come now, there's no such thing as "never" while there is life and hope, you know that. People change their minds; children grow old enough to wander from home – there is no telling what may happen.'

'Please leave me alone.'

'I will then, but I will be back soon. I am leaving some willow bark powder for the fever, and some drops that may ease you a little. Try to rest.'

Bodkin left and closed the door behind him, but evidently Mr and Mrs Linton were waiting outside to hear what he had to say, for I soon heard the three of them talking. Perhaps the Lintons were accustomed to the thicker doors downstairs, or perhaps they wanted me to hear – at any rate, they were loud enough for me to hear their conversation distinctly.

'She has become ill from strain and grief,' said Bodkin. 'The separation from Hareton was very painful for her, and hearing that she was not even to visit was too much to bear. There is a collapse of the whole system. She must have complete bed rest, for a week at least, if she is to recover properly.'

'I hope you see now, my dear,' said Mr Linton to his wife, 'how wrong it is not to maintain a strict division between

413

servants and family. You can see that it has been harmful to both her and the child.'

'Nelly is only sulking. I don't see why we should indulge her further,' his wife replied.

'There is nothing wrong with a nurse becoming attached to a child she reared from birth,' Bodkin snapped. 'It is only too natural that she should – so much so that I doubt you would wish to employ one who didn't. And you of all people, Mrs Linton, should understand how it is that grief and worry can make one ill. But whether you approve of its cause or not, I can assure you her illness is real now. She needs rest and treatment, or she will get worse. Mrs Linton, you wanted her service badly enough to drag her here against her will – I only hope that means you care enough for her to let her have the care and rest she needs now.'

I had never heard Bodkin truly angry before. It seemed to surprise Mr and Mrs Linton, too, for they replied in soft, conciliating tones, and the three of them moved out of earshot. I carefully pushed myself up into a sitting position, and performed the examination of my breasts that I had refused Bodkin. They felt hard as stone, hot, and painful to the touch. I tried to press some milk out, but none would come, and binding them was too painful to endure. What was I to do? And what would happen if I did nothing? I ought to confide in Bodkin, I knew, and get his advice, yet I felt no inclination to do so. The pain felt right and proper. Perhaps, I thought, what was happening to me now was a punishment for what I had done at Pennistone Crag. A feverish waking dream took hold of me, in which I seemed to see my breasts swelling until they burst open. Streams of blood and milk poured down my front, weaving themselves in and out of my long, loose hair until they formed a thick rope, which writhed like a snake and crawled up to wrap itself around my neck – I screamed.

A housemaid came running in, looking flustered. I told her that it was only a nightmare. She must have reported to Mrs Phillips, though, for a few minutes later that personage arrived, puffing a bit from her trip up the stairs. She felt my forehead and nodded grimly.

'It's a fever all right. Now there's a fine start to your employment – scarcely two days in, and already you're a burden on the household.'

'I'm very sorry,' I said. I felt miserable, and tears were already filling my eyes.

'Oh, I'm sure it's not your fault,' she said, softening just slightly. 'Do you get fevers often, girl?'

'Never before,' I said. 'Nor colds, either.'

'Mmm. You don't look like the sickly type, that's true. Well, no one escapes for ever, I suppose. It's time for your medicine now anyway – I've just sent the housemaid for some tea and honey to help it down. I'll just sit here until she gets back.'

'Thank you,' I said, though in truth her presence was anything but comforting. Was I to talk to her? And if so, what about? After a few moments of awkward silence, though, Mrs Phillips took the conversation upon herself, and commenced telling me the names, duties, age, and history of every person, male or female, who worked in the house and grounds. I had scant hope of remembering half of what she said, but still, it was needful information for me, and certainly preferable to answering questions or making conversation myself. At last the housemaid arrived with a tray bearing tea, dry toast, a pot of honey, and a glass bottle half filled with golden liquid. Mrs Phillips poured some tea into a cup, measured in a dose of the willow powder, and added a spoonful of honey before mixing it all up and handing it to me.

'Drink that,' she ordered, and I obeyed.

'And now I'm to give you some of these drops, Dr Kenneth says. I'm putting them in a little glass of my own cowslip wine, which is a fine medicine in its own right.' This too, I was ordered to drink. I found it very pleasant, and said so. 'It's a recipe as belongs to the household here – perhaps you'll help me make more, next spring when the cowslips are out,' she said. 'This here's from last year's crop – it's best to let it sit for a year or so.'

The medicine administered, Mrs Phillips encouraged me to eat some of the toast, but I had no appetite. So she piled everything back onto the tray, and left. The drops and wine had made me sleepy, and after she left I did sleep for a while, but the pain in my breasts was intense, and kept waking me up again, so that I drifted in and out, wavering between nightmares and my waking pain. It was so bad that I was half resolved to confess it to Bodkin on his next visit. But something else happened, to make that unnecessary.

The next morning, Mrs Phillips came as usual to administer my doses, but before leaving this time, she gave me an appraising look.

'I've a job for you, Nelly, if you can manage it,' she announced. 'It's one you needn't leave your bed to do, but it would be a help to us.'

'Is it sewing?' I asked. 'I think I could sit up to do some.'

'Nay, not like that, but no harder, certainly.' Mrs Phillips went to the door, and called out, 'Abel, you may bring her up.'

A loud clomping followed, and then a weather-beaten man appeared at the door, holding in his arms a tiny lamb – small even for a newborn, I thought.

416

'Born too soon, and the dam died not long after,' he said, by way of explanation. 'She'll need to be kept warm all the time, and fed every few hours. Can you manage that?'

'What am I to feed her?'

'We'll give you a bottle with a leather teat, and bring you a pitcher of milk each morning to fill it from,' said Mrs Phillips. 'Abel here will put a packing crate filled with straw next to the bed, so she won't soil the bedclothes.'

'It seems like a great deal of trouble for you all,' I said doubtfully.

'She'll be more trouble downstairs,' said Mrs Phillips irritably, 'with every lass in the place hovering over her, and fighting over the chance to feed her, there'll be no work done at all. It's always that way with the orphan lambs, till where I think we shouldn't bother with them at all. But they say Heaven rejoices over every lamb saved, so I suppose we must do our best. Anyway, Dr Kenneth says you'll need a week in bed at least, and you've nothing better to do in the meantime. And who knows, maybe she'll be a comfort to you, and help you get well that much quicker.'

Abel gently deposited the lamb in my arms, and promised to send a boy up with the crate and a bottle as soon as possible. Then he and Mrs Phillips took their leave, and left me in possession of my new charge.

The lamb was a stroke of luck. As soon as the lad had come and gone, and I was sure of not being disturbed for a while, I put her to my own breast, but it was so painful that I gasped and pulled her away instantly. If I were to go through with this, I realized, I would need something to bite down on, to bear the pain. I cast my eyes about the room, but saw nothing that would serve, until my eyes lit on my little copy of *Paradise Lost*. It was the right thickness, and dense enough to bear the pressure of my teeth, but I hated to damage it. Still, there was nothing else that looked as if it would serve. I put the bottom corner of it into my mouth, bit down gently, and put the lamb to my teat again.

I have never felt such pain, before or since. It was as if my flesh was being ripped off me. But then, when I thought I could not bear another moment, the pressure suddenly released. I pulled the lamb away and saw the tiny white threads of milk spraying out of their own accord. I hastily put a towel over them, and got ready to put the lamb to the other side. Before I did, though, I took the book from my mouth and looked at it. The impress of my teeth had gone deep into the cover and partly compressed the pages inside. I turned the book to another corner and bit down again before recommencing my operation. If anything, it was more painful than the last. The lamb, frustrated at being pulled from her meal, suckled harder than ever, and I bit down so hard I felt the cover giving way in my mouth. Then I snatched up a pillow and held it over my face so that I could cry out without being heard. By the time I felt the release, and could relax a little, the pillow was wet with my tears, and the corners of my poor book's covers were bitten clean off. But the worst was over. I could manage now, I knew, until my milk dried up properly, by binding my chest during the day, and turning to the lamb only when the pressure grew uncomfortable.

The poor lamb was not so pleased by the operation. Twice she had been pulled off a teat, and she was objecting now in no uncertain terms. I gave her the bottle, which she eagerly sucked dry before falling asleep in my arms. I bedded her down in her crate. Now that my bodily pain was gone, the deeper pain from which it had distracted me surged to the fore again. I was never to see Hareton again. He would think I had abandoned him – perhaps Hindley would tell him so, for spite. He would be so grieved, and his grief would make his father angry, and then – it did not bear thinking of, yet I could think of nothing else. Over and over I plodded in the same weary circles, like a donkey turning a mill. I was dead to everything but the leaden pain in my heart.

I am not the first woman to lose a child – children die every day hereabouts, all too readily, and their mothers grieve for them bitterly, every one, I am sure. Yet I almost envied such women their grief: it was so clean, so final: they could at least no longer be tortured with fruitless hopes and cankering fears. The worst was come; they would never see their child again. But then, they could be sure it was safe in Heaven, and in time that must bring some comfort. And then, too, those around them would understand their claim to grief, and sympathize in it. I had left my child in a very Hell, that no one seemed to see but me, and my grief was treated as a mere inconvenience by those who had caused it. Is it any wonder I turned my face to the wall, and wished never to rise from my bed again?

Bodkin returned the next day, felt my forehead and my pulse, and declared me somewhat improved. Mrs Phillips hovered nearby, offering information on what I had taken, and when, interspersed with her own observations. Bodkin listened patiently, but as soon as she paused, he asked her to leave us.

'Why, I don't know,' she began, looking flustered.

'Please, ma'am, I am a married man and a doctor – there is nothing improper in it. Nelly and I are old friends, and she scarcely knows you as yet – she will speak more easily between the two of us.'

Mrs Phillips looked at me, and I nodded. She left. As soon as the door was shut, Bodkin leaned in close to me.

'I have been to Wuthering Heights,' he said softly.

419

'You have?' I gasped. 'When?'

'Shh, speak more softly – the dragon is just outside the door, I'm sure. I went there yesterday, after I left you. I thought it would do you more good than all my powders and pills, to hear that Hareton is well.'

'And is he? How did he seem? Is he very unhappy?'

'He misses you sorely, I will not deny it. The poor fellow seemed sadly puzzled that you had not returned, but I was able to explain that that was not by your choice, and that you were at least as grieved by it as he could be. That seemed to comfort him a little.'

'How does Hindley treat him? I have been so afraid of what he will do if I'm not there to protect him!'

'Well, I won't pretend that Hindley has suddenly turned into a loving father – and you wouldn't believe me if I did. But children adjust to new circumstances faster than you might think, and Hareton is a sturdy, sensible lad. He's found his feet pretty well – he seems to know when it's safe to be around Hindley, when to disappear, and when to run to Joseph for protection. Joseph grumbles at him, as might be expected, but in his own sour way he's devoted to the lad, and makes sure he's decently fed and clothed at least. Mostly the boy is left to himself, except for meals, and he seems happy enough when he's playing by himself. He's got hold of a kitten, too, that he takes about with him, and talks to a good deal, and I think that's been a comfort to him.'

'He will forget everything I've taught him.'

'Yes, very probably he will. He'll run as wild as a little moor pony for a few years, growing healthy and strong rather than learned. And then when the time comes he'll learn it all over again, and be surprised at how fast it comes back to him.'

The picture Bodkin painted was not a cheerful one, but it was a good deal better than the ones conjured by my fevered imagination. Hareton alone and unmolested, amusing himself on the moors for hours on end, as I knew he could do, with a kitten for company . . . my heart unclenched a little. But I was not ready to give up all my worries yet.

'But how long will that be? Do you think Hindley will ever get round to sending him to the curate?'

Bodkin hesitated. 'No, I don't,' he said frankly. He paused a moment, then took both my hands in his. 'Nelly, I know you are fond of Hindley, for all his flaws.' I shook my head, tears streaming. I didn't know what I felt for Hindley, any more. 'The truth is that he is destroying himself. I never saw any man set at it with such determination. In a very few years, he will be bankrupt, or mad, or dead – if not all three in turn. When that happens, Hareton will naturally fall to his uncle's care, and you may be sure Mr Linton will see to it that he gets a gentleman's education. And then he will have you back again as well, to give him love and guidance. Think of this as but a season in the wilderness for both of you.'

'I wish I could,' I sobbed. 'But who will even notice if Hindley runs mad, and kills his own child, as I have seen him come near to doing before?'

'I will,' said Bodkin firmly. 'That is the other thing I came to tell you – I have made up with Hindley, and have agreed to join him and some other fellows for cards and drink at his house each Tuesday evening. Sometimes I will be out on cases, of course, but more often than not I'll get there, and have a chance to check in on the boy and Hindley both.'

'But you promised Mrs Kenneth you wouldn't!'

'I have spoken to Anna about it, and she understands the need. And Nelly, I will promise you this' – here he pressed my hands firmly – 'I will tell you if anything changes there, and if I see real danger to the boy, I will take what action I can. Do you believe me?'

I nodded. 'Thank you,' I whispered.

'Have I comforted you?'

'A little.'

'Good. And now to my usual Nelly Dean pharmacopoeia: have you clean linen? Can I fetch you a cup of tea? I know better than to try to make you laugh just now.'

'You have made me smile, at any rate.'

'So I see – I am glad of it.' Until now Bodkin had scarcely glanced at the lamb, but now he turned his attention to it.

'And who is this little creature?'

'I was wondering when you would notice her. I was beginning to think you thought it so commonplace to keep a lamb in a sickroom that it was not worth remarking on.'

'Ah well, I had heard something of her from Mrs Phillips already. But how are you getting on with her? It is not too much trouble?'

'Oh, scarcely any, to me. Someone brings up the milk for her, so I've very little to do really. Mrs Phillips claims she'd make the housemaids neglect their work if she were kept downstairs, but I can't help thinking that it's a great deal more trouble having her up here. I suspect they mean her to be a comfort to me,' I added bitterly.

'And is she?'

I snorted. 'I am not a child, to be consoled with a peppermint stick for the loss of a playmate. I'm only glad it's a ewe lamb, and not like to be butchered for table. To raise up a creature from birth, and then have it ripped from my arms to be slaughtered, would be a bit too much like what I've been through already.'

'Perhaps Mrs Phillips thought of that, and made sure it was a ewe.'

'Perhaps she did,' I acknowledged. 'And if so, it was a kind thought. The creature is some company, to be sure. I suppose I would rather have her than not.'

'Have you named her?'

'No.'

'Why not?'

'Why should I? It's not as if I need to call her, or distinguish her from all the other lambs in the room.'

'Come now Nelly. I know you of old. The cat in the barn could not finish licking her newborn kittens before you had them all named.'

'Perhaps I have learned my lesson.'

Bodkin's face grew serious, and he took hold of my hand again.

'God knows you have cause enough to feel both grief and anger, Nelly. I don't dispute that. But do not cling to those feelings, nor get in the habit of feeling that taking pleasure in anything again is a betrayal of your love for Hareton. It will do no good to him, and it will only undermine your own health. I am speaking as a doctor now – I have seen it too often.'

I felt my face flush, and looked down. What he said was only too true.

'Take comfort and cheer where you can find them,' he went on, 'and keep yourself well. Then you and I will both do what we can to see that you and Hareton are reunited in time. Will you promise me that?'

'You have taken a great deal of trouble on yourself to ease my worries about Hareton a little,' I said, 'and I suppose that gives you the right to offer advice, too. It's good advice. I will try to take it. But I feel as if my heart is broken. I cannot just tie it up with string, and go bounding on my merry way.'

'Of course not. It will take time for you to recover – I don't deny that. Only don't stand in the way of your own recovery.'

'Yes, Dr Kenneth. I will obey your instructions.'

'See that you do. You don't want to find out what I do with refractory patients.'

'I have already found that out, and it is really nothing very frightening. But I will try to do as you say anyway.'

After Bodkin had left, I picked up the lamb to feed her again. What Bodkin said was true – my heart had yearned towards her, her tiny warm body so similar in weight to a human infant, and like one in being dependent on me for all her needs, but I had fought the yearning. I fought it no longer. I named her Leveret, and for the remainder of that week she spent more time in my arms than in her straw-filled crate. She did not heal me altogether, but, together with Bodkin's assurances, she gave me my first hint of ease from the gnawing pain at my heart. Lambs grow a good deal faster than children, of course. Leveret was slower than most, from having been born prematurely, but even so, by the time I was deemed ready to rise from my bed she was more than ready to try her legs in some space larger than my tiny room, and that added to my own drive to be up and about as soon as possible. On the appointed day, I rose at dawn and carried her down to the pen that had been rigged up for her near the kitchen door. She bleated piteously when I left her there, but I was not too much distressed by it, knowing that I would see her again at her next feeding. Then I went back upstairs and washed and dressed to be ready to wait on Cathy when she woke up.

That was the real beginning of my work at Thrushcross Grange. In some respects, it was like beginning service all over again, for the household was run on very different principles from Wuthering Heights, so that I had a great deal to learn – and to unlearn. There were a great many rules, not only about when we rose and went to bed, and what work we did and when, and how, but about what to wear while we did each task, and how to speak and behave in the presence of the family or of each other, and what we might or might not do with our time off. There was, furthermore, a strict order of status among the servants themselves, to which I was obliged to attend. At Wuthering Heights I had learned how to do a great many different things. Now I learned that some of these things were 'beneath' me and would damage my standing if I did them, while others infringed on the rightful territory of some other servant. Servants defined their status as much by what they could not be asked to do as by what they actually did, and woe betide the servant who dared to ask something of another that she had not the authority to command!

Much of this seemed to me merely silly. Why should I wear a different apron for starting the fire in the mistress's room than I wore for polishing silver? Why must some tasks be done only before noon, and others only after? And if something clearly needed doing, what did it matter which of us did it? There was little satisfaction in learning it all, for it seemed only to restrain, rather than expand, my capacities. It was like learning the rules of some vastly complex card game, which would never be played for pleasure. Still, I am blessed with a quick mind, so I picked it up rapidly enough, along with some of the real skills of being a proper lady's maid, in which in truth I was somewhat deficient.

As the mistress's own maid, answerable only to the house-keeper and the butler, my status among the servants was officially high, but that did not mean I was immediately accorded respect. I had got off to a strange start, for my first few days I had gone about like a sleepwalker, barely able to answer when spoken to, let alone make friendly conversation, and then, of course, I had been stricken with a mysterious illness. 'Standoffish, sickly, and probably simple-minded, that's what we thought of you then,' Wilson confided in me later. Fortunately, I did not know that then, but certainly I knew that I had some work to do to make a better impression than I had at first.

Some were inclined to sneer, for they thought their master had married beneath him, and that Wuthering Heights itself was little better than a poor farmhouse on the moors. I remember when I first saw the great hearth in the kitchen, fitted with an elaborate machinery for turning meat by clock-work, with a different spit for each sort of roast, I exclaimed at it in some wonderment, and then heard sniggers and slighting remarks behind me. I rounded on them sharply.

'The Earnshaws have been held in honour in this neigh-bourhood since 1500,' I snapped. 'They never had need of ironmongers' fancywork to prove their dignity. It was only Mr Linton's grandfather who bought this place, wasn't it?' I meant only to defend the Earnshaws, but found I had ruffled feathers in my turn, for of course the servants all held the family honour dear. 'Still,' I added, 'I can see that it would be a wonderful convenience when there are large numbers of guests to feed. We did not entertain much at Wuthering Heights, you know, being so far from town. It is to old Mr Linton's credit that he equipped his kitchens so handsomely,' here I turned to the cook, 'and I am sure you put them to very good use.'

'Oh, we do, we do,' she replied happily. 'It's a pleasure to work in such a place, I can tell you. We have all the best equipment here, and if any new thing comes out, that will make our work easier, the master is always happy to buy it.'

'I shall look forward to seeing more of it, and perhaps making use of some, to help you out when you are busy here.'

In suchlike manner, by being always a friendly and willing worker, but at the same time showing that I would not tolerate slights to my mistress or myself, I came in time to earn the respect of most of my fellow servants, and the friendship of one or two. Mrs Phillips remained a gruff, grumbling body, but I remembered Leveret, and gave her credit for a kinder heart than she generally showed me. She in her turn seemed relieved to find that I really could do a great many different things competently, and would do them without complaint, and grudgingly allowed that I was 'pretty handy, all told'.

At this time I learned what Mr Linton had meant when he told his lady that it was best to keep a strict separation between servants and family, an idea I had thought merely ridiculous when I first heard of it. The truth was that at Thrushcross Grange, as at most great houses, the servants formed a little society among themselves, sleeping, eating, and spending their leisure hours in rooms that their employers almost never entered, and interacting with the latter, for the most part, only in very formal ways. This will come as no surprise to you, Mr Lockwood, for you are accustomed to living that way, but it was a new experience for me. And while I remained a little scornful of the formality and strict notions of rank that informed it, I came to see that it allowed both masters and servants a greater degree of privacy than anyone had ever had at Wuthering Heights.

One afternoon not long after this, I went out to feed Leveret in her pen and found Abel there, examining her.

'Ye've done a fine job,' he said to me with a smile. 'She's near enough ready to go and join the flock now. Have ye given her a name?'

'Yes, I call her Leveret.'

'Well, now ain't that a coincidence, for I've a baby rabbit named Lambkin.'

'Do you really?'

'And a cat named Pup, and a dog named Calf – no, miss, I'm only teasing ye. It just seems funny to name the young of one beast after the young of another.'

'It has some meaning to me,' I said.

'Well, ye may call her whatever ye like, I'm sure.'

'You say it's time for her to join the flock? Will you take her up there tomorrow?'

'Could do. Unless you'd like to do it yourself. Thursday's your day, isn't it?'

'Yes, and next Thursday I have the whole day.'

'Ah, that would be grand. Ye could take her up there early in the morning, and bide with her a wee bit – that's if ye don't mind.'

'I should be glad to,' I said. I had not been up on the moors since I left Wuthering Heights. It would do me good, I thought, and my weekly visit to the Kenneths could be made in the evening.

Accordingly, the following Thursday I rose early and dressed myself in my old, comfortable work clothes. At my request, the cook had set aside for me a slice of cold pork pie and some bread and butter. These I wrapped in a large napkin and put in a small canvas rucksack, together with a jug of the thin beer the servants drank at table. Before I could leave, the cook tried to urge on me a large square of oilcloth to sit on.

'So ye don't mucky your clothes,' she said. 'It's right dirty up there. And bring an extra shawl – ye've no idea how cold and windy it is up there, e'en when it's warm here.'

I laughed. 'You forget I grew up on those moors,' I said. 'I can assure you the heather is quite clean and dry. And as for the wind, it sets my blood running, to keep me warm, besides which this shawl is quite thick. I have all I need, truly.'

She fingered the shawl, and pronounced it adequate, but would not let me leave without the oilcloth. 'Ye forget ye've recently been ill,' she said. 'Take it, dear, else I'll be worrying about ye all the day.' I gave in then, and took it, with thanks. I would not need it, I knew, but it was pleasant, for a change, to have someone show such concern for me. Then I added a bottle of milk for Leveret, and swung the whole onto my back.

Thus laden, I met Abel at Leveret's pen. We let her out, and set off on our way. The lamb followed close behind us, baaing for her breakfast all the way. When she grew weary, we stopped and I fed her a bit, then we continued on. We soon came within sight of the flock, spread out over a large stretch of moorland. Abel took leave of me then, and strode off on business of his own. I threw down my rucksack and shawl, retaining only the bottle, and took off in the other direction. I suddenly felt an urgent need to be alone.

I had thought I would be glad to get back to the moors – and certainly my heart had lifted when I saw them before me. But as the green pastures gave way to heather and ling, and the unobstructed wind swept into my face and whipped my skirts about my legs, bearing with it all the familiar smells and sounds, what I felt was something much stranger and stronger than mere pleasure. How can I explain it? It was as if, in leaving Wuthering Heights, I had left behind, not only that house and its inhabitants, but the moorlands too – and more than that, the Nelly Dean who had lived and worked there. Or not left behind, it now appeared, but only sealed off unchanged, like the locked room of a dead loved one. And now the moorland wind had blown open the door, and it all rushed back around me, a whirlwind of feeling.

I lay myself down on the heather and held up the bottle to bring Leveret to me. As she eagerly nursed, I clutched her to my chest and sobbed as I had not done since my illness. I don't know how long I might have kept it up, for my sobs seemed not to release but to deepen my sorrow, but Leveret, her hunger satisfied, scenting the entrancing odours of the moors and spotting other creatures very like herself for the first time in her life, was struggling with all her might to squirm out of my grasp. I let her go, of course, whereupon she began running about with the other lambs and kicking up her heels with a most lamb-like glee. My breath was still quivering and my cheeks were wet with tears, but I could not help laughing to see her, for she was unaccustomed to the uneven ground, and tumbled over with every second leap, only to scramble up looking greatly puzzled, and then start again. After a particularly bad tumble, which sent her head over heels down a small slope, she came running back to me and began nuzzling me insistently for the bottle, just as any startled lamb would do with its natural mother. I let her finish the bottle I'd brought, then smiled as she ran off to practise cropping the grass with her new playmates, imagining much the same smile hidden in the stolid faces of the nursing ewes. Then I lay on my back with my head on my arms and gazed up at the sky.

Directly above me was a brilliant blue sky strewn with billowy white clouds that moved gradually across it, not advancing in fixed formation, but slowly turned and broken and swirled into ever-varying shapes, which I gave shape to in my imagination, tracing the forms of animals and landscapes, and most often faces. Every now and then the likeness of some beloved or fearful face would emerge, so striking that it would make me gasp and sit up, only to find it already shifted out of recognition. I think I must have dozed then, for a time, for when I next noticed it, the sun was past its zenith, and I was very hungry. I made my way back to my things and ate my lunch, then lay back on the heather again and resumed gazing at the sky.

Advancing from the left was a cluster of low, dark, heavy clouds, bringing in their wake an unbroken mat of dark grey, like a shade being drawn slowly over a window, or a lid closing over an eye. As I looked upwards into the clear sky that remained, I saw that the white clouds in the middle distance were drifting in the opposite direction from the dark clouds below, as if moving to shelter behind them, while far above both was a layer of white wispy streaks, faintly brushed onto the distant blue, that appeared as fixed in position as I was myself. It was the steadiness of those high white wisps, I realized, against the movement of the middle clouds, which made my pictures form and deform so quickly, while providing the subtler shadings that now and then brought a likeness to startling life. In an hour or two, I knew, the dark would cover the whole of the sky – would *be* the sky, so far as we below were concerned. But above it all, the white clouds would continue in a different direction altogether, taking paths and forming patterns unseen by me. I tried to imagine our positions reversed – that the distant blue was really the ground, and the sky these purple-and-brown billows about me, and that I was gazing down from these impossible heights, trying to make out the movements of white beings on a blue earth below. And then all at once I succeeded, and felt such a rush of dizzying vertigo that I clutched at the heather, and feared my delirium had come upon me again, till I sat up and brought myself to my senses.

I set out for the Grange, wrapping my shawl about my head as I went, for the first light drops were already falling. The shepherd had advised me to leave at a brisk pace at first, without looking back, and let Leveret stay or follow me as she chose. 'Shoo's old enough t' be weaned, and shoo'll manage well enow wi' t' flock on 'er own, but there's no 'arm in letting 'er follow ye back hoom, and I'll bring 'er back out with me tomorrow – that's if ye don't mind the trouble, miss,' he added politely, which I assured him I did not. I tried to follow his directions, but like Orpheus, I found the urge to look back irresistible. My first glance showed her still with the other lambs, but on my next she caught sight of me, and alarmed at the distance I had already covered, came running up to butt me reproach-fully for my attempted abandonment.

'So, Leveret,' I said to her, 'you wish to play Mary's little lamb another day, and follow me everywhere I go. Well, so you may.'

I left Leveret at the Grange, and continued on into Gimmerton to see the Kenneths. When I got there, Bodkin had more substantial news to give me.

'Hindley has engaged the curate to teach Hareton,' he announced.

'Really! Does he pay him?'

'Well, I doubt Mr Withers would go there for nothing,' said Bodkin, but a quick sideways glance at his wife told me there was more to tell. Shortly afterwards Mrs Kenneth was called out of the room to attend to something in the kitchen, and Bodkin leaned in confidentially.

'It is shamefully easy to beat Hindley at cards,' he said in a low voice. 'I thought to just hold back in my play, but his other companions have no such compunction, so now I play to win.'

432

'And you win enough to pay Mr Withers?'

'Not always. But it turns out that Withers is a dreadful hypochondriac, so I make up the difference by supplying him with harmless syrups and pills for his imaginary ills, for which I might otherwise be ashamed to charge.'

'And Hindley doesn't mind you paying?'

'Hindley doesn't know, though I'm sure he could guess if he put his mind to it. I told Withers to name him a low fee, and not to dun him for payment if it wasn't forthcoming. Hindley passes him the odd shilling now and again, and imagines he is stringing him along.'

'How long do you think that can last?'

'I've no idea. But Hindley has grown accustomed not to being held to account for what he owes others – as you know to your cost – and Withers has grown fond of the lad. It might last for years. At any rate, we must take things as they come.'

'Do you think I might talk to Mr Withers about how his lessons are going? He might like to know what I did with him before, and what I have learned about how best to teach him.'

'I think that is unwise. I don't know that he is very discreet, and I am sure that he is not very brave. Keeping one secret from Hindley is probably the most we should expect. But I get reports from him.'

'And how is Hareton getting on?'

'Slowly. Not from incapacity, Withers says, but because he only studies when the curate is there to oversee him. He likes his studies, though, and as he gets older he will probably do better at making time to study on his own.'

Mrs Kenneth returned to the room then, so we both turned to more general subjects. Then I thanked them both sincerely, and took my leave. My heart was lighter than it had been since I left. Hareton now had two people who saw him regularly and

433

cared what became of him, and his education was once again underway. It was strange to think that, while I had been watching the clouds up on the moors, this news had been waiting for me, like the white clouds tumbling on their own way above the grey. And somehow that image became attached to the thought of Hareton for me, and gave me comfort. It was not exactly that I ceased to miss him, or worry about him, or to grieve for the real discomforts of his condition, but – how shall I say it? – I relinquished the deep and urgent terror I had felt on his behalf. I saw that he had his own path that he would have to follow without me, but I knew now that he would not walk it wholly unwarded. And while I was not yet healed, I saw that I would heal.

TWENTY-SIX

I have told you already how Heathcliff's return that September, after three years away, disrupted all the peace we had grown accustomed to at Thrushcross Grange, and caused great strife between Cathy and Edgar, and between both of them and poor deluded Isabella. I myself was perhaps not blameless in all that, and I have played many a weary round of 'what if?' about my actions at that time. Yet I acted without malice, and usually in hope of doing some good. In the tornadoes that afflict the central plains of America, I have read, one must open up windows, else they will explode outwards, yet in the hurricanes that batter the coast, they must be closed and battened, or they will shatter inwards. I knew not what kind of storm Heathcliff was, and so I opened some windows, and fastened others, and generally, as it appeared later, the wrong ones. But there is no sense in returning to that now.

As soon as I learned that Heathcliff was staying at Wuthering Heights, I took the first opportunity of being alone with him, to accost him on Hareton's behalf.

'He's a hardy little brat,' he told me, 'and he likes his father scarcely better than I do, which shows he has some grains of sense in him, anyway.'

435

I took hold of his hand, and held it hard in both of mine, though he tried to tug it away.

'Promise me,' I said fiercely, 'if you have ever owed me any gratitude for the past, or if you hope for any favour in future, promise me that you will not harm that boy, nor stand by to see him harmed.' Before I finished, Heathcliff twisted his arm up and over, and wrenched it out of my grasp. But instead of being angry, he gave me a grim smile.

'I will promise you that, Nelly,' he said, 'as regards bodily harm – though not out of any gratitude to you for once saving my sorry life, nor because I expect to require any generosity from you in future. Seeing Hareton injured in that way has no place in my plans.'

'What are your plans, then?'

'That is none of your business.'

'But you swear that you mean him no harm?'

'I mean to do all I can to ensure that he is healthy and sound of limb, and lives a long life.' I searched his face. There was something about his words that I did not quite like the sound of.

'Will you swear it? Swear it by—' I thought for a moment, rapidly discarding both the Bible and the Devil. 'By your love for Cathy.'

'Not by that,' he said bitterly. 'My love has undergone some rather violent changes lately. I will swear it by something much steadier: by my hatred for Hindley.' I opened my mouth to remonstrate with him, but he turned away and strode off, and I was obliged to be content with what I had got.

Not long after this, Bodkin informed me that, not only had Heathcliff driven away the curate, but that he himself had been obliged to give up his visits.

'Why? Heathcliff bears you no enmity, surely?'

'None to me personally, as far as I know, but he always seeks to draw Hindley ever deeper into dissipation, and he has noticed that I am no friend to that project. Besides that, since he came I cannot win at cards any more, and am in danger of losing more than I can afford. I call myself a skilful player, but Heathcliff is something of a different order.'

'Do you think he cheats?'

'Either that or he is preternaturally lucky in his cards, or at least in the timing of them. For perhaps four hands out of five, he will seem to be more unlucky than otherwise, but no sooner do his opponents gain confidence, and begin raising the stakes, than his luck suddenly turns, and he sweeps the table.'

'Are the other men losing too? I wonder that they keep coming.'

'Heathcliff plays them like a trout on thin line. One or another of them usually comes away a little ahead by the end of the evening. But never me – and even if I did, Hindley's losses grow so deep now, I cannot in good conscience take further part in his fleecing. I am very sorry for it, though, Nelly, for I know I promised you I would keep an eye on the lad.'

'You must do as you think best,' I said sadly. 'I am most grateful for all you have done until now. But tell me, how does Heathcliff behave towards Hareton?'

'You will scarcely credit it, but he is actually kind to the boy, and makes a point of protecting him, whenever his father grows rough. Hareton adores him, and seeks to imitate him in all things, although—' Here Bodkin hesitated, and flushed.

'Although what?'

'Well, let's just say that Heathcliff doesn't make the best use of his influence. He has acquired the manners and habits of a gentleman himself, as you can see, but that's not what he shows Hareton, nor encourages in him. It's as if he wants him to grow up rude and uncultivated.'

I nodded. 'I think that is just what he wants. It's of a piece with some things he has said to me.'

'You seem less worried than I expected, Nelly,' he said, looking puzzled. 'I thought we should have a storm, for sure.'

'It's odd, isn't it?' I said. 'I worry more about everyone else since Heathcliff came, but less about Hareton. Do you know how sometimes you listen to someone speaking fair of a person they mean to like, and yet you hear through it all that they hate him, and wish him ill?'

Bodkin nodded. 'I know just what you mean.'

'Well, it is just the opposite of that with Heathcliff and Hareton. When I hear him speak of Hindley, I know his hatred and his ill wishes are real. But when he speaks of Hareton, there is something else – a kind of softening of his whole face, an unbidden smile quickly suppressed. Did I ever tell you, that once, when Hareton was only a baby – it was the very night Hindley tried to drown you in the bog, in fact – Hindley dropped him from the top of the stairs? It was an accident – he was drunk, and Hareton was struggling to get free – and he would have been killed for sure, but that Heathcliff just chanced to be passing underneath at the same time, and caught him. Heathcliff looked as if he would like to undo the act, right after, but in that moment, when he caught him, there was something – a gentleness, an instinctive care in the way he took hold of him, and dipped his knees to ease the child's landing – that I had never seen in him before. The next day, Hareton followed after him like a lamb. If anyone was by, he would scowl and tell him to be off, but when he thought no one was looking, he smiled at him. It was only a few days after that that he ran off, so I forgot all about it, but now . . .'

'I'm not sure that Heathcliff's affection is much more of a boon than his hatred. It has certainly done little good to Mrs Linton.'

438

'No,' I sighed, 'but my hopes are so far reduced these days, his mere bodily safety seems enough to be grateful for, though he sacrifice his education to get it.'

All the rest of that weary, sad time – of the strife Heathcliff sowed amongst us, of Catherine's illness and Isabelle's elopement – I have told you already. And then my little Cathy was born, who was to bring us such a long spell of peace and happiness at the Grange.

Yes, I nursed her too, in secret, but it was no such dark and difficult thing as it had been with Hareton. As soon as I heard her cry, the ache in my breasts told me the milk would come. Mr Linton was willing to hire a wet nurse, but I told him that I had raised Hareton by hand without difficulty, and recited for him some of the cautionary stories of Dr Perkins, and he soon agreed to let me do as I thought best. As she was left entirely in my care, I had no difficulty in keeping the secret, and then, as I mentioned before, she weaned herself before she was a year old.

It was when the milk came for Cathy, all unbidden, that I lost my superstitious fears about what sort of bargain I had made with Hareton that night at Pennistone Crag. The Devil's dealings are obscure, to be sure, but he does not give away his wares for free, like a baker tossing in a sweet bun with the purchase of a loaf, for mere goodwill.

I did see Hindley once more before his death. It was about four months after little Cathy was born, in the height of the summer. During those first months, I had had her with me nearly always when she was awake, and even when she slept I was scarcely ever more than a few steps from her side. But the intervals between her feedings had now stretched to where I felt I could safely leave her in the care of a maid for a few hours, and venture to Gimmerton on some long-deferred

439

errands. The day was fair and warm, and, much as I loved my bonnie nurseling, and cherished my time with her, it felt sweet to be alone and unencumbered for the space of a bright afternoon, so I did not hurry. My errands took me from shop to shop, and on the way I encountered a number of acquaintances, who were all eager for news of the family, for, as I told you before, Mr Linton had shut himself up since his wife's death, neither visiting nor receiving visitors. And so my errands stretched themselves out, until I saw I must be on my way.

Just as I was passing the inn, my foot slipped on a loose cobble, my ankle turned, and down I went, face forward, with a thump and a cry, and my basket spilled packages in all directions. I had just got onto my knees, and was beginning to collect my things and trying to ascertain if I was injured, when I felt myself being supported up by a strong arm, and heard a familiar voice.

'There you are, Nelly, come, let me help you stand—'

'Hindley!' I cried. I was so addled with the pain and shock just then, and so relieved to see a familiar face, that I greeted him like an old friend. Then consciousness returned, and I began stuttering, 'I mean, ah, Mr Earnshaw, how kind . . .'

'Oh, leave that alone,' he said with a grin. 'I'm not your master any more. Is it your ankle that's hurt? Here, put your arm over my shoulder, and we'll get you inside that way, and see what's amiss. And don't worry about your parcels: Arthur the pot-boy is picking them all up, see? He'll bring them after you.' He helped me hobble into the inn to a seat, and called for the landlord to bring me a glass of wine. I accepted it gratefully, for my heart was pounding and my nerves jangling. A few sips calmed me, and I began to catch my breath a little. Then Arthur brought my things, and I occupied myself with checking over my parcels and replacing them in the basket, so I would not have to look at Hindley, but I chattered to him as I worked, expressing relief at each undamaged purchase, and thanking him again and again for his help.

'How is that ankle, now?' he asked when I was done. 'Shall I fetch Kenneth?' I turned my foot about a few times and pressed it against the floor. It hurt a little, but the pain was fading already.

'No harm done, I think,' I told him.

'I'm glad to hear it,' he said, 'but let me at least arrange a cart or a donkey for you, to get you home safely.'

'No, no,' I said, 'that won't be necessary at all. It's only a little distance, and the pain will go off with walking, I'm sure. Coddling it will only make it go stiff, you know.'

'Ah, that's the spirit. Nelly. Living at Thrushcross Grange hasn't softened you up too much, I'm glad to see.'

'No.'

An awkward silence followed.

'And how are you, Hindley?' I ventured at last.

'Oh, you know me, going to the Devil as fast as ever I can,' he said, with forced heartiness. I glanced at his face, which I had not ventured to do before. He looked awful: his eyes bloodshot and watery, his nose puffy and red, and his skin blotched with ugly eruptions. I looked away.

'And Hareton?' I forced myself to keep my voice light. 'Is he going to the Devil too?'

Hindley snorted. 'Long gone,' he said, 'but to a different Devil from mine. That black bastard, Heathcliff, has him in thrall. He's taught him to hate his own father – he'll not be sorry when I'm gone.' He paused. 'No one will.'

'I will be,' I said firmly. I looked at him again, and held his eyes this time. I could not resist a final attempt. 'Hindley, surely it's not too—'

'Stop,' he said harshly, but his eyes were soft, and did not leave my face. 'Don't try to save me, Nelly. Just don't. I am

441

like a man running down a steep slope, faster every minute. If I try to pull up now, I will only tumble arse over teakettle, and land at the bottom just as surely. Let me at least finish as I began, with my legs under me, and the wind in my face.'

I could not speak, and my eyes were streaming, but I nodded. I could give him that. I took a final sip of my wine, and gathered my things.

'Farewell, Hindley,' I said at last.

'Why fare-thee-well thaself, Nelly lass,' he said lightly, and turned away.

I headed home. The ankle was painful, but it would bear my weight, and I was not sorry for something to distract from the tumult of my feelings. I was about halfway home when I heard a shout, and turned to find Hindley running after me. I stopped and waited, thinking I must have left something behind, but he stopped about a dozen yards short of me.

'Hey, Nelly,' he cried, 'remember this?' Then he stretched his face into a solemn scowl and began sawing at an imaginary fiddle while his legs danced wildly beneath him, as he had done on that long-ago night. I laughed and clapped.

'Always!' I called. Then he swept me a deep bow, turned on his heel, and danced back up the road, fiddling as he went. I watched him for a time, until the ache in my breasts reminded me that I had been too long gone already, and I turned to hurry on my way.

I never saw him again. Two months later, he was dead, and I grieved for him with all my heart.

*

As Mr Linton became a recluse, the household shrank a little, and its strict orders and divisions softened. I was nearly always with Cathy when she was little, and he liked her company as well, so he would often have us both sit with him, of an evening. On one of these occasions – it would have been when Cathy was about three years old – my little lady chanced to stub her toe on a piece of furniture, and began to wail. Her father, who was nearest to her, ran to her to comfort her, and she accepted his embrace willingly enough, but at the first opportunity she wriggled out of it again and ran to me. She climbed into my lap and nestled in my arms, while I exclaimed over her injury and kissed it better. Then she nodded off to sleep, and I sat with her a while longer, till she should be deep enough in slumber for me to carry her upstairs. The silence was broken by Mr Linton.

'I wronged you, Nelly,' he said quietly.

'Wronged me, sir? When would that be? I'm sure you have always been a just and kind master.'

'When I took you from Hareton. I look at you now with Cathy, and I cannot imagine how I ever thought it right to separate you from him so casually as I did.'

I opened my mouth to reply, but my throat closed, and it was a minute or two before I could speak.

'I am sure you meant no harm, sir,' I said at last. 'You were young, and did not know any better.' A long silence greeted this. He seemed to be waiting for something.

'If there is anything to forgive, I have long since forgiven it,' I said at last.

'Thank you,' he said.

We never spoke of it again.

When Cathy was eight, Mrs Phillips announced that she was retiring to live with her sister by the coast, and it seemed natural that I should step into her place as housekeeper. She seemed pleased at the prospect.

'Well, Nelly, I thought you a poor enough choice when you first came here,' she said in her usual blunt manner, 'but you have proved your worth since. I shall be easier knowing I have left Mr Linton in your hands.'

I thanked her, and then, on a sudden impulse, added, 'I have long wished to thank you too, for your help in my first illness here – and especially for bringing me the lamb to raise.' Mrs Phillips looked a little uncomfortable at this, but I ploughed on. 'I know it was not for your convenience that you brought her to me, but for my comfort. It was a kind thought, and a wise one, and I have always honoured you for it.'

'Aye, it did do a good deal to bring you round,' she said, 'but I may as well tell you, it wasn't my idea at all. Dr Kenneth told me to do it. A puppy or a ewe lamb he said you must have, and if we couldn't find one we must buy one, but not to tell you it was done for you, or that he had ordered it. I thought it a foolish indulgence, and said so, but he was adamant – he said you might die without it. And right he was – not about the dying, of course, for we can't know that, but certainly that lamb set you up again, better than his powders and my syrups.'

'And all this time . . .'

'All this time you've thought me wiser and kinder than I was,' she laughed. 'Well, I suppose it did no harm, for it made you behave more respectfully to me, and that made me like you better, and on the whole we got on better than we otherwise might.'

'I'm sure you have earned my respect, many times over, since then.'

'Well, thank you for that, but still and all, I'm glad to leave without that undeserved credit on my conscience.'

And that brings me to the end of my secrets, Mr Lockwood. The rest of my story you know. This final sheet will rest on the stack, and I will wrap it up in paper, and tie it with string, and . . . then what? Not send it to you, that much is certain. You are only a name – I have known that for a long time. So why did I write it?

I told you once that at the wedding of Cathy and Hareton, I would be the happiest woman in England, and so I ought to have been and so I believed I should certainly be. But after the wedding, instead of happiness, a great weariness fell upon me. I could scarcely drag myself from bed in the morning, and when I did, I would sit over my morning cup of tea, running my mind over the various tasks that needed doing, and finding not one that could motivate me to action. Yet when I turned to amusements instead, they were no better. Even books could not hold me. I told myself that I was worn out from all the preparations, and allowed myself a few days of rest, but instead of becoming more refreshed by my idleness, I seemed only to grow wearier. At last I grew concerned, and sent for the doctor.

Bodkin questioned me closely, and examined me, and then he sat back, his face solemn.

'You are suffering from atlasiensis,' he announced.

'What on earth is that?' I asked, frightened. 'It sounds dreadful.'

'It is the disease that afflicts those, like Atlas, who carry the world on their shoulders. As long as they are carrying it, they go on well enough, but as soon as the weight is off their shoulders, all the weariness catches up with them.'

'I don't think I have carried the world, or anything like it. I have done no more than my duties.'

'Yes, your duties as housekeeper to two houses, mother of the bride, mother of the groom, and manager of two estates. That makes at least six people whose duties you are doing, and doubtless I am missing some.'

445

I smiled. 'It is really not so much as all that. Many of those duties overlap, you know, and sometimes it is easier to manage things yourself than to hire others to do it – there is less time spent consulting and giving instructions.'

'Very true, and for that reason I suggest that you also take over as mayor of Gimmerton, and perhaps curate as well. Clearly, the more roles you take on, the less you will have to do.'

'But it is no use telling me I have too many duties. The truth is that for almost a week now I have neglected them all, and yet I only seem to grow wearier.'

'You cannot rest properly with them weighing on you.'

'What am I to do then?'

'I am going to prescribe for you a month by the seaside.'

'A month! Good heavens! I cannot be gone half so long as that.'

'You must. I am serious, Nelly. You must make arrangements to have someone – or some three or four, more like – to take care of things here, and really go away. Take at least two long walks by the sea daily. Make friends with your landlady. Take out a subscription to the local library, and read all the latest books. Collect shells, and glue them to boards. And for a full month, be responsible for no one but yourself. Doctor's orders.'

I declined his advice, of course, but a few more days showed no improvement, and then Bodkin spoke to Cathy and Hareton, and they entered into the plan with enthusiasm. I suggested that we all three go together, but they had been warned off this arrangement. And so a room with a sea view was engaged by proxy, and a post-chaise hired, and I was bundled off to the sea by myself.

I don't know that my malady was quite what Bodkin had diagnosed, but certainly his treatment was effective. I had never seen the sea, and found it wondrous and delightful. Gradually my walks grew longer, and the sea air seemed to drive the weariness from my limbs and spirits. With little to demand my attention in the present, and almost no one to talk to, I found my mind turning more and more to the past. And so, instead of gluing shells to a board, I began to write. And then when I returned home, I continued, on and on, until I had produced the whole of the stack now before me. And now that it is all done, I wonder what I am to do with it.

Mistress of a snug household of my own. That is what my mother wanted for me, once. What I wanted, more than anything, was to be one of the Earnshaws, to be truly a member of their family. A foolish wish, and one that has led many situated as I was to a lifetime of faithful service with little return. No wonder my mother wanted me out. But I cannot complain: I have been more fortunate than most. Cathy and Hareton both love me and look up to me as to a mother. I am more mistress here than many a real mistress, and I cannot be divided now from those I love.

So why am I still sad? Ah, when I search it to its core, I wonder if it is not just the mother's sadness after all, the mother's sadness that is also her joy: they will thrive without me. I am no more the centre of their world.

TWENTY-SEVEN

Dear Mr Lockwood,

It feels strange to take up the pen again to write to you. I thought I had finished with all that. I had quite a sizeable pile of paper by the end. I tied it all up with a red ribbon, wrapped it in an old linen pillowcase, and put it under some blankets in a trunk. But I have pulled it out again. I find that my story is not finished after all.

When Hareton and Cathy and I all settled at Thrushcross Grange after the wedding, Wuthering Heights was left to the care of old Joseph, with a boy to assist him. Finding a boy to put there was no great difficulty – there is no shortage of idle lads in this neighbourhood – but keeping one there was another matter altogether. Joseph proved such a harsh master that one by one the boys abandoned their posts, until the position acquired such a reputation that finding another lad for it became impossible. One day Bodkin stopped in for a cup of tea and some talk after a professional visit to Cathy, who was nearing her confinement. The poor man had lost his wife the year before, in a fever that followed on the birth of their youngest daughter – I had been away at the time, on my trip

448

to the seaside – and he was still wearing mourning. I knew he would prefer to talk of other things, though, so I brought up the matter with him.

'I don't know what I am to do about Joseph,' I said. 'He is too old to be left alone all the way out there, but he drives the boys away faster than I can find new ones.'

'Perhaps you are choosing the wrong boys. I could name some whose homes have been made so unpleasant to them that Joseph could not but be an improvement.'

'I thought of that already, but it is no use. The ones who are welcome at home return there; the rest merely run off to sea, or to the Army, as inclination takes them.'

'What, they think Joseph is worse than the British Army and Navy? Well, either he is a greater terror than I can conceive of, or the lads hereabout are exceptionally stupid.'

'His temper has not sweetened with the years, nor has his arm lost strength with a switch. His Bible tells him not to spare the rod, and that at least he is prepared to obey to the letter. Perhaps he thinks his excesses there will make up for some deficiencies in other areas, such as loving his neighbour.'

'So they prefer the devil they do not know, to the devil they do. And to think the government is paying good money to press gangs and recruiters to lure unsuspecting young men into service, when, did they but know it, Joseph is performing the service for free!'

'Make light of it if you will, but what am I to do? He is really too old to be left all alone, even if he can still find the strength to drive away those meant to care for him.'

'Well, why leave him all the way out there at all? Let the Heights to some young family who can make the farm pay a little, and get Joseph respectable lodgings in town. I could name a few landladies who are as honest and clean as you could wish,

449

but yet have a strength of character that could quell even Joseph. Mrs Greene, for example: it is said of her that she scrubbed her late husband as vigorously as she did her floors, until he was worn away to a scrap, and simply blew away.'

I laughed. 'I would dearly love to see Joseph matched against Mrs Greene,' I said. 'It would be a clash of Titans, indeed. But there is a difficulty which perhaps you have not heard of. Joseph has been collecting notes of hand in lieu of part of his wages for as long as he has been at Wuthering Heights – dating back all the way to when Hindley's grandfather was master there, if you can believe that. Hindley's father would gladly have paid him in full, for he had a horror of debt, but it had become a kind of fixed idea to Joseph that his "notes" were more precious than money, and Mr Earnshaw was not fool enough to force cash on him if he preferred mere signatures on scraps of paper. And of course Hindley, and then Heathcliff, were only too happy to follow suit. When we tried to dislodge Joseph from the Heights – for his own good, mind you, for however little I love him, God knows the man has earned his retirement – he dug out a whole chest full of these chits, which added up to nearly a thousand pounds, and said that if we were to send him away, he "mun have his wage".'

Bodkin whistled. 'A thousand pounds! An impressive total for such a man. I can see that it would be a pull for the young Earnshaws to come up with such a sum all at once, but still, it could be done – Thrushcross Grange is a rich estate, after all. And the man really is owed the money.'

'So I told them, and they agreed. None of us wishes to cheat Joseph of his hard-earned wages. But the man really is a little mad on this subject: to hear him, you would think that instead of wishing to pay him what is rightfully his, and help him to retire comfortably, we were trying to rob him of his employment, his home, and his money all. Nothing will do for him but to continue at Wuthering Heights, and continue to add new signatures to his ancient pile. We have not the heart to cross him in this. I am not sure we have even the right to.'

Bodkin looked thoughtful. 'Has he any relatives, who might take on the task of caring for him there, in hopes of gaining such an inheritance?'

'He had a sister, but she died a few years back. I don't know if she ever married – Joseph would scarcely ever talk of his family.' Then I remembered. 'Of course she did! And had at least one child. Joseph attended the wedding of a nephew of his, let me see, it would have been August of 17—.'

'What an almanac you are! Do you have every casual little memory filed away by month and year, that way?'

I flushed. 'No, of course not. But that was the summer Hareton was born, and it was in the midst of his . . . difficulties then. That is how I remember it.' Bodkin did not appear to notice my discomfort in the least.

'Ah yes,' he said with a smile, 'it's funny how children anchor you that way. For me lately the years all seem to run together, but if I need to know a date more precisely, I need only remember that at that time Ricky had the cast on his arm, or Kate had just learned to crawl, and between that and the season I can usually pin it down within a month or two.'

'Well, thank you for making me think of it. A grand-nephew or someone of that sort may be just what we need. I will speak to Joseph about it. And, speaking of the children,' I added, 'how are yours faring?'

'They still miss their mother,' Bodkin said, 'all but Sophie, who doesn't remember her. But Maggie does for us very nicely during the day, and the children love her. Her own two boys come in with her, so the five of them all tumble about together quite happily. Have I ever told you how grateful I am, that you sent her to us?'

'Only about a hundred times, and she says the same. And it's not a problem, having her gone in the evenings?'

'Her husband doesn't come back from the mill until late, so she's able to give us supper before she goes. And she's added a little maid-in-training to the household, Sarah, who is with us at night, so that if I am called out the children will not be left alone. But in truth we scarcely need her. Peter is so proud to be the man of the house when I am out, he'll pop out of bed the moment Sophie cries, and have her walked or rocked back to sleep again, before Sarah has rubbed the sleep from her eyes.'

'Do you ever bring him about to your cases, as your father used to do with you?'

'I take him with me now and then, for he's keen to learn, but not nearly so much as my father did. There is more at home for him than there was for me. There'll be time enough for him to see cases, when he is properly apprenticed. I am glad he's taken to it though. Ricky never did, you know: he's much happier as a clergyman.'

With that we parted.

I did speak to Joseph on the subject of his relations, and discovered that the marriage of his sole nephew, all those years before, had borne fruit in the form of a numerous family. I obtained their address from him and wrote to them, telling of Joseph's condition and hinting at his wealth, and sure enough, they found they could spare their second son, a lad of fifteen years, to 'do his duty' by his great-uncle. This boy had been saddled with the august name of Abraham, though, when he arrived, it struck me that a less patriarchal figure could scarcely be imagined, for he was slight and timid.

It was on a grey morning in early spring, about a year later, that this same young man came dashing into my sitting room, wide-eyed and breathless.

'Uncle Joseph is dead,' he announced, and then collapsed into a chair and buried his face in his hands.

'There, there,' I said soothingly, 'you've had a shock – let me get you some tea and you can tell me all about it.' I filled him a mug, and when I could see that he was a little recovered, pressed him to tell me how Joseph had died.

'I don't know,' he said. 'I found him dead in his room this morning.'

'So he died in his sleep?'

'No – I mean – I don't know. He was not in his bed, but slumped against the wall. His eyes were open, and his face—' He buried his head in his hands again.

'His face was what?' I asked gently.

'Horrible. It was horrible.'

'Well, he must have had some kind of fit, or perhaps a nightmare. Did you hear anything in the night?'

'I did,' he said, without lifting his head. 'I was woken up by a commotion, and I leaped out of bed, thinking we had robbers in the house. When I got out into the hall, I could hear that it was all coming from Joseph's room – he was shouting, and stumbling about, as if he were crashing into things. I tried to open the door, but it was locked from the inside.'

'Was that unusual?'

'No, he always locked his room. I was never allowed in there. I called out to him, but he yelled at me to go away and leave him alone. Then things quieted down, and he told me again to go away, so I went back to bed. He always woke me before dawn to get up and make the fire, but this morning he didn't, and when I knocked on his door and called out to him, there was no answer. So I fetched the toolbox and took the door off its hinges. And then I found him.'

'Do you think there had been anyone in the room besides him that night?'

'I . . . I don't know,' he said. 'The window was latched on the inside, and you know it is very high up, but—'

'Did you hear any voices besides his, or any noises than could not have come from him?'

'No, I don't think so.'

'Then it was only a bad dream he was having, you may be sure of it. It must have frightened him more than his old heart could bear. He was a very old man – it's no surprise his time had come.'

'I suppose so,' said Bram doubtfully.

'Well, what do you think happened? It's clear enough no one could have got into the room and back out again without leaving any sign.'

'No human, perhaps. But I tell you, that house is haunted. I felt it, many times. I am sure there was . . . something . . . in that room with him.' He shuddered. 'Something that killed him.'

I laughed more heartily than I felt. 'The only bad spirit haunting Wuthering Heights was your uncle Joseph's,' I said briskly, 'and it was ill-tempered enough for a host of angry ghosts. That is all you felt, you may depend upon it – that and sheer starvation, for you look like you haven't eaten in a month, poor boy. Go down to the kitchen, and the cook will give you a good solid breakfast – everything will look better with some food in your belly. Go on with you.' This prospect appeared to cheer him considerably, and he hastened to obey. I sent one of the stable boys with a message to Bodkin, that Joseph was lying dead at Wuthering Heights, and he should meet me there as soon as he could manage. Then I set out to walk there myself, as briskly as I could. I had no love for Joseph, as you know, but still, the thought of him lying alone in that desolate house touched my heart. He had been a faithful servant, after all, in his own sour way, and he deserved better than that.

When I reached the house, I saw Bodkin's horse already tethered outside – he had made better time than I had, evidently. I found him upstairs, in Joseph's attic room, with the body. Bodkin was bent over Joseph, who was as his nephew had described him – on the floor, slumped against the wall, and with a scowl that might have been horror or rage frozen on his face.

'What do you think?' I asked.

'There's no mark on him,' said Bodkin. 'What does the nephew say happened?'

I relayed young Bram's account.

'Death by haunting? I can't put that on the death certificate. It seems clear enough he died of a heart attack. At his age it is not uncommon to find disease of the heart.'

'Do you think the attack might have been brought on by a nightmare? That might explain what Joe heard.'

'Very likely. Or the other way around – he was staggering about from the attack, and its stress brought on delusions. Either is possible. What do you know of the nephew?'

'A surprisingly decent boy, considering his parentage. Easily cowed, I think – it was that, more than the hope of gain, that made him bear with Joseph longer than any of the other lads.'

'You don't suspect foul play?'

'Not in the least. Do you?'

'I see no sign of it, but I have to ask. Still, I trust your judgement, and I'm content to call it death by natural causes if you are.'

'Can we move him onto the bed, and shut his eyes for him?'

'Of course, I'll help you with that. He can lie with some dignity until the undertaker arrives – I took the liberty of telling him we'd be needing him here later this afternoon.'

'Thank you.'

Together we lifted Joseph up and laid him out in the bed with his hands folded on his chest. When we were finished, Bodkin asked me what I planned to do until the undertaker arrived.

'I'll stay here,' I said. 'Someone should keep watch.'

'Well, I'll stay with you then, if you don't mind. I've no calls on my time just now, and Peter knows where to find me if something comes up.'

'I'd be most grateful.'

I blew up the fire, still banked from the night before, and made us both a pot of tea. The storeroom was still reasonably well supplied – evidently the abstemious old man had made few inroads on its little luxuries. I found a pot of jam and some oatcakes, and carried them out to have with the tea.

'This is like old times, isn't it?' said Bodkin. 'You and I, drinking tea and eating oatcakes and jam, here in the kitchen of Wuthering Heights.'

'It is,' I said, and suddenly felt my eyes fill with tears. 'It's strange – with Joseph gone, I am the only one left now, of all the people who lived here then.'

'Were you fond of him, in the end? I hadn't thought so.'

'No, not really, but he was my last tie to my childhood here, you know. I thought I hated him, but now I find I can wish him no worse than that he will meet a more forgiving God than the one he prayed to.'

'Amen.'

We sat for some time, sipping tea and crunching oatcakes

in companionable silence. Bodkin seemed as lost in reverie as I was. At last he spoke.

'How I envied you all, back then!'

'Envied us? Really?'

'Oh yes, back when we were all children, before Heathcliff came. Father would bring me to Wuthering Heights every few weeks, and drop me off for half a day or so, remember?'

'Of course – that was when we started calling you Bodkin.'

'Yes, well, you and Hindley would be let off lessons when I came, so that we could all play together, and it seemed to me that you were always free that way, since I never saw you otherwise. And then you and Hindley were such good friends to each other. I thought it must be a fine thing, to have a friend and playmate always to hand like that.'

'It was, often,' I said, 'but we certainly had our lessons and other chores to do, much of the time. Your coming always made a holiday for us.'

'I suppose that is why you were always so glad to see me.'

'Oh, you were good company too. We did have fun, didn't we?'

'We did.' We lapsed into silence again.

'Poor Hindley,' said Bodkin at last. 'What a mess he made of his life, in the end.'

'Yes,' I said, and then, moved by a sudden impulse, added, 'so much so that it is hard to believe it could have been any worse, if he had married me after all.'

Bodkin looked startled. 'Married you!'

'We wanted to marry. What is so astonishing about that?' I snapped. 'We were not so far apart in birth – I was as well brought up as old Mrs Earnshaw, and of the same family, for that matter. I don't know why you all should talk as if I was some filthy tinker sleeping in a ditch, whom it would be shocking

457

for him even to know, let alone marry!' But Bodkin's shock seemed only to deepen at my words.

'I thought you knew,' he said.

'Knew what?' I was still angry, but the look of dismay on Bodkin's face disturbed me, and my heart began to pound. 'What?' Bodkin reached across the table and took my hand in both of his.

'That you were Hindley's sister,' he said gently. His words seemed to knock the breath out of me. I sat staring, mouth agape, for a long minute.

'How do you know?' I breathed at last.

'My father told me – wrote it out on a scrap of paper not long after he had his stroke, and made me burn it after. He had kept it a secret until then, but he worried that with your mother so far off, there would be no one in the neighbourhood who knew, in case . . .'

'In case we tried to marry?'

'Yes.'

I sat still, his words sinking into my mind like rennet into milk, curdling memories, changing everything at once, though it would take time, later, to strain them and see what remained.

'Did Hindley ever know?'

'I really don't know,' said Bodkin. 'I don't think Father did either. What do you think?'

I thought back. So many things were recurring to my mind in a new light now. Had he known? Was it that, and not my lowly status, that made him rush to put a wife between us, and after her death, gave the edge of disgust to his longing? *There is no degradation of mind or body I will not embrace, except you.* He must have known. And that night, when he finally turned to me, and said, 'Nelly,' in that sweet, calm voice, and I turned away, what had I refused, after all? Had I unwittingly saved us

458

from a terrible sin? Or only forestalled a confession that might have eased us both, and set Hindley on a path to healing at last? I would never know.

'I think he knew,' I said finally. 'It would explain . . . some things. Not all, but some. But what made you think I knew?'

'I wrote to your mother, when you told me she was ill, to ask if she wanted the secret to die with her. She sent a note to say that she had told you already, that you knew everything.'

'She never told me anything! When I got to Brassing, she was past speaking. She only kissed my hands, and wept, before sinking to her final rest. Perhaps she only said she meant to tell me.'

'She was very clear in saying that you knew already. Perhaps her mind was wandering at the end, and she believed she had told you, when she only wished to do so.'

'I don't think so,' I said. 'Mrs Thorne told me she had her wits about her all the way through, that she met with people, read and wrote letters, and gave orders, all as if her death were just another household event, to be prepared for thoroughly and carried out efficiently.'

'Well, that is a puzzle, then. And you mean to say the thought never crossed your mind?'

I let out a bitter chuckle. 'There is very little that didn't cross my mind at one time or another,' I said. 'I had a very active imagination, and there were enough silences around the subject of my birth to give rein to all sorts of wild ideas. I even recall a time when I tried to believe I was secretly heir to the French throne, hidden in Yorkshire for safety – but I could not make it work. I certainly would have liked to believe that I was not my father's child, and that I was rightfully part of the family at Wuthering Heights. But it was clear as day that I was my mother's own child, and she was such a plain, sober, upright

459

woman, I could not imagine her being swept away by passion, nor could I imagine Mr Earnshaw in the character of her ravisher. And she was so devoted to the mistress!'

'That puzzled me too, but when I asked Father about it, he only shook his head and shrugged. He knew the bare fact, apparently, and nothing more.'

'I suppose we will never know, then.'

'No, I suppose not.'

But we were mistaken. We found a letter in my mother's hand, opened, among Joseph's papers. Her mind must have been wandering a little at the last, after all, for it was addressed only to 'Nelly, Wuthering Heights'. I suppose the post-boy was too young to connect that personage with the Mrs Dean who lived at Thrushcross Grange, and so had delivered it here. Joseph would have been unable to resist the temptation to add it to his hoard of secrets. It was dated to about a week before her death. I sat down to read it. Here it is.

My dear Nelly,

There are things you ought to know about your past, and mine. I made a solemn promise not to tell you of them, but I suppose death dissolves all promises, and if it does not, and I do wrong here, I will have answered to my Maker for it, and for all my other sins, before you come to read this.

Thomas Dean is not your father. When I found I was with child, I saw that I needed a husband to cover my sin, and that I had best find one soon, before my condition began to be evident. Tom was doing some work for Mr Earnshaw at the time, so that he was about every day. I knew that he was unmarried, and believed him to be kind and decent, though not over bright, and he had sent some admiring looks my way. So I met his looks with smiles of my

*own and, in short, soon gave him reason to believe I was
with child by him, and so he married me. I knew that I
wronged him so, but I told myself that I would bring him
more good than harm, by being a good wife to him and
making for him a better and more prosperous home than he
would have without me – for Mr Earnshaw had said he
would give us the lease of this farm at easy rent, and I knew
I could work it all but single-handedly myself. But I
presumed too much on Tom's simplicity, and on his
gratitude to me for marrying him. When you were born only
seven months after he thought you were conceived, too large
and vigorous to pass as a seven-months child, I saw that he
suspected that he had been duped. But he liked the comforts
I brought him too well to challenge me on it, and he was
ashamed to acknowledge it. And he proved to be one of those
men who take out their anger on the powerless, and so you
bore the brunt of his disappointment, until I had to send
you away, in fear for your very life.*

*I know, Nell, that you have often wondered what about
you could make him hate you so, and my heart bled that I
could not give you an answer that would make you see that it
was through no fault or shortcoming of yours, but so it was.*

*But I have not told you who your father was. And I find
that I cannot write it out, even now. But you know now, do
you not? And you see why I had to interfere between you
and Hindley, and why I could not let you bear his child? I
have wronged so many people: my husband, your father, and
her whom I loved more than anyone on earth save you –
and I know that I have wronged you too. Now that Death
approaches, it is mostly my wrongs that are before me, so
that my life seems made of wrongs – but I did not wrong
you then.*

461

*But how could I do such a thing? I was not young and
thoughtless, nor deceived in my innocence as many a servant
girl has been, or led astray by the urgency of my affections.*

How can I tell you?

*I did it for her. She never knew of it; she would have been
wounded to the core had she known, yet I did it for her. Or
so I believed then.*

*In the first twenty years of their marriage, the Earnshaws
had been given but one child who lived longer than a week.
That was Heathcliff, the first, and even he lasted only a
month. There was a stillborn daughter, and another
daughter and a son who each lingered only a day or two.
And miscarriages, one after another, some early, some later.
But the memory of little Heathcliff still gave them hope of a
living child to come.*

*At first the mistress's pregnancies had come every two or
three years, and she was able to regain her strength
between them. But then they began to come closer together.
Three within three years brought forth living children, but
each died within a week of its birth, and the mistress grew
weaker and weaker. Finally Dr Kenneth told them flatly
that her next confinement would kill her, she was so worn
out. But the master never wholly believed that her
weakness was more than a failure of will, and he was still
desperate for a son. She confided in me about it,
frightened for herself, but sharing her husband's longing
for a child.*

*And so, unbeknownst to her, I did a terrible thing. I
convinced the master that I could be to him as Hagar was to
Abraham, to bring him a child. I said that we could hide my
pregnancy from her, and pass a child off as an orphan
abandoned at his door – but in fact, with help from Elspeth,*

I took care not to conceive. For two years I kept him from her, and as she grew stronger we deceived ourselves that our sin was for the good of another, whom we each loved better than ourselves. But then he began to grow frustrated that there was still no child. And so I saw no alternative but to allow myself to conceive you.

Our plan was to tell her that I must go to America, that my brothers needed me there. But instead of going there, I would hide myself away in another part of the country until the child was born, and then make arrangements for it to be left on the Earnshaws' doorstep, a foundling. We had no doubt that Mrs Earnshaw would adopt the babe as her own, for her heart was broad, and she longed for a child. Mr Earnshaw intended that I should never return after that — that I would live henceforward in exile from her and from my child, as much as if I had gone to America in truth. But I had plans to find a position somewhere near enough to visit occasionally at least, for I loved Mrs Earnshaw too well to resign myself to never seeing her again.

We never carried out our plan. As soon as I told the mistress that I needed to leave, she became extremely distraught. She could not believe, she said, that I could prefer my brothers, who had 'abandoned' my mother and me, over herself, when we had always been 'more than sisters' to each other. I stayed firm, for I had made a promise, and knew not what else to do, but then she became quite hysterical. Her children were all dead, she cried out; her husband had forsaken her bed, and now her dearest friend and sister was leaving her too. She had nothing more to live for, she sobbed, and could only pray that death would take her soon. In this manner, she soon made herself really ill.

463

I could not refuse her. I told the master that I would stay, and then I made arrangements to marry, as I told you. He returned to his wife's bed, and she conceived not long afterwards. Had you been born a boy and Hindley a girl, or had their child not lived, I think he might have still have adopted you as his heir, without ever acknowledging himself your father. But Hindley was born instead, and that convinced him that he had been right to cast me off. Yet I do think that for him Hindley's birth was still tainted by our shame – and the more so when I came back to the house to nurse him. He was always but too ready to believe that Hindley would be a disappointment to him, and that had its influence on the poor lad's character. And then, too, I think Joseph suspected something of what had occurred, for he took to needling the master in small ways, hinting at buried sins, and he could see that his barbs hit home.

When you told me that he had walked to Liverpool, and brought home an orphan to raise as his own, I guessed at once that he was attempting some sort of penance for his past sin, and it made me angry that he should do so without thinking about how it would affect the rest of his family. But that was unjust of me, perhaps. It was I who led him into sin, after all, so who am I to speak against his effort at atonement? Then I saw but through a glass darkly, but now I begin to see clearly. I see my sin: how I longed for the power to set things right by my own act, to be the one who could give her ease, even if she never knew it. And I see other things too, that are harder to name.

Our secret stained your young life, Nelly, and caused you much pain, without your knowing whence it came. But you are strong, my daughter. You have a clever head and a skilful

464

hand, good practical sense, and the will to work steadily. You
got those from me, I like to think, but your heart is broader
than mine, and your need to order and manage is less, and
so I think you will find, if not perfect happiness, at least
contentment in your life. Keep well, my daughter. Return
good for evil; forgive those who sin against you, and most of
all forgive

Your loving mother,
Mary Swithin Dean

I finished the letter in silence, hesitated for a moment, then
pushed it across the table for Bodkin to read.

'Are you sure?' he asked.

'Go on,' I said. 'You might as well know the rest.' I watched
Bodkin read, and saw him nodding as he read. He finished,
and handed the letter back to me.

'A woman of powerful character, your mother,' he said.

'She was that.' I waited, but he made no further comment
on what he had read. 'So now you know my secret as well,' I
said at last. 'Or did your father tell you that one, too?'

'He didn't. But I had guessed something of the sort. I could
not see how else you could have come to nurse Hareton as you
did.'

I froze. 'You knew that? How?'

'Again, I guessed. We had little Ricky around then, you may
recall, and Anna was nursing him, so I noticed things on your
rare visits to us I might not have otherwise. How your figure
had altered, for example. How you never fed Hareton in my
presence, and how he nuzzled into your bosom when you held
him. How you would make some excuse to disappear with him
for a few minutes, and then come back with your tucker tied
a little differently. Small things in themselves, but they added up.

Especially since you had never told me how you had solved the problem of his feeding, as you evidently had. And that was unlike you.'

'Well, what a day of revelations this is. Why did you never tell me you knew?'

'It was evident that you did not want me to know. I thought I was respecting your wishes. Do you wish I had?'

'I do. It would have been a comfort to confide in you. But then, it is easy to say that now. At the time . . . perhaps not. There were so many other secrets contained in that one, including Elspeth's part in bringing it about. There were' – I blushed at the memory – 'spells, rituals, that sort of thing. I was afraid I had done wrong.'

Bodkin smiled. 'There would be. Elspeth was no fool.'

'What do you mean?'

'Something my father told me when I started practice. "The less you are sure of the efficacy of your treatment," he said, "the more precise you must be in prescribing it. Do not say to take about so much, about so often – tell them to measure it to the grain, and take it on the minute of the clock. Tell them what to take with it, and whether to sit, stand, or lie down after they do. Insist that your instructions be followed to the letter. The more precise they are, the more your patient will believe in them, and that belief will often heal them, where the medicine alone would be sure to fail." There, and now I have told you *my* great secret. You must never tell anyone of it, or I shall be completely done in as a doctor.'

I shook my head and managed a smile, but in truth my mind was spinning so, I felt dizzy. Everything I remembered, everything I thought I knew, was shifting and changing at once. I thought of what I had learned from Mrs Phillips, about the lamb.

'At Thrushcross Grange, when I fell ill,' I said, 'did you know—'

'That you had still been nursing Hareton, and were suffering from leaving off too suddenly? Yes.'

'And that was why you told Mrs Phillips to find me a lamb.'

'Ah, another of my secrets betrayed. When did she tell you?'

'Not until she left service, years later – she kept her word to you.'

'I'm glad of that.'

'Are there any secrets of mine that you *don't* know?' I said at last.

'A great many,' he said with a smile. 'I don't know most of what you were thinking, or feeling, during all that time. I don't know how you endured all that you had to, and still found it in yourself to give such loyal service as you did, to those that hurt you.'

'Not so loyal, always.'

'I don't know that either.'

'And have you any more great secrets to tell me?'

Bodkin reached across the table, and gathered both my hands in his, his voice suddenly serious. 'Only one,' he said.

I looked at his face. I had known it since childhood, watched it grow and change over thirty years and more. In youth, sir, we show the world the face God gave us, for good or ill. But in later life, we must wear the face we have made for ourselves through a lifetime of habitual expressions. Joseph's upstairs was so deeply seamed with ill-temper that, had his heart undergone a miraculous transformation in his late years to universal benevolence and love, I do not think his face could have made shift to show it. The creases in Bodkin's tanned and weather-roughened skin told a different story: one of much laughter,

467

and some sorrow, of great kindness, and little anger. All my life, he had been a steady and true friend to me, steadier and truer even than I had known.

'Tell me,' I said, though I already knew the answer.

And writing now, I find I have another answer too. I know who will read this.

In reply to yours of the 18th of June

Dear Mr Lockwood,

What a surprise it was to hear from you again, and with such news as you had to share, too! First, let me congratulate you on your engagement to the Honourable Miss De Lacy. Of course I could never agree with you that any woman is beyond your deserving, but if your betrothed be but half as noble and gentle in character as she certainly is in her lineage, you will be a very happy man, I am sure.

Speaking of young love, I am sure you will be pleased to hear that Cathy and Hareton's modest wedding went off as planned, and the pair are now happily settled at Thrushcross Grange. Hareton will never be as cultivated as Mr Linton was, but he has gone far to mend his deficiencies. If you met him now, you would never guess that he had only but lately learned to read: you would find him just the sort of plain-spoken, down-to-earth country squire – more interested in his horses, his dogs, and his crops than in ideas – as can be met with in many a great house in Yorkshire. Cathy has come into her own as a lady, and is none the worse a mistress for having been for a time little more than a serving-maid herself. They have a little girl now, and Cathy is expecting her second confinement in December.

Old Joseph has been gathered to his forefathers. He had accumulated quite a fortune in savings from his wages – well over a thousand pounds – and we all thought he would leave it to his nephew Bram, who had cared for him patiently in his last months at Wuthering Heights. You may imagine our surprise, then, at finding that he had bequeathed the whole sum to Hareton! The young couple consulted with me about it, however, and we concluded that it would be an injustice to accept the inheritance, and so it has been put in trust for Bram, until he comes of age.

Now on to the substance of your letter: how very kind of you to offer to take me on as the housekeeper of your London establishment, and at double my present wages, too! I feel honoured that you should think of me. Yet if it be true, as you say, that servants in London are all 'rascals, layabouts, and thieves', why, I should think it would be uphill work to manage a house full of them – and a lonely post, too, for an honest woman. As for your claim that I owe you this service as compensation for the damage done to your health by our 'dastardly climate', why, the climate is not my doing – and if your health had not sent you to Italy, you would never have met the Honourable Miss De Lacy, who it appears has effected your total cure, since you think of settling again in England. And so you have some cause to be grateful to our climate, after all!

But I am only teasing you, Mr Lockwood, as I think you were teasing me. The truth is that I have agreed to take up a position of a different kind. Next Saturday, Ellen Dean, housekeeper at Thrushcross Grange, will be transformed into

470

Mrs Robert Kenneth, wife to a doctor and mother to four children, ranging in age from two years to twenty-five. Not so different from what I have done already, you may say: managing a household, and raising the children of another mother, but there is a world of difference to me. And who knows, I may yet have a child myself – I am younger now than my mother was when she bore me.

You took such a kind interest in all I told you of my masters and mistresses – of the Earnshaws, and Lintons, and Heathcliffs – that I have presumed you will not be averse to hearing a little more, and will even extend your interest to a line or two about myself. If I have presumed too much, let me offer my apologies for wasting your time with such a long letter as this has been.

Sincerely,
Nelly Dean

ACKNOWLEDGEMENTS

This novel grows in large part out of the experience of teaching *Wuthering Heights* to generations of Williams College students. I thank them for the curiosity, intelligence and insight they have always brought to those classes. I am additionally grateful to Arletta Bussiere and Samreen Kazmi for assistance with research, and to the latter for her many insights into servant/employer relations. Thanks are also due to Williams College and the Oakley Center for supporting this project financially and collegially. I would also like to thank the Brontë Parsonage Museum and the people of Haworth for their part in ensuring that Haworth, the Parsonage, and the lands around it remain a place where visitors can connect with the spirit of the Brontës' novels. Special thanks to Brenda Taylor and Julie Akhurst for the private tour of Ponden Hall.

Ilon Specht and Elinor Case-Pethica listened to every piece of this novel as it was written. They were my first audience, and their encouragement and understanding have been vital to me throughout. Many thanks to my agent, Deborah Schneider, and to Katie Espiner and Cassie Browne of Borough Press for all they have done to bring this project to fruition.

Thanks most of all to two writers, Paul Park and Tracy Chevalier, who have generously offered expert advice and practical assistance at every stage of this project, while serving as role models of excellence in this curious enterprise of writing fiction. Their inspiration and their friendship are pearls beyond price.